Mistaken Beliefs

M K Turner

ISBN: 978-0-9927529-8-9

By M K Turner

Meredith & Hodge Series

The Making of Meredith

Misplaced Loyalty

Ill Conceived

The Wrong Shoes

Tin Soldiers

One Secret Too Many

Mistaken Beliefs

Quite by Chance

Family Matters

Not If You Paid Me

Bearing Witness Series

Witness for Wendy

An Unexpected Gift

Terms of Affection

The Murder Tour Series

Who Killed Charlie Birch?

Others

The Cuban Conundrum

The Recruitment of Lucy James

Murderous Mishaps

ACKNOWLEDGMENTS

Editing by Sharon Kelly

Cover Design by www.behance.net/lwpmarshala1e9

Photography by: Joshua Patterson and Katie Harp

1

A iden O'Brien's knuckles dragged through the dregs of beer as he reached for the bottle. He gave a roar as his fingers found it, he tightened his grasp, and rapped it neatly on the edge of the bar. Staggering to one side as he slid from the bar stool, he lunged towards one of the men jeering at him, and swung the jagged edges of the broken bottle towards the grin he intended to cut away. The struggle that followed lasted no more than seconds, and O'Brien's hearing seemed to become enhanced. He was aware of tense whispering, and the sound of sobbing as his life began to slip away. Someone was speaking to him, and cutting out the background noise clamouring in his ears, he lifted his head and focused on their words.

"Come on, mate, that's enough. Know when you're done."

O'Brien tried to answer, but his tongue was too heavy, the process too complicated. His head was placed back on the dirty carpet. He was alone.

His eyes opened a little as a piercing scream clawed at his consciousness. He saw Ben Jacobs standing over him, and he watched blood drip from the knife in Jacobs' hand. Aiden O'Brien was still frowning as his last breath left him.

~ ~ ~

DCI John Meredith attempted to pace the floor of the cupboard-size interview room.

"You're innocent? You need to do better than that! I need more than that. For God's sake, Ben, that's what ninety-nine percent of people say when they sit in this room. You're up before the magistrates later today if they can fit you in. I'm not the OIC on this case, he's pissed off because I'm here. He doesn't want me interfering, but I'll try to help. Give me something to work with, there's next to no chance of you getting bail."

Meredith looked at his friend, placing his hands on the table and leaning forward, softened his tone. "Start at the beginning and tell me exactly what happened. Everything you remember, even if it doesn't seem relevant." There was a tap on the door. Meredith paused and looked up in irritation as DI Jamie Wessex poked his head into the room.

"Sorry to interrupt," there was no apology in his voice, "but the duty solicitor is here, I've told him your friend needs to see him, he'll be ten minutes or so." His tone was accusing as he looked at the two men. "You'll have to leave then," he nodded at Meredith. "I have to get on with the *formal* interview." His emphasis on the word confirmed his displeasure at Meredith, a senior officer, having a private meeting with the suspect.

"Who is it?" Meredith asked, and rolled his eyes at the answer provided.

"What was that look for? Is he useless? Who would you recommend? I'll find the money if necessary." Ben Jacobs was desperate.

Meredith waited for the door to close behind Wessex. "He'll do for now, as I said, bail is a long shot at this stage so it will make little difference. Quick now, bring me up to speed before he gets here, what happened last night?" Sitting, Meredith tapped his pen on the pad indicating the urgency. He looked into the eyes of his oldest friend and nodded encouragement.

Ben Jacobs closed his eyes, he could see Meredith's belief in him was hanging in the balance, and he couldn't blame him. It looked about as bad as it could get. He should have smelt something was wrong, he'd been set up, and he didn't know why. If it didn't make sense to him, how could it make sense to Meredith? He groaned and opened his eyes.

"From the beginning," Meredith encouraged.

2

It had been almost eight o'clock when Ben Jacobs arrived at BB's nightclub. It had become the hottest club in town, and with his singing engagements at an all-time low, Ben worked there a couple of nights a week when needed. He could handle himself well enough, but muscle was rarely required, it wasn't the sort of club that catered for punters likely to cause trouble. Barry Brooker, the proprietor, was aiming for a moneyed clientele, and whilst a few lesser beings were granted access, at weekends they only stepped over the threshold, if, as Barry put it, they would fit in with the classy mob.

"Whoa, look at you. New DJ, Ben, and you've pressed your shirt, you on a promise tonight?" Pete Beresford, more commonly known as Big Pete, punched Ben on the arm as he passed.

Dan Jones sniggered, and knowing it would irritate, he tousled Ben's hair.

"Come on, Ben, why the new gear? What's the SP? You can tell us, we know how to keep a secret. Is it the tall one with the legs that go all the way up to her armpits?" Dan Jones hugged himself and blew Ben a kiss, "Is it? I could waste time with her."

Ben smiled his perfect smile. He really liked the two men, and while he hated working the door to supplement his income, he enjoyed their company and the banter that came with it. Big Pete was six feet six inches tall and weighed in at eighteen stone. Deceptively light on his feet, he was a good man to have with you should there be trouble. Generally he was the typical gentle giant, but his size tended to intimidate, so he suited the job. Dan was a different kettle of fish altogether. He was short, something Ben knew shouldn't be mentioned unless you were looking for trouble, and he was stocky. His philosophy was to get in first, attack definitely being the best form of defence. Dan was also what Ben's father would have called a lad. Never shy of boasting if he had scored with a girl the night before. Balding slightly, but good-looking, he was more than a little vain.

Ben Jacobs was the better looking and most charming of the three, this, together with his minor fame as a local singer, brought the girls flocking, particularly during the week when there was a shortage of single men in the club. Ben tried not to take advantage, he'd had a lifetime of one-night stands - it came with the territory. In an about-turn on his past, he attempted to make sure he actually liked the women he picked up for more than their looks, much to the amusement of the other two. Ben felt little need to settle down, he'd tried a couple of times, and found people got hurt that way. All Ben wanted were a few more venues to book him as a singer, and to give up working the door, which seemed to be becoming a more permanent fixture.

"Well lads," he finally answered, having popped his head through the double doors that led to the main bar and dance floor, "it's like this . . ." he paused and smiled, before shaking his head. "No, you don't want to know. My life must be so boring compared to yours. Anyway, I doubt you know her."

"You wind-up merchant!" Dan laughed as he pulled Ben's arm up behind his back in a mock hold. "Spill the beans; you're getting past it, I'm sure she'd like a younger, more active bloke."

"Okay, okay, get off the cloth and I'll tell you." Ben was released as Barry Brooker entered the foyer.

He halted his confident stride and fixed his eyes on the two men. "Is this what I pay you for?" His tone was calm, but his demeanour menacing. "One of you go in there and check it out." He indicated the bar with a jerk of his head. Throwing his cashmere coat over the desk, he asked, "Where's the girl that should be doing this? Oozing charm and flashing her cleavage at our customers? If she's late again, she's out. I've told her before; I don't pay good money for old rope." He sighed deeply as though the late arrival of the cloakroom attendant had ruined his night.

"Don't panic, boss," Big Pete smiled amiably, "there's nothing doing in there yet, and Sandra is having a pee."

Barry Brooker shook his head, disappointed at the lame excuse.

"Keep on your toes tonight, I've got company coming and I don't want any trouble. Do you understand?" Brooker's neck jerked forward to assert his words.

Ben thought he looked like a bulldog with a toothache, and smiled.

Starting to climb the stairs to his office, Brooker called back to Ben. "I don't know what you've got to smile at, Jacobs, although I'm glad you've smartened yourself up, you might pick up a trick tonight, we have a coachload of grannies coming in from the salsa club." He finished his ascent grunting out a laugh.

Once he was out of sight, Ben tugged his forelock. "Glad to have pleased you, squire," he said in a thick West Country accent.

The three men laughed. To them Brooker was a pretender.

Barry Brooker had been brought up by working class parents in Hartcliffe, a rough estate on the south side of Bristol. His parents had worked hard to provide him with a better chance in life. Much to the amusement of his peers, living in the redbrick streets surrounding their modest home, he had taken and passed the entrance exam to attend the Queen Elizabeth Hospital School. It was at QEH he perfected his skill at charming those around him. His Bristolian brogue all but disappeared, and he made sure he made friends with those who would be of use to him. Brooker homed in on people's weaknesses, and either took advantage, or helped them overcome them – but always for a price.

It was onwards and upwards for young Brooker, from the moment he stepped through the impressive entrance, and with a quick swing of his new leather briefcase, took out Fatty Morris who was in the process of pulverising Henry Chapman. When he later looked back on that moment, Brooker could never recall what had possessed him to come to Henry's aid, but they became lasting friends. It helped that Henry's father was rumoured to be a millionaire, and that he had two pretty younger sisters, Penelope and Susie.

Brooker charmed his way into their lives, and in the fullness of time, their family, by marrying Penelope. His charm offensive had paid huge dividends, he'd made it out of Hartcliffe and had a rosy future ahead of him. Although, those that knew him best, knew to give him a wide berth when the façade retreated to be replaced by a cold stare and a merciless heart.

Dan waited until they heard Brooker's office door bang shut.

"You lying sod," he accused Ben. "You let us believe you were on a promise, when it was Brooker sounding you out."

"It was not. As it happens, my old DJ fell apart. This is the one I wear for gigs, so it'd better not get damaged, I've got a rat pack gig at The Tunnels the day after tomorrow."

"We'd better look after you then, don't want that pretty face getting injured, takes longer to heal at your age . . . uh oh. Eyes front, men. No looking, first one to ogle buys the beers." Dan wagged his finger at the other two men.

Sandra, the cloakroom assistant teetered into the foyer. As usual her heels were two inches too high, and her ample bosom was spilling out of the low neckline of her blouse.

"Sandra, you look delightful as always, my precious," enthused Big Pete. "The punters will pay to get in just to look at you." He grinned as Sandra shoved her nose into the air.

"If you're being sarcastic, you can take it and shove it, I've had enough of you lot taking the piss. Now, clear a space and let me get on with my job." She paused, and the scowl fell away to be replaced with an innocent smile. "By the way, have any of you got a ciggy? I left mine on the bus."

As Dan put his hand in his pocket, Sammy Gregory, another doorman, came running in.

"Bloody car is playing up again. Three miles I've had to walk. Is Brooker in yet? If he knows I'm late again, I'll get the push for sure." He stopped to catch his breath as the others confirmed he was. "I'm going to the locker room to get changed, if Brooker comes down, tell him I'm checking the carpark or something."

"Will do, but you're his blue-eyed boy, don't panic." Placing his hands on his hips, Dan frowned. "Why does he need four of us in? It's Thursday night, are we expecting any large parties other than the salsa group?"

"No idea, he called me this afternoon," Sammy called as he bounded up the stairs. "Who cares? I need the money."

Sammy disappeared into the locker room as Brooker appeared at the top of the stairs. He shouted down to them.

"Oi, you lot! Someone will be in for me shortly, don't give him a hard time, show him up and buzz me to let me know he's on his way." He walked back to his office and slammed the door.

"Well, he's a ray of sunshine tonight I see. Who's pissed him off?" Sandra observed as she clambered onto the bar stool behind the counter. "He's such a W. Nice as pie one minute, cut your throat the next."

"He'll never change, but he pays well. Anyway, at least you've got me." Big Pete winked at her, and rested his shoulder on the wall next to the counter.

"Beers are on you."

Ben laughed and Big Pete tore his eyes away from Sandra's cleavage with a groan.

Dan pulled several cigarettes from the packet in his hand and placed them on the counter. "You can have a quick one with me later."

He grinned as Sandra snorted. Scooping up the cigarettes, she balanced them on the shelf of the small till.

"In your dreams. I've got better taste." She flipped her hand at him. "Out of the way, punters arriving."

Dan stepped to one side, as three young women hurried through the door, each rearranging their hair before approaching Sandra.

"Bit windy out there, is it?" Big Pete remained leaning against the wall, and smiled as the girls used various descriptions of how bad it was.

Dan watched them disappear into the bar. "I might take up salsa you know. They know how to use their hips." He went to the door as the sound of clicking heels warned of more approaching customers. Pulling it open he swept his hand forward in welcome. "Come in, come in, get out of that wind and warm yourself up." He wiggled his eyebrows at the two women. The older of the two smiled at him.

"Play your cards right, and I might let you help me." She threw her head back and laughed, before pushing him in the chest. "But to earn that, you have to dance with me." Catching sight of Ben, who had moved to open the bar door for them, she added, "Now you look like a man who knows how to move."

Ben appraised her quickly, the movement of his eyes was subtle, his smile disarming.

"Two left feet I'm afraid," he lied. "But Dan was just saying he wanted to learn to salsa." He grimaced at Dan as the woman looked momentarily disappointed. "He says he's a good mover." Ben pulled open the door to the bar and waited until the women were out of earshot. "You see, Dan, you may be younger, but you've either got it or you ain't." He looked up as Sammy appeared on the stairs. "Take Sammy here. Thick as shit, but a full head of hair, massive biceps, and a smile that reminds you of a spaniel. Can't even tuck his shirt in, but they still flock to him."

"Who do what?" Sammy asked as he swung his legs forward using the banisters on either side of the staircase for momentum. He cleared the last five stairs, and managed to land neatly on his toes in the centre of the foyer. He tucked his errant shirt tail in.

"Nothing," grumbled Dan. "Jacobs thinks he's a bloody comedian all of a sudden."

"Are you doing stand-up now as well?" asked Sammy. "I thought the singing would be enough . . . What?" he demanded as his colleagues sniggered.

The next hour or so passed peacefully. It was busy for a Thursday, and there were only two young men in who seemed to have drunk too much. Any trouble would be handled easily. Having walked the perimeter of the bar and dance floor, Sammy returned to the foyer. He placed his elbows on the counter and rested his chin on his hands.

"Come on, Sandra, let me share your taxi. You don't pay for it and you could drop me home on the way. Of course, if you're feeling lonely you could always spend the night with me, or me with you, if that suits. I haven't got to work tomorrow," he lied.

A bricklayer by trade, Sammy was twenty-three, and something of a local hero, being a successful amateur boxer. He earned reasonable money, and worked at the club for the easy access to women. He was obsessed with women. Knowing he was the only one of the doormen who had yet to bed Sandra, and having heard stories of her exploits in the bedroom, he'd made it his quest to wear her down.

Sandra opened her mouth to answer and snapped it shut again as a burly man, with a mop of dark hair, burst into the foyer. He was slightly flushed, and swayed as he came to a halt.

"Where's Brooker?" he demanded. With a look of distaste, he scanned those in the foyer. Not finding Brooker, he snapped, "Tell him O'Brien is here and I want to see him, now!" He glared at Sandra as he ran his hand through his hair in an attempt to tame it.

Ben exchanged a knowing glance with Big Pete. This was clearly not a happy man, and they hoped Brooker would pacify him and not wind him up, or they would be picking up the pieces.

Sandra lifted the receiver. "There's a Brian here to see you, shall I send him up?" She shook her head as she listened to Brooker's response. "Of course." Replacing the receiver, she adjusted her top to hide the lace of the bra that had appeared and looked at Ben.

"Show Mr . . . Er, Brian, up to Mr Brooker's office would you please." Turning back to O'Brien she smiled her sweetest smile, and affecting an upper-class accent, said. "Ben will show you up to Mr Brooker, who asks if you would like a drink. In which case I will have a barmaid bring it to you."

"Forget the drink, take me to Brooker," O'Brien snapped, and followed Ben up the stairs. Reaching Brooker's door, Ben lifted his hand to knock, but O'Brien shouldered him out of the way, opened the door himself, and strode into Brooker's office.

"Go in, why don't you," Ben muttered, and looking over O'Brien's shoulder, he saw the look of surprise on Brooker's face. "Everything okay, Mr Brooker?" he asked, looking at O'Brien who had stopped abruptly at the desk and now loomed over Brooker.

"Of course! Get on with your work." Brooker spat his response. Then, catching himself, he smiled and looked up at O'Brien, "Aiden, come on in, sit down. Did the girl on the desk offer you a drink? I think   . . ." He stopped and looked at Ben. "Are you still here? Close the door behind you."

Closing the door firmly, Ben heard O'Brien ask, "Where is he?" before he returned to the others in the foyer. The others looked up expectantly.

"Well," chirped Sandra, "I've never seen him in a mood before, have you, Ben? He's always such a nice polite chap. I could quite fancy him, all rugged and Gaelic." She smiled, ignoring the snorts from the men. "By the way, Brooker says to have one of the girls take up a bottle of Irish, even if he said he didn't want a drink. He's such a pushy bastard."

"I'll do it." Dan walked away to the bar.

Ben cocked his head puzzled. He'd never seen O'Brien before, and he wondered how Sandra knew him.

"Who is he?" he asked. "Can't say I've ever had the pleasure . . . or misfortune." He watched the frown appear on Sandra's brow.

"No, you probably wouldn't have. I think he drives for one of Brooker's other businesses, he's been in a few times on a Saturday. You don't do Saturdays, do you?" Turning her attention to the couple entering the foyer, the frown dropped away to be replaced with a smile. "Ten pounds each as it's before eleven, shall I take your coats?"

Ben left her to it and opened the door to the bar as Dan returned with Brooker's order.

"Everything all right in there?"

"Yeah, fine, but there are a lot of thirsty people at that bar. Those girls are nice to look at, but your pint's flat by the time they've finished pulling it." Dan laughed. "I don't know how Tania does it, but they work faster when she's around." He nodded at the tray in his hands, "Better get on, the boss is waiting for this. I hope they don't want ice. Someone forgot to switch on the machine."

Ben turned his attention to Sandra. "Hey, Sandra, where's Tania? She didn't say she was taking holiday."

Ben had a soft spot for Tania. She was the events manager at BB's, arranging themed nights, private parties, and live acts. It was how Ben had come to work there, both as a singer and a doorman. Tania was a nice-looking woman with a sweet personality, but of late she always seemed a little preoccupied, sad even. Ben had tried his luck with her a few times, but Tania had rejected his advances. They all knew she had a boyfriend, somewhere, but she wouldn't speak about him, so they'd stopped asking. They didn't even know his name. Ben had given in gracefully, more to protect his pride than to respect her wishes.

"As far as I can make out, she's going away with Mr X. She came in on Tuesday all excited and said next time we saw her she'd have a gorgeous tan." Sandra sniffed, "Lucky cow. I know the weather here hasn't been too bad, but a bit of non-stop sunshine would suit me down to the ground."

Dan stood outside Brooker's office. He knocked at the door once and entered. The sound of raised voices caused him to pause momentarily.

"Give me some credit. You're telling me I got it wrong? I don't think so. I want answers and I want them fast!" O'Brien bellowed.

"Sit down will you!" Brooker shouted, then, softening his tone, added, "Relax, Aiden, look, the firewater is here. Let's have a drink and I'll explain." Brooker held his hand towards the free chair before returning his attention to Dan. "Put it there and get out!" He pointed at the desk in front of him. "I don't want any interruptions. Not any. Tell the others." He snatched the bottle from the tray before Dan had set it on the desk. Dan turned away as Brooker cursed. "No fucking ice, peasants."

"Who is he, Dan, any idea?" Ben asked, when Dan returned to the foyer.

"Not sure, something to do with a transport business the family have an interest in." Dan grinned, "Probably been robbed of his overtime, once too often." He shrugged, "Although, why Brooker would take shit from a driver is beyond me, so perhaps I'm wrong."

"You may be right," chipped in Sandra. "If I didn't need the money, I'd have given Brooker the rough side of my tongue long ago, that's for sure. All that false charm, he thinks we don't see through it."

"Do it to me, do it to me. I've never had the rough side of a tongue. All the girls I know are too boring," joked Sammy, who had fallen to his knees in a gesture of prayer.

"Everyone's a comedian, a bloody comedian. Get up, you stupid sod. I doubt you'd know what to do, even if someone drew you pictures."

They were still laughing as Big Pete returned from his carpark inspection. Dan recounted the episode, and Big Pete cuffed Sammy around the ear, and looked at his watch.

"Nearly twelve, brace yourselves troops, the pubs will have chucked out, the masses might arrive any minute."

"Is that all it is?" Ben screwed up his nose, "I thought time was supposed to fly when you were having fun. I'll pop to the gents before I take up my position, just in case it goes mad," he joked, "if that's all right with you, General?"

Giving Big Pete a sharp salute, Ben took the stairs two at a time, and went to the locker room. He studied his reflection as he washed his hands. A couple of his laughter lines had deepened, and he decided he needed a haircut as he flattened down a tuft of hair over his ear while his hands were still wet. He smiled as he thought about the wickedly funny Jane, who worked in the salon on the High Street. She'd been in the club the previous Thursday, and he hoped she might come in tonight. His thoughts were interrupted by the sound of raised voices, angrily protesting, and giggling coming from the foyer.

"Let the fun begin," he muttered, and shaking water from his hands, he hurried to the door. As he dashed out of the locker room and turned the corner to the stairs, he crashed straight into Aiden O'Brien. "Sorry, mate. I didn't see you there. Are you okay?" He placed a hand on O'Brien's upper arm as he cast a glance down to the foyer. O'Brien shook his hand away, and Ben attempted to sidestep him.

"What if I wasn't? Would you give a shit? I doubt it," O'Brien snarled, blocking Ben's path.

"Okay, steady on. It was an accident, and I've said I'm sorry. If you'll excuse me, I've got matters to attend to." Again, Ben tried to sidestep O'Brien, but O'Brien grabbed his lapels.

"Business? What sort of business would that be I wonder? You make me sick the lot of you." With a sudden lunge, O'Brien pushed Ben back against the wall. There was a ripping noise and part of a lapel tore away from the jacket.

Ben's patience gave out, and with a quick movement he brought his arms up through O'Brien's with some force. O'Brien's hands lost their grip on Ben's jacket, and taking advantage of his opponent's surprise, Ben forced his forearm against O'Brien's throat and pinned him against the wall. Ben was unaware that the merry party in the foyer had fallen silent, and were watching the encounter with interest. Opening his mouth to tell O'Brien in no uncertain terms that he was about to be ejected, he snapped it shut as Brooker came hurrying out of his office.

Brooker pulled at Ben's shoulder. "Leave the man alone, you animal. He's my guest, no need for fisticuffs," Brooker forced a smile for O'Brien. Looking down into the foyer he saw the gaggle of guests watching him. Releasing his grip, he patted Ben's shoulder. "Take him down to the bar, and ask Tania to look after him." His face screwed up as he remembered Tania's absence. "Shit. Get one of the others to look after him, I need to make a phone call."

Ben released O'Brien, and Brooker stepped back. The crowd at the bottom of the stairs had yet to disperse.

Brooker looked down on them. "There's nothing to see here, move along to the bar." He attempted a smile, and one of the girls shouted that there was plenty to see. The pretence was dropped. "Get in the bar or fuck off. Do I need to bar you?" Brooker put one foot on the top stair, and shrugging, the girl led her friends away.

Big Pete appeared in their place, and ignored Brooker's presence. "Everything all right, Ben?"

"Get a grip on your staff," Brooker spat, "or you'll all be out of a job. Mr O'Brien is a friend of mine, make him comfortable, and keep this lunatic under control." He pulled O'Brien forward and patted his shoulder. "Go on down, Aiden. I'll be with you in two minutes, and if this idiot gives you any more grief, let me know." Making a dismissive gesture with his hand, he turned and went back to his office.

Ben followed O'Brien down the stairs, a face like thunder, and his hand smoothing the damaged lapel as though it could repair it. O'Brien waited for Ben in the foyer, and Ben eyed him suspiciously as he left the final stair. He was surprised when O'Brien held his hand out.

"Sorry about that, I didn't mean to get you into trouble with that prick. I'm wound up tonight as you might have noticed. Let me buy you a drink, I'll get that jacket sorted for you too."

Ben took the man's hand. "Don't worry about it, go and have a drink, you look like I feel."

O'Brien bellowed out a laugh and pumped his hand up and down.

"Trust me, it's not possible for two of us to feel that bad." Releasing Ben's hand, he turned and nodded thanks to Big Pete, who showed him through to the bar.

When Big Pete returned, his disapproval was evident. He wagged his finger at Ben. "I could do without you playing up when there's trouble on the door. Dan's well pissed off with you, had you been here, you might have saved him."

"Oh shit. Is he badly hurt?"

"Oh, it's bad. One of the punters threw up all over him, he's had to go home and change." Big Pete almost reached the end of the sentence without his face cracking into a smile.

"You rotten . . ." Ben never completed the sentence as Brooker came running down the stairs. He rarely moved quickly. He braced himself for Brooker's next verbal onslaught, but to his surprise Brooker slapped him on the back, told him he was a good man, and went through to the bar to join O'Brien.

The next hour was fairly standard for a Thursday evening, with customers coming and going, and little for the doormen to do. As it approached one o'clock, they questioned again why Brooker had felt the need for four of them to be present. The salsa club was entertaining, and other punters were being taught how to flip their hips with each step, the more hardened drinkers sat near the bar keeping themselves to themselves, and a few couples canoodled in the darker corners. O'Brien and Brooker appeared to be getting quietly plastered on Guinness and whiskey chasers. As nights went, it was a doddle. Big Pete said as much, when the door opened, and two well-built men, he'd not seen before, sauntered into the club.

Sandra smiled at them. "Evening, gentlemen, that'll be twenty pounds each please." Her face registered the shock she felt as the larger of the two men removed his wallet. The club officially closed at two o'clock, and with barely an hour to go, customers tended to argue the odds at this time of night, it was a sure way of blocking a late entry.

"There are four of us, darling." The man smiled a dazzling white smile, and Sandra smiled back. "They're parking the car. They won't be a minute. Might even be a few more by and by." His large hands deftly fanned four twenty-pound notes from the bundle. He wafted them at her, and when she took them, he pulled another free and dropped it on the small china plate, carefully positioned to encourage tips.

Sandra snapped the till shut. "Thank you, sir, much appreciated. I don't think we've seen you here before. I'm Sandra." Her eyes twinkled as the man winked.

"Nice to meet you, Sandra, I'm Eric." His deep voice seemed to rumble up from his chest. "Is Mr Brooker in the bar?"

Hoping her eyebrows hadn't risen too far, Sandra confirmed he was, and watched the two men disappear. When their companions arrived, she waved them on through, and turned to Sammy.

"I liked him. He's just like that actor, Idris Whatsit, and what a voice, sent shivers down my spine, and so smart. I bet that suit was handmade."

"We're going to have trouble." Big Pete was looking into the bar. "O'Brien is smashed, Brooker looks concerned, and those blokes have just joined them."

Ben stepped over to join him. "Shall I go and ask if all's well?" He looked at the odd group and shrugged. "Brooker seems comfortable with their presence. Oh . . . perhaps not, he's trying to move away."

"What's going on? I can't believe I had to go and change, was hardly worth coming back," Dan complained as he came to stand behind them. It was a futile exercise, he was too short to look over their shoulders and into the bar.

"Nothing yet." Pete turned away and looked down at Dan. "Brooker's on his way out, get in the bar and keep your eyes on O'Brien and his new friends. All calm at the moment, let's keep it that way."

"It had better stay that way. I'm all out of clothes." Dan pulled the door open, and Brooker appeared in the void.

"Are you lot still standing around? I've got some calls to make, I'll . . ." He stopped speaking and stepped to one side as a group of four lads left the bar. He listened to their banter as they exited the club. "Pete, go out and watch them clear the carpark, I don't want the punters having their cars damaged. Dan, go around to the yard, one of the barmaids said she heard something. Ben, get in and keep an eye on the bar, we've got a few drunks, and Sammy, you stay on the door."

Brooker rarely got involved in organising the door staff, and was irritated by the look of surprise that most of them displayed.

"Get on with it, I'm not paying for a male knitting circle. Earn your keep or bugger off." Stepping forward he clapped his hands, "Now." He didn't wait to see if they responded, but hurried across the foyer and up the stairs.

Big Pete shook his head as the door to his office banged shut. "Those lads had better accents than him. Don't reckon they'll be keying any cars, but the man has spoken, so jump to it, boys."

Dan and Ben entered the bar. Dan sauntered off to the far side of the dance floor, where two middle-aged salsa club members were putting lads, young enough to be their sons, through their paces. Ben took up position at the top of the steps leading down to the dance floor. From his vantage point he glanced around the room. O'Brien was talking to the four men, and from the sway of his shoulders, it was clear he'd had more than enough to drink, yet there he was taking a shot glass from one of the men. He knocked it back, and in the process slid off the bar stool. Eric helped him back up. Ben smiled as O'Brien slapped him on the back in thanks. At least he was a happy drunk.

The smile became a frown as the door opened and a group of six men came into the bar. What was Sammy thinking? It was almost closing time. Brooker should have left Big Pete on the door. He caught Dan's eye and jerked his head towards the bar, and they watched as the new arrivals exchanged bear hugs and high fives with Eric and his friends. O'Brien sat in the midst of this frivolity, smiling aimlessly at one of the lads, attempting to engage him in conversation. Ben's observations were interrupted by a tap on his shoulder.

"Hello, Ben. I thought you would've come over for a chat seeing how it's quiet tonight. I haven't upset you, have I?"

Ben looked down. Dawn's pretty little face was aglow. But then, it always was. She was wearing a tightly fitting mini dress that showed off her superb body. Ben liked Dawn, but she wanted more than he was prepared to give, and he didn't have it in him to be blunt with her. He smiled. "I am busy as it happens. It doesn't look like it, but Brooker is on the warpath, and I've got to keep on my toes. I've already had trouble from him tonight." He nodded at O'Brien as he bellowed out a laugh, and for good measure held up the torn lapel. He leaned forward. "Perhaps I'll come over for a chat a little later." His face was close to hers and he felt her shiver. Suppressing his smile, he looked into her eyes, "I'll come over later, I promise."

"It's nearly closing, why don't I go and wait in your car for you." Dawn pouted, determined to have her way.

"I'm not . . . hang on." Spinning away from her, Ben looked towards the shouting coming from the bar. Two of the later arrivals were clearly poking fun at O'Brien. Ben couldn't hear the words but it was clear they were taunting him. O'Brien was shouting and pointing his finger. Sighing, Ben took a step towards the bar, hoping that Dan wasn't far behind.

As he walked towards the group, he watched O'Brien take a bottle, smash it, and lunge at the men in front of him. Increasing his pace, Ben reached the group as the tussle that had ensued calmed down. He pushed one of the men out of the way, and looking down was pleased to see the broken bottle on the floor. That was one less thing to worry about.

"He's mad. Off his rocker," called a voice.

Ben didn't see the face of the man who spoke, but his hand accepted the hard object pressed into it. He had no time to respond, as O'Brien staggered forward and the weight of his body fell onto Ben.

"Come on, mate, know when you're done," Ben grunted as O'Brien's knees buckled. Manhandling him awkwardly, he managed to lay O'Brien on the floor. Someone was crying, but it was the piercing scream that made him jump up and turn around.

"He's knifed him." Dawn threw her hands over her mouth, and eyes that had previously lusted after him now looked fearful.

Ben turned back and looked down at O'Brien. O'Brien frowned, and seemed to be peering at Ben's hand. Ben had eyes only for the vivid patch of red growing larger on O'Brien's exposed white belly.

"We need help," he shouted. "Someone call an ambulance." Even as the words left his mouth, he knew it would be too late. O'Brien's eyes were open, but there was no life left in them. Ben flinched as someone tapped his shoulder.

"Drop the knife," Dan's voice was sharp, and he jumped back as Ben spun round.

"Do what?" Ben demanded, and looked at Big Pete walking purposely towards him. "I think he's dead."

"I think you're right mate. Drop the knife. Now."

Big Pete's tone wasn't as sharp as Dan's had been, and Ben looked down at his hands. He gave a small gasp of amazement as he saw the knife. Looking up, his eyes darted around the circle that now looked in on him. His thoughts were running wild. How did he get a knife? Who had stabbed O'Brien? Why was everyone looking at him? How did he get a knife? Surely, they couldn't think that he'd done it? How did he get the knife? How dare they think it was him? With a final glance at the knife, he looked up defiantly.

"What are you all looking at?" He threw the knife to the floor. Unfortunately, it bounced, and it hit the side of O'Brien's leg. One of the women screamed. "That man is dead." Ben pointed at O'Brien. He was disgusted with them, were they truly entertained by a dead man? "Get out of here." He jerked his head towards the door and his eyes met Barry Brooker's.

Brooker was shaking his head as he strode forward. "What have you done, Jacobs?" Stopping, he looked at his customers. "The police are on their way. Ignore this man, the police will want to speak to all witnesses. We've locked the doors at their request. Please take a seat and we'll arrange drinks for you." He smiled warmly before turning and walking to Big Pete. "Get him covered up, then get your mate up to the locker room and hold him there until the police come, and get these people seated with a drink in their hand."

"Will do. But where are you going?" Big Pete asked as Brooker made to leave. He saw Brooker's shoulders tense as he stopped, his head whipping back to Pete.

"I am going to make some phone calls if that's all right with you, damage limitation is necessary. Knowing that one of the door staff knifed a customer could kill this business. Now, do -"

He was unable to complete the sentence, as Ben rushed forward and punched him full in the face.

Ben opened his mouth to speak, but was silenced by the arrival of two paramedics hurrying forward to offer now unneeded assistance to O'Brien. They were followed by a man who looked as though he'd been called from his bed.

"I think that's enough for one night, don't you?" DI Jamie Wessex had indeed been called from his bed. He'd only managed two hours sleep as it was his turn to do the last feed. Sore eyes burned into Jacobs, as several uniformed officers arrived to back him up. He looked at Brooker. "Did he do this?" he asked.

Brooker didn't have time to answer.

"Yes, he did. I saw him, but I don't know why." Dawn's beautiful face crumpled, her lip quivered and she blinked back tears. "I don't know why."

Wessex looked from Big Pete to Dan, searching for confirmation. Ben's heart sank as Dan shook his head and raised his shoulders, and Big Pete merely shrugged and held out helpless hands before looking down at his shoes.

Brooker looked at Wessex. "I'll be upstairs in my office, if you need me." He hurried away. Once in his office he pulled his phone from his pocket and tapped his foot impatiently as he listened to the ringing tone. When it was answered, he snapped, "It's done, and one of my boys is in the frame. It's a fucking nightmare, it shouldn't have happened here." He listened for a few seconds. "I'll leave that with you, but get it done quickly, they're bound to ask."

Hanging up, he grabbed the bottle of whiskey and poured a generous measure. Leaning back in his chair, he stared at the ceiling. His thoughts were interrupted by a tap at the door. Dan's head appeared.

"The police want all staff in the locker room, including you." He gave a useless shrug. "They've arrested Ben."

"Of course they did, he had the bloody knife. Easy case for them. I hope this isn't going to take long, I'm knackered." Pushing Dan out of the door, Brooker closed it behind him.

3

Ben Jacob's world had imploded, and he looked at his friend, his eyes searching Meredith's features for a glimpse of hope. He found none there.

"I know it sounds lame, but I didn't do it. I had no reason to. One of those blokes shoved that knife into my hand. And, before you ask, I don't know why I took it. I was more concerned about protecting O'Brien than killing him. There are cameras in the foyer, on the dance floor, and at the bar. Check them out, you'll see that I'm telling the truth."

"I will but . . ." Meredith looked up as DI Wessex strode into the room. "You'll have to go now, sir."

The fact that the word sir was spoken more as an insult than a mark of respect was not lost on either of the two men already occupying the room, or the dishevelled duty solicitor who followed him. Meredith pursed his lips and contemplated his response.

Wessex forced a smile. "If you please." His hand indicated the door.

Slowly uncrossing his legs, Meredith pushed himself up. "No problem, you have a job to do." He picked up his notepad, flipping the cover over as Wessex's eyes scanned the page. "Have my seat, it's warm." He smiled at the duty solicitor. "This is my friend, he's innocent, look after him for me. If you need anything doing, give me a call."

Instinctively, his hand reached for his business card, he allowed it to drop to his side, task incomplete. "Anyone here will be able to put you in touch." His eyes found Wessex. "I'll be taking a look at the CCTV while you conduct the interview. I trust you don't have a problem with that."

There was the challenge.

Wessex nodded. He didn't speak until Meredith had left the room.

Meredith thumped the wall repeatedly as he made his way to the incident room on the next floor. His team greeted him with smiles as he strode to the

17

board on the far wall. He glanced at the photographs waiting to be pinned up before he turned to face them. The one he didn't want to see, was the one a customer had taken on his mobile. It showed Ben Jacobs standing over Aiden O'Brien, knife in hand. He hoped that the phone had been confiscated, or it would be all over the media within hours.

"What are you doing here, Gov? We weren't expecting to see you until tonight. Come to give us a speech, have you?" Dave Rawlings joked, but frowned as Meredith looked at him.

"No, Dave, I've come to brief you on this case." Meredith simply nodded at the look of surprise.

"But, sir, I thought we were working for DI Wessex on this one, that is _"

"Shut up and listen, Trump." Despite his sharp words, Meredith smiled. He was going to miss Trump the most. "I have an interest in this one, and before Prince Edward sends you off in the wrong direction, I wanted a word."

The team tittered at the use of nickname for their newly assigned boss. Meredith leaned against the table behind him ignoring the photographs.

"It will come as no surprise that Ben Jacobs claims he's innocent. I believe him, so it's up to you lot to prove that. He was given the knife at the height of the drama, and didn't realise what it was until the crowd had dispersed. He had no axe to grind with O'Brien, in fact, he was trying to protect him. A group of men had wound O'Brien up and he had tried to bottle one of them. Ben says there were cameras, have you got the recordings?"

"We have, we were about to look at them, but should . . ." Jo Adler fell silent as Meredith held up his hand.

"I have royal assent, begrudgingly given, but permission none the less. Let's have a look."

~~~

Down in the interview room, Ben Jacobs was in a state of panic. The detective interviewing him was clearly hostile, and it had taken the duty solicitor ages to find a pen in his jacket pocket and then open his notebook to a blank page. Meredith hadn't instilled him with any sense of hope, and after repeating several times that he wasn't guilty, he'd clammed up, refusing to speak unless Wessex acknowledged that it was possible that he hadn't knifed O'Brien.

Wessex threw his arms into the air after thirty minutes. "That's it, I have work to do. Your client is going back to the cells," he informed the solicitor. "We'll speak again once we've been to the magistrates."

"Ah yes, I meant to say," stammered the solicitor who had thus far only uttered a handful of words. "They want us there for two-thirty. I shall meet you there."

"With Mr Jacobs preferring to stay silent, rather than explain what happened, there's little point in wasting any more time. I'll question him again once he's on remand." Wessex got to his feet. "Now, if you'll excuse me, I have a case to build."

Jacobs snorted as the door shut. He looked at the solicitor, who was attempting to shove his notebook into an already overstuffed briefcase. "Did you hear that? Build a case, not solve it, build it."

The solicitor considered this. "He did, didn't he? Quite wrong of course, but it will all come out in the wash." Ben wrapped his arms around his head and groaned, the solicitor smiled at him. "Have patience, Mr Jacobs, these things take time."

Ben bit back a caustic comment, and, his voice flat, asked, "If I'm going to court later, I'm assuming I'll be able to get some clothes, tell me I haven't got to go in these." He pulled at the shapeless boiler suit he was wearing, his own clothes having been taken for forensic examination. The solicitor glanced up at the clock, his eyes told Ben that would be unlikely. "Get me Meredith. Now!" he shouted, thumping the table.

Twenty minutes later, Meredith dropped open the flap, and peered into Ben's cell. "I've got your keys from evidence, anything in particular you want?" He took a step back as Ben launched himself towards the door, his eyes eager.

"Meredith, thank God. That bloke Wessex has got it in for me, doesn't seem to like you much either. Did you get the recordings? What have you found out?"

These and many more questions tumbled out at Meredith.

"Ben, Ben, calm down. I've explained it's not my case, but it's my team working on it, so relax." Meredith tried to calm him.

"But you've seen the recordings?" Ben leaned his face towards the small opening. "Tell me you've at least done that."

"I have, but they're inconclusive. You walk into the crowd, there's a bit of movement, and when the dust settles, you're the one holding the knife. It doesn't look good, but both recordings are being examined, frame by frame, so don't lose hope. They are also going to get some stills of two of the blokes that slipped away circulated. Caught them on the foyer camera, and they'll get names for the rest of the group around O'Brien, but it all takes time. Now what do you want to wear?" Meredith couldn't lie to his friend, it didn't look good.

"Something smart. It's all in the wardrobe, and get underwear. They even took my socks," Ben mumbled. Suddenly he became alert. "You said both. There are three cameras not two, what happened to the third one?"

"Three? I don't know, but I'll find out. I'll see you in court."

Meredith left the flap open, unable to close it on his friend's desperate face.

~~~

"Here you go, son." George Davis, the duty sergeant opened the door to the cell. "Meredith says he'll see you in court."

"What, to see me sent down without a trial," Ben retorted angrily. "Because from where I'm sitting that's what it feels like. Nobody wants to hear the truth!"

"The way I heard it, you didn't want to speak, so how's anyone going to listen to you? You'll do yourself no favours with this no comment malarkey." George held out the bag. "Meredith said he chucked some deodorant in there as you whiff a little." He smiled as Ben took the bag with one hand, and raised his free arm and sniffed. "If Meredith believes in you he'll sort this out, and he does believe in you. He might be leaving the force, but he's not the type of bloke that goes back on his word, whatever the circumstances."

Ben's head jerked up. Meredith was leaving the police force! How could he help Ben if he wasn't a copper? With the smell of the stale sweat still lingering in his nostrils, he looked at George and forced a smile.

"I do whiff a bit. Any chance I could have a quick wash? I don't think deodorant will mask this."

George nodded. He didn't believe Jacobs had done it either. He'd heard him sing, he was good, not that that made him innocent, but if Meredith trusted him, then so did he. He stepped back and jerked his head down the corridor.

"Come on, look lively, the van will be here any minute." He led the way down the corridor, Ben's eyes darted back and forth, the sign for the toilet was getting closer.

As they approached their destination a door at the end of the corridor opened, and a young man with a tired face hurried past them. The smell of cigarette smoke wafted in.

"Fire escape," explained George, "it's where they all smoke. Meredith's favourite spot."

Ben forced a laugh. "Thought he'd given up again. What's he going to do when he leaves the force? I've not seen him in a while, and he probably thought now wasn't the time for small talk." Ben forced a lightness to his voice that he didn't feel.

George chuckled and nodded agreement. "He's taking a sabbatical I think they call it, going to become a private investigator, working with Patsy. Odd if you ask me. Do you know Patsy?"

"Of course, poor girl, fancy working and living with him. Glutton for punishment." He nodded his thanks as George opened the door to the gents' allowing him to enter. Ben unpacked the things Meredith had collected and placed them on top of the waste bin next to the sink. He waved a pair of boxer shorts at George. "These are what I was after. Now avert your eyes, I don't want to make you jealous." He forced the joke as he pulled on the zip of the boiler suit.

Laughing, George stepped to the side and stared at a cubicle door. Ben stepped neatly out of the boiler suit and pulled on the boxers.

"You're safe now, no need to worry about what your missus is missing." Ben forced a laugh, trying to convince himself that he was capable of hitting the old man, or at least manhandling him into the cubicle.

His hand shook as he moved the lever of the tap to the correct temperature. Squirting some soap onto his hand, he lathered his face before splashing copious amounts of water to remove it. He repeated the action with his right armpit. The water gurgled and splashed, and had now formed a small puddle around his feet. From the corner of his eye he caught George's shuffle. "You okay?"

"Peeing myself now, thank you very much. Not too good on bladder control with running water." George paused and pointed at Ben, "If I go and take a leak, you'll not do anything stupid, will you?"

"Like what? Make a run for it?" Ben laughed as he splashed water under the second arm pit. "Give me a break." He smiled in the mirror as George closed the door to the cubicle. Before it had shut tight he had his trousers on. Keeping the water running he shoved the jacket and socks back into the bag, and forced his bare feet into his shoes, while buttoning up his shirt and shoving it in to the waistband. Picking up the bag he called to George, "Thanks for this, George, might give me a chance if I don't stink."

He grabbed the carrier bag, and hoping there was no one in the corridor or on the fire escape, he opened the door. The corridor was clear, and closing the door softly, he hurried to the fire escape. He paused for one second, fixed a relaxed smile, and pushed open the door. The metal platform at the top of the escape was also empty. He allowed himself a smile of relief as he surveyed the carpark below. Two officers had climbed out of a patrol car and were arguing about something as they made their way to the station. Once they had entered the building there was no one else in sight. Ben flew down the steps wondering why he had run. He had no plan, no means of escape, and at the precise moment, he had half a dozen cameras following his every move. Reaching the final step, he eyed the huge double gates, which stood open to the street beyond. Filling his lungs, he prepared to break into a run, when he spotted it. His hesitation only momentary, he sprinted to the bicycle propped up against the wall screening the recycling bins. It wasn't chained up. Hanging the bag on the handle bar, he swung his leg over the saddle and steered it to the gate. Within seconds, he was pedalling for all he was worth down the side street that led from the station carpark and to some sort of freedom.

Knowing it would only be minutes before the alarm was raised, Ben turned left at the end of the road, and headed towards Cabot Circus shopping centre. Once there, he swerved into the service area, and paused to catch his breath and work out his next move. He had no money for a taxi or a bus, if he continued on the bike, the cameras would probably pick him out in seconds, and he had neither the knowledge necessary, nor the inclination to steal a car. If he could make it to BB's, he could pick up his car. A spare key was hidden in the back bumper, and there was a little cash inside. If he took the bike, it would take him less than ten minutes to get there, but they'd be looking for him on a bike. Deciding he'd have to go on foot, which would take twice as long, he reasoned that at least by mingling with the shoppers, he'd be far less likely to be found quickly. He pulled the bag free from the handle and put on the jacket. Leaning against the wall he removed his shoes and pulled on his socks, finally, he rummaged amongst the toiletries and found a comb. He was mid-stroke when a voice came from behind him.

"What you doing over there?" A short balding man in brown overalls left the door to his van open as he stepped forward to investigate. Ben continued combing his hair to give himself time to think. Tucking the comb into his inside pocket he stepped forward.

"Are you a man's man?" he asked with a wink, and what he hoped was a cheeky smile.

The man stopped walking. "What does that mean?" he asked looking at Ben as though he were speaking a foreign language, but automatically took Ben's hand when proffered.

"I'm Meredith." Ben peered at the badge on the lapel of the overalls, "Are you off now, Andrew? If so I could do with a favour."

"Andy, call me Andy. I'm off to Cribbs, why? What's it to you?" Andy had relaxed and pulled a cigarette from behind his ear. Holding it between his lips, he slapped his pockets until he discovered his lighter.

"I've been caught with my trousers down, quite literally as it happens, managed to shove my stuff in here," Ben held up the plastic bag. "Stole his bike," he nodded towards the bicycle, "but forgot my wallet. I'm after a lift to my car."

Andy blew out a plume of smoke and grinned. "Married was she?"

Ben glanced at the wedding ring on Andy's finger, and reminded himself to stick close to the truth.

"Not that I knew. Went out to a club for a beer with some mates, some bloke gets stabbed, and we have to hang around for hours with the police. When I finally get released, they've all buggered off and I'm left with this girl . . ." He paused and shrugged. "Okay, woman. But I'd had one too many, her offer of going back to hers seemed attractive." He gave a laugh. "I never got to see her the morning after, when I wake up, she's gone, and I'd only just got my pants on, when she flies into the room and tells me to sling my hook because her husband was home early. May I?" He took the cigarette from

Andy and drew in a deep draft. "Anyway, I grab a bag, shove the rest of my gear into it – except the wallet, and have it away out of the window. Nearly break my neck, as I didn't see the bike there. In the event, it was useful, but I'm knackered and I have to get to my car. Any chance of a lift?" He took another drag, and when Andy refused to accept the cigarette, he dropped it to the floor and ground it out.

"Where you going?" Andy had already turned away and was walking back towards the van.

Ben followed closely. "Do you know BB's night club? My car's around the corner from there."

"Jump in, I'll make a detour."

The two men got into the van, and Ben blew out a sigh of relief.

"What you going to do about the bike?" Andy enquired as they drove past it. "Won't stay there long, I'll guarantee."

"Well, they've got my wallet, there were a few notes in it, I'd been to the casino earlier." Ben gave a growl. "Don't you hate the way that alcohol makes your brain sink south." He joined in with Andy's laughter.

"I've got a brother with a brain in his dick, he doesn't need alcohol though, it lives there permanently."

~~~

Meredith continued to bite into his pasty, despite the concerned look on Trump's face as he hurried towards him. He dropped it onto the plate as Trump squeezed around the table in front of him and announced.

"Jacobs has done a runner. Poor old George is in a right state."

"Tell me you're kidding." Meredith knew he wasn't and was already pulling on his jacket. "Talk as we walk, Trump." Grabbing the remains of the pasty, Meredith ate as Trump kept up with his stride, and updated him.

"George took Jacobs to the gents' for a wash and brush up. He needed to pee, Jacobs took the opportunity to get away via the fire escape. To add insult to injury the camera has picked him up stealing George's bike. The team are trying to track him via CCTV, but he headed off towards Broadmead and it's busy. DI Wessex is not a happy bunny, and whilst I understand his frustration, he was too harsh to old George. Unnecessarily so in my opinion, George will be in enough trouble when the Super gets to hear about it."

"What's Wessex doing now?" Meredith took the stairs two at a time, and at the top paused to cram the last of the pasty into his mouth.

"Shouting mainly, but working on getting the CCTV footage to hand. Several of the witnesses from last night are due in later, and he wants Jacobs back in custody before then." Trump stopped in his tracks as Meredith opened the door to the carpark. "Where are we going?"

"BB's. I want to know where this missing footage is, and to speak to Brooker if it's possible."

"But, sir, do you think that's wise?" Trump still hadn't moved, and jumped forward to catch the door before it closed behind Meredith.

"I'm a wise man, Trump." Meredith paused as he opened his car door. "And on that note, you may wish to stay here so Wessex doesn't get his knickers in a knot, keep your mouth shut about where I'm going though." Meredith climbed into the car.

Trump hesitated for a second, before pulling open the passenger door and climbing in. "I doubt he'll miss me, and if he does I'll tell him I didn't want to miss the lead on the lost footage." Once on the road, he asked, "How does it feel knowing that you'll be free of all this answering to superiors soon?"

"There's always someone requiring an answer, Trump, it simply means I don't have to be so nice."

Trump turned quickly to face him as he asked, "Do you do nice, sir?"

Meredith bit back a smile. "Not for the next hour or so. We're here." Meredith pulled up on the double yellow lines outside the entrance to BB's. "And before you say it, I know there's a carpark, I'm choosing not to use it." Climbing out of the car, he pulled his warrant card from his pocket. "I'll do the talking, that way you can't get yourself into trouble." The doors to the club were closed but not locked, striding confidently into the foyer Meredith looked around. "That's a shame, no one here, let's check out the bar."

When they entered the bar, they were greeted by the sight of numerous white-suited forensic officers going about their duty. Numbered cards littered the scene where photographs had been taken of evidence collected.

"Stay where you are, Meredith. This scene has been contaminated enough already." Frankie Callaghan got to his feet. "Why are you here? I thought DI Wessex was heading up this case."

"He is, but he's busy, he's allowed the suspect to escape. How are you, Sherlock?" Meredith smiled briefly and glanced around the room. He found three cameras as promised by Ben Jacobs. He turned his attention back to Frankie Callaghan as he approached. "I could ask the same of you, thought you only did bodies these days?"

"I do as a rule, but it's been quiet on the homicide front. I finished the PM, which was straight forward, and came to have a look. Does DI Wessex know you're here?"

Frankie placed an evidence bag in a blue plastic crate.

Meredith looked at the collection of bags and ignored the question. "Only the fatal stab wound, or did you find anything else?"

"Nothing out of the ordinary, except enough alcohol to comatose a man. I'm surprised that didn't kill him, but as I say straightforward. To answer the question you were actually asking, one single stab wound, blade entered and was given an upward thrust just under the rib cage, punctured a lung, nicked an artery, and was then dragged down and out, causing more damage. We have the knife, it has one set of prints which I am reliably informed belong to your suspect."

"Anything else?" Meredith rummaged through the evidence bags and lifted the one holding the broken bottle. "Used?" he enquired.

"Only for holding alcohol. Numerous prints, but they've not been run yet." Frankie took the bag and replaced it. "Why are you here, Meredith?"

"Only two lots of camera footage were collected, and there are three cameras. The suspect claims he's innocent, so I thought I'd better check. Where's the machinery for the cameras?" Meredith was now scanning the room. There were four exits, one to each toilet, a fire exit which he assumed opened into the carpark and one back out to the foyer.

"In the staff room, upstairs. The suspect says he's innocent?" Frankie sounded incredulous. "And you believe him? Don't they all say that?"

"That's what I told him when he said it." Meredith gave a shrug. "You never know, this one might mean it. Where do I find the staff room?" Meredith turned towards the main exit.

Frankie looked from Meredith to Trump.

"The suspect is Ben Jacobs," Trump explained. "DCI Meredith is lending a hand."

Frankie raised his eyebrows. "Ah, I see, the singer chap. Top of the stairs, door on the left. Not sure any of the staff are still here though, I think they were all released a while ago."

"Cheers, Sherlock." Meredith was already walking away. "Trump, this way. Let the man do his job."

"Don't worry, Louie, not long to go, you'll soon be free of him," Frankie whispered with a smile.

"I heard that. He'll miss me, as will you, Sherlock." Meredith disappeared into the foyer.

"I think we will, Frankie." Trump gave a small smile and turned to follow Meredith.

Trump was genuinely sad that he wouldn't be working with Meredith, and while his new boss, DI Jamie Wessex came with good reports, he hadn't yet formed any kind of bond with him. Meredith had never been easy to work with, but one always knew where one stood, and never doubted Meredith's intuition on an investigation. It seemed to Trump that DI Wessex followed the text books too closely, and didn't allow the team an opinion. Trump sighed as he followed Meredith up the stairs, it was early days, he needed to give the chap a chance. He caught the door to the staff locker room before it closed on Meredith, and looked around.

"I suppose it's functional," he commented as he walked along the row of pale wooden lockers, and pushed a chair under the chipped matching table.

He pointed at the kettle sitting next to the sink. "Shall I pop that on? How long are we staying?"

"As long as it takes. Put it on." Meredith walked to the metal shelving unit holding a small screen and the recording machine. He tapped the top of the machine. "Where do you put the tape in?"

"I think it's digital, sir." Trump came to stand behind him and looked over his shoulder. "Held on some sort of disk and downloaded if necessary."

"Do you know how to work it?" Meredith pushed the button on the screen, and the view of the carpark greeted him. There were several vehicles parked there, one being Frankie Callaghan's Land Rover. To the right of the view was the entrance to the carpark. Meredith leaned forward and peered at it as Trump told him he had no idea. Straightening up, Meredith snapped, "Well go and find someone that does, I'll make the coffee."

As Trump disappeared, Meredith hurried to the window at the other end of the room, and, as he expected, he saw Ben Jacobs, walking along the street adjacent to the carpark. Ben stopped running and disappeared below the wall for a while. Before Meredith realised what was happening, Ben had opened a car door, and driven away quickly, but not fast enough to draw attention from the public. Meredith's hand flew to his phone, but he didn't use it, instead he ran his fingers through his hair and considered the stupidity of that failure, but before he'd formed a conclusion, he could hear shouting and then Barry Brooker flew into the room.

"What's going on, and who the fuck are you?" he jabbed his finger at Meredith.

"DCI John Meredith, and you are?" Meredith flipped open his ID.

"Barry Brooker, owner. I've already spoken to your lot. I'm going to the station later, and we've given you the recordings, so you tell me why he walks into my office without so much as a by-your-leave." Brooker jerked his thumb towards Trump who had appeared behind him.

Meredith ignored the question and his eyes moved to Trump. "What was he doing that was so private?" he asked.

"Speaking on the telephone, sir, I did knock but evidently he didn't hear me." Trump's lips twitched.

"And what was he speaking about that was so private?" Meredith persisted, and Brooker's eyes grew wider.

"I don't know, sir, he hung up as I entered."

"Well, we'd better get hold of his telephone records." Meredith returned his gaze to Brooker. "Unless, of course, you wish to tell me who you were talking to and what it was about?" He tilted his head slightly as he watched Brooker struggle to control himself. It took a while, but eventually Brooker responded.

"It was private. It has nothing to do with you, or the murderer Jacobs, so, correct me if I'm wrong but you'll need a warrant to get hold of my records." His voice was calmer and his stare cold.

"Which I will have shortly. For the record, Mr Brooker, we have reason to believe Ben Jacobs was set up. We're collecting evidence which is pointing that way, so everything to do with you and this club, is relevant. Now, before we get back to the phone call, where's the third recording?"

"I have no idea what you are talking about. Set up? By who?"

Meredith smiled and his eyes darted to Trump. "Tell him, Trump."

"But, sir," Trump began to protest as Brooker turned to face him.

Meredith grinned at the back of Brooker's head "Tell him," Meredith insisted, and for the second time in minutes, questioned his own actions. Was it Brooker or Trump he was attempting to make feel uncomfortable?

"It's whom," Trump stated.

"What is?" Brooker snapped.

"Your question, it should have been, by whom?" Trump blew the word gently from lips that looked poised to whistle.

Brooker spun around and faced Meredith again. "If you're trying to wind me up, it's working. I don't need a fucking grammar lesson. Who set Jacobs up? *If* he was set up. Is that what he's saying?"

"It's what the evidence is saying . . . as for Jacobs, he's out there somewhere no doubt planning his revenge."

Brooker screwed his eyes shut, and missed Trump raise his hands questioning Meredith's statement.

"You let him go?" Brooker was incredulous. "I've seen the footage, he approached O'Brien, O'Brien dropped to the floor, and Jacobs was holding a knife. And you let him go?" He looked surprised when Meredith clapped his hands.

"Which brings us neatly back full circle. Where is the third recording? You have three cameras and only two recordings were sent to us. I need the third, please. Now."

Brooker waved his hand dismissively in the direction of the machinery.

"I don't deal with the technical stuff. I can only just about manage to switch the thing on." His smile was forced. "As I can't help you, if that will be all . . ." He turned back to face the door, but Trump blocked his path.

"Who supplied the team with the footage we do have?" Meredith was becoming irritated, Brooker was being obstructive, and apart from the fact that that indicated he may have something to hide, Wessex could turn up at any time. He placed his hand on Brooker's shoulder and turned him to face him.

Instinctively, Brooker knocked Meredith's hand away. "Hands off!" he warned. "Like I said, I've already supplied your lot with everything they needed." Unable to outstare Meredith, he looked at Trump. "What's his problem?"

"Ah, well that's simple, sir." Trump smiled warmly, "DCI Meredith can't understand why you're not helping us. A customer was stabbed to death in your club, a member of your staff arrested on suspicion of murder, now at large, and you seem too preoccupied with other things to want to help. I'm sure DCI Meredith is wondering what could possibly be more important. Perhaps you'd like to share that with us, after you've told us who can explain the missing footage." Trump walked to the table and pulled out a chair. "Here, take a seat."

Brooker snorted in frustration, but walked to the table without further encouragement. Meredith joined him in sitting down and pulled out a notepad from his jacket pocket.

"That's better. Now, name and contact number of who supplied the footage, and anyone else that can set or access the recordings, and uses this room."

"But that's all of the staff, I don't have that information in here." Brooker tapped the side of his head.

"No, I'm sure. Let's start with those that you do have, shall we?"

4

Having reached his car, Ben wasted no time in driving away. It wasn't until he approached the M32 motorway that he relaxed a little and wondered where he should go. He didn't want to run, he wanted to find out why O'Brien had been murdered, and who had set him up. He believed that the only man that could give him that information was Barry Brooker. He swapped lanes, and avoiding the motorway slip road, pointed the car in the direction of a smart suburban estate, and Barry Brooker's home. Ben had no idea how he would convince Brooker to help him, but he had little to lose by confronting him.

Ben had only been to Brooker's home once before, he hadn't been driving and he didn't know the address, however, he knew he would recognise it when he saw it. What he did remember it was a left turn off the main road. Careful to keep within the ridiculous twenty miles an hour speed limit imposed by the former Mayor of Bristol, he entered the estate. Taking the first left turn, he knew immediately this wasn't the street, the houses were too small. He turned around and took the second turn. Driving along slowly, peering at the houses at the ends of the long drives, he knew Brooker's house had a balcony on the front bedroom, but it wasn't in this street. Retracing his route, he returned to the main road to take the third turning. As he drove along the street, he knew as he turned the bend he would see Brooker's house. Slowing, he looked up the drive as he drove past, and saw one of Brooker's many cars parked outside the garage. He drove on, considering his best course of action.

When he got to the end of the road, he turned back and parked on the opposite side of the road. He glanced at the clock on the dash; he should be in front of the magistrate now. The thought renewed his anger; thumping the steering wheel, he freed his seat belt and was about to jump out of the car, when a car drove towards him and pulled onto the drive. A man, whose face

29

was vaguely familiar, got out and knocked on the door. When Brooker's wife answered, the man held up his ID. Replacing his seatbelt, Ben turned the key in the ignition, cursing himself for his stupidity as he drove away. Of course the police would be talking to Brooker, he'd have to catch him before he went to the club, assuming the club would open. He drove away, and parked up on a little used lane to await nightfall.

~~~

Meredith looked at the man standing in front of him. He was huge, and looked like he should be on some sort of television show demonstrating his strength and his ability to pull trucks with his teeth.

"If you didn't send the recordings, who did?"

"I don't know, I've told you that, I don't know why the boss got me in. I've got to get to the station to give a formal statement, and I have to work tonight." Big Pete gave a bitter laugh. "Yes, the bastard says it's business as usual. So, if there's anything else, can we get on with it?" He didn't know who had sent the recordings, and he didn't like it that one was missing. He wasn't convinced that Ben hadn't done it, it looked that way to him, but if there was a chance that the recording would help, he wondered who would have withheld it. The sooner he could ask some questions of his own the better.

"How well do you know Jacobs?" Meredith leaned back in the chair and folded his arms across his chest.

"Well. Like I said, we're mates." Big Pete linked his fingers on the top of his head, his frustration evident.

"Do you think he did it? If so, why? Why would your mate stab a total stranger?"

"I don't know, it looked like it, but looks can be deceptive." Big Pete released his hands and tapped the table with his finger. "But I'll tell you why he wouldn't have done it, he wouldn't have done it because the bloke ripped his jacket. That's a certainty. So, anyone trying to fob you off with that bullshit is grasping at straws. Ben's a decent bloke, he doesn't look for trouble, he's too pretty for that," he held up a finger of warning, "not a coward either, but he wouldn't get involved unless it was necessary. Do you know what I mean?"

"I do." Meredith pursed his lips. "In your opinion, was it necessary, from what you know? I mean, did he need to get involved?"

"Yes, that was his job. The dead guy was pissed, and swinging a broken bottle, so yes, he had to do something, but stab him? No. Where did the knife come from? Ben had no need to be carrying, that's asking for trouble. Not his style anyway, I know when the bloke hit the deck Ben had the knife, so it looks bad, but something ain't right, and you lot better find out what."

Meredith smiled at him and flipping to an empty page, he wrote in his notebook and tore out the page. "When he calls you, tell him to ring me." He held out the paper, which Big Pete took and stuffed into his pocket.

"I'll take it, but he won't phone me, why would he? Can I go?" Big Pete leaned forward ready to push himself up when given permission.

"Because he needs help from someone. Who else might he call if not you?"

Slumping back in his chair, Big Pete sighed and shrugged, "Dan, possibly, but he has other friends I don't know." He held out his hands, "His life doesn't revolve around the few nights he works here you know."

"I do know, yes. But as what happened, happened here, my guess is he's going to want to find out what happened to that recording, and who better than his trusted workmates? Now, who else might have sent on those recordings?" Meredith jotted down the names dictated to him, and slid his notebook into his pocket. He jerked his head towards the door, "You can go now, but don't forget, tell him to call, he knows he can trust me."

Big Pete was up and out the door in a flash, both Meredith and Trump were surprised at how light he was on his feet.

Opening the door, he turned back to them. "Like I said, *if* he calls I'll pass it on. Not convinced he'll believe he can trust you though."

"He will. Give him the number." As he left, Meredith lifted his phone from the table. "Not a word, Trump. Not a word." He held up his finger to emphasise the point before greeting Patsy. "I might be a little late, something's come up." He grimaced as he listened to her response, and nodded as Louie Trump silently excused himself, not wishing to listen to what Meredith was about to say.

~~~

Patsy dropped her phone onto Linda's desk to demonstrate her frustration. Linda Callow had worked with Patsy for some time, they had met while Patsy was still a police officer, and she was now officially living with Louie Trump. She was more than used to the volatile relationship of Meredith and Hodge.

"Do you know what he's done now?" Patsy demanded.

"Told you he's going to be late again?" Linda didn't bother looking up from her screen.

"He's got involved in someone else's case. Today of all days. I know Ben Jacobs is a good friend, but he's stepping on toes. I can't see that Jamie Wessex will relish his interference, and that's what it is, and Wessex is more than capable of dealing with it, and Meredith . . ." She stopped ranting and closed her eyes for a second, before completing the sentence. "But, it is Ben, and I can see his point, but . . ."

"But what? Ben Jacobs? How is he involved?" Linda had abandoned her work and was now leaning forward expectantly. "From the beginning, otherwise you know I'll only make up the bits you omit."

"Ben Jacobs stabbed someone at BB's last night. Or, I should say *allegedly* stabbed someone, but he escaped custody this morning, and there's a missing recording that Meredith is convinced will help him. He's going to tell Wessex what he should do I think." She grimaced, "Not his case, even if he was going to be around, it wouldn't be his case, and today of all days."

"What's today of all days?" Sharon Grainger bustled through the door followed by a man wearing grey overalls. "Today is a momentous day. Well, to be more accurate, tomorrow will be, but what's happened today that's making you look like you're sucking a lemon?" She turned to the man behind her. "Toilet's through there. Put the seat back down."

Patsy and Linda watched the man exit through the door to the kitchen and restroom.

Patsy pointed at the door. "Someone you met on the street?"

"Don't worry about him. What's happened?"

Sharon Grainger was the widow of Chris, Patsy's former partner in the private investigation business. Chris Grainger had also been working for the SIS, unbeknown to all but a few, and his unintended involvement in a massacre in the former Czechoslovakia had resulted in him being shot and killed in revenge for his actions. Only a privileged few, including Meredith and Patsy, were aware of this fact. His wife had no idea, she believed he had been killed in a mix-up with the Russian mafia, and worshipped his memory.

"Meredith has become involved in a murder case. Ben Jacobs was arrested and charged, but escaped before he even got to the magistrates' court." Patsy shrugged, "Tonight might be a total washout." Patsy threw her arms into the air. "Why am I surprised when most of the things I arrange with him are a washout."

"He'll be there. If it's Ben you can understand it, bless him. Now, give me a moment," she turned to the man who had reappeared behind her. "Is that better? Now off you go, get on with it, I'll be out in a moment."

"Should I ask?" Patsy watched the man leave.

"Yes. Who is that?" Linda asked.

"A workman. Call yourselves detectives. My turn, I'll make the tea on the way back." Without further comment, Sharon disappeared towards the restroom.

"Probably her car again, the electrics are playing up. Meredith will be there, don't worry." Linda pulled her keyboard forward and began tapping away, effectively dismissing Patsy.

"I'm not worried for me, it's the others I don't want him to let down." Patsy recovered her phone and walked towards her office. "If you find out what Sharon's up to, let me know. Did you put that new file on my desk?" Linda confirmed the file was there, and she closed the door.

Sitting at her desk, Patsy opened the file and skimmed the summary page. Her new client, Aiden O'Brien, wanted his daughter's boyfriend checked out. Friends, home, work and lifestyle – that meant surveillance. Patsy hated surveillance, and prayed silently that the relationship would break up before she'd spent too many hours sitting in her car. She picked up the photograph of Sian O'Brien and tutted.

"Who have you got mixed up with young lady, did no one tell you that the boy next door makes great boyfriend material?"

Picking up her pen, Patsy made notes from the information provided, and formulated a plan of attack which would hopefully lessen the amount of surveillance. Once the plan was sketched out she opened her laptop.

"Right, Gary Mason, do you use social media?"

Patsy opened her Facebook account and typed in Gary Mason, Bristol, she found him listed tenth. His account didn't appear to be blocked in any way, and after a cursory glance at the photographs, she read posts on his home page. The most recent was two days ago, he had been tagged by Sian O'Brien at a local cinema, and it announced that *Finding Dory* had been amazing. Patsy checked for Gary's and Sian's mutual friends, there were thirty, and she jotted down their names before setting up a bogus account posing as a twenty-year-old student. She used the photo of a cute puppy for her profile picture, before typing in her first post as Alice Brown.

OK, OK - I give in. So, Facebook - I've arrived – show me what you've got. PS. Please be my friend.

Making friend requests to the thirty mutual friends, Patsy set about sharing what she believed would be of interest to them should they check Alice Brown's activity. She had ten new friends within the hour. They were clearly not discerning people. She looked up as Sharon entered carrying a mug of tea.

"That took you long enough," Patsy observed, before thanking her.

"I've been busy. Have a sip, and follow me."

"But I'm in the middle -"

"Leave it, this won't take long." Sharon walked back to the door. "Come on, follow me." Smiling as Patsy slipped her shoes back on and did as she was bid. "You too," Sharon beckoned Linda, who joined them. Opening the door to the office, she led the way out to the carpark.

"Where are we going? Have you bought a new car?" Linda asked, looking around the nearby cars. She halted as Sharon stopped and turned to face them.

"Turn around and tell me what you think? I reckon it has a certain class. It's fabulous, isn't it?"

Patsy and Linda turned around to look back at the building. The workman in the grey overalls was kneeling by a toolbox, packing away his tools, he glanced over and smiled. Their eyes travelled upward.

"Nice!" exclaimed Linda, and looked at Patsy who was standing open-mouthed. "Don't you think?"

"Why? I mean, who . . ." Patsy was clearly at a loss for words, and Sharon walked to stand beside her.

"Do you like it?" She put her arm around Patsy's shoulder and gave it a hug. "It's just right, perfect, in fact."

"I think I'm in shock." Patsy screwed her eyes shut and reopened them. It was still there. "Oh boy!" she exclaimed.

Sharon removed her arm and clapped her hands.

"I knew you'd love it. Now, back inside, that tea's getting cold."

~~~

By six o'clock hunger got the better of him, and Ben pulled the concealed drawer out from beneath the driver's seat and recovered the emergency fund of fifty pounds he had left there. Tucking the notes into his breast pocket he drove to a popular burger van, and was pleased to see that there were only a handful of people about. Purchasing food and several bottles of water, he ate in his car as he watched the sun set on the horizon. He had long since stopped trying to work out how he'd ended up in the predicament in which he found himself, but his boredom had fuelled his anger, and tossing the now half drunk bottle of water into the passenger footwell to join the burger wrapper, he headed back to Brooker's. Slowing as he approached the estate of impressive modern dwellings, he yawned, he'd barely had three hours sleep in the last twenty-four. He rubbed an eye with his knuckles as a further yawn overcame him. Blinking, he looked back at the road in time to see the startled cat freeze in his path.

"Shit," Ben cursed, as he swerved to avoid the cat, and seconds later realised the bend in the road would not favour such a manoeuvre. He tried to correct his error, only to make it worse, and the last thing he remembered, as he raised his hands to protect his face, was the solid wall of red brick hurtling towards the car.

~~~

The loud bang made Hannah Godfrey freeze. Standing under the running water, she waited for a few more moments expecting more to happen. It didn't. Maybe it was nothing. She welcomed the cold water cooling her tired body. Her workout had lasted over an hour in the basement gym of her unique home, but neither the exercise, nor the refreshing shower could dispel her feeling of numbness. She had a fabulous home, an intelligent, successful husband, a daughter she adored, and more money in the bank than they had ever dreamed possible, but something more crucial was missing. Something she couldn't put her finger on, but the need of it was sapping her energy. Sighing, she stepped out of the shower cubicle and grabbed a towel from the shelf. Throwing her wet hair forward she wound the towel into a turban and reached for another.

Hannah looked out the window and couldn't believe what she saw. A car had crashed into the garden wall. Looking around for something to wear, she settled for one of her husband's tee shirts and the panties she had worn while exercising. Casting the turban aside she thrust her wet hair through the neck of the tee shirt, and hurried up the stairs to the hall.

Running into the front garden she surveyed the scene. The driver was slumped over the wheel. Hannah rushed forward, her eyes searching the street beyond for someone, anyone, who might also be rushing to find out what had happened. There was no one, and she paused for a second, her hand on the car door.

Yanking it open, Hannah spoke softly to the driver, "Can you hear me?" She waited a beat. "I'm going to help you sit back in the seat, let me know if it hurts." Receiving no response, she dipped her shoulders into the car and placed her arms around the man. She could see blood on both his brow, and dripping from his right hand, which hung uselessly by his side. "I'm going to try now. One, two . . ." Taking the weight of the man, she grunted, and pulled his body away from the steering wheel, before panic took hold. "Why didn't I simply call an ambulance? What if I'm doing more damage? Oh shit, what if he's dead?" She bit her lip as she positioned the man's head back against the headrest, and peered closely at his face. "Please don't move again. I'll call an ambulance, I know that's what . . . anyway, I won't be long." She snatched back the hand that had intended stroking his face. "Two seconds. I'll be two seconds."

Turning quickly, she had taken only a few steps before she heard the groan. She hesitated, knowing she should remain on course, but against her better judgement she returned to the car. The man was dabbing his fingers on his forehead and wincing.

"Shit, shit, SHIT!" he cursed. "I don't need this." Sensing her presence his head snapped towards her, he groaned, and screwed his eyes shut.

"I don't think you should move. Stay there, I'm going to call an ambulance." Hannah turned back towards the house.

"Don't! I'll be fine. I am fine . . ." Ben held in the groan, as he swivelled and lifted his legs out of the car. If he were a betting man, he'd put money on at least one broken rib. He lifted his hand. "Would you mind?"

Hannah moved forward, her eyes wary. It was clear the man posed no threat, her concern was for the damage he may be doing himself. Once out of the car, Ben stretched his back, and let out a groan that came from deep within as though he were attempting to empty his body of pain.

"I really don't think you should be doing this."

Hannah studied Ben. His eyes were closed and he was leaning on the car for support. She watched as he composed himself, knowing he was about to lie to her. Despite the pallor of his skin, and the blood congealing on his temple, when his eyes opened and found hers, he forced a smile. She looked away momentarily, embarrassed that she found him attractive.

"It's only a couple of bruises. Please don't concern yourself. Is it possible for me to use your phone? Then I'll be out of your way." He smiled again.

Hannah looked back at the house. "This way." She held her hand forward.

Ben pushed himself away from the car, and tentatively stepped forward. A pain shot up his right side which took his breath away, and he stumbled towards her. Hannah grabbed his arm, and placing it across her shoulder, she wrapped her arm around his back.

"You're going to have to let me help you. I don't think you'll make it otherwise." She held him tight as step by step, they slowly made their way to the house.

Even in his condition, Ben appreciated the smell and the feel of the woman pressed against him. His right arm hung limply over her shoulder, and his hand brushed against her breast with the motion of their movement, the nipple responding accordingly. He timed his steps with hers, his eyes watching each movement of her shapely naked legs as he tried to concentrate on a plan as to what to do now he had no transport, but he found it difficult to focus on anything but the pain and those legs.

Hannah helped him through to the kitchen and onto a chair. Ben looked around the room at the glossy white cabinets, black slate and sparkling chrome, and whistled.

"Wow. I knew the houses on this road were on the large side, but I reckon that my whole apartment would fit in here." He glanced at Hannah and hoped his surprise didn't show.

She was beautiful. Dark almond-shaped eyes returned his gaze, and full lips pouted at him from between flawless cheeks. Even with her damp hair hanging in rat's-tails around her shoulders, she looked stunning. His eyes travelled down, her tee shirt was damp from her hair, causing it to cling to her breasts, and then he was back to those legs. He tore his eyes away, knowing he had to focus on this latest predicament.

"It's wonderful. Perfect even, it was built to our specification . . . but not all that glitters, et cetera."

Hannah turned her back on him, and opening a wall cupboard, she stood on tiptoe to lift out a first-aid box. Ben saw the lace on the edge of her red panties.

"We need to get you cleaned up a little."

"Thanks." Ben looked away as she turned back. "I would also like to borrow a phone if possible."

For a brief moment, Hannah was concerned. Everyone had a mobile these days, why not this man? Perhaps she had been too hasty letting this stranger in when she was home alone. Opening the box, she lifted out a small bottle of antiseptic and a bag of cotton wool pads. She placed them on the table, and as she put water into a small bowl, she wondered how she could alert someone without drawing his attention.

"I left mine at work," Ben continued. "That's where I was going in such a hurry. Had I been driving slower I wouldn't have had to swerve to avoid that cat."

Hannah relaxed as he provided the answer to her concern. She smiled as she dipped the cotton pad into the water.

"Ah, it was a cat. I wondered how you'd managed to crash, we've been here for almost eight years now, and never a hint of a problem with the road. Where do you work? Keep still now, I need to find out where this blood is coming from. Let's clean you up."

Ben cursed silently. He'd put himself in a position where he had to lie again. Lies should be kept to a minimum – otherwise they always caught up with you. He avoided the question.

"I wouldn't mind, but I don't even like cats that much, it was instinct." He raised his eyebrows and winced as the action caused the hair to pull against the dried blood on his forehead. "It wasn't your cat, was it?" He pulled his head away from Hannah's approaching hands. "You will be gentle, won't you?"

Hannah laughed, and placing her hand on his shoulder pulled him forward carefully.

"No, not my cat, and yes, I will do my best. Now hold still." Hannah cleaned away the blood with a few gasps from Ben, and found that the wound was a small gash above his right temple. Now clean, the injury didn't look that bad. "I think you'll live, it probably needs a stitch or two though."

"I don't think so! I have an aversion to needles. I'll take my chances, but thanks for cleaning it up." Ben smiled. "I confess I'm a coward."

"In which case, I'll use some of this magic skin glue. Hold still."

Hannah applied the glue along the wound and pinched the skin together as gently as she could. Ignoring the jerk of Ben's body, she held it for what she guessed was a minute. She repacked the first aid box, explaining it would take a few minutes to set fully, and he'd be able to wash his hair if he wanted to. Knowing she was prattling on, she turned away and replaced the first-aid box. When she turned back she caught the quick movement of his head as he looked away. Suddenly aware of her lack of clothing, she felt the flush rise to her cheeks. Grabbing the hem of the tee shirt she tried to stretch it down.

"What must I look like? Wait here, I'll go and get dressed properly." She left the bloodied cotton pads on the work top and stepped towards the door.

"Don't bother on my account," Ben joked, adding quickly, "after all, look at the state of me." He grinned. "I think I win the 'who looks a mess' competition. I wouldn't mind splashing a bit of water over my face."

Hannah turned back and looked at him. His white shirt had several darkening blood stains, and a large damp patch, tinted pink, from where she had cleaned his forehead, causing the shirt to stick to his shoulder.

"Okay, I concede. Strip that shirt off and I'll throw it in the wash." She looked at his trousers which were in a similar condition. "I'll ruin them if I wash them, I expect they're dry clean only. But you can't sit around in them. Follow me."

"Look, you've done enough. I'm not sure how your husband will feel if he comes home and finds me in a state of undress. If I could use the phone."

Ben's smile was genuine, and Hannah was convinced she blushed again as she replied, "Jerry's in Canada. Not back for two weeks, so depending on how long it takes you to shower, you'll be safe . . ." Hannah realised how that must sound, and stuttered, "S . . . sorry, you probably want to get away. Use that one." She pointed at a handset on the wall. "Sorry, I'll be back in a moment."

Ben jumped to his feet. "Please stop apologising, I didn't mean that, I was trying to avoid any awkwardness. There's nothing I'd like more than a shower." He unbuttoned his shirt. "Look, I'm almost ready." He grinned, as she flushed again. "Am I embarrassing you?" He pulled the shirt together coyly.

"No!" Hannah snapped. "This way."

Walking down the stairs to the basement, she led the way to the shower room. Her heart beat a little faster, and she tried to answer the questions that her sensible self was asking. Why had she let this stranger into her house? What did she know about him? What *would* Jerry say? Was she safe? Even if she was being a good Samaritan, why was she taking him to the shower room? How did she know he wasn't some deranged axe murderer, she didn't even know his name? She stopped abruptly as Ben followed her into the small tiled changing area, and turned to face him.

"What's your name?" she demanded.

"Ben," he said without considering his answer, and looked around. A large plate glass shower cubicle filled half the room, and judging by the array of chrome attachments, he would be able to shower from any angle he chose. Stepping forward he peered through a smoked glass panelled door, and found himself amazed at the gym equipment filling the room behind. He gave a low whistle, and turned to face Hannah. "Well you'll certainly never be out of shape." His lips twitched into a smile as she flushed again.

Hannah thrust out her hand, "Hannah, Hannah Godfrey, nice to meet you. The shower is simple to use," she spun round and slid open the cupboard door behind her, "dry towels in here, and you should be able to find a tee-shirt and jogging bottoms on those shelves there." She indicated the shelf below the towels. "Bring your things up when you're done and I'll throw them into the machine. I'll be in the kitchen."

Forcing a smile out of politeness, Hannah hurried from the room, not stopping to think until she was in her bedroom, stripped of the clothes she had been wearing, and securely ensconced in a pair of jeans, and an oversized sweatshirt. Sitting at her dressing table, she dragged a brush through her hair, and secured it in a topknot. Only then did she relax and allow herself to wonder what on earth she was playing at. A smile crept to her lips, she felt like an errant teenager, she was enjoying this drama, and why not? She wasn't doing anything wrong; he, Ben, would be gone in a short while, and she'd be alone, and bored - again. Studying her reflection, she wondered if he'd want to eat with her, or perhaps she could give him a lift somewhere. "Only one way to find out," she announced to the mirror, and grinned at the twinkle she caught in her eye.

5

Patsy brushed a stray hair from Meredith's shoulder, and standing on tiptoes kissed the tip of his nose.

"You'll do, I suppose. Now, we really must make a move. Amanda is meeting us there." Throwing the strap of her bag over her shoulder, she grabbed her car keys and opened the front door.

"I said I didn't want any of this. I don't see the point. It's not like I'm emigrating." Meredith rolled his head in a circular motion in an effort to release some of the tension in his neck.

"Meredith! Now!" Patsy pointed at the open door. "One, you shouldn't be so ungrateful. Two, you love these things, despite the moaning, and, three, if you really are suffering we can escape after a couple of hours, if you want." She pulled the door closed behind them. "I know you have other things on your mind, but haven't you always?"

Ten minutes later, Patsy pulled into the carpark which was surprisingly empty, and glanced at the clock on the dashboard. It was past eight o'clock and it was supposed to have started at seven. She didn't say anything to Meredith, but locked the car and followed him into the pub.

Dave Rawlings came to greet them. "Welcome, Gov. I thought you'd stood us up for a while, what can I get you?" He leaned around Meredith and kissed Patsy on the cheek.

Meredith surveyed his surroundings. A small banner proclaiming "Good Luck" hung lopsidedly over a table laden with the expected buffet fare. The handful of people watching him waved and called out greetings; he raised his hand and saluted them.

"This is going to be a long and painful night," he murmured to Patsy before accepting his pint from Rawlings. "Cheers, Dave. How are they doing?"

"Early days, Gov. Jacobs has vanished off the face of, and no one who knows him is talking. Except to say they can't believe he did it."

"He didn't." Meredith emptied his pint, and beckoned the barmaid, "Fill that up, and whatever anyone else is having." He raised his voice, and a few of the guests got up and came to the bar to place their orders. He acknowledged their thanks, spoke to a few, before returning his attention to the barmaid. He handed her his bank card. "Have one yourself and you'd better keep hold of that."

He watched Patsy seat herself with Rawlings' wife, Eve. "What's Wessex doing about the missing footage?" He was surprised when Rawlings laughed.

"Not funny I know, but trying to stay a step ahead of you, he was a bit heavy handed when he questioned Brooker. Brooker's brief got snotty, it got messy, and the Super had him in his office for half an hour. He wasn't happy." He took a swig of his pint. "What do you know about Keith Chapman?"

"Name's familiar." Meredith shook his head, "Who is he?"

"Brooker's father-in-law, and as far as we can make out, financier."

"How is he involved? Is he . . . Oh boy, here she comes." Meredith forced a smile and held his arms out. "Linda, you look as . . . unique, as always. Beautiful." Meredith hugged Linda and attempted to rub her lipstick from his cheek while she was still speaking to him.

"Hello, Meredith, thank you. You look as handsome as ever." She glanced over her shoulder at Trump. "But not as handsome as Louie, obviously. I'm so excited we've finally got here, I can't wait until tomorrow. I've baked a cake to celebrate, and wait until you see . . ." Linda stopped speaking as Patsy grabbed her arm.

"Don't go stealing anyone else's thunder. Come and sit with me, do you know Eve Rawlings?" Guiding her by the elbow, Patsy led Linda away.

Meredith handed Trump a pint. "What will Linda have, and what is that she's wearing?"

"A red wine, it's a cat suit apparently." Trump sipped his pint. "She thinks it makes her look taller."

"I've never seen a cat covered in . . ." Meredith squinted towards Linda, "Hippos. Blue hippos, with their crotch down by their knees, before," he handed Trump the drink. "I'll let you do the honours." He smiled as Trump shrugged.

"She made it herself, I have no idea where she keeps finding the fabric. Still, it makes her happy." He looked over his shoulder and found Dave Rawlings was now in deep conversation with the landlord. "May I have a minute later? Couple of things I think you might want to hear. Nothing urgent."

He wandered away and joined the women at their table. Meredith looked around, and the pain gripped his chest again. A razor sharp, penetrating pain, and he gasped and drew in a deep breath which he held while he silently counted. Eleven! The pains, which had been increasing in frequency, had only ever reached a nine before. He tried to relax, perhaps he should see a doctor. He was still considering this when a large hand slapped his shoulder.

"A pint, a whiskey chaser, and you're paying, you bastard. It was you that got me into this mess." George Davies tapped the pump on the bar, and barmaid smiled at him as she pulled his pint. "And a single malt, please, love. The good one, not that cheap crap you keep for the drunks." He looked at Meredith as he lifted his pint from the bar, "Tell me that wanker Wessex isn't invited."

"Not that I know of. What's happened, and why's it my fault?" Meredith pulled up a bar stool and perched waiting for George to half empty the glass.

George smacked his lips together in appreciation, picked up the whiskey, knocked it back, and handing the empty glass back to the barmaid, he ordered a refill.

"Same again, he's paying." He looked at Meredith and shook his head. "You don't know? Over thirty years I've been a copper, last ten as duty sergeant, not even a coffee stain on my record, and here I am, couple of years before retirement, and bang!" He wandered off to collect a bar stool and dragged it back. Sitting to face Meredith he shrugged helplessly. "Suspended, gross misconduct, if he makes it stick my pension will be halved, not to mention my reputation." He took the fresh whiskey and repeated his earlier actions. The beer glass, which he turned in continual circles on the bar, remained half empty.

"Suspended? Gross misconduct?" Meredith glanced at the barmaid, "Make that two. A disciplinary I'll grant you, but that's over the top, even for Wessex."

"Yeah, well, there you have it. You've knackered my career. I intend to drink this place dry tonight, at your expense."

Meredith had said nothing to George, other than to mention that Ben Jacobs was a good bloke, and asked that George keep an eye on him. He'd have trusted Ben not to do a runner too, but he had played no part in George's misjudgment.

He sighed. "I'll have a word, George," he said quietly.

George snorted. "You won't be any good to me now, will you? I've got to work out how to tell the wife, she had plans for my pension money." He picked up the latest whiskey and knocked it back in one. Meredith ordered him another drink.

"I need a word with Trump. I'll be back, take it steady, George." Meredith worked his way across to Trump, shaking hands and exchanging words with a few of the others there, and when he caught Trump's eye, he jerked his head towards the door. "A word," he mouthed, and Trump, glad to have an excuse to get away from the table of women, picked up his drink and followed him to the door.

"Is this about George?" Trump asked, as he walked to the perimeter wall of the carpark, and leaned against it.

"Partly," Meredith replied. "But first, you said you wanted to speak to me." Meredith joined Trump by perching himself on the low wall. "Tell me what I missed back at the station."

Trump settled his pint on the wall next to him, and turned to face Meredith. "When I arrived back at the station, some of the staff from BB's had already been in, some were waiting for a formal interview. The one overriding thing that came out of it, was that with the exception of Brooker, and I'll come back to him, everyone is shocked that Ben Jacobs could do such a thing with such little provocation. Nobody really saw anything until the poor man hit the floor, and the girl, Dawn, screamed. They didn't realise that the fracas had become so serious. When Brooker arrived at the station, he became irate about you, and your interview techniques. By which time of course I had arrived back and explained to DI Wessex about the missing recording. He became quite animated and went off to interview Brooker."

Trump lifted his glass and sipped his pint; keeping hold of it, he gave a shake of his head before continuing. "He demanded Brooker tell him where the missing tape was. Brooker was pretty much as he was with us. Said he had no idea who had sent them, and that it was nothing to do with him. He added that having thought about it, it may have been his nephew. Then, without warning, and for reasons which are beyond me, DI Wessex lost it. He screamed questions at Brooker. Did he not know what was going on in his own business? Did he think we were idiots? How could he not know? Were we expected to believe that such a crucial piece of evidence had gone missing without his knowledge? He rounded off by telling Brooker, that if that were the case, he was clearly a total idiot that didn't know what was going on under his nose. DI Wessex announced he was arresting Brooker for obstructing the course of justice."

Trump took another sip before turning back to Meredith with a grin. "And then all hell broke loose."

Meredith returned the grin. "I like a bit of loose hell. What happened?"

"Brooker stood up and told DI Wessex he was a total wanker, and that it was he who didn't know what was going on. He tried to get to the door, but DI Wessex blocked his way, they . . ." Trump paused looking for the right word, "scuffled, I think covers it, and I stepped in and asked Brooker to take his seat. He did, but not before demanding a phone call, and his solicitor. He also told DI Wessex to arrest him formally and to stop playing at being a copper. If it weren't such a serious case it might have been amusing."

Trump's expression became serious. "Between you and I, I think something must have happened to cause DI Wessex to act like that. He's been so formal, everything in order, all by the book, so I can only assume something has seriously wound him up. I hope he calms down, if he gets this wound up over nothing, what will he be like when he's really up against it? You've not said much about him, is this normal, do you know?"

Meredith gave a non-committal shrug. "How would I know? What happened then, did he arrest him, tell me he wasn't that stupid? Meredith smirked as Trump nodded.

"He did I'm afraid, had him in the cell for almost an hour. When the solicitor arrived, we had an attempt at an interview, but the solicitor shot everything Wessex said down in flames, mostly correctly, and demanded we release Brooker, which after a call from the Super, we did. Before he left, Brooker threatened him. He told DI Wessex that he had messed about with the wrong man, and that he would have his career. He pointed out that we had allowed a murderer to escape, while his only misdemeanour was to not know what had happened to a recording he'd never seen. He said DI Wessex should think about that. Wessex was fuming, he established where he could find Brooker's nephew, and released him. He was not a happy man."

"Did you find the nephew?" Meredith emptied his pint.

"Jo and Tom went to question him. They found him at his grandfather's house. Keith Chapman, have you heard of him?" Meredith shrugged and Trump continued, "The lad, Gary, agreed to accompany them to the club to show them how the system works, and the email with *all* the recordings he sent in. Chapman went with them as well."

"Who is this Chapman? Rawlings asked me if I knew him too. Should I know him? The name rings a bell, but I can't place him. Oh dear, here comes Patsy, I think I'm in trouble."

The two men watched Patsy stroll across the carpark, she was shaking her head as though in disappointment.

Meredith held his hands up in surrender. "I know, I know, I'm being naughty. Give me five minutes, and I promise you I'll be the perfect host." He forced a smile and waved jazz hands at her.

"Five minutes. I know you're worried about Ben, that's understandable, but as of now, other than to be a concerned bystander, there is nothing you can do. Don't get your team into trouble by interfering. They'll get it sorted with Wessex. You're only almost, but not quite, indispensable you know."

She looked at Trump, her face stern. "Don't encourage him." Glancing at her watch, she added, "You have five minutes from now." She returned her attention to Meredith, "Apart from anything else, someone needs to keep an eye on poor old George. If what he says is true, you were right, Wessex is a gung-ho bastard!" Keeping her face straight, she added, "Two in a row, you have to feel for the team." Turning she walked back to the pub grinning.

"Gung-ho bastard? I thought you didn't know anything about him?" Trump challenged.

"What I know is irrelevant to the case, no point in distracting you, hard enough to keep you lot on track at the best of times. Don't change the subject, tell me about Chapman, and the recordings."

As if on cue, Jo Adler and Tom Seaton pulled into the carpark.

"You can get it from the horse's mouth, but I'd do so inside, I don't think Patsy was joking." Trump stood and picked up his now empty glass. "My round."

"How bad was it for George?" Meredith asked as they walked to greet the new arrivals.

"Appalling. DI Wessex had him in his office, left the door open and laid into him. Much of what he said was unnecessary, most unfounded, but give the old boy his due, he took it like a man. He did whisper something at the end of the tirade of abuse thrown at him, but I didn't catch it. DI Wessex went scarlet and barely had the ability to tell him to get out."

Meredith chewed his lip. "He'll get his. It's only a matter of time." Opening his arms, he greeted Jo and planted a noisy kiss on her forehead. "Come on you two, hurry, the drinks are on Trump, and I want information without arousing Patsy's wrath."

Once back in the bar, Meredith made a show of making his way around the gathered guests, shaking hands and reminiscing with them to placate Patsy. Believing he'd done enough, he made a beeline for Jo Adler and Tom Seaton. Making sure they had drinks, he turned his back to the room his face as serious as if he were interviewing a suspect.

"Right you two, bring me up to date. What's the latest on the missing recording, and any news on Ben?"

"No news on Ben at all, Gov. He has disappeared. DI Wessex has requested we be allowed extra overtime to enable us to follow those closest to him." Jo Adler shrugged, knowing it wasn't what Meredith wanted to hear.

Meredith grinned. "Ha! I wish him luck with that. Now, what about the recording?"

Jo perched herself on a bar stool, and placed her drink on the bar next to her. Meredith wasn't going to give up.

"Not a lot to tell, Gov. At the moment, it's a needle in a haystack. Brooker's nephew, Gary, showed us how to access the recordings, seemed a nice lad, but very distracted, nerves I expect, unlike his grandfather, who was extremely calm. He showed us how they're all stored in the cloud," she held her hands up, "I still don't know what that means. He showed us the email that forwarded the recordings was from BB's general email account enquiries@BBnightclub. He explained that anybody who had access to that email account could have sent the recordings. He opened up the file," she raised her hands and made speech marks with her fingers, "in the cloud, and there are two or three months' worth of recordings from all three cameras in the bar, until the twenty-four hours which includes the murder of O'Brien."

She paused to sip her drink, and Meredith wound his finger in circles, indicating she should keep going.

Tom Seaton grinned at her. "Two bosses now, Jo. Dear God, how are we going to cope?"

"Can we get on with it, please? If Patsy comes over and finds me talking shop, I'll have to phone you in the early hours. Quickly now, and laugh Tom."

"What?" Tom looked at Meredith as though he'd gone mad, but caught on when Meredith threw his head back, laughed heartily and slapped him on the back. Glancing along the bar, Tom saw Patsy ordering a drink. She smiled and waved, he returned the gesture and beamed at her.

Turning back to Meredith he took up where Jo had left off. "To summarise, one, there is a missing recording, two, that recording has vital evidence which may possibly put Jacobs in the clear, and three, it will be somebody that has access to the club's account. We asked for a list of who had access to that account, and were redirected to Brooker. We found him emptying a bottle of whiskey in his bar. We ended up with eleven names, which he claims is, to the best of his knowledge, the full complement of those with the ability to access the account. So, tomorrow -"

Meredith thumped the bar in irritation. "Okay so eleven people have access, eleven people could have sent them, but who was asked to? It's not fucking rocket science, is it? We asked for them, they arrived, who sent them?" He picked up his glass and took a large swig. "For Christ's sake, this is elementary stuff. Who asked for the recordings?"

Tom Seaton cleared his throat. "Wessex."

"And who did Wessex ask? Does he remember? Has that person been interviewed? What did they say?" Meredith's tone was sarcastic, and he knew he was taking his irritation out on the wrong people.

"Wessex asked Brooker. Brooker spoke to the staff as a group, as by that time they had been gathered in the locker room. He dropped DI Wessex's business card on the table, and told someone to get him the recordings. Wessex has confirmed this, he and Brooker then left the room," Jo Adler explained.

"Okay, so now we're getting somewhere, who was in the room, and how many of them had access to the club email account?" Meredith asked.

"I can't remember all the names, Gov, but there were three doormen, the receptionist, two barmaids, and a cleaner who turned up after the event to clean the club. My guess is it's not her, and therefore one of the others."

"So where was the email sent from? I've been in that locker room, the recording equipment is in there, but I didn't see any computer."

"That's where we were when we left to come here. We need to question them all again to see who took it upon themselves to send the recordings. Apparently, there is a small office with a desk and laptop, next to Brooker's office. Did you go in there too?" Tom Seaton smiled, "You know Wessex is going to get mightily pissed off with your interference, don't you?"

Meredith stared at him. "Do I look like I care? Get me the names first thing in the morning, and we'll see what we can do."

"But, Gov," protested Jo, "you really should back off now, we'll keep you informed, but you can't take this any further."

"I think I can do what I like, Jo, I'm a big boy. In fact -" Meredith was interrupted by a screech at the door. He turned to look and Peggy Green waved at him.

"Yoohooo. Merewinkle," she called. "I can't believe you're here. How did Patsy manage that?" Peggy walked towards him grinning. Realising there was little else he could do, he fixed a grin and walked to meet her.

"Hello, Peggy, I wasn't expecting you."

"That's because you never invited me. I'd never leave the house if it wasn't for Patsy."

Peggy Green had been a vital witness on one of Meredith's previous cases, and though brash and outspoken, with a tendency to challenge Meredith, the two hit it off, and she'd become an adopted member of Meredith's somewhat disjointed family.

"Never get out?" questioned Meredith. "The last I heard you were in Spain with whatshisname and the baby. Don't try and pull the wool over my eyes, old woman."

"Less of the old woman." Peggy poked him in the ribs. "And Pablo is not so much of a baby anymore, he's walking now. Poor little thing. Young Pablo could do with a few more visits from his godfather. He won't know what you look like if you don't get your arse around to see him soon. But wait a couple of weeks, they're still in Spain." She stared at Meredith's hands. "I could have sworn I was a guest and would be offered a drink. Are you buying?"

Meredith kissed the top of her head and pushed her towards the bar. "Of course, Peggy, what are you having?"

Over the next hour or so, more people arrived who had worked with Meredith over the years, including Sharon Grainger, and Frankie Callaghan. Patsy was delighted that Meredith appeared relaxed, and was enjoying socialising with his guests. Several of his old team had tried to escape a few times, but Meredith had managed to convince them to stay for another ten minutes, numerous times, and a real party atmosphere took hold as more and more alcohol was imbibed.

A little before ten-thirty, Rob Hutchins, a promising young detective constable, whom Meredith had encouraged into CID, opened the door and looked around nervously. He had been sent by DI Wessex to round up the team for a debrief before an early start the next day. Wessex was not best pleased that they hadn't returned after an hour as instructed. Hutchins didn't fancy his chances of success as he stepped into the bar, and was immediately spotted by Meredith.

"About time, Pa, I didn't think you were coming." Meredith slung his arm around Hutchins' shoulder. He had nicknamed Hutchins, Pa, when he had become a father for the first time while working on his first case with Meredith's team. "What's your poison?"

Hutchins tried to make an excuse, but Meredith ignored him, and when he turned to the bar to order a drink, Hutchins gestured wildly to Trump and Rawlings in an effort to save himself. Meredith turned and caught him in the act.

"Are you doing semaphore now, Pa?" he asked, knowing full well why Hutchins was there.

"Sorry, Gov. The Gov, that is, DI Wessex, has sent me to round everyone up. He's back at the station waiting to brief them."

Meredith put an arm around Hutchins' shoulders, "Have you been there all night?"

"Yep," Hutchins grimaced, "and he's not in the best of moods, so I'd better get on with it."

Meredith nodded and shoved the pint glass in his hand. "In which case, drink that, and I'll let you get off."

As Hutchins took the first sip of the pint, Meredith nudged him, "What's the latest?"

As Hutchins' throat welcomed the comfort of the cold liquid, he wondered how much he should say, and deciding Meredith would find out anyway, he wiped his mouth with the back of his hand and stepped closer to Meredith.

"I'm not sure what you already know, sir, but I can tell you that there is a list of people that may have sent the recordings. Some of them have been telephoned and deny it was them, the others we'll track down in the morning. DI Wessex has the tech team working on finding an IP address for the computer which sent the email, and running face recognition on some of the stills. That way we can establish if the email came from the club, if it was, we're back to square one, and we've yet to find any of those surrounding O'Brien at the bar."

"That's it? That's all he's got? What about motive? What about finding out why O'Brien was there, and what had made him so angry? Anything new on that?" Meredith was incredulous.

"No, sir. DI Wessex has arranged to go and see the widow tomorrow, she was too distraught today and the doctor had given her a sedative. The family we did manage to speak to had no explanation, and Brooker says they were simply discussing work." Hutchins eyes glanced from side to side. He didn't want to get caught giving out this information, even if it was to Meredith. No one was listening and he relaxed a little.

Meredith released his clenched fists, and ran his fingers through his hair.

"Just discussing work? Wessex accepted that, did he? Our friend Brooker knows a lot more than he is saying, that much is clear. Has anyone established what O'Brien did for Brooker? I don't accept this 'he was simply a driver' crap. A driver wouldn't have got into his office to shout and bawl at him."

Hutchins was relieved when Trump came to join them at the bar, he felt he'd said enough.

Trump patted Meredith on the shoulder. "I think it's time for us to make a move, sir, but before we do, we'd like to present you with a small token to help you remember us. So, if we could have your attention please…"

Trump turned and swung his arm to the other guests, who had fallen silent, all eyes on Meredith. Rawlings picked up several small packages which had been carefully gift-wrapped. He handed the first to Meredith, who took little time in removing the wrapping. It was an expensive pen set, and Meredith was touched by the amount of money that had been collected. He waved the box at his guests before sliding it into his inside pocket.

"Thank you very much. I'm touched, I have to say I wasn't expecting that, thank you. Of course I was hoping to forget you all, despite being unforgettable myself." He smiled. "You all know me well enough to know I wasn't looking forward to tonight, but I'm glad I'm here, and I know some of you should be elsewhere, so please do feel free to leave now, I promise I won't stop you. Thanks again." He patted the pocket containing the pens before holding out his hand towards Trump.

Rawlings stepped forward again. "Not so fast, there's a couple more for you to open here." He shoved another gift into Meredith's outstretched hand. When Meredith opened it, he found a magnifying glass. "I'm reliably informed all private detectives need one of those, Gov." He laughed as he handed him the last package.

"If this is an effing deerstalker . . ." Meredith laughed as he unwrapped the tweed hat, and popped it on his head, before placing the magnifying glass in his breast pocket so that it was clearly visible. "Very funny. I'll have to find you a new nickname now, Sherlock," he called to Frankie Callaghan, before falling serious. "All joking aside, thank you once again. I will never wear this hat again, I will never use the magnifying glass, but I am sure the pens will be put to good use. Now, those of you that have to bugger off do so now, because I am going to have a serious drink."

He turned to the bar, but someone in the group sang out, 'For he's a jolly good fellow', and he turned back, flapping his hands in an effort to halt the singing. "There's no need for . . ." he was stopped mid-sentence as the barman appeared carrying a yard of ale.

Patsy groaned, this could get messy, Meredith rarely refused a challenge. Meredith removed his jacket, hung it on the back of the nearest chair, and rolling up his shirt sleeves he took hold of the yard.

"I can do this easily, you must know that, but if anyone fancies a challenge, time me, and I'll choose the next contestant."

Placing the glass against his lips, he bent his knees slightly, and opening his mouth, he slowly tilted the yard, until the liquid started pouring into his mouth. The crowd clapped and cheered encouragement. He was about half way through when the large brass bell hanging over the bar rang out noisily. It was only used to signal last orders, and Meredith lowered the glass and glared to his left to see who had caused the interruption. His eyes locked onto DI Jamie Wessex.

"I wasn't expecting to see you." He held the yard towards Wessex, "your turn."

"Sorry, no can do. I've got a murder investigation to run, and half my team are here." His eyes sought out Rob Hutchins, "I sent him to get them, but apparently even such a simple instruction was too complicated." He looked around the bar, his eyes making contact with those that should be back at the station. "Outside – two minutes," he snapped. Looking back at Meredith he added, "Happy retirement, old boy." He left the bar without further comment.

There were grunts, groans, and murmurings, not least from George, who told anyone that would listen that he was going to punch the bastard on the nose, if he could get out of the chair. Meredith shook the hands of those who were leaving, and promised he'd keep in touch. They knew this wasn't a false promise, particularly until the Ben Jacobs case was solved to his satisfaction.

~~~

Ben Jacobs pulled the clean white tee shirt over his head, and winced as it rubbed against his wound. Walking to the mirror, he carefully ran the comb through his hair, before packing his meagre belongings back into the carrier bag. Taking it up to the kitchen, he placed it by the door, he planned to make his phone call and leave at the earliest opportunity.

Hannah smiled at him as she pulled a large pizza from its box. "I'm going to pop this into the oven, you're welcome to join me, unless you need to leave once you've made your call." She opened the oven and slid the pizza onto the top shelf.

Despite the plans he'd made not five minutes before, Ben found himself smiling and nodding in agreement.

"That sounds great, thank you. I could eat a horse." His smile faltered and he cursed silently, he pointed to the phone, "I'll use that one, shall I?"

"Yes," Hannah opened a drawer and pulled out a notepad, "I've got a shopping list to write."

Ben lifted the receiver from the wall, and walked back into the hall. He didn't want Hannah to hear the conversation.

With a poor memory for numbers, and lost without his own phone, he had two choices, call his local Chinese takeaway or call BB's. He dialled the number for the club, hoping that Big Pete would answer. His heart sank as Sandra's standard greeting was called. He hung up, and considered his options. Without his friend's numbers, he had little choice but to go via the club. Sighing, he walked back into the kitchen.

Hannah noticed his long face. "Oh dear, could you not get who you wanted? You look cheesed off."

For some reason, which he couldn't explain, Ben placed his trust in Hannah, but not with the complete truth.

"It's a long story, I'm trying to get hold of a friend, but have to get past his girlfriend first." He called up his most charming smile. "I don't suppose you'd do me a favour and make the call, would you?"

Hannah agreed, and Ben redialled and handed her the phone.

"Ask for Big Pete, if she gives you any trouble tell her it's none of her business, she won't take offence don't worry."

Sandra looked at the phone in irritation as it rang again. She placed her nail file on the till and snatched it up. "BB's, how can I help you?" she snapped.

Hannah glanced at Ben, "I'd like to speak to Big Pete if possible, please." Hannah replied, and smiled encouragingly at Ben.

"Who is it? What do you want him for?" Sandra asked, clearly not interested in the answer.

"I don't think that's any of your business, I'm a friend, and it's important. That's all you need to know. Now, may I speak to Pete, please." Hannah was not used to being curt with anyone, she glanced at Ben and grimaced, and he nodded encouragement. Hannah heard the exasperated sigh from Sandra.

"If you don't give me your name I'm not putting you through to anyone, I don't care if you're the queen mother."

"I think you'll find that the queen mother is dead. Big Pete, please, now. I don't think he'll be best pleased if he knows you're messing me about." Hannah was warming to her role and grinned at Ben.

Sandra didn't reply. Placing her hand over the mouthpiece she called to Pete, who was speaking quietly to Brooker at the entrance.

"Pete, some woman wants you. Won't give her name." She pouted as Pete turned to her. "Said it was important."

Pete shrugged. "I don't know any woman that has anything important to say." He grinned at Brooker. "Get her name, I expect she's one of my admirers."

He waited while Sandra relayed the message. Brooker patted him on the shoulder and walked towards Sandra as she returned to the call.

"Pete says, emergency or not, he won't come to the phone unless you give your name."

Sandra sounded smug, and Hannah was at a loss. Glancing at the handset, she hit the speaker button.

Pushing a pen and paper towards Ben, she asked. "He said what?"

Ben listened to Sandra's responding sigh echo in the kitchen.

"He said if you don't give your name, he won't speak to you. It's not that difficult to understand, surely? Name or I'm hanging up." Sandra was now bored and wanted to get back to her nails.

Ben scribbled something on the pad and pushed it back to Hannah. She glanced at him before responding to Sandra.

"Tell him it's Nancy, Big Nancy." They waited, this time Sandra didn't place her hand over the receiver but called to Pete.

"Nancy. She says she's Big Nancy."

"I don't know any Nancy." Pete shrugged, and then the penny dropped. He stepped forward his eyes on Brooker. "Oh, I know, I'd better speak to her, she's a pain in the arse. If I don't, she'll be calling all night. Sorry, Boss," he added, as he reached Brooker at the reception desk.

"Hello, Pete here, what do you want?" His tone abrupt, he walked back to the door. Ben snatched the phone from Hannah, forgetting it was on loud speaker.

"Pete, it's me mate, Ben. Can you speak without being overheard?" His voice rang out around him and he looked startled. Hannah switched off the speaker.

"Yes, my love, it depends what you want. I have my boss with me, so keep it short."

"Shit! Is Brooker there?" Ben paced into the hall and sat on the bottom stair.

"Yep, but busy though. Where are you calling from?"

"That's a long story you don't want to hear." Ben ran his fingers through his hair. "I need help, I've smashed the car up. I need rescuing, a bed for the night, and some transport."

"Well you don't want much, do you?" Pete glanced at Brooker who had finished his conversation with Sandra and was now climbing the stairs to his office. For his benefit, Pete raised his voice a little, "I've got to be quick, the boss doesn't pay me to chat to you. A friend of yours, or so he claimed, has been in touch."

"Friend? What friend?" Ben queried.

"Hang on a minute," Big Pete pressed the phone to his chest as he pulled open the door allowing Sammy to enter. Once Sammy was in conversation with Sandra, he stepped outside hoping he wouldn't lose the signal. "Meredith, John Meredith. He's a copper. He said you'd want to speak to him."

"Was a copper," Ben replied standing up. "Thinking about it, that's not a bad shout, did he give you his number?" Ben strode back into the kitchen and grinned at Hannah.

Pete pulled Meredith's card from his pocket and read out the number to

Ben. Ben was having second thoughts as he wrote the number on the pad. Meredith would try and talk him into giving himself up, which he had already considered and dismissed. He wanted a word with Brooker first.

"Okay, I've got that, I don't want him to know where I am. Second thoughts, would you call him for me, I need to think this through. Tell him I'll speak to him tomorrow and give me your number too." He scribbled the number beneath Meredith's. "Thanks, and finally, a big ask I know, but is there any chance you could put me up tonight?"

His face fell as Big Pete said he thought it would be too dangerous, as there were still police officers at the club, and friends may be followed on the chance they were harbouring Ben. Ben thanked him anyway and promised to keep in touch. He sighed and replaced the receiver.

Hannah had busied herself laying basic dinner settings on the breakfast bar. She pulled the cork from a bottle of wine and held an empty glass towards Ben.

"Would you like one? It sounds as though you could do with one."

Ben nodded and she poured a generous measure into the glass and slid it towards him.

"I know it's none of my business, but are you in some kind of trouble?" A light flush coloured her cheeks as she asked the pertinent question.

Pulling out a stool, Ben sat opposite her. She didn't need to know the full story, but he had to tell her something, he left out the key details.

"Not trouble so much, as a predicament." He shrugged. "For reasons I won't bore you with, I can't go home tonight, so I'll have to find a B & B or cheap hotel locally. If I'd not left my phone at work, I could have called a few mates."

"Wouldn't it be easier to simply get your phone? I can give you a lift if you like." Hannah checked the pizza. "Nearly done. We can eat this, and then I'll give you a lift." She smiled at him.

"Unfortunately, head office is in Cheltenham, a little too far for a lift at this time of night. Don't worry I'll get a room somewhere. Do you know anywhere locally?"

Hannah considered this, it wouldn't be difficult to find somewhere fairly close, but she wondered if she should let him stay the night. She was enjoying having someone in the house, and he seemed a nice enough chap, but that was ridiculous. Wasn't it? What would Jerry say? Her hand flew to her mouth. She'd forgotten to call her husband. He'd asked that she called before his scheduled seminar. She looked at the red digits of the timer on the oven. She might be able to catch him.

"Damn. I forgot to phone my husband. Do you mind if I do it before we eat?"

"Of course not, would you like me to leave?" Ben responded, sliding off the stool as she lifted the handset.

Hannah waved him back. "Not at all, it'll only take a minute," She scrolled through the address book, and before hitting the dial button, she turned back to Ben. "I need to get this out, so I'll put him on speaker, please don't speak, I don't know how I'll explain a strange man in the house."

Ben nodded, and held back a smile as the now familiar flush rose to her cheeks. He sat back on the stool, and doodled on the pad. The sound of ringing filled the kitchen as Hannah opened the oven and took out the pizza. She slid it onto a large wooden board as the hotel receptionist answered in a perky Canadian accent.

"Hi, may I speak to Jerry Godfrey, please, room three-two-two," Hannah asked as she sliced into the pizza.

"Certainly, mam, transferring you now."

The phone rang for a while, Hannah was about to hang up when a sleepy, female voice, murmured hello. Hannah stopped slicing and looked at the phone. She didn't speak.

"Hello, hello. Is anyone there?" The woman's voice was clearer now.

Hannah recovered her senses. "Valerie. I'd like to say what a surprise, but that would be lying, may I speak to my husband please?" Her tone was crisp and efficient. Valerie managed an "Oh" before the sound of muted voices filtered through.

Ben sneaked a sideways glance at Hannah, her face was stern as she glared at the pizza. He would have wagered his last month's earnings that his guess as to what was going on was correct.

In Canada, Jerry Godfrey snatched up the phone. "Hello, Hannah. How are you?"

Ben knew his guess was right, the question was too formal, delivered too crisply.

"I'm fine and dandy as you would expect. I'll be quick as you're clearly busy. The contract arrived from Dance Electronics. Where would you like me to send it?" From the corner of her eye, Hannah saw Ben turn to look at her, she tilted her chin and stared at the clock on the opposite wall.

"Send it? What do you mean? Look, Hannah, I can explain."

"No need, I'm not stupid," Hannah snapped. "Where?"

"It was a fluke that Valerie was here, I bumped into her yesterday, quite by chance . . . I . . ."

Jerry was saved further explanation.

"Save it," she said sharply. "I listened to all this the last time, I have neither the energy, nor the will to live through it again. Answer please."

"Answer? To what question?"

Ben could hear desperation creeping into Jerry's voice. He looked back at the pad as Hannah stabbed at the pizza with the cutter she was clutching.

"Where do you want me to send the bloody contract, and your other belongings, Jerry? It's a simple enough question. Still, your mind has been on other things, so I'll send everything on to your mother's address. I'll speak to the solicitor in the morning, and we can sort the rest out via her." Hannah dropped the cutter and her hand shot to her face and brushed away the single tear. She would not cry.

"Hannah, please." Jerry now sounded irritated. "I deserve better than that, Hannah, you won't even hear me out? I can -"

"Better? Better?" The words were spat out rapidly but Hannah remained static. "I'm the one who deserves better. I know this has been going on for months, and I'm prepared, Jerry, perfectly prepared."

"If you knew, then why didn't you say? You're trying to call my bluff," Jerry sounded more confident.

"Oh, for God's sake, put Valerie on." Hannah tutted as though speaking to an errant child, and raised her hand to her hip. "She'll speak the truth, she's always wanted you to put a ring on her finger, well, now she can have her wish."

There was a short silence before Jerry mumbled, "No, I won't. We need to talk, but now is not a good time."

"Of course it's not a good time. Your mistress is, what, lying naked on the bed looking at you? As I say, I'm prepared, I knew I'd get confirmation during this trip, so I've arranged a little . . . what would you call it? Oh yes, a little distraction of my own, after all what's good for the goose . . ."

"A little what? What does that mean?" Jerry bellowed into the receiver, but a moment later he laughed. "Do me a favour, don't kid a kidder, Hannah. You haven't got it in you. I'll give the airport a ring and get the next flight back." There was still amusement in his tone.

Hannah glanced at Ben and pulled her shoulders back. "Don't bother, Jerry, stay and enjoy the trip. I have plans, I'm going away for a few days."

"Away? Where, and with whom?" Jerry had lost some of his confidence.

"Ben." It was a simple announcement, but she could feel the tension building in her shoulders. She looked at Ben and mouthed 'Sorry'. She gave an apologetic shrug and Ben grinned and returned the gesture.

"Ben who? Stop buggering about, Hannah, this is serious, and messing around won't sort this out."

"No, only the solicitors will be able to do that now. I must go I have a case to pack."

"I asked who?" Jerry was shouting now, "Ben, WHO?" Valerie could be heard speaking in the background but her words were not clear.

"I have no idea, we only met a couple of hours ago, Ben is my distraction, so, no formal introductions are necessary. Say hello, Ben."

Ben eyes widened in surprise, "Hello, Jerry." He hoped he'd used his deepest and sexiest voice. He'd be out of here in a couple of hours, and if she thought it would help, who was he to question her actions?

"What the . . ." was all Jerry managed before he hung up.

Hannah replaced the handset, and Ben noticed the slight tremor in her hand.

"I'm so sorry you had to be witness to that." She brushed her hands over her cheeks. "Not pleasant for you. Now, we'll eat pizza, and drink wine, and not brood on things which we can't change."

She lifted the cutter and her hand was shaking. Ben got to his feet and went to her. Removing the cutter from her fingers, he pushed her in the direction of her stool.

"Allow me." He finished the job, placing a slice on each plate, and topped up the wine glasses before returning to his side of the breakfast bar. "Do you want to talk about it?"

"No." Hannah blinked rapidly to disperse any tears trying to form. "I don't." She sipped her wine. "You don't need to find a hotel, you can stay the night. I don't need to worry about what to tell my husband now." Realising what she had said, her hand flew to her mouth. She shook a finger at him, "No, no. I didn't, that is, I meant in the spare room." The now familiar flush also covered her neck, and Ben laughed.

"Thank you, and relax. I know what you meant."

They ate in silence, with Ben polishing off most of the pizza, before carrying their drinks and the bottle of wine into the comfortable and homely sitting room. Hannah asked what type of music Ben liked, and as he liked just about everything, they settled on something soothing, and she opted for Nat King Cole. They fell silent. Hannah trying to remain calm, and hold back the wave of panic that threatened to engulf her, and Ben, wondering how he'd ended up in the middle of a domestic when he was already living a waking nightmare. He made up his mind to take his leave first thing in the morning, and as he did so he remembered the car.

"Shit," he cursed and got to his feet a little too quickly, and groaned as the pain shot through his torso.

Hannah jumped and her wine splashed over her hand. She wiped it away on her jeans. "What's wrong? Are you okay? Do you need a doctor?"

"No, no, I'm fine," Ben lied. "I've just remembered I've left my car sticking out of your wall. I need to move it before it causes more accidents."

He wanted to move it before it was reported, and the police ran a check on it.

"I don't think you should do it, you're in no fit state." Hannah held out her hand, "Give me the keys, I'll do it."

"They're in the car." Ben attempted a smile. "Still, I doubt anyone would want to steal it."

Twenty minutes later, under Ben's direction, Hannah had moved the car to the top of the drive, and helped Ben stack the bricks which had been dislodged as tidily as possible a little inside the gate. They walked back to the house as a flash of lightning lit up the garden. The thunder that followed sounded as though it were immediately above them. Large splats of rain had already begun to darken the ground by the time they'd reached the porch.

"Get another bottle, or make some coffee if you prefer," she directed as the heavens opened. "I'd like to catch the weather report. My parents are in Cornwall with my daughter, they had a trip planned tomorrow."

Ben felt sick as he made his way to the kitchen. He had no idea whether he was newsworthy, but he didn't want the television switched on just in case, but with no way of stopping her, he filled the kettle. If he needed to be away quickly, too much alcohol wouldn't help. He took his time, not wanting to be confronted by his own mug shot on the screen, but eventually, he had to carry the mugs through to Hannah. As he entered the room she looked at him, back to the television, and then back at him.

"What?" he asked, knowing the answer.

"Should I be in fear of my life?" Hannah pointed at the screen, "You made the local news, Ben Jacobs, small-time entertainer and suspected murderer."

"Hey, less of the small time," Ben attempted a joke as he placed the mugs on the coffee table. He jumped back as Hannah flew at him, but her aim was good, and the slap knocked his head sideways.

"Don't you dare. Don't you bloody dare!" she shouted. "I am having the worst day of my life, my husband is screwing someone else, and I have a murderer in my living room. Don't you dare treat me like a bloody fool." Rant over, she sank to her knees, covered her face and sobbed.

With some difficulty, Ben joined her on the floor, and placing his arm around her shoulder, he pulled her close. She sobbed for a few minutes, and then stilled, remaining in his embrace, her only movement was the hand that swept away the remnants of her tears.

Eventually, she looked up at him. "You have some explaining to do." She sniffed. "Give me your side of the story, and if I believe you, you can stay, if not you can go and I'll give you thirty minutes before I call the police."

Ben pulled up his tee shirt, and used it to wipe the dewdrop from the end of her nose.

"Sounds like a fair deal," he spoke quietly. "But can we get off the floor? I'm in agony here."

Twenty minutes later he had told Hannah what happened. He explained he would be speaking to a friend, an ex-police officer the next day, and that he was sorry he had brought more grief into her life. Hannah accepted his explanation, and agreed he could stay until he had spoken to Meredith. She opened another bottle of wine leaving their coffee to go cold.

Wine finished, they went to bed in separate rooms. Hannah lay awake wondering how her life had been upended in a few hours, while Ben did pretty much the same thing in the room next door. When Hannah fell asleep, it was with a feeling of relief, the events of the day seemed to have lifted a weight from her shoulders, and she felt a sense of freedom. Ben on the other hand felt his troubles had multiplied, he was now relying on a total stranger, and one that had no reason to like men at the moment. His frown remained as he drifted off.

~~~

Once his old team had gone, the enthusiasm seemed to drain from Meredith, and he found himself sitting next to George, sipping a pint of lemonade.

"They'll mish you, we'll all mish you. Mind you I might not have to, I might need a job." George laughed into his pint.

"And I'd give you one, George, if I had one to give. But this isn't done yet, you never know what's around the corner. I'll have a word with the Super tomorrow." Meredith nodded solemnly.

"Kind of you, Meredith, but I don't think you have much shway with him now," George attempted to push himself out of the chair. He gave up and nudged Meredith, "Help me up, I need a pee."

Helping him to his feet, Meredith slapped him on the back. "Do you need any help? And I'm not offering to hold it." He smiled at the man who had encouraged him to join the force.

George declined. "I need a lot of help, but I don't think you're the man that can give it now. I'm on my own now, on my own."

George's shoulders slumped, and he stumbled off towards the gents. Watching him until he'd reached the door, Meredith sat heavily and stared at his glass. George was probably right. He asked himself again if he had made the right decision, and couldn't come up with an answer. As his eyes searched the room for sight of Patsy, the pain returned. His hand flew to his chest, and he counted. One, two, three . . . He managed to count to twenty before the pain subsided, he really did need to see a doctor. As though reading his thoughts, Amanda, his daughter arrived at his side. She placed her hands on his shoulders and bent to look into his eyes.

"Dad, what's wrong, are you all right?" She noted the paleness of his skin, and the perspiration on his brow.

"I'm fine." Meredith shrugged her hands away. "Get off me, you'll have Patsy worried."

Amanda lowered her hand and found his wrist, she held it to take his pulse. "Well you don't look all right. In fact, you look most peculiar."

Meredith snatched his wrist away. "Will you pack it in! You're not even qualified yet. I told you, I'm fine. Let's find Patsy and make our way home. She promised me I could leave early if I behaved, and I reckon I've ticked all the right boxes."

"First, tell me what happened then," Amanda persisted.

"Nothing, nothing at all, I'm just tired. Go and find Patsy."

"Well, at least that's a good idea. I'll grab your jacket." Amanda went to collect it. As she lifted it the phone rang. She pulled it from his pocket, and a number flashed across the screen. It clearly wasn't someone in his contact list, so she rejected the call.

Thirty minutes later, their goodbyes had been said, and the three climbed out of a taxi. Meredith opened the door and unloaded the contents of his pockets onto the hall table; wallet, change, keys, phone . . . he retrieved the phone and checked it. As he hung his jacket on the newel post, he listened to the message and smiled. It was from Big Pete. Ben Jacobs had agreed to speak to him the next day.

6

Meredith had been awake for over an hour when the alarm clock sounded, but for the last few moments he'd been staring at the ceiling counting. The pain had only lasted for a count of fifteen this time, and he wondered if that was significant. Throwing his arm out from under the duvet, he switched off the alarm, and turned as Patsy mumbled into the pillow.

"It can't be time to get up yet. Tell me you set the clock for the wrong time."

"You stay there, I'll make the tea." Meredith swung his legs around and sat up. "But first a shower."

Standing in the shower, he turned his face into the stream of water, allowing it to pummel his face, lost in thought. He was startled when he heard Patsy's voice.

"Have you fallen asleep in there or something?" she asked.

"Something like that, yes. It's weird not having to go into the station for a briefing, or worry about who may have cocked up on collecting some evidence. I feel weird." He stepped out of the shower and wrapped a towel around his waist. "I can't explain it, and I can't get my head around it."

"That'll soon pass." She ran her hand over his wet shoulder. "It's Friday today, don't come into work, take the day off to get your head around it. We'll manage until Monday," her eyes narrowed, "and it will give you a chance to catch up on what's happening with poor old Ben. You'll only be thinking about it anyway. I'm still finding it difficult to believe that he's in this situation, so I'm sure you're thinking of little else."

"I might take you up on that. But poor old Ben? I'll give him more than poor old Ben when I speak to him."

Patsy paused, her toothbrush halfway to her mouth. "Ah, so you are going to speak to him. I knew you were up to something last night, be careful you don't get yourself into trouble." She waved the toothbrush at him.

"I was speaking figuratively, and I did say *when*." Meredith walked from the bathroom.

"I know exactly what you said, Meredith, and don't leave that wet towel on the bed."

~ ~ ~

Patsy had been gone less than thirty minutes before Meredith drummed his fingers on the kitchen table. Peering into his empty mug, he pondered if he should make a fresh brew, and glanced at the clock. It was five minutes later than the last time he'd looked. Cursing, he stood and pulled his jacket from the chair. With had no idea what time Ben would call, he couldn't sit around doing nothing. He decided to buy some cakes and surprise the girls by going into the office. He'd only visited once since he'd accepted half of the business as a gift from Sharon, making him a director, and joint owner with Patsy. He still questioned how wise either action had been. But, he had to look at the bigger picture. What was done was done, it was he who had been looking for a change, and he had to get on with it sometime.

Striding into the hall, he snatched his keys from the table, and the pain came from nowhere. Staggering sideways, he clung to the banister for support, and unable to draw a breath, he dropped the keys and thumped his clenched fist repeatedly against his chest. It wasn't until Amanda called to him, that the internal vice-like grip eased enough for him to gulp in air, he drew it in slowly until he was able to stand upright. Amanda's feet appeared through the banister next to him.

"Did you not hear me call? I said if you were on your way out would it . . . Jesus, Dad, what's wrong?" Clearing the remaining stairs with a small leap, she placed her hands on her father's shoulders. "Look at me!"

Meredith tutted and raised his eyes to hers and gave her a wink. "There is nothing wrong, stop fussing."

"Oh, really?" She turned him to face the mirror. "If that's nothing, I think I've chosen the wrong career."

Meredith's face was almost beetroot in colour, and beads of perspiration glistened on his forehead.

"I was choking, last piece of toast," he lied, as she lifted his wrist her fingers pressed against his pulse.

"Now tell me the truth. Your pulse is rocketing, sit down, I'm worried you might fall." Pulling him forward by his wrist, she pushed him to sit on the stair. He didn't resist or argue, which confirmed she was right to be concerned. "The truth please, Dad, you're scaring me now. I know you're big, strong, John Meredith, but even big strong men get the stupid gene, and ignoring signs that something serious may be happening to your body, confirms you have that, as if it needed confirming."

"Indigestion, that's all it is," Meredith rubbed his palm across his chest. "Big, strong John Meredith can't party like he used to. Too much beer, too much food, too late a night. It seems I can't take it anymore. I'll be fine in an hour."

His pulse had slowed and Amanda released his wrist. His colour was returning to normal.

"I don't believe you. You need to see a doctor - it could be your heart." Kneeling, she looked into his eyes. "I've not had you back for long, I don't want to lose you too. Please see a doctor."

"I will, I promise. Not now, I must get to work, but I'll make an appointment." Pulling her forward he kissed her forehead. "I promise. Now, what were you going to ask me?"

Even as he placated her, he knew that would be unlikely. He couldn't even remember his doctor's name, it had been so long since he'd last seen him.

Amanda pursed her lips, her likeness to her father undeniable, her face set, she shook her head.

"I wanted a lift, and I know you don't need to go to work, Patsy told me you were starting on Monday." She raised an eyebrow, "I'll do you a deal. You see a doctor within the next three days, and give me a lift to work, and I'll not mention anything to Patsy until we know what's wrong with you." She grinned as her father's eyes narrowed.

"I'm offended you think I would lie to you, I'm offended you think you need to blackmail me with Patsy, and I'm surprised you need a lift. What's wrong with the car I bought you?"

"Then you're easily offended, and nothing's wrong with the car, but I'm going out straight from work so I don't want it with me." Amanda stood and took her coat from the newel post. "You are okay to drive, aren't you?" She made to grab her father's wrist again but he put his arm behind his back.

"Perfectly, thank you. Now, if you're ready."

Twenty minutes later, Meredith pulled up outside the entrance to the hospital.

"Thanks Dad, your next task is to book an appointment. You don't want both of us on your case, it wasn't an idle threat."

Kissing her fingers, Amanda pressed them on her father's cheek, and slammed the door before he could respond.

Meredith pulled a face as he saluted her.

Driving away, he decided he'd give it a few more days, and eat healthily as that was supposed to cure all ills, before making a decision. Driving past the bakers he'd intended on visiting, he smiled at his willpower, and headed for Grainger & Co.

His phone rang as he parked the car. Releasing his seat belt, he pulled his phone from his pocket and climbed out of the car. It was from an unknown number.

"Meredith."

"It's me," Ben Jacobs announced. "I think I need your help."

"You need a kick up the arse, is what you need, and you always need my help. Where are you?"

"Well, that's open to debate. I want your word that my location will remain between us, I don't want you going all prim and proper on me. I know you're not a copper any more, but I want your word."

"You have my word. Stop buggering about and tell me where you are."

Meredith confirmed he knew how to find Hannah Godfrey's house, and turned towards the office. "I've got to pop into the office for a while and . . . what the . . ." Meredith looked up at the façade of the building and closed his eyes. "Second thoughts, I'll come straight there."

Climbing back in the car he took a moment to collect his thoughts. The pain wasn't as bad as it had been earlier, but it was now too regular to ignore. He started the engine, but before pulling away he searched the number of his doctor's surgery, and waited until it was ringing before he drove back out on to the main road. It rang for a few moments before a crisp voice asked how she could help him. He asked for an appointment with his doctor.

"Dr Williams retired nearly six years ago," there was amusement in the receptionist's voice. "Shall I book you in with one of the others, would you prefer male or female?"

Meredith said he didn't care, he simply wanted an appointment as soon as possible. There was a brief silence.

"The next available appointment is ten-thirty on Wednesday morning with Dr Towers, will that suit, Mr Meredith?"

"That's six days away!"

"Is it an emergency? What's the problem?"

"I'm not discussing my health with some nosey receptionist, what if I said I thought it was an emergency?" Having joined the ring road, Meredith's speed increased with his annoyance.

"I would suggest you phone the NHS helpline, and they will tell you if you need to go to hospital." The receptionist's irritation matched Meredith's. "Do you want this appointment or not? I have patients waiting." Smiling as she heard the sigh of defeat, she hung up when Meredith confirmed he'd take it.

Meredith slowed, and pulled onto the exclusive estate. As he followed Ben Jacob's directions, he drove past Barry Brooker's home and spotted Rawlings' car. He slowed a little more as his eyes travelled up the drive. Dave Rawlings stood, hands in pockets, staring at the ground, as Wessex rang the doorbell. Although he kept his eyes on the rear-view mirror as he drove past, Meredith didn't witness the opening of the door, or hear the echo in the street as it was slammed shut. Returning his attention to the road, he drove on. Minutes later he pulled onto the drive as directed, noted the pile of bricks to his right, and spotted the rear of Ben Jacob's car at the far side of the house. He nodded his appreciation as he took in the property, and wondered whose home it was, and how they were connected to Ben. The door opened before he could ring the bell.

"Come in," Ben ushered him quickly into the hall. "Kitchen's this way, the kettle's on."

Meredith followed, his eyebrows raised as he took in his surroundings. Ben was clearly comfortable in the house, and he assumed it was a relative's home until he entered the kitchen and found Hannah Godfrey. She smiled, held up a mug and asked if he'd prefer tea or coffee. Meredith returned the smile, but wasn't amused. Ben had a piece of skirt with money, and he appraised her as he answered. The second thing he noticed was the white mark on her finger, evidence that a wedding band had lived there for some considerable time.

"Coffee, black with two, please." He sat himself at the breakfast bar as indicated by Ben. "I'm Meredith, nice to meet you."

"Hannah; I'll make this and I'll get out of your way." She lifted the kettle, "You two have a lot to sort out."

"We do," Meredith watched Ben's fingers lightly drumming the breakfast bar, "and you two know each other how?"

"He drove into my wall." Hannah gave a laugh and placed the sugar bowl in front of him as he frowned.

"Recently? I saw the pile of bricks." He caught the exchange of looks between the pair.

"Last night," Ben snapped. "Not sure how that's relevant, we need to get on." He looked away as Meredith's eyes widened.

"And how much has he told you?" Meredith failed to keep the irritation from his voice, and pursed his lips as Hannah placed the coffee in front of him.

"I saw the news, Ben tells me he didn't do it, and that you're an ex-police officer here to help him prove his innocence."

Hannah smiled warmly, but it wasn't reciprocated, Meredith was barely holding his temper.

"And you believed him. Just like that?" His eyes told Ben how foolish he thought she was.

"Yes." Hannah had picked up on the hostility and became defensive. "Was I wrong? Have I harboured a murderer? In which case, why are you here? To make a citizen's arrest?"

"Yes, you were wrong. He could be anybody, he may have done it, I don't think so, but then I've known him most of my life. You however, have had the benefit of what? Eight hours, maybe ten?" Meredith pointed to her left hand. "That band hasn't been missing for long, a flash of his pearly whites, and a wink, do not a good man make. Where's your husband?" Meredith looked to Ben who had jumped to his feet.

"Now hang on a minute, Meredith, you have no right -" He stopped speaking as Meredith slammed the flat of his hand onto the breakfast bar.

"No, pal, you hang on. I have every right." He jabbed his finger at Hannah, "You don't know her from Adam and vice versa. You're wanted for murder and I've compromised myself coming here, for what? So you can show off your latest shag? What are you playing at? I -"

Meredith fell silent as it was Hannah's turn to bang the breakfast bar, although she chose to use a wooden spoon. Whacking it repeatedly until her anger had subsided. She turned to point the spoon at Meredith.

"I am still in the room. My personal life is just that. Personal. I am not his latest shag." She moved the spoon to point at Ben, "I gave someone the benefit of the doubt, if I'm wrong, so be it, but I have your measure. Rude, arrogant, and full of self-importance. Who do you think you are? How are you compromised? You're no longer a policeman, so if you don't like being here, if you don't want to help him, leave!" She moved the spoon towards the door. "But if you're going to dob him in, at least have the courtesy to give him time to move on." Clearing her throat, her cheeks flushed, she lay the spoon quietly on the breakfast bar hoping she'd made her point.

Meredith laughed out loud. "Dob him in? We're not in the playground, love." He pinched the bridge of his nose.

"Then stop acting like it, and get on with it. I'll be in the office if you need me."

The last comment was for Ben, who nodded and mouthed 'sorry'. When she had left them alone, he rounded on Meredith.

"What the fuck was that all about? She's a decent girl, and helped me when I needed it. I thought I was going to be safe here while we sorted this mess out, but she's more likely to give me my marching orders than a bed now. Cheers, mate, thanks a bunch. What's the plan now that you've queered my pitch, we'd better get on with it."

"I don't have a plan. How could I have a plan? I wasn't expecting you to do a runner, and certainly not expecting you to shack up with a member of the public." Meredith had calmed down and sipped his coffee. "She makes a good coffee though, and you can't blame me for jumping to conclusions, she's a looker." He watched a little of the tension leave Ben's face, and the twitch at the corners of his mouth.

"But a classy looker, unfortunately she has taste." Ben ran his fingers though his hair and leaned forward, his elbows resting on the breakfast bar. "We need a plan. Big Pete is going to come round, if he's not being followed. This place backs on to fields, he'll take the dog for a walk, and if he thinks the coast is clear, he'll come in the back way." He looked Meredith in the eye,

"What news on the third recording?"

Meredith pulled his note book from his pocket and flipped it open to a blank page.

"None. It's obvious that the third tape was omitted from the email, and deleted from the system. Hopefully, someone somewhere has kept it, our priority is to find out who sent the email to my . . . former team. There were seven people in the room when Wessex left his card. I've ruled out the cleaner, so that leaves three door men, two bar staff, and the receptionist. I haven't got their names, so let's start there."

Ben was shaking his head. "I can't believe it was any of them, it's obvious someone stitched me up, but not one of them surely."

"Names. Not everyone is as nice as your hostess. Don't get sentimental, let's get facts." He watched Ben's features harden.

"Big Pete, hopefully you'll meet him in a minute, the other two doormen were Dan Jones and Sammy Gregory, the barmaids -"

"Sammy Gregory? The young boxer?" Meredith interrupted.

"Yes why?"

"Because we'll rule him out for now, I saw him being interviewed on the local news, and I doubt he has the wherewithal to be involved in this." Meredith tilted his head to one side, "Although, I suppose he could be stupid enough to be coerced. Hmm." He pencilled a star next to Gregory's name. "And finally, the barmaids." He looked up, pen poised.

"Both Eastern European, Lithuanian, I think," Ben shook his head, "I've not had much to do with them, but I can't see it, why would they have access to the club's email? They can barely speak English, let alone write it."

"Who knows? Why would you be standing over a dead body with a knife in your hand?" Meredith tapped his pad. "Names."

"Bridget and Kat. Don't ask me to pronounce their surnames, I can find out though. I'll give Tania a ring once Big Pete gets here, he'll have her number."

"Who's Tania?"

"Brooker's secretary, or PA, I don't know what he calls her this week, but she basically runs the club. Hires and fires the staff, arranges theme nights, books the acts, she might even do the books. That's how I met her."

"And you think if you call her she won't mention that to the police. I never realised how trusting you were." Meredith gave a shake of his head. "Surname."

"Davidson. She's a good sort, firm but fair, grounded. She'll know it wasn't me. Shit." He slapped his hand against his forehead. "She's on holiday at the moment, and that being the case, she won't know much anyway, other than names of course."

"And addresses." Meredith tapped his pad. "That leaves us with the receptionist." He looked up as Ben laughed. "Funny? Why?"

"Sandra. I have no idea of her surname, never had the need to know it, but if we're talking intelligence, she's one rung above Sammy. Now you have the names, what do we do?"

"Tell me about their relationship, if any, with Brooker."

Meredith was about to say more, but was interrupted by the phone ringing. He looked around the kitchen and spotted it on the wall as it stopped ringing. They heard Hannah's footsteps cross the hall. Ignoring the two men she walked through the kitchen to the back door, and out into the garden.

Ben got to his feet. "It must be Pete." He too left the kitchen and disappeared into the garden.

Meredith took the opportunity to have a look around. Walking to the fridge, he scanned the items held in place by colourful magnets. There were several pictures drawn by a child, a list of grocery items, a dental appointment card, and several photographs. One, taken with the sea as a backdrop, showed Hannah sitting with a young girl on her knee, holding hands with a man who he assumed was her husband. The man was well-built and clearly kept himself in shape. Meredith wondered where he was now.

Stretching out his hand he opened the nearest drawer, and found neatly folded tea-towels. He opened the one below, an assortment of cling-film, baking paper, and foil. Pushing it shut, he questioned what he thought he might find. There was a sudden movement behind him, and something hit him behind the knees causing him to lose his balance for a moment. He spun around, and the bouncy spaniel jumped up against his thighs, before retreating to the sound of his master's voice. Meredith looked at the paw prints which now decorated the kitchen floor, and the front of his trousers. He closed his eyes. It was going to be a long day.

"Sorry about that. He's very friendly." Big Pete pointed at Meredith's legs and turned back to Hannah, "Have you got a mop and an old towel love, he's made a bit of a mess. Sit."

The spaniel sat, and looked adoringly at the man towering above him, and didn't move when Hannah stepped over him.

"Don't worry, I'll see to it later, but I will get you a towel." She disappeared into the hall and returned with a large fluffy towel. Falling to her knees she held it towards the dog. "Come on, puppy, let's get you cleaned up."

The dog tail wagged against the floor, and he looked from his master to Hannah.

"Go on." Permission received, the dog flew to Hannah, and proceeded to fight with the towel as Hannah attempted to dry him. "Rollo, SIT." The dog stilled and allowed Hannah to complete her task.

"Can I get you a drink?" she asked, clambering to her feet.

"Not for me thanks. He could do with some water though. He's had a fair old romp this morning."

Meredith closed his eyes in disbelief. This was a murder investigation, of sorts, and his team was made up of the suspect, a giant, a woman who didn't like him much, and a spaniel. He opened his eyes to find everyone looking at him, except the dog, who was trying to grab the corner of the towel.

"Shall we get on?" Meredith sounded as weary as he felt as he walked back to his seat.

"Yes," Ben agreed. "Pete, take a seat and talk to us about who would have access to the club's email account, and what happened after the copper, Wessex, left."

Pete joined Meredith and Ben sitting at the breakfast bar, and Hannah enticed the puppy out of the room with the towel.

"Happened in what way?" He took a biscuit from the plate in the centre of the table.

"We're told that DI Wessex left his business card and asked that the footage from the bar the previous night be emailed immediately." Meredith flipped his notebook open. "It was, but as one recording was omitted, and now has disappeared, we need to know who sent the email. We've ruled out the cleaner, Ben is convinced it wouldn't be the bar staff, so that leaves you, Dan Jones, Sammy Gregory, or Sandra. Who sent the email?" Meredith bit his lip as Big Pete shrugged again.

"I don't know, I didn't stop. My mate," he jerked his thumb at Ben, "had apparently stabbed someone, and I went to ask Brooker who the other blokes drinking with O'Brien were. Can't you find out where it came from? I thought no one had secrets from anyone anymore where internet stuff was concerned."

"If we had access to it, yes. But that's with the police, I'm sure they have people on it, we're trying to shortcut the process. Let's go back to the men you wanted to see Brooker about. What did you ask him and why?" Meredith flipped over a page of his notebook.

"I thought it was odd, well you did too, didn't you?" Big Pete looked to Ben for confirmation.

Ben nodded his head to encourage him, although he didn't know what was coming.

"Brooker had four of us working the door. There's usually only three, sometimes two, we only have a full complement when there's some gig on, and we're expecting a full house. It was busy enough, but not so much as four of us were needed. I asked him point blank. I told him it looked bad for Ben, and what did he know about the blokes who were drinking with O'Brien, because the way Dan told it, they'd wound O'Brien up to such a frenzy, that he was trying to bottle one of them, but didn't manage it 'cos Ben stepped in and knifed him. I explained to him that it could have been me trying to calm it down if we hadn't been top heavy on staff, so I wanted to know who they were, if they were connected to him in anyway, and if not, they wouldn't be coming in again."

"What was his answer?" Meredith jotted something on his pad.

"Told me they were associates of a friend of a friend, and that they were unlikely to return, but if they did I was welcome to bar them." Big Pete scratched his head. "Not much use, is it?"

"He didn't give the names of these associates or the friend?" As Big Pete shook his head, Meredith was asking the next question. "What did you do then, and did you see what happened to the others? I understand that you can't send emails from the staff room, although there is a smaller office where it could be done, did you see anyone enter that room?"

"I went back to the locker room. Sandra and Sammy were leaving, she was upset and had agreed to let him share her taxi," he looked at Ben and winked, "the cleaners were cleaning and talking in their own language. Dan was staring out of the window, watching the punters who had yet to drive off. Then we left together."

"Why was he watching them?" Meredith asked.

"No idea, I didn't ask. We were all shocked, some bloke had been murdered, and our mate had apparently done it, we didn't say anything. 'Night, and see you tomorrow if it's open, was as complicated as it got." Big Pete stood up, "I think I'll have that drink now, do you think she'll mind if I help myself?" He didn't wait for an answer, but walked to the kettle. "Not much to go on is there?"

"But you have access to the recordings and the email system?"

Meredith kept the questions coming, and affronted, Big Pete swung around to face him, causing water to slop from the kettle.

"Are you suggesting that I did it? Why would I be here?" He looked at Ben, "Tell your mate to wind it in, or, copper or not, I'll see to him." He banged the kettle down and switched it on. Jabbing his finger at Meredith, he added, "Be careful."

"I was asking because I need you to send me some recordings. Are you always this touchy? I haven't got time to pussyfoot around egos."

"For Christ sake, can we get on with it, I don't need you two squaring up. What recordings do you want and why?"

"I want everything you can send me. I'll start with the lobby. I haven't got access to the names of people in the club, so I'd at least like to see their faces, it's a long shot but some might be known to me. I'd also like to check out what went on in the carpark, both before and after the event, and if and when we have the time, we can work backwards and see who, if any, of the lot taunting O'Brien had been in before and who they spoke to." Meredith tilted his head, "Is that something you could do?"

"I don't know. I'm not gifted technically. How would I attach them, is there a button, and if this is supposed to be done on the sly, where would I do it?" He held up his phone, "I only have this, I've not got a computer."

Meredith resisted the urge to bang his head on the breakfast bar. "Then why do you have access to the club's email account if you are so technically challenged?"

"I don't, well I did, they thought it might be needed when they introduced the digital stuff, but I've never used it. I sit and watch replays of the recordings if someone's had a slap or their car keyed, but I've never used the email, why would I?" He looked at Ben, "Sorry mate."

"Tania," announced Ben. "Tania will do it for us I'm sure."

"I thought you said she was on holiday?" Meredith asked flipping back in his notebook.

"I did -" Ben was interrupted by Big Pete.

"She can access remotely." He gave a shrug, "I have no idea how that works, but she did something for Brooker via her phone one day. Something about sending out Christmas invitations, so she may be able to access the security recordings too. Shall I give her a ring, she might pick up?" He looked to Meredith for an answer.

"It's possible she has that sort of access, but will she do it?" Meredith questioned, and looked from one to the other, "Because if she does, she'll need to be able to keep her mouth shut. Are you sure you can trust her - absolutely?" They confirmed they could in unison, and for the first time Meredith allowed himself a smile. "Good, because if she'll do that, and she works closely with Brooker, we may be able to get more information out of her. Give her a call, see if she can access the recordings, and find out when she's back."

"Now?" Big Pete asked.

"No, tomorrow. There's no rush," Meredith threw his arms into the air. "Where's the toilet?" Looking at Ben, he shook his head as he got to his feet. "Sort it out."

Ben gave directions and Meredith left the kitchen.

"I don't think I like his attitude," Big Pete commented as he scrolled through his contacts.

"Not many people do, but he's a good bloke. Do you think it would be best if I spoke to her?" Ben held out his hand for the phone.

"Nope, 'cos she may say no, given the circumstances, and then it would be awkward. She'll do it for me."

~~~

Patsy carried the tray of tea into the main office and set it on Linda's desk.

"I spotted the cake, Linda, it's fabulous, Meredith will love it." She resisted the urge to tut as Linda pouted.

71

"It'll be stale by Monday. No one thought to tell me that he wasn't coming in until next week."

"I've already apologised on his behalf, Linda, I'm not going to repeat it. He had loose ends to tie up, and make way for a clean start on Monday." Lifting her mug, Patsy walked to her office, "I'm going to give Mr O'Brien a call and see if he can get me copies of his daughter's phone account. We need to find out who she's been speaking to."

"Good idea," commented Sharon Grainger. "Well, in Meredith's absence, and unless either of you have anything you want me to do, I'm going to drink this and go shopping." She smiled as the others shook their heads. "Good. That's that settled."

Patsy dialled O'Brien's mobile, and found that his answer service picked up the call immediately. Hanging up, she flipped a page in the file on her desk, and called his home number. Ten minutes later she hung up on a tearful Mrs O'Brien, and opening her on-screen calendar she inserted the appointment they had agreed.

Scrolling through her contacts she hit the call button for Frankie Callaghan. As she listened to the ring tone, she logged onto Facebook and went to Sian O'Brien's home page. There had been no post from Sian herself, but many of her friends had left messages of condolence, expressing their shock that her father had died. There was no message from Gary Mason. She looked away from the screen as Frankie answered her call.

"Hi, Frankie, I'm after a favour of sorts. I don't suppose you're dealing with the post-mortem on Aiden O'Brien, are you?"

"I am as it happens, but you know the rules, I can't give you any information as it's an on-going murder investigation. What's your interest anyway?" Frankie was hesitant in his response, and Patsy wondered if he were distracted.

"O'Brien had hired me to work for him. I called to speak to him on something trivial, only to be told by his wife that he'd been murdered here in Bristol, and naturally I thought you might be dealing with it. Come on, Frankie, I don't want anything too detailed, simply an idea on how he was murdered. Surely that can't be asking too much." Patsy smiled into the receiver, knowing Frankie would be weighing up how much information he should divulge. Her smile became a frown as Frankie responded.

"He was stabbed, Patsy, why don't you speak to Meredith?"

"What do you mean speak to Meredith? What's he got to do with it?"

"I have no idea. I don't suppose he's still involved now that he has officially left the force, but he was at the scene the morning after. Hold on," he held the phone away from his mouth and called an instruction to someone, and on returning his attention to Patsy, added, "Patsy, I have to go, as I say, speak to Meredith."

Patsy hung up and placed the phone carefully on the file in front of her, it took seconds for her to link the information she had, and she hit her forehead with the palm of her hand.

"Oh, dear God, it can't be! Ben's victim?" Snatching up the phone she dialled Meredith, and had to leave a message. "It's me, please give me a call as soon as possible, and hopefully before you speak to Ben Jacobs. I've got news on Aiden O'Brien. It's urgent, Meredith, don't ignore me."

~ ~ ~

Meredith closed the door of the cloakroom behind him and crossed the hall; his eye caught the movement in the sitting room and he walked and stood in the doorway. Oblivious to his presence, Hannah clapped her hands and called the puppy to her. He flew across the rug, slipper in mouth, his tail wagging furiously. After a little persuasion, he dropped the slipper and sat in front of her, his tail swishing against the rug, and his eyes darting from her face and back to the slipper. In one quick movement, she snatched up the slipper and tossed it behind the sofa.

"Fetch. Go on, Rollo, bring it back." She grinned as the puppy skidded off the end of the rug and disappeared behind the sofa. Her hand flew to her chest as Meredith spoke.

"You've done that before," he observed.

Hannah's smile faded as she turned her head towards him. "Always had a dog in the house when we were kids. You forget how energetic they are, and how much fun." She tilted her head, "Not sure why we don't have one now."

"You have a child, that's hard enough work." Meredith grinned as the returning puppy crashed into Hannah. "I'll leave you to it. Apologies if I was rude, difficult situation. I'll find him somewhere to stay so as not to compromise you further."

"Thank you," Hannah relaunched the slipper as Meredith turned away. "If you can't find anywhere, it is safe for him to stay here," she called as he crossed the hall.

Meredith paused but chose not to reply.

"Did you get hold of her?" he asked as he entered the kitchen, and sighed as the two men shook their heads.

"I left a message, she might call back." Big Pete held up his hand as Meredith opened his mouth, "Before you say something that might irritate, no, I didn't say why, just that it was urgent." He smirked as Meredith shut his mouth and seated himself opposite.

"What now?" Ben asked. "Who knows when she'll call, or if she'll get the message, should we give Dan a call? Perhaps he can do it."

"I don't think we should get anyone else involved, the more people who know where you are, the more likely you are to be picked up. Although, you could give yourself up, it will look much better for you, I'll keep working it out here for you."

"That's never going to happen. I'll go to the police when we have something we can give them to work with. I'm not placing my liberty in the hands of Wessex." Ben shook his head, "You can forget that."

"Okay, then while we wait and see what happens with Tania, we need to find out who O'Brien is, what his connection with Brooker is, and why it was necessary for him to be killed. I need to get to a computer to do some basic searches. I'll also have a word with some contacts."

"Do you think it was intentional," Big Pete looked upset, "in as much as, he wasn't in the wrong place at the wrong time, it was a set-up from the beginning? How did they know that Ben would step in?"

"They didn't. Yes, I think O'Brien's card was marked, and that it was Ben who was in the wrong place at the wrong time. If he hadn't been there they may have tried something else, or simply dropped the knife. The success of deflecting attention was access to those security cameras, it had to be guaranteed, and that brings us full circle to Brooker, and, who sent those recordings."

Meredith drummed his fingers, "There's little more I can do here. I'll get to the office and see what I can find out about O'Brien and his dealings with Brooker, you go about your normal business and keep your ears open," he looked from Big Pete to Ben, "and you need to find somewhere else to stay. Have a think about your options, and keep your fingers crossed that she'll keep her mouth shut," he nodded towards the door. Standing, he added, "I'll pick you up a 'pay as you go', and call back later. You have my number if you need me. Let me know if you're moving on."

Ben's shoulders sagged. "I don't know where I can go, but I'll give it some thought." He looked at his mug as he added, "It might be best I stay here, to keep her on side you know."

Meredith and Big Pete exchanged glances but neither spoke causing Ben to raise his eyebrows. "What?" he demanded.

"Engage your brain, mate. The other part of your anatomy can wait till you've sorted this mess out."

Message delivered, Meredith left the kitchen, and he allowed himself a smile as he heard Big Pete laugh at the first pitiful excuse put forward by Ben. He called goodbye to Hannah as he opened the front door. Checking the road was clear, he pulled off the drive, it wouldn't do to be seen in the area. However innocent his visit may have been, it would raise questions, and he didn't need that. He drove straight to the office.

~~~

Trying not to look up, Meredith hurried across the carpark, and pushed open the door. He forced his warmest smile for Linda.

"Loopy, a sight for sore eyes as always. Hope you're ready to be put to work, I've got a lot to do."

Linda paused for a second before she grinned at him. "Ready, willing, and able, sir!" she gave a sharp salute. "But before we get started, have you spoken to Patsy? She's not best pleased you're ignoring her again, *and*, tea and cake as we work. Sharon will be miffed she didn't stick around." Linda stood, and smoothing down her multi-coloured sweater, teetered off to the kitchen.

As that door shut, Patsy's flew open. "Why didn't you call?" She threw a hand into the air. "Not to worry, you're here now. We need to talk, come on."

Following her back to her office, Meredith pulled out his phone. He noted the missed calls and saw he had a message waiting.

"Sorry, I had it on silent. Not sure why, wasn't expecting to be in demand, I suppose." He sat on the opposite side of her desk. "Anyway, what's the panic?"

"I'm assuming you've been with Ben, and are about to launch yourself into some covert investigation into the death of Aiden O'Brien, recently deceased husband of Rosie, and father to Sian?"

"What? How do you . . ." Meredith smiled, his eyes twinkled and he held her gaze until she returned the smile. "That's better. If I were a betting man, I'd say that yet again our paths have unexpectedly crossed, and that, yet again, you are one step ahead of me."

"She is. You're right there," Linda bustled into the office carrying a tray. "I made this to celebrate your arrival."

Meredith looked at the highly-decorated cake, the word 'Welcome', written in tiny sugar-coated jellies, had been pushed into the thick butter icing. He guessed it would be approximately a million calories a slice.

"That looks almost too good to eat, but I'm going to give it a shot. Cut me a large slice and I'll eat while Patsy explains herself." Meredith's healthy eating plan flew out of the window.

"Yes, sir." Linda sliced into the cake. "You are going to be amazed."

Meredith assumed she was referring to the cake, and watched patiently while she cut three slices, and handed out the mugs of coffee. To his surprise, she carried her own to the other end of the desk and sat on the vacant chair. He eyed her warily, before looking to Patsy for help.

"What's wrong?" Patsy asked before biting into the cake.

"I take it you'll be stopping." Meredith looked at Linda, making no attempt to hide his irritation. It was Patsy who responded.

"Of course she is, she's part of the team, Meredith. Linda will carry on with whatever we need her to while we go to Abbotts Leigh. Fab cake, Linda, well done. Shall we proceed?"

"Thanks, new recipe as well, always a bit dodgy." Linda put her hand behind her back and pulled a note pad from her back pocket, and retrieving the pen from behind her ear, pointed it at Meredith. "Fire away, sir." She looked at Meredith's pout. "If you are worried about me discussing anything that happens here with Louie, relax. I am the soul of discretion, he rarely even asks about my work, I mainly do the IT stuff, and he can't get his head around it."

Meredith considered this. He doubted if Trump discussed his work with Linda either, but there was a chance he would, and that might be useful. After an encouraging nod from Patsy he beamed at Linda.

"Okay, let's get this show on the road. Aiden O'Brien, find out all you can about his work, any associates, and business connections. Although I believe he's a driver, so that might not be many. Barry Brooker, owner of BB's nightclub, and fingers in other pies. Which ones, how and why, and is there any obvious connection to O'Brien? Keith Chapman, father-in-law of the aforementioned Brooker, he's obviously involved in the club in some way, but what, why, how, et cetera. Cross-check all three as best you can. Finally, if you have time, Hannah Godfrey lives around the corner from Brooker, see if you can find anything on her or her husband." He paused and bit into his cake. "Mmm." He grunted his appreciation as he took another huge bite.

"Name?" Linda looked up from the neat row of notes she had made which now almost filled the page.

Meredith shrugged and swallowed. "Don't know, but it'll be on the electoral register." He slurped his coffee.

"Connection to the case?" Linda persisted.

"No idea, none probably, but they are on the peripherals, so when you have time." He turned to Patsy, "Why are we going to Abbotts Leigh?"

"To meet the grieving widow, Rosie O'Brien. She doesn't think her husband was killed in a bar fight, she thinks he was murdered deliberately to shut him up."

"Shut him up about what?"

Patsy now had Meredith's full attention and he pushed the cake away, and leaned forward with his arms folded on the desk.

"I have no idea, that's why we're going." Patsy glanced at her watch. "We have to leave in thirty minutes."

"And she contacted you why?" Meredith didn't like coincidences, and was clearly concerned about this one.

"She didn't, her husband did. He was worried about their daughter, Sian. He thinks . . . sorry, thought, that she's got in with the wrong crowd, becoming secretive, and a general pain in the butt. He came to see me the day before he died, and before you ask, no, he didn't seem concerned for himself in any way. He was simply a concerned father, who felt that he and his wife had lost their connection with their daughter. He said he was ashamed to admit that he didn't even know who her friends were any more, although he feared she was knocking around with a lad called Gary Mason, who he clearly didn't like. He didn't say why, and I have set up a face -" She jumped back as Meredith gave a shout and threw his arms into the air.

"Halle-bloody-lujah!" He reached across and tapped Linda's pad. "Write that name down. Same required." Turning his attention back to Patsy, he winked. "And there we have the connection. And . . ." he gave Linda a warning glance, "I reckon we're one step ahead of Wessex and the team. Gary Mason is the grandson of Keith Chapman, and nephew to Barry Brooker." Meredith put his hands behind his head and leaned back in the chair. "I think we need more of that spectacular cake, Loopy."

Linda grinned at Patsy. "I'm going to like having someone that appreciates my culinary delights working here." She placed another slice of cake on Meredith's plate. "I'm sorry it only said welcome, if I'd have known we were changing, I'd have done that instead." Collecting the mugs, she placed them back on the tray, before tucking her notepad back in her pocket. "I'll make more tea and get on with this, sir."

"Meredith will do, you don't need to call me sir." Meredith watched her make her way to the door, his smile had disappeared at her words.

"I'll come up with something, I like PHPI for Patsy, but MPI sounds wrong. Give me a couple of days."

He ignored her comment and sat up straight to face Patsy. "I'd almost forgotten. Did you know about that?" his thumb jerked over his shoulder, "That was a surprise I wasn't expecting."

"No, Sharon organised it without a word. Too soon?" Patsy had known he wouldn't like the new facia, but had thought his reaction would have been a little more explosive, so a smile twitched as she added, "You don't like it?"

"No, I don't bloody like it. I don't want everyone to know my business, especially its location. It's ridiculous. I don't know what she was thinking of! This was a one year leave of absence, a sabbatical negotiated by your spooks, it may not work out, you know that."

Undeterred, Patsy continued, "I thought it had a nice ring to it: Meredith & Hodge – Private Investigators." She moved her palm through the air as she spoke.

"What's that got to do with it? Do you know how many people out there don't like me?" Meredith glanced over his shoulder as Linda returned and answered the question.

"No one knows that many people!" Linda laughed at her own humour. "I think it looks classy, but the website and stationery are all still in the name of Grainger & Co. Is that being changed?"

"It had better not be." Meredith took the plate from her hand as he got to his feet. Taking a large bite, he added, "It's that sign that will be changing. Hodge grab your coat, we have a visit to make. Loopy get on with those searches, and shout if you find anything I need to know."

"Will do." She pretended to brush away some of the crumbs that had flown from Meredith's mouth. "I'll keep you posted . . . Gov?" She shook her head as she left the room, "No, that's not right, not here."

Meredith shook his head at Patsy, who was buttoning her jacket. "She gets worse." Holding his hand towards the door, he asked, "Who's driving, me or you?"

"Actually, she's getting better, you aren't used to her yet, that's all. I'll drive, you can tell me about your meeting with Ben. I'll drive your car though. You'll only moan about the leg room in mine." Patsy held out her hand for his keys as she called goodbye to Linda, and Meredith dropped them into her hand.

Fifteen minutes later, almost at the end of his update, his hand had relaxed enough for the blood to circulate properly, although he still kept a hold of the corner of his seat, and Patsy caught the odd twitch of his knee as his feet sought non-existent brakes.

Meredith paused his briefing as Patsy dropped the coins into the toll basket and the barrier lifted to allow them access to the bridge. He looked up and down the Avon Gorge as they drove across the Clifton Suspension Bridge. The tide was rising, and would soon cover the muddy banks, the sun caught the ripples of the sludge coloured water as the tide pushed towards the city. Not even the graffiti on the cliff face could mar the magnificent scenery for him.

"I'll never tire, or cease to be amazed by this," he let go of the seat and held out his hands. "Two minutes from the city centre and Bristol says, ta-da, look what I've got, bet you weren't expecting that. It's Amanda's favourite view."

He sighed, and Patsy glanced at him.

"Have you gone all poetic on me?" She was genuinely shocked.

"Well, it is magnificent, shame about the colour of the water though, always ruins any photographs." Patsy manoeuvred around the traffic control on the other side of the bridge, and his hand returned to its former position. "To finish, we have to get him out of there. I don't know when that ring left her finger, but it was recent. The last thing we need is some errant husband turning up and finding Ben shacked up with his missus."

"Shacked up? That's a bit of a jump, isn't it? He only met her last night. I know he's a good-looking chap, but given the circumstances I doubt anything is going on." From the corner of her eye she saw Meredith turn to face her.

"Good-looking?" He coughed out a laugh. "You've always had a soft spot for him, haven't you?"

Patsy tutted. "He reminds me of you. He clearly went to the Meredith school of chat-up lines, but most of his manners remain intact. But if your ego is bruised, I think you are handsome, whereas Ben could be described as pretty." Stopping at red traffic lights she turned to face him. "You wouldn't want to be pretty now, would you?" Returning his smile, she pulled away as the lights changed.

"But, if you think he's nice looking, why wouldn't she, because she's a looker too? There is no way he's not interested, and she was more than happy for him to stay."

This time she heard the amusement in his tone.

"Not everyone has your high standards," Meredith continued. "I don't know how you resisted me for so long, and I'll wager that we'll have a bigger mess on our hands if he stays there." He lifted his hand and pointed at a building on the next corner, "There's the pub, next left."

They missed the O'Brien house on the first drive past as they weren't expecting it to be so large, and continued along the lane. When they realised their error, Patsy turned the car around and headed back.

"Slow down a bit," Meredith ordered. "I want to speak to Loopy before we go in, that's a big property for a driver." He called Linda and asked for an update on what she had found on O'Brien.

"He's listed as a director of a haulage company called Flood's Transport, his wife is too, Rosemary O'Brien. In 2005 Keith Chapman appeared as a director and was allocated thirty percent of the shares, but there's no mention of Barry Brooker. I checked back a bit further and the main shareholder was one Michael Flood. In 1987, Rosemary Flood, became a director with a ten percent shareholding, and in 1989 Aiden joined the board. Rosemary's name changed, and it appears her father gave a thirty percent share in the business to O'Brien when they married. Michael Flood is no longer a director, he disappeared in 2007, and Chapman retained his thirty percent shareholding as did Aiden O'Brien, with Rosemary becoming the majority shareholder. I've also found out that Chapman is a shareholder in -" Linda paused as Meredith interrupted.

"Good work, Loopy, that's enough for now, we're at the house. Keep at it, we'll check in later."

~~~

Rosemary O'Brien opened the door before they reached it. An attractive woman, with close-cropped red hair, she bore the tell-tale signs of the recently bereaved. The dark circles around her eyes were a stark contrast to her pale complexion, her shoulders sagged, and it seemed the exertion of holding out her hand in greeting was almost too much effort.

Meredith took hold of her hand and encased it in his own. "Thank you for seeing us at this time, Mrs O'Brien, we are sorry for your loss, and appreciate you agreeing to meet us. I'm John Meredith, and this is Patsy

Hodge." He didn't smile, there was little to smile about, but he did hold her gaze a while, and his eyes told her all she needed to know.

She nodded as she reclaimed her hand and offered it to Patsy. "Call me Rosie, only my mother called me Rosemary, and that was when she was angry." She patted Patsy's hand. "Aiden told me about you, he said he had little doubt that you would find out what's going on, and if he did, then I do too. Come in."

She led them into the wood-panelled hall, through the kitchen, and into a sunroom which ran the length of the rear of the house. It was effectively sectioned into three areas. At the far end a round table was surrounded by four chairs, and the window overlooked a large rectangular pond, providing a wonderful spot to eat a late breakfast or lunch. In the centre of the room, attractive wicker furniture housed plump floral cushions, and faced out to the attractive garden and the woods beyond, and on its left, a large modern desk and chair faced the side garden, and a square of earth which looked as though it had recently been dug over. Patsy guessed it was a vegetable patch.

Rosie led them to the table. "Take a seat, I'll make some drinks, what would you like?"

They both opted for tea, and waited in silence, taking in the view, while listening to Rosie move around the kitchen. When she returned, she wasted no time in getting down to business.

"Sian is just eighteen, we'd almost given up on children when she arrived. She's doing her A- levels, although I have a suspicion she's been bunking off school, who knows if she'll pass them. Never thought she'd do that, but she's changed so much. She's always been a happy, outgoing, family-oriented girl, but in the last six months she has changed. Still outgoing, if you count wanting to go out every night of the week, and stay over at friends at the weekend." She looked down into her lap. When she looked up she sought Patsy's eyes. "With Aiden gone, I'm relying on you to help me get my daughter back."

"Where is she now?" Meredith placed his mug back on the tray.

"With her grandmother, Aiden's mum. Aiden's murder has hit us all hard, but his mother is eighty-three and wasn't expecting to bury her son . . . if she lives that long." Rosie coughed out a bitter laugh. "They can't tell us when they will release his body."

"That's because of the way he died. They need to be absolutely sure no one will request a second post-mortem before they do that." Meredith's voice was gentle, and leaning forward he linked his fingers together, resting his hands on the table. "Patsy tells me you think his murder may have been planned."

Rosie's back straightened, and she pulled her shoulders back. Her eyes challenged Meredith to doubt her. "It was. I'm sure of that, I know it. I can only hope that the police do their job properly and prove that."

"Do you think that Ben Jacobs, the man arrested at the scene, had reason to murder him? What reason would he have?"

"He works for Brooker. Brooker is Chapman's son-in-law. They probably planned it between them." She lifted her hand and pointed at Meredith. "I don't know who Jacobs is, but as I told the police, his only personal connection to my husband may be that he was *personally* paid to kill him. You don't get much more personal than that. This was not Aiden getting into a fight and it ending badly. This was Aiden being placed so that he was an easy target. Why else would they want him to go to that club, and at that time of night?" Once more her energy levels plummeted and her hand fell to her lap.

"Who arranged the meeting?" Patsy asked. "Did your husband want to see Brooker, or was it the other way around?"

"Chapman. Keith Chapman arranged it." Rosie frowned, "Why do you ask?"

"Do you know why?" Patsy answered the question with one of her own. She watched as Rosie placed her hands on the table and stared at them as though she'd not seen them before.

"Aiden will have told you that Sian did some work at the office during the Easter holidays. She met Gary there, Gary Mason, Keith Chapman's grandson. He's a few years older than her, but there seemed to be no harm in it. We allowed him to take her to the pictures, out for a pizza, you know normal teenage dates. Aiden made him promise no alcohol, and all was well for a couple of months. Then something happened between them and they split up. She was devastated for a week or so, and then she seemed back to normal."

Rosie had drifted back to her daughter, and taking her eyes away from her hands, she lifted her tea and sipped it as she started into the garden, her mind somewhere else. A frown creased her brow and she put the cup down abruptly.

"Things were back to normal for about a month, before her attitude suddenly changed towards everything. She answered back, she stayed out all night, and she purposely looked for arguments. No one and nothing seemed to matter, not even her grandmother. Although, since Aiden . . . perhaps at least that relationship will recover." She rapped the table. "I've lost my husband, and I need my daughter back." She blinked back tears as she looked from Patsy to Meredith. "Help me."

Meredith felt the guilt hit him as though it were a physical punch. His chest tightened at the blow, and a wave of heat spread around his body. For a moment, he wondered if he was about to have one of his episodes, but this pain was different. It wasn't physical, it was emotional. He lowered his head in thought. He'd come here not to help this woman deal with a wayward teenager, but to glean as much information as he could on her husband and his dealings, in an attempt to help Ben Jacobs. But seeing her pain, reminded him of losing Amanda. Clearing his throat, he raised his eyes, deciding to remain on the subject of Sian for a while longer.

"We will do all we can, I promise you that, and I realise sometimes you know you're right without being able to qualify why, but I have to ask, could this not simply be teenage angst? Pressure of splitting up with a boyfriend, starting A-levels, the hormone thing?"

"No. That's what we thought, we also considered drugs," Rosie was still shaking her head, "it was none of that. Something made her hate the life she lived. It was like a button had been pushed, and I pray to God she can forgive herself for how she treated her father. Sian treated him as though he had ceased to exist, she went days without even acknowledging he was in the same room." Rosemary put her hands over her face. "It broke his heart" Her voice cracked and she held her hands in place while she composed herself.

"How do you know it isn't drugs?" Patsy's tone was gentle.

"Because she has allergies, sometimes the reaction is severe and she takes constant medication to keep it under control and help her body deal with it. She has quarterly blood tests to monitor something or other, I don't fully understand it, but it's been three years now, and although she still has to avoid certain substances, nuts, feathers, even tree bark, we no longer live waiting for the next episode. Her glands would balloon, her face looked like she'd been a boxing match, her tongue would swell and she felt as though she was choking." Rosie's hand rested on her throat. "No, hopefully that's all under control. But before the last test, I did speak to the doctor, and ask him to check if there was anything else in her blood – drugs. They tested and she was given the all clear. Not that she knew."

"What else could have triggered this change, did she have a row with Aiden? Could it have been splitting up with Mason?" Meredith asked.

"No row. One day she was Daddy's girl, the next she could barely look at him." Rosie sighed. "We've been over and over and over it. To our knowledge nothing out of the ordinary happened. As for Gary, I think she's seeing him again."

"Because . . ." Meredith prompted.

"Because, a week or so ago, Aiden followed her after she'd slammed out of the house. She drove to the shopping centre and went inside. Aiden waited for a while, but not wanting her to know he had followed her there, he decided not to go in. As he was leaving he saw Gary drive up and park near her car. There were lots of spaces nearer the entrance, and Aiden believed they had arranged it."

"You didn't ask?"

"No point, every question was answered in the same way. What's it got to do with you? Why do you think you can control me? Or silence. We have barely exchanged a dozen words in the last two weeks."

"Even since Aiden died?"

"Was murdered," Rosie's chin tilted upward. "But no. She was shocked, I thought she might faint, the police liaison officer was here when she got home, and later I heard her crying, but she'd locked her door and ignored me when I went to her. This morning she came down with a bag packed and announced she was going to her grandmother's." Rosie gave a brief smile, "She did apologise for going though. I've called, and she's there, and I'll get a call if she leaves."

Rosie blinked back the tears and clasped her hands together.

Meredith nodded and waited a beat as though considering the information, then, pulling a note pad from his pocket and moving the conversation back to the reason he was there, he asked, "Why do you think Brooker and or Chapman wanted your husband dead?" And knowing she might question what that had to do with sorting out her daughter, added quickly, "Because, from the information you've given, it seems that Gary Mason is very much involved in your daughter's problems, and given his relationship with the others, there might be a link."

Rosie's head tilted and the frown was back.

Meredith kept talking, "Did Aiden warn Mason off? Did he perhaps go to Chapman about his concerns for Sian? If we knew why he went to the club, it might help rule that out." He paused as though awaiting an answer before asking, "How did he know them by the way, Brooker and Chapman? Did Gary Mason work for your husband?" He scratched his head. "Apologies for so many questions, but I'm having difficulty in working out the connections." He watched Rosie's chest rise and fall as she sighed, her shoulders sagged a little more.

"It's a long story, but I'll keep it as brief as I can. My father started up the business when I was young, he was very successful, and the business grew year on year until he was working flat out, and at full capacity. Aiden came to work for him as a contracts manager, and ended up doing everything that was necessary to deal with the volume of work, even driving." Rosie paused, as memories from happier days filled her mind. "It was how we met, Aiden and me, almost thirty years ago."

She smiled as the memories tumbled around, before giving herself a shake. "Anyway, Aiden had gone to the same school as Brooker, and at a school reunion he happened to mention how busy things were, and that we needed to invest more, and at least double our fleet to cope with demand. My father didn't approve of debt, he would never have borrowed the money required, and was planning on extending the fleet one truck at a time once there were sufficient funds to cover each purchase. Brooker told him he needed to find an investor." She glanced at Meredith's empty cup, "Would you like another drink?"

Keen to keep her talking, Meredith shook his head. "What happened then?" he prompted.

"Nothing for a while. Barry Brooker married Chapman's daughter, Penny, we went to the wedding, and later that year they came to ours. We drifted apart over the years, seeing them less as our lives moved on, you know how it is," she glanced at Patsy who nodded. "It was only on rare occasions we got together. A few years after we married, we were all invited to a party. A grand opening of something or other connected to a school friend. Barry had a stomach bug, and Penny brought her father instead." She waved her hands, "I don't know how it came about, but my father got talking to Chapman, and within months, Chapman had checked the books, and invested a huge sum into the business for a thirty percent share. Sian was eight or nine by then, and times were good, we doubled the fleet, doubled our business and everyone was happy. Keith took a hands-on role, which surprised us, and he brought in lots of new clients. It gave my father the opportunity to step back a little. He never really liked Chapman, although he wouldn't say why, but it worked. When my father died, it was unexpected, a stroke from which he never recovered, and we were in disarray. Keith Chapman was a great help, but after a month, he thought he should take control, and suggested that he take the role of managing director. Aiden had never much liked the way Chapman worked, thought he was too abrasive with some of the staff, and as we were majority shareholders the job eventually fell to Aiden. Things have never been the same since."

Rosie got up and walked to the window, lost in her own thoughts. Meredith and Patsy allowed her a moment, and Patsy was about to speak when Rosie returned to her seat, and her story.

"A year or so later, Chapman wanted to buy us out, or at least buy a controlling share, he offered a lot of money, it was a generous offer, but we refused, and that didn't go down too well. With the insurance money from Dad, we didn't need the money. Afterwards, he and Aiden were frequently at loggerheads about one thing or another." Sighing she sank back into her chair. "So, that's how we're connected. Aiden wanted to buy back Chapman's share earlier this year, we had the finance all ready to go, but he refused, so we muddled along. I have no idea why he didn't accept; it was a good offer – more than good. I don't know what I'll do about it all now . . ." Rosie closed her eyes.

"Nothing quickly, and certainly nothing before you've taken advice," Patsy answered. "You need things to settle, to make sure you are thinking clearly before you do anything."

"How did Chapman and Brooker respond to your husband's death? You said earlier you believe they had set him up, did either of them contact you?" Meredith asked.

Rosie opened her eyes. "Chapman called and left a message of condolence, and sent a ridiculously huge bouquet of flowers, and Brooker called me a little after your officer left. At least Brooker sounded genuine, Chapman was merely going through the motions and couldn't wait to get off the phone." A wave of exhaustion swept over Rosie, and she seemed to deflate a little. "Anyway, that's not relevant to Sian. What was it you wanted to speak to Aiden about?"

"We'll come to that, but first it would be useful to know why you think they were in some way responsible for your husband's death. It may be relevant, and we shouldn't rule anything out," Meredith coaxed.

Rosie looked troubled, and it was clear to both Patsy and Meredith that she was considering her words carefully, eventually she straightened up.

"I don't know the full detail, it could be nothing I suppose, but two days before, something happened, or was said, that set Aiden off. He was in a foul mood, at first I thought it was due to Sian, as he'd been to see her, but later I heard him on the phone to Brooker. I'd never known him be so angry." Without warning, she jumped to her feet, "I'm being rude, let me refresh your drinks." She collected the empty cups and disappeared into the kitchen.

Patsy waited until she was out of earshot, and leaned towards Meredith. "She's not going to tell us something," she stated simply. When Meredith inclined his head, she explained, "She was clearly working out how to answer your question, and at this very moment will be rehearsing the explanation. Listen carefully when she comes back, you'll see what I mean."

Meredith didn't have to wait long. When Rosie returned with the replenished tray, she was speaking as she approached the table.

"I have no idea what had wound him up, but I heard him say to whoever he was speaking to, *"You're lucky your brother-in-law is a dentist, because when I've finished with you, you'll need his help."* Having placed the tray in the centre of the table, she sat to face Meredith. "That told me it was Brooker, his brother-in-law, Ross, is a dentist. Aiden demanded to meet Chapman and hung up moments later. He refused to discuss it with me until he'd calmed down, and went out for a jog," she pointed to the woods at the bottom of the garden, "that was how he de-stressed, running through those woods."

"What happened next?"

Rosie's head snapped up as Meredith spoke. She looked startled for a moment.

"He came home, showered and sat at this table, to tell me all. But his phone rang and it was Chapman. I don't remember exactly what Aiden said, but he became angry again, and after asking why, agreed to meet Chapman at BB's."

"But Chapman wasn't there." Meredith pursed his lips.

Thinking Meredith had asked a question, rather than make a statement of fact, Rosie shook her head.

"No. I've been told that much, but little else, other than Aiden started a bar brawl and was stabbed. He didn't, he wouldn't. He called me a little after getting to the club, said he'd spoken to Barry, but was going to wait for Keith Chapman to arrive. The next I knew was a knock on the door and my husband was dead."

Unable to contain her grief any longer, Rosie dissolved into tears, her quiet sobs causing her body to jerk.

Patsy went to her. "You poor thing, this is clearly too much for you. Can I get you something, or call someone to be with you?" she rubbed her hand across Rosie's shoulders.

Pulling a tissue from her pocket, Rosie shook her head as she blew her nose. "No, it's fine. I need you to get on with the job in hand. Let's get back to why you wanted to see Aiden."

"We wanted access to Sian's phone bill. If we can see who she's been calling, that may help," Patsy explained.

Rosie pulled her fingers across her eyes to remove any remaining tears and sniffed loudly. Standing, she pointed to the desk at the other end of the sun room.

"Of course. All the family paperwork is in there. Phone, gas, cable TV. We had online accounts for most of it, the passwords will be on the inside cover of the file." She shrugged as Patsy's eyes widened. "Not the most secure of places I know, but . . . lazy, I suppose." Standing, she walked towards the desk, but the phone in the house rang before she got there, and she changed direction. "I'd better get that. Help yourself."

Patsy located the file for the household bills and switched on the O'Briens' computer. Logging into their telephone account, she quickly copied and emailed the accounts for the whole family, for the last six months across to Linda, before rummaging through the other paperwork while Meredith paced around waiting for Rosie O'Brien's return. Patsy found nothing else of interest in the file, and opened the shortcut to an email account. It was Aiden's account, she found nothing of interest on the first screen, but she noted his address and password from the file to enable Linda to take a deeper look.

Rosie O'Brien returned. "It was my mother-in-law, after news." She shook her head despondently before turning to Patsy, "Did you find what you were after?"

"I hope so. I've sent copies to the office so we can start work immediately. Given the circumstances, would you mind if we spoke directly to Sian, if we feel it necessary? We could always say we are helping investigate her father's death."

"Her father's *murder*. But yes, if it helps. Do whatever you feel is necessary, but please keep me updated. I need a straw to grasp." She lowered her head. "I shouldn't have sent the liaison officer away, at least she was company, but I was only ignoring her."

"Is there no one else who can come and stay with you?" Meredith asked.

"Many, but I'm better on my own. I would prefer Sian was here though. Was there anything else?"

Confirming they had everything they needed for the moment, Patsy and Meredith said their goodbyes, and drove back to the office. Linda had reams of information on the Chapman connection awaiting their attention, and was about to make a start on the telephone records.

She smiled as they entered the office. "Meredith & Hodge are back! I like that, it's got a nice ring to it." She ignored Meredith's snort. "It's all on Patsy's desk, which of these accounts would you like me to attack first?"

"How long will it take?" Meredith walked to look over her shoulder.

"Depends on who they've been speaking to, about thirty minutes each for the basic breakdown."

"Start with Aiden, and move on to the others, we're going nowhere." Meredith walked into Patsy's office. "If there's any of the cake left, it'll go nice with a black coffee, two sugars," he called, as he picked up a document on the top of a neat pile on Patsy's desk. Looking up at Patsy who had followed him in, he waved it at her. "Old Loopy is more efficient than I realised. One clearly has to look past the clothes."

"And I suppose all this time you thought I was stupid employing someone for the sake of it," Patsy tutted and picked up the next document.

"Not stupid, no, soft, I realised she was refreshing company . . . in small doses." He tapped the file. "This is going to take an age, we need somewhere to jot down the relevant stuff so we can see if anything pops out."

"Like an incident board you mean?" Patsy shook her head sympathetically as she sat and logged on to her computer. "We live in a technological age, Johnny, it's all done on here now, it cross-references for you, and you don't always have to look for it. Last month -"

"What does?" Meredith frowned, he didn't want to spend hours inputting information. Key words were enough for him, he rubbed his chest.

"Linda's spreadsheet," Patsy held up a hand. "Don't worry, it doesn't look like a spreadsheet, it looks like this. She calls it her contaminator." She grinned as Meredith grunted. "Because it cross-contaminates if there is a connection." She spun her screen around, and placing his hands on the desk, Meredith stooped to look.

"That's a bloody incident board if ever I saw one, only neater. Why not a crosschecker or something less dramatic." Pushing Patsy out of her chair, he took a seat and studied the detail. Grabbing the mouse, he scrolled through the document.

"How has she done all this so quickly? We've only been gone a couple of hours. Too much information in places, but I like this. I like it a lot."

"I knew you would. She copies and pastes stuff in which she thinks is relevant, and does some jiggery pokery magic stuff, which she calls a formula to crosscheck against whatever she wants crosschecked. You see?"

"Clear as mud, but I'll take your word for it. How does she know what to cross-reference though?"

"On our instruction, and her own initiative. We allow our staff to use initiative. Hang on let me show you." Patsy pulled the chair from the other side of the desk and sat next to Meredith. "You asked for stuff which may connect Aiden O'Brien to either Chapman or Brooker." She pointed at the heading, now we need to expand that so we put another name in here." She typed Gary Mason, and hit return, before going to the next box and typing in Sian O'Brien, and hitting return again. "Then we drag the formula across like this, and . . . Hey Presto!"

Meredith's eyes widened as a neat column of information appeared below the names.

"Why haven't we got one of these at w . . . Ugh." The pain gripped his chest and unable to move he closed his eyes and counted, aware that Patsy was shouting something he couldn't make out. As the pain subsided he gave a low groan. "Bastard, up to twenty-three." He murmured before filling his lungs with air which he blew out noisily.

"Skipper, do you want to tell me what just happened? Are you okay?" Meredith looked up to see Linda peering at him. "Patsy's calling an ambulance."

"Don't be bloody ridiculous, it's heartburn. Where is she?" Meredith pushed himself to his feet calling Patsy who hurried back into the office, her phone clamped to her ear. "If that's the emergency services, tell them it was a false alarm. NOW." He shouted and jabbed a finger at her when she hesitated.

Reluctantly Patsy murmured that assistance was no longer necessary, hanging up she put her hands on her hips. "What just happened? It looked like you were having a heart attack!" she demanded.

"Don't be so dramatic. Heartburn caused by my ulcer," Meredith lied smoothly, before he turned to look at Linda.

"I know I'm new, and I don't want to upset the applecart, et cetera, et cetera, but if you ever call me skipper again, you're sacked." He waved his finger, "No nicknames, it's Meredith, get it?"

"Yes, but -"

"Can we get back to your health? What ulcer?" Patsy remained arms akimbo, and he knew he'd have to compound the lie.

"I have an ulcer, not serious, but it flares up occasionally and causes the most God-awful heartburn. I used to have something to take, but it's been so long I have none left." He held up a hand as she opened her mouth, "But, yes, I've made an appointment to see the doctor and get some more. Now can we get on with . . ." He pulled his ringing phone from his pocket and looked at the screen. "Trump. Excuse me ladies." He walked out into the reception area as he took the call.

"I'm not sure the skipper is telling the truth PHPI." Linda shook her head. "You need to keep an eye on him."

"I intend to, and skipper? Where did that come from?"

"Well, I thought about an appropriate name for him, and as he's going to take the helm, so to speak, I thought captain, that wasn't right, but skipper seemed perfect, and skipper it is. Do you think he should have any more of my cake? It is rather rich."

"I'm going out," Meredith called from the front office, and was out of the door before the two women could react.

Patsy assumed it had something to do with Ben Jacobs, so she didn't pass comment other than to give a warning to Linda. "He won't like it if you ignore him." She smiled as Linda flapped her hand dismissively.

"He'll love it when he gets used to it. Take me, for example, I don't mind him calling me Loopy any more, in fact I quite like it. It's a sign of affection." She sniffed and picked up the cake. "I'll pop this back in the kitchen, the skipper can have it tomorrow. Give me a shout if you need any help. In the meantime, I'll get back to those phone records."

~~~

Barry Brooker gripped his phone a little tighter as he listened to words he didn't want to hear. Eventually they merged into one and all he heard was noise. He was about to hang up, when he decided it was time to take a stand.

"I hear what you say. But enough . . . Yes, that's what I said. ENOUGH! I'm not interested anymore. It's over. Finished. The End. Don't call me, I won't change my mind. Don't make me do something you'll regret. Now, I don't want to be rude, but I've got to get to the police station. Another fucking complication I didn't need."

He hung up and dropped the phone onto the coffee table, where he stared at it for a few moments. He knew his words would cause shock waves, but he didn't care. He'd had enough, his life was too complicated, it needed to be simplified. When he got back from the station, he'd sever a few more ties too, and sod the consequence. Snatching up his phone, he walked briskly to the hall, collected his car keys, and called up the stairs,.

"I'm going to the police station, and on to the club. I'll sort my own dinner out."

"Why do they want you back at the station?" Penny Brooker hurried to the top of the stairs, and watched her husband check his appearance in the large ornate mirror. "Do they think you had something to do with it? Shall I call Dad?"

"Don't be fucking stupid, Penny, I wasn't even in the bar. They want names, dates, who, what, why. I don't know why they think I can help, but they do. And, no, your father does not have the answer to everything, despite what he might think."

Penny walked down the stairs, "But -"

"No buts, Pen, enough now." He kissed her forehead. "Don't wait up."

"I'll come with you. We can go to dinner together when you've finished. It won't take me . . ." Her face fell as Brooker shook his head.

"No need. I don't even know how long I'll be there. Perhaps we can go somewhere nice tomorrow." He turned away and Penny caught hold of his arm.

"But it . . ." she let go of his arm as he spun back to face her.

"No! No, buts. Not today." He saw the moisture building in her eyes and sighed. "I don't need tears, not now. Get a grip. I'll call you later." He pulled her forward and kissed her again before he turned away, and hurried out of the house, not wanting to hear one more but.

Brooker had married Penny Chapman for convenience, for access to her family's money, and access to her father's contacts. It had surprised him when he realised he loved her. They had been sitting in a consultant's room, and had been told that due to an issue with Penny's deformed fallopian tube it was unlikely they would ever conceive naturally. The consultant had left them alone, having given various leaflets on infertility treatment, and he'd held her as she wept. Once composed, she'd looked up at him, and he saw her fear, and her love, and her need of him, and just for a moment, for the first time in his life, he felt content.

"You won't leave me, will you?" she'd asked him. "I can live without a baby, but not without you."

Everything had clicked into place. She loved him. Wanted him. Needed him. And he realised he loved her because of that. She had nothing to gain, she was independently wealthy, but still she felt that way about him. Until that moment, Brooker's world had been based on what he could gain from relationships, romantic or otherwise. Penny became the one exception. He dumped his mistress the next day, and had not cheated on his wife since. He cheated at most things. But not at his marriage, not any more.

Driving away from the house, he glanced back, and wondered what would happen now he'd pulled the plug. Fireworks, without a doubt, but he would be okay, he knew too much. Perhaps they would sell up and buy a nice villa in Spain somewhere, life in the sun was appealing, and the family would be at arm's length, which suited him nicely. Now all he had to do was get the police off his back and he could start making plans. He glanced at the display on his dashboard as his phone rang. Keith Chapman's name flashed at him, and he wondered if she'd called him. His top lip curled as he called 'Reject'.

7

Meredith climbed out of his car as he saw Trump striding towards him. "With the detail this time, what happened?" He grinned at Trump.

"Can we walk, sir?" Trump looked back at the police station, "If we're seen it might not be smiled upon."

"Why would anyone be watching? Get in the car, I'll drive somewhere."

Meredith headed out of town, and Trump began to relax.

"If I hadn't been there, I wouldn't have believed it. While I agree that Brooker was confrontational, DI Wessex really let the side down."

"Let the side down? Is that what you'd call it?" Meredith laughed and thumped the steering wheel.

"Well, he shouldn't have been provoked, it was clear Brooker was trying to intimidate him, and he flipped."

"From the beginning, Trump, I'm going to enjoy this."

Trump explained how their investigation, as to who had sent the recordings in, had come full circle back to Brooker, and Wessex took Dave Rawlings to bring him in for questioning. Brooker had refused to travel with them as he wasn't under arrest, and by the time they reached the station his solicitor was waiting for them. Wessex purposely kept them waiting for almost an hour, and Brooker was seething by the time Wessex and Trump had arrived to interview him.

"We went through the usual protocol, the recorder was on, we read him his rights, and I gave him the document, which explained that the recordings had been sent via his laptop. He denied it, saying he rarely used it, and he didn't even know where it was. DI Wessex asked if Brooker was suggesting it had been stolen, and Brooker shrugged and said possibly, as he didn't know where it was how could he tell?"

Trump scratched his head. "I swear I've never met someone with a temper like that. DI Wessex got nasty and told him he'd have a warrant to search all associated premises within the hour, and would have great pleasure in arresting him thereafter."

"How did Brooker react?" Meredith was smirking. He had no time for Jamie Wessex, and he was enjoying being in Trump's company.

"Cool as a cucumber. He stood and held out his hand, and said, he'd helped as much as he could and he'd be off. We couldn't hold him, well we could, but not without the same kerfuffle as last time, so I ended the interview and shook hands with his solicitor. Pleasant chap."

"Trump, get on with it."

"DI Wessex opened the door, and as Brooker passed him, he said something like, 'Are you running off to Daddy to ask him to clear up your mess again?'. Well, Brooker didn't like that and reverted back to seething. He stopped walking and leaned forward, they were now forehead to forehead, and he told DI Wessex he'd made the biggest mistake of his life."

Trump glanced at Meredith and grinned. "And then he did it. Wessex pulled his head back and head-butted Brooker! Right in front of the solicitor. I can't condone his behaviour, he was in trouble, solicitor or no solicitor, and with such little provocation." Trump shook his head, still amazed at what he'd witnessed.

"How much damage did he do?"

"This is amusing you, isn't it?" Trump tutted.

"Can't stand either of them, so yes, I'm amused."

"There was a fair amount of blood, but in the end, nothing that won't mend. DI Wessex had split his eyebrow, and Brooker had a bruised, possibly fractured cheekbone, and lost at least one tooth."

Meredith raised his eyebrows, Aiden O'Brien's prophecy on Brooker needing a dentist had proved accurate, just not at his hands. "And then . . ." He prompted Trump to continue his story.

"Wessex went upstairs and resigned. Just like that. We now have to pussyfoot around Brooker while we try and find this damned laptop – and of course the recording." Trump glanced sideways at Meredith, "What news on Jacobs?"

Meredith didn't flinch. "It should be me asking you that."

"I thought he might have been in touch, you know me, sir, off the record."

"Trump, you're too straight for off the record, so it's lucky I haven't heard from him. Do you know who's taking over yet?"

"Tom Seaton has been put in charge until they find someone. Safe hands."

"Indeed. Do you want a pint, or do you have to get back?"

"No can do, I've agreed to go back and give Tom a hand."

"Good man, keep me informed." Meredith turned the car in the opposite direction and drove back to the station. He dropped Trump around the corner before heading home.

Now alone, he wondered if Patsy had managed to get anything worthwhile from Linda's findings. He let himself in, and cursed Trump for not joining him in a drink as Amanda marched up the hall to confront him.

"So it's happened again! What ulcer? I don't know anything about an ulcer." She stepped to one side to halt his progress.

"That's because it was being medicated. Where's Patsy?" Loosening his tie, Meredith began to remove his jacket.

"Don't take that off. We're not stopping." Patsy appeared from the kitchen, coat on, and bag over her shoulder.

"Are you taking me somewhere nice?" Meredith smiled at her.

"Yes, to the doctor. He said he'd fit you in between other patients, we simply have to wait."

Meredith continued to remove his jacket. "I am not a child, and I have an appointment next week. That's soon enough."

Patsy heard the edge in his voice, and knew an argument was moments away, so she changed tack.

"But next week you may not be able to make it. With this O'Brien case taking off, and whatever else may come in, not to mention Ben, I thought it might be wise to get it done and out of the way. We can't have you gripped by your ulcer playing up when you're with a client or witness. Please, Meredith, for me."

Meredith was well aware Patsy had given him the ability to save face, and as he was concerned himself, he pushed his arm back into the sleeve of his jacket, and grumbled, "I would have gone whatever we had on. But if it stops you two nagging, I'll go now." Picking up his car keys he turned to Patsy, "I never had you down as a nagger, and I don't need a chaperone." Turning away, he opened the door. "I'll see you eventually, who knows how long this will take. And I'll be hungry when I get back."

"You're always hungry, I promise dinner will be waiting for you." Watching the front door close, she turned to Amanda, "He's worried."

"Yep. Not even a half-hearted fight. Oh boy, whatever it is I hope he listens to the doctor. I have to go out now, give me a call when he gets back."

Surprisingly, Meredith didn't have to wait long, after five minutes he was called through as someone had cancelled their appointment. He nodded a greeting as he sat in the chair at the side of the doctor's desk.

"Mr Meredith, chest pains, I understand. Remove your jacket and unbutton your shirt please, and tell me what's been happening, and for how long."

"I think it's heartburn." Meredith hung his jacket on the back of the chair and unbuttoned his shirt.

"Mr Meredith, I'm a busy man, and no doubt you are too. It would be easier if you didn't self-diagnose, and simply answer the questions I ask."

Meredith rubbed his brow. The doctor was right of course, he had to find out what was going on.

"It's been going on a little over a month. Started with a mild stabbing pain in the centre of my chest which lasted seconds, and gradually the pain has increased, and the time it lasts has become longer. It varies in intensity, and it does incapacitate me momentarily, so I've been counting." He gave the doctor a shrug. "It varies."

"Counting?" The doctor's frown was deepening as he removed his stethoscope from its box.

"Yes, I hold my breath and count slowly. The average was eleven but the one today was twenty-five."

"At what speed do you count?"

Meredith demonstrated, and complied with the doctor's instructions as he was given a thorough examination. As the doctor noted the last result, he cocked his head and looked at Meredith, "Is your life particularly stressful at the moment?"

"It's always stressful, it comes with the job, or rather, it came with the job, we'll see now I've moved on. This week as it happens."

"You've changed job?" When Meredith confirmed the change, he replaced his stethoscope and nodded, "And that's worrying you?"

"Of course not! Is there anything wrong with me or not?"

"You have a strong heartbeat, your lungs are clear of fluid, however, to be on the safe side, I'll make an appointment for an ECG when we've finished, but, I believe, you are having anxiety attacks. Probably caused by worrying about the change in circumstance. It happens. I'll prescribe you some medication which should keep you calm. Two tablets a day to start with, reduce that to one after a week, and after a month you can start to phase them out."

Meredith grunted a laugh. "Anxiety? You want to give me happy pills? Because it will be a waste of time, I won't take them. I saw how they affected my ex." He watched the doctor lean back in his chair and fold his arms across his midriff. "Sorry, but there's no point in wasting money."

"Why did you bother coming if you don't want to deal with what's wrong with you? Anxiety attacks can be severe, and can cause you to lose consciousness. The happy pills as you describe them will relax you, and so head off attacks."

"I came because I thought there was something wrong with my ticker. As that appears to be okay, I'll deal with the pain. I am not anxious." Pulling the jacket from the back of his chair, he felt his chest tighten, it was mild, but he didn't want to let the doctor know. "I'll tell you what, you give me the prescription, make the appointment for the ECG, which I'll attend, and if it doesn't go away I'll take the medication. Will that do you?"

"It's a start. It's nothing to be ashamed of you know." The doctor tapped on his keyboard, and a few seconds later a prescription churned out of the printer, which he signed with a flourish. He handed it to Meredith. "No shame at all."

Meredith thanked him, and shoving the prescription into his pocket he waited while the doctor logged onto his system and made an appointment for the hospital. Once done, he couldn't get out of the surgery quick enough. He sat in his car and smoked a cigarette before making a phone call.

"I need to see you as soon as possible. Are you available now?"

Fifteen minutes later, Meredith watched the automatic door of the underground carpark slide up slowly, and drove in before it had fully opened. He was met by a smart young man in a pinstriped suit, who said nothing as he escorted Meredith through the building to a small meeting room, where he left Meredith alone. Meredith sat at the empty table and drummed his fingers as he searched for the right words. He gave a cursory glance at the man who came to join him.

"What do I call you? Are you still insisting on Burt?"

The special agent who had been appointed Meredith's handler took a seat at the other end of the table and smiled at him. "Does it make a difference what my name is?"

"No, seems a little unnecessary though." Meredith shrugged, "You're not going to tell me?"

"Burt will do fine. What did you want, Meredith, it sounded urgent?"

"I've been dragged into a case, one that has personal connections, but that's not the reason."

"Reason for what?" Burt frowned as he watched as Meredith shifted position, clearly uncomfortable.

"The bloke they brought in to replace me has resigned, I need to go back, can we square that?"

"Nope." Burt's face relaxed. "We've gone to a lot of trouble getting this sorted, and it won't be undone because your friend Jacobs has found himself in a spot of bother. We agreed a year and we'll stick to that." He got to his feet. "If that's all it was -"

"It's nothing to do with Jacobs. I can handle that from where I am. You've given me nothing to do, so it fills the time." Meredith's eyes narrowed as Burt sighed to express his irritation, but he halted his progress to the door, and half turned to face Meredith.

"What is it, if it's not Jacobs, what is it?"

"I made the wrong decision, I'm a copper, not a – what do you call it – an operative. I can still do what you want and remain a copper. It was only ever a trial thing anyway, you can't have forgotten the meeting with the Chief Constable."

"No, you can't. If you are a serving police officer you will be compromised, you can't respond as required. You signed up for this, Meredith, we can't force you, won't want to, but if you renege . . . well, whatever else it is you do you won't be going back to the police force, and . . ." Burt took a step towards Meredith, "Has this got something to do with your planned visit to the doctor next week?" Burt took a half pace back as Meredith banged his fists on the table.

"You fuckers had better not have bugged my house again."

Meredith had come into contact with Burt and the SIS when a previous case had thrown them together. Burt had bugged Meredith's house to make sure he wasn't withholding information.

"Calm down, Meredith, we've done no such thing. You're in the system, every time you do something which goes on line we know about it." Burt pulled out his phone and tapped the screen several times. "Here we are. John Meredith, appointment to see Dr Towers at three-thirty on the twelfth." He held his hands up, "No bugs."

"And that is of interest to you why?" Meredith was barely holding his temper.

"It wasn't, not until you asked to meet with me, so I checked what you'd been up to. Is it to do with your health?"

"No. I was under the mistaken belief it might be time to move on. I was wrong. I want my old job back." Meredith bit his bottom lip as Burt shook his head.

"No, Meredith, the mistake you made was agreeing to come on board and thinking you could jump ship and reclaim your previous life on a whim. You can go back, that was agreed, but not until we're ready for you to do so, and that won't be now. If that was all . . ."

Meredith wanted to grab Burt by the throat and pin him to the wall, and wondered if he told the truth about the panic attacks they would release him. He decided that although they might, probably would in fact, they wouldn't consider him for his old job if he did, and then he'd have nothing except the detective agency, and quite apart from not knowing how working with Patsy would pan out, that wouldn't fulfil him. He'd put the attacks down to feeling useless, and if that were the case, he'd need to keep himself busy.

He nodded. "It was worth a try. But get me something to get my teeth into. I'll continue working on the Jacobs case as a sideline, but I need more than that. That was the deal." He stood and added, "Do you know anything about Keith Chapman? Have your mob take a look and let me know?"

Burt grinned and looked positively chipper, and as Meredith walked past him, he said, "It's a small world, Meredith, smaller by the day. I'll call you later. And by the way, Meredith, you are one of the mob now." His smile remained as Meredith raised his hand and waved without turning back.

8

Keith Chapman paused at the mirror and straightened his tie. Once satisfied with his already immaculate presentation, he allowed himself a moment and closed his eyes to compose himself. He considered Barry Brooker to be an idiot, and had warned him to keep his temper, but he never could when it was necessary. The family didn't need this sort of attention. He'd only just managed to keep his other idiot son-in-law out of the newspapers when he'd been caught in a compromising situation with the local Conservative Chairman's wife, and in the back of a car of all places. The last thing he needed was the police digging deeper than necessary. He loved his daughters dearly, but they had both chosen idiots for husbands. He blamed himself, he should have had more control over them, but he'd not allowed for just how stupid the men actually were. His thoughts were interrupted as his grandson, Gary, ran down the stairs, and ignoring Chapman, headed towards the front door.

"Where are you going?" he snapped. Even Gary, the apple of his eye, had caused him unexpected difficulties. He'd expected more loyalty from him.

"Home," came Gary's surly response.

"Do you need money?" Chapman had barely finished the sentence when the door slammed shut. Tutting, he walked to his study. Tapping the phone, he considered his options before dialling Brooker. "I thought we'd agreed you were going to calm down?" he snapped as Brooker answered.

"I was calm. If I wasn't, he'd be in hospital. Was there something important? I've got to go and see Ross. Anyway, how did you know?" Brooker was not in the mood to placate his father-in-law, he knew Chapman would take offence, but right at that moment he didn't care. He was almost at the stage where he could walk free of him.

"Word travels fast when there's trouble on my doorstep. Keep your head down, you stupid man. You're always attention seeking, you've never changed." Chapman hung up before Brooker could respond, and making a decision, he made a second call. "It's me. I need you to sort Brooker out." He sighed as he listened to the response. "That's exactly what I mean, I know what I said before. I lied. Do it. You'll be rewarded."

Content his instructions would be carried out he made his third call.

"Hello, darling, it's me. I'm sorry but I won't be able to make it. Not for the foreseeable, you stay and have a good time though. Relax and enjoy yourself." There was no response. "Are you still there? Oh." He pulled the phone away from his ear as the other person slammed down the receiver. He hoped she wasn't going to cause him grief, not at the moment, that would be too sad to contemplate.

Getting to his feet, he walked into the living room where his wife sat reading. "Do you fancy going out to dinner? I thought we could invite the girls and their useless husbands." He smiled as she got to her feet agreeing. "Go and get ready, I'll give them a ring." Having spoken to his daughters, he went to the foot of the stairs and called to his wife. "Just us and the girls I'm afraid, their idiot spouses aren't in." Walking back to the mirror, he checked his appearance again.

~ ~ ~

Barry Brooker stepped into the gleaming reception office and looked at the girl smiling at him. She wore a crisp white overall and had a large chest, and he knew, without her moving from behind the desk, her skirt would be short. Ross had a liking for tarts in uniform. He looked towards the door of the surgery.

"Is he in there?" he lisped, wincing at the pain the movement of his jaw caused.

"Yes, I'll let him -"

"Don't bother." He dismissed her with a flick of his hand and walked across and opened the door without knocking. "For fuck's sake, put her down."

Brooker held the back of his hand to his mouth to catch the drool as the dental nurse jumped away from his brother-in-law, and tidied her clothing before making herself busy at the other end of the room. Brooker climbed into the chair.

"Calm down, Barry. I know you get wound up coming here, but we're all ready for you, don't overexcite yourself." Ross Mason smiled at his brother-in-law.

"I'm not fucking excited. I'm in agony," Brooker cursed as the chair flattened out beneath him. "Don't you hurt me."

"Let me take a look."

Ross Mason laughed as Brooker flinched when he put the mirror into his mouth.

"Barry! I'm not doing anything yet." He leaned closer to inspect the damage. "Can't do much with that, best plan of action is to get it out and build a bridge. And I promise, because I can see your hand shaking, that that is the best course of action. We'll only do the extraction today, though, the gum needs to heal." He extracted the mirror. "And a policeman did this?"

"Yep, but I'll have him, don't worry." Brooker closed his eyes. "Are you going to numb it, because I'm already in bloody agony, you'd better have some strong painkillers too."

"Of course, let's get a check-up done before we get on with it, who knows when I'll next see you. Nurse."

Ross Mason stepped away from the chair, and the nurse placed a bib across Brooker's chest, and went to sit at a computer to the left of Brooker. Brooker heard her fingers tapping the keys as Ross called out information about his teeth. When he'd finished, Mason tilted his head and looked at Brooker.

"You also need two fillings, shall I do them now, while you're numb?"

"No, just get the tooth out, and let me get out of here. Get off." Brooker pulled away the hand that Mason was patting.

"I was trying to help calm you. You're still shaking."

Mason's exchange of glances with the nurse didn't go unnoticed by Brooker, who silently cursed his weakness.

"Get on with it."

"In which case I shan't need you, nurse, would you get some painkillers for Mr Brooker to take away, and I'll have a coffee." Mason turned his attention back to Brooker. "Now, close your eyes, you don't want to see the size of this needle." He winked at the nurse as Brooker groaned. "But you are going to have to open your mouth."

Brooker obliged and clasped his hands together to hide the shaking. Mason administered the injection with a further groan from Brooker.

"That won't take long. You should sue."

Mason leaned over to peer at Brooker, he pulled his face away seconds later as Brooker's hands flew apart, and his arms were flung wide. Brooker gasped for air as he tried to lift his shoulders from their prone position. Mason placed a hand on his chest.

"Calm down, calm down." There was panic in Mason's voice. Brooker's body jerked as his chest cramped, and he lost the ability to fill his lungs. "I NEED HELP IN HERE." Mason yelled at the top of his voice as he unlocked the secure cabinet and lifted out a phial of adrenalin.

The nurse appeared at his elbow, her hand covering her mouth as Brooker convulsed, and she watched Mason lean forward and grab Brooker's arm to insert the needle.

"Call an ambulance. Now," Mason commanded.

The nurse hurried to the phone but by the time she had finished the call, Brooker had stopped moving.

"We should do CPR," she stated as she turned to the pale-faced Mason. "Shall I do it?"

Mason nodded and stepped to one side. Brooker was pronounced dead at the scene by the paramedic who arrived some minutes later.

~ ~ ~

Keith Chapman waited while the waiter settled his wife at the table before taking his own seat.

"Would you like something while we wait for the girls?" he asked.

"No, water will do. Still. Thank you." Alice Chapman smiled at the waiter and waited for him to leave. "Is something going on that I should know about?" she asked quietly.

"No, my darling, of course not. Why would you think that?" Chapman's smile didn't reach his eyes. This was a worrying turn of events.

Alice Chapman had been diagnosed with dementia. She was currently going back and forth to the specialists as they did various tests and tried different drugs to halt its progress. Once sharp and all-seeing, she now drifted off mid-sentence, forgetting what she had been talking about, and had found herself in various locations, although she didn't know why. There had been many tearful phone calls asking to be rescued before she'd agreed to see a doctor. Perversely, this suited Chapman, his wife had never approved of certain involvements, and as she held the balance of power and he loved her dearly, he'd all too frequently had to bend to her will. But, since this illness had developed, he'd been able to relax and not have to cover his tracks so carefully.

"I don't think anything," Alice tapped her temple, "I'm going mad remember. It's a feeling that's all." She watched her husband formulate a tempered reply, and her hand dropped to the table and formed a fist, knowing he was about to lie to her.

"You are not mad. Forgetful, my darling, that's all. The medication will help. You are taking it, aren't you?"

"Oh yes. If nothing else, it does seem to make things clearer. For instance, I remember you saying you had to go away for a few days, and you haven't, but I can't remember you saying why."

Chapman inclined his head and smiled, but inside was silently cursing. This wasn't good. Perhaps he should try and substitute the medication. He gave a laugh.

"I did, my sweet. It was a business I had an interest in buying, they changed their minds, they decided not to sell. It's of no . . . Oh look, Susie is here." Chapman pushed his chair back, and stood to greet his daughter.

She turned her head allowing him to kiss her cheek, before fussing over her mother. "How are you? You look well. Have you looked at the menu yet, a friend told me . . ."

Chapman sat and watched his wife carefully. All mention of his trip forgotten, as she discussed the merits of the menu with her daughter. He made a mental note to look at her medication the next day.

The waiter returned with the water, and Susie Mason ordered a large gin and tonic.

"We'll be having wine in a moment." Chapman's words were clipped.

"But, not now. I need a drink. What's happened between you and Gary?" Susie settled her bag on the floor. "I wish you could still smoke in these places. Where's my drink?" She glanced over her shoulder in search of the waiter. Chapman didn't respond to her question, and busied himself with the menu.

"I think the rack of lamb sounds good. Did you say you were having the duck?"

"What's wrong with Gary?" Alice looked from her daughter to her husband.

"He's in a strop. He was so bloody rude to me this evening. I asked if it was to do with that girl, whatshername, and he went ballistic. Told me it was none of my business. When I told him I was coming to dinner with you, and asked if he wanted to join us, he told me he'd rather eat shit! I assumed you'd had a row." She turned in her chair again, "Where is that . . . Oh, here he comes."

The waiter delivered the drink and was waved away when asked if they were ready to order. Chapman glanced at his watch.

"Where is Penny? It's not like her to be late." He tapped the table in irritation.

"Am I allowed to use my phone? I could find out, and we can get on, I'm starving." Susie grimaced at her father. He had a strict rule about no phones at the table, and following an embarrassing outburst at a previous dinner, when Ross's phone had been flung across the restaurant, the family always set their phones to silent when dining with Keith Chapman.

"Give her five more minutes," Chapman snapped. He knew he was the butt of many jokes in this regard, and the lack of respect irritated him.

"Who?" Alice asked.

"Who what, Mum?" Susie patted her mother's hand, for it to be snatched away.

"Don't treat me like an imbecile. Who are we waiting for?"

"Penny, my love, we are waiting for Penny." Keith Chapman smiled. That was better.

Susie finished her drink and snatched up her handbag. "This is ridiculous,

I'm calling her." She found her phone and looked at the screen, before worried eyes found her father's. "Something's happened, I have six missed calls." She held up a finger, "Let me listen to the messages."

Chapman watched the look of horror develop on his daughter's face and pulled his own phone from his pocket. He too had several missed calls. He listened to the first message as Susie's hand covered her mouth.

Replacing his phone, he stood and held his hand towards his wife. "Alice, we have to leave. Barry is dead, we must go to Penny."

"Who's Barry? I'm hungry."

"I'll buy you some of that disgusting fried chicken you like on the way, but come now, we must go." He looked at his daughter, "Help your mother with her coat, I'll go and settle the bill."

~ ~ ~

Meredith had not reached home before his phone rang.

"You're in luck, Meredith, you pushed the right button," Burt announced. "You're going back, at least for the duration of the Jacobs inquiry, but you're there for a reason. Be at the station to meet with the Assistant Chief constable first thing in the morning. I'll see you there."

Meredith's smile was wide, he didn't care what the reason was. He didn't know what button was linked to Chapman, but he was glad to have found it. Pulling onto the drive, he saw Patsy at the window. All he needed to do now was explain it away to her. She opened the door for him.

"How did you get on? What did the doctor say?" She groaned as his phone rang and he raised a finger to silence her.

Emptying his pockets with one hand, and allowing her to help remove his jacket, he took the call.

"Trump, how can I help you?"

"I thought you'd like to know that Brooker is dead," Trump stated simply.

"What? When did this happen, and how? Please don't tell me Wessex hunted him down."

Meredith was joking, but in his world stranger things could happen. He pulled the phone away from his ear and hit the speaker to enable Patsy to listen.

"No, but it was his fault." Trump paused, knowing he had Meredith hanging.

"You are kidding me. Trump, don't fart about, get on with it."

"Brooker was frightened of the dentist, but had to go due to the damage DI Wessex caused, and he had heart failure in the chair apparently. Literally scared to death."

Meredith didn't respond, that was too close to home if he was having panic attacks, and he told himself that even if he didn't get the prescription, he would go for the ECG.

"Are you still there?"

"I am, Trump, yes, I was thinking about the implications to the case."

"In what way? It's not really your problem, but I thought you'd like to know."

"In the way that, if it looks like Brooker withheld the recording and now he's dead, if anyone else is involved they'll be free and clear, and we'll never get that footage. Bollocks! Oh, and by the way, it is my problem, I'll see you in the incident room as soon as I've met with the ACC in the morning."

"Are you serious? What -" Trump was interrupted by Patsy.

"You are kidding me!" Groaning, she placed her hand on her forehead and walked away to the kitchen.

"Yes, I'm serious, Trump, but I've got a domestic to sort out. See you tomorrow."

"Delightful news. Good luck, sir."

Meredith hung up, and dropping his phone on the hall table, followed Patsy into the kitchen. She was pouring wine, and handed him a glass.

"I can't wait to hear this. We've discussed nothing else for weeks. You've been gone less than two days."

"I know, I can't explain, not until tomorrow, once I've met with the ACC. I got a call saying my involvement was crucial, and that I was to be at the station first thing." He held up hopeless hands, "What could I do?"

"Say no! That's what! Say, no, I'm terribly sorry, but I have another job now. One I thought about for weeks, and decided it was the best thing for me. You have *sooo* many other policemen, please choose one of them, there's only the four of us, and quite apart from anything else, I'm personally involved with the bloody suspect. That would have done for a start." She shook her head, "I should have known better."

She banged her wine onto the table. "Your dinner is in the oven, I have a headache and I'm going to take a long bath." Brushing past him, she ran up the stairs and slammed the bathroom door.

Meredith had no defence he could put forward, so he pulled out a chair, and sipped his wine as he listened to the running water above him. After a few minutes, he opened the oven and smiled. Hotpot was one of his favourites. His meal finished, and as Patsy had yet to appear, he topped up his own glass and carried both upstairs. Lifting his foot, he placed it on the door handle to the bathroom, and opened the door.

"Knock, knock. You forgot your wine."

Patsy's hand appeared from beneath the bubbles and accepted the glass. Placing his own on the basin he stripped off.

"Have you come to explain or apologise?" Patsy was still fuming and her tone was not welcoming.

"Can't explain, not until tomorrow, but I do apologise. Move up." He climbed into the bath behind her and gasped. "How do you stand this heat? I think I agreed because it was about Ben," he lied, "but I won't dissolve our partnership, I won't step away from the business. I'll let them know that, I promise."

"You have already stepped away." Patsy slapped the water in frustration, and some bubbles landed in her wine, which she attempted to scoop out. "Shit! So, you're going to tell them that you know where Ben is, that you've met with him, or are you going around to arrest him?"

"Bollocks! I haven't called him." Meredith fell silent and watched the back of Patsy's head move from side to side as she despaired. "Bit of a mess, isn't it?" he mumbled.

"Everything seems to become a bit of a mess with you." She finished her wine, bubbles included.

"But . . ." Meredith slid his arms beneath the water and around her waist, "it always works out in the end." He kissed her neck and she pulled away from him.

"Don't even think about it. You've got a mess to sort out, and that won't help."

"It will help me."

"Tough." Patsy lifted his hands away and stood up. "Because right at this moment, the only thing I want to do to you would be very painful." Stepping out of the bath she wrapped a towel around her body. "Hurry up, we've a lot to sort out."

When Meredith appeared downstairs ten minutes later, empty glass in hand, and looking sheepish, Patsy sighed and closed her eyes. "What do you want me to do?" she asked.

"How do you know . . . Oh forget it, you always know. I need you to move Ben. I can't bring him in, not yet, not until I know what's what, and once I do know what's happening, I can't know where he is. Does that make sense?"

"Perfect. Except it's wrong. I remember the Meredith that was straight down the line. That Meredith would have brought him in, and then proved his innocence."

"Well, that Meredith was a policeman, and at this moment I'm not. I need to sort a few things, Ben being top of the list." Meredith made no attempt to hide his irritation. "And I know I've pissed you off, but I'm stuck between a rock and a hard place here, so -"

"Of your own making."

"Of my own making," Meredith conceded, "so I'm asking for your help. Do I take by your attitude the answer is no?"

"You can take this, I am so angry with you, I have no idea why you are still able to walk. You've let me, and Sharon, let's not forget Sharon, with her new shiny sign over the door, you've let us down. She signed over fifty percent of the business in good faith, and you took weeks, going back and forth, before you agreed. And now, only hours in, you've pulled out again. Arggh!" She covered her face with her hands. "Get me wine."

Meredith smiled as he walked quickly to the kitchen, he knew she was going to do what he'd asked.

9

Patsy drove to the office and collected one of the 'pay as you go' phones from the cupboard in her office. She saved a number that Ben could contact her on, before heading for the home of Hannah Godfrey. Ben was not expecting her, nor did he know of the change in Meredith's circumstances. They had decided that it was best that neither of them had a traceable link to him, so they hadn't called to update him.

Hannah Godfrey opened the door and smiled, but her frown remained as she looked at Patsy's car parked on the drive. "Can I help you?"

"Yes, I'd like to see Ben please." Patsy's lips twitched into a brief smile. "Don't look so shocked, I'm working with Meredith."

Hannah stepped back giving Patsy room to enter. "He's in the kitchen, straight through."

Ben looked up from the newspaper, and was clearly shocked to see Patsy. "Where's Meredith?"

Sarcasm apparent, Patsy snapped her answer. "I'm fine, thank you, Ben. Sorry to hear about your spot of bother. We need to move you."

"Sorry, Patsy. You look great, but are clearly pissed off with me. Not sure why Meredith has roped you in. What's happening?" Ben shot a glance at Hannah who was watching his interaction with Patsy closely.

"I'll tell you what's happening. Meredith has decided to become a police officer again, which means it will be me on the wrong side of the law, and not him, as we're going to move you, now, and then he won't know where you are." She glanced at her watch, "I doubt you have much with you, so if you could grab it, we need to make a move."

"Where?" Ben rested his palms on the breakfast bar. "Where are we going?"

"I have no idea, but even if I did, I wouldn't say, because this poor woman shouldn't know either, that way if anyone knocks at her door, she won't be lying." She looked towards Hannah and her expression softened, holding out her hand she stepped forward, "Patsy, Patsy Hodge, apologies for this rude interruption, but it's unavoidable, and I'm sure you don't want to be harbouring him any longer than is absolutely necessary."

"Hannah, and it's not a problem, I don't mind . . . that is . . ." Hannah stumbled trying to find the right words.

"Oh boy, he's worked his charm on you hasn't he? They should come with a health warning, him and Meredith both." Patsy held her hands up. "I'm sorry, Hannah, but this is serious, a man is dead, he's chief suspect, and if Meredith is right, the man who set him up and destroyed the evidence is also dead, so -"

"Brooker is dead?" Ben jumped to his feet, "How, when?"

"This afternoon, scared of the dentist apparently, he had a heart attack."

"You'd better be kidding me." Hands on head, Ben paced to the end of the kitchen, "Now what do we do?"

"What we do is move you. DI Wessex has resigned, and Meredith has been asked back to take on the case as far as I understand, we'll know more tomorrow. God forbid, I should be in the loop, but now he's a copper again, he can't know where you are. Pack your stuff."

"He'd tell them where I was? Is that what you're saying?" Ben shouted. "He told me I could trust him, he told me that he'd help."

"And he is, why do you think I'm here? Now stop wasting time." Patsy banged her hand on the breakfast bar, "Because I'm not happy about this turn of events either, so the sooner we get you settled elsewhere, the better."

Patsy didn't miss the silent exchange between Ben and Hannah before he left to collect his things.

"I'm sorry if I sound sharp, it's been a long and irritating day. Here, take my card, give me a call if you want an update. But, please don't try and contact Ben. Wait until this thing is over." Patsy smiled as she handed over her card.

"Thank you, but nothing's going on. I am worried about him of course, but only because he seems a nice man." Hannah looked at the card.

"He is a nice man, and I don't think he did this, so if you are interested in him I'll give you his number when this is done and dusted." She looked up as Ben returned, "Are you ready?"

"I think so." Ben pulled at his shirt, "Is it all right if I keep hold of these for a while? I'll need a change of clothes." His smile was awkward. "And if I can have a bag please." He put the neatly laundered clothes on the breakfast bar.

"Of course." Hannah pulled a carrier from the cupboard, and slid the clothes into it. "The trousers washed up well, they didn't shrink," she commented quietly.

"They'll be fine." Ben took her hand and lifted it to his lips. "Thanks again, I don't know what I would have done without you."

Patsy turned away, knowing that they would be meeting again, and not wanting to ruin the moment. "Two minutes, I'll be in the car." She lifted the bag and took it with her. Ben joined her several minutes later. She smiled at him. "She seems nice."

"Too nice for me, I think. Where are we going?" he asked as Patsy reversed back into the road.

"I have no idea. I thought I might drive to a seaside town and get you a B & B sorted, unless you'd rather have a hotel, somewhere busy, where you won't stand out like a sore thumb. What about Weymouth?"

"No! I'm not leaving Bristol. You may as well stop the car now. I need to be here."

"Why, what can you do?" Patsy glanced at him. "Look, Ben, this is difficult enough already. I don't know where else I can take you. Your face is plastered all over the local news, so Bristol is not a good idea." Patsy indicated and turned onto the main road as Ben fell silent.

As she approached the motorway, he slapped the dashboard. "Tania's. I can go to Tania's, she's away for another week, if this isn't sorted by then, I'll go with your plan. Head towards Downend."

Patsy drove past the slip road for the motorway, and turned the car to face the other direction at the next roundabout.

"Who is Tania?" she asked.

"A girl from work. I don't know how much Meredith has told you, but she's going to help us work out what happened to the missing recording."

"Okay, and she's away now? Where?"

"She is indeed, big secret where, she didn't tell anyone, only that she'd be back with a tan. Weird that, but she won't kick up a stink if she comes home before I've gone."

"I hope you're right."

As they drove to Tania's house, Patsy explained about the telephone, and that she'd put a basic wash bag together, along with some of Meredith's clothes. Ben thanked her, and they fell silent until he told her they were at their destination.

"It's the last but one on the left, no lights on. Good, park over there."

"How are you going to get in?" Patsy asked as she applied the handbrake.

"Key around the back, under the dustbin," Ben lied. "Give me two minutes and I'll let you in the front door." Crossing his fingers, he sprinted to the end of the road, and up the lane behind the rank of houses. There was no key, and he hoped, no alarm.

Hopping over the fence, he made for the back door and tried the handle, knowing it was a long shot. The door was, of course, locked, he looked around for something to break the glass with and eyed the collection of pots to the right of the door. Picking one up, he weighed it in his hand, ensuring it would be heavy enough, he drew his hand back hoping the noise wouldn't attract the neighbours. As he did so, he saw the key, sitting in the circle of dirt left by the pot, and he grinned as he picked it up.

"Please work," he whispered, as he slid it into the lock. "Thank you, God," he murmured, as he stepped into the kitchen. Leaving the lights off, he tentatively opened the door into the hall and braced himself for an alarm to sound. When nothing happened, he hurried to the front door, and opening it, waved Patsy in. She collected the bags from the boot and hurried to join him. Ben patted the wall for the light switch. "That's better. I could do with a drink. Will you join me?" He turned back to the kitchen.

"Not alcohol, put the kettle on," Patsy answered, following him. As he stepped into the kitchen, someone put a key into the lock of the front door. "Someone's coming in," Patsy warned, and gasped as Ben shoved her to one side and knocked off the light switch before pulling her into the kitchen. His hand went over her mouth until she bit into his finger and he released her.

"Please keep still, don't move. I have no idea who that is," his whisper was harsh as the front door opened.

Standing perfectly still they listened to the movement of someone entering the house, and heard the footsteps coming along the hall towards them. Ben made ready to pounce, and was blinded by the light that flooded the kitchen. He squinted at Tania and his body relaxed.

"What the bloody hell is going on here?" she demanded. Looking at Ben, like he was dirt on her shoe, she spat, "I'd never have thought it of you, you bastard. What did you think, that you could use my home as some sort of shag pad while I was away?"

Turning her attention to Patsy, she snorted. "Are you married, love? Is that why you had to come here . . . thinking about it, why did you have to come here? What's wrong with your flat?" She was back to Ben. "Breaking into my home, MY HOME! You bastard, you'd better have a good explanation, or I'm calling the police."

"Tania, calm down. I'm sorry. I didn't break in, I used the key. And by the way, under a flower pot? That's the first place anyone would look!"

"Fuck off! You can lecture me about security when you've told me what you're doing here." Putting her hand into her pocket she pulled out some cigarettes and walked to the back door. She paused, her hand on the handle, she turned to Ben, "Unlocked I assume . . . Ah yes." She pulled open the door, "Get your arse out here, I need a fag, and I'm not smoking in there."

"It's a bit complicated, and very messy." Ben stepped forward ignoring the clenched fist Patsy held towards him.

"Oh, I've no doubt, life's like that. Explain." Tania stepped into the garden and lit her cigarette before turning back to Ben.

Ben stood in the doorway and looked at her. Her face was blotchy and it was clear she'd been crying.

"Are you all right, Tania, you look a bit upset?"

"EXPLAIN!" Tania's hand was shaking as she lifted the cigarette to her lips.

"Okay, okay, don't get the neighbours involved, it's a long stor -" He grunted as Patsy pushed past him.

"May I have a cigarette please? We'll have a smoke and then go back inside. This is not something we want to talk about out here."

"Really? Well it's my house, and I make the rules." Despite her harsh retort, Tania handed the packet to Patsy. "Who are you?" She accepted Patsy's card and read the detail. "Okay, that doesn't explain why you're here in my house, with him," she nodded at Ben, and waited while Patsy lit her cigarette, but tutted at her response.

"We really need to do this indoors."

"Whisper then." Tania leaned towards Patsy who nodded.

"Ben's wanted for murder, and Barry Brooker is dead," Patsy said quietly.

"Shit!" Tania's head shot up. "Smoke fast, I need to sit down!"

Having ushered Patsy and Ben into the living room, Tania put the kettle on, stating she couldn't cope without some caffeine in her system. Ben paced the living room inspecting the knick-knacks and photographs displayed on the various shelves. He stopped at the photograph of a young boy and lifted it from the shelf. The child was clearly related to Tania as he had both her eyes and her smile. Tania appeared behind with a tray.

"Put it down please, Ben." She waited until he'd done so before handing out the coffee.

"Who is it, a nephew? He looks like you." Ben sat on the chair in the bay window.

"Don't change the subject. Who are you supposed to have murdered, and how did Brooker die and when?"

Between them, Patsy and Ben explained what had happened.

"I'm not sure if you got Pete's message, but that's what he wanted," Ben concluded, "we still do. I'm not sure how far the police have got with it. Have you spoken to Pete? Actually, why are you here? Shouldn't you be laying on a sunbed somewhere?"

"Yes, I should, but that went tits up, and I don't want to talk about it. Explain again about this recording." She held her hand up to Ben, "Not you, I want to understand this," she said, looking directly at Patsy.

"As far as we can make out, there are three recordings made each day in the bar at the club. When the police asked for those that would have been made when the murder took place, only two were sent. It's believed they were sent from Brooker's laptop, but which he denied sending and the laptop is missing, and what we want to know is can we work out if it was Brooker who deleted the missing recording or sent the email, or both. It's a long shot, I know, but with Brooker dead, that avenue of investigation will die with him. If it does, that makes Ben's position even more precarious, and he will more than likely be tried for the murder of Aiden O'Brien."

"Aiden O'Brien is dead?" Tania looked shocked. "And Brooker?" she shook her head and stared at the carpet.

"Did you know O'Brien?" Patsy asked.

"He's one of Keith's friends, Keith Chapman. I say friend, I don't think Mr O'Brien liked him much, but I think they had a business together. I can't believe it, I only spoke to him a couple of days ago, and Barry too, God, I can't get my head around this."

"Can I ask why you had to speak to Aiden?"

"I didn't have to, I answered the phone, he wanted, K … Barry." She looked away from Patsy. "I met him a couple of times because he used to come to the club, nice guy. Shit! Not wanting to make light of Barry's heart attack," she glanced at Ben, "or you of course, but have I still got a job? And if so, for how long?" She covered her face with her hands, "I don't believe this, I need that job." Clearly distressed, Tania attempted to get control of her emotions.

Patsy gave her a few moments before speaking. "Perhaps the club will stay open. Do you think you can help us, or should we leave?"

"I don't know if I can help you. I haven't got a computer here. My laptop is at the club, but he can stay," she nodded towards Ben. "Only for a week though, if you haven't got this sorted by then, you'll have to find him somewhere else." She flexed her hands, "I need another ciggy, are you joining me?"

Patsy studied Tania as she looked heavenward and blew smoke into the sky. She was hiding something, and that something had connections with Chapman.

"Can we go to the club and get your laptop?" she asked.

Ben had gone to the toilet, and Tania looked up at the bathroom window as the flush sounded.

"Not today. I don't think I can face them today." Taking a long drag on her cigarette she blew the smoke towards Patsy. "I'm not trying to be awkward, I'm trying to work this out. I don't want to get dragged into this or . . . can I sleep on it?"

"Of course, I could get it for you if it would help."

"How?"

"This chap, Big Pete, could get it for me if I go to the club and if he's working. Would it be easier if we did it that way?" She smiled as Tania nodded, and glanced at her watch. "Time's getting on, you call Pete, and I'll go home and get changed. She turned to Ben as he appeared in the doorway. "I'm going to get Tania's laptop. You stay here, no calls, no going out."

"I'm not stupid." Ben looked past her at Tania, "Are you okay?" He'd had a look around while upstairs, and knew an awkward conversation was coming.

"I'll be fine. Get that kettle on." Tania dropped her cigarette into a flowerpot, and stepping into the kitchen took a key from a hook which she gave to Patsy. "For my locker."

Patsy called Meredith on the way home. "Get your glad rags on we're going clubbing," she announced as he answered.

"To BB's I take it?" He smiled into the phone as she gave confirmation. "In which case, I'll be ready before you get here."

They strode into the club an hour later, and a surprised Pete pushed himself upright, he'd been leaning on the counter deep in conversation with Sandra.

"I wasn't expecting you two," Pete shook Meredith's hand and gave Patsy a nod. "Come on through to the bar, for some reason it's quiet tonight. Can't think what's keeping the punters away." He led them through to the bar, and taking the key from Patsy, disappeared while Meredith ordered the drinks.

"Very quiet for a Saturday. Nothing like a stabbing to kill off a business." Meredith looked across at the DJ who was tapping away on his phone, and counted only ten customers, all of whom looked bored, and he doubted they'd stay long. "He's back," he commented unnecessarily as Pete approached.

Placing the bag at Patsy's feet, Pete jerked his head towards the door. "I've got to get back out there, the boss is on his way in."

"Boss? If Brooker is dead, who's the boss now?" Meredith asked.

"Chapman is my guess," Patsy answered and Big Pete nodded.

"Yep, and he's a miserable bastard too. Called earlier and said to carry on as usual, and report any problems to him. Didn't say he'd be coming in, but . . . Oh, he's here. I don't know you okay."

Big Pete initially ignored the distinguished looking man standing in the doorway, and surveying the room, walked to the DJ and had a quiet word before turning back and going to greet him. They left moments later.

"So, that's Keith Chapman. Smart looking man." Meredith pursed his lips. "Looks a lot younger than I thought he would. How did you get on with Linda's findings?"

"He's sixty-eight, father died when he was young, his mother was poor, but she married well when he was nine, and he was sent away to boarding school. He went to Exeter university, where he was quite political, as was his stepfather, who by the way, later went on to become an advisor to Maggie Thatcher, no less. Chapman met and married his wife, Alice, there. Rumour has it she was pregnant and their son, Henry was not premature. When he finished university, he worked for Alice's father.

"Chapman himself was active in the conservative party in his younger days, but that seemed to fall by the wayside for a while as he began to build his empire," Patsy continued, "but he became active again, and was an MP for a short while before giving up his seat due to illness. We couldn't find anything on the illness. By this time, the couple had three children, the other two were girls, um . . . I can't remember their names. He has business interests as long as your arm, some of them most peculiar in relation to the others. For example, a pottery business in Cornwall, and a llama farm in Wiltshire. He is listed as a board member for a school and several charities, both local and national. Estimated to be worth in excess of ten million by an online business rating site that Linda found. In the nineties, he was voted best looking business man." She smiled, "Is that enough to keep you happy?"

"For now," Meredith leaned forward and kissed her on the forehead, "it will be interesting to see what my lot turned up when I go in tomorrow." He watched her features harden a little. "It will all work out in the end, Patsy, you know that."

"Indeed, I do. I could do without all the bloody messing about in the middle though." She glanced behind him, "The giant's back."

Meredith turned to look, and Pete came to stand a little further up the bar. He called an order to the barmaid, and without turning towards Meredith, said,

"I don't know you, leave now so he doesn't recognise you. He's good with faces. He's not said a word about Brooker, but wants all the staff in tomorrow afternoon, yes, a bloody Sunday, so he can speak to them about Ben. Apparently, he feels we owe it to the deceased, to assist the police with their enquiries." He smiled as the barmaid brought his order, "Don't know about you, but that doesn't add up for me. Anyway, you get off, I must dash, apparently, I'm now a butler too."

Lifting the tray, Big Pete turned away from the bar without another word.

Meredith knocked back his drink. "Drink up, let's do as the man says. We've got a laptop to deliver."

Patsy glanced at her watch, "It's midnight. You have to meet the Assistant Chief Constable in the morning, do we want to do this tonight, or shall I get it sorted tomorrow and let you know? In addition, of course, you will then know where Ben is."

"Bugger. Okay you win, give Jacobs a call and let him know."

Ben accepted the delay without question, he'd had a heart to heart with Tania, and she was in no state to be dealing with this, he hoped that after a night's sleep she'd be a little brighter.

10

Meredith was at the station before most of the team had arrived. Only Dave Rawlings was in the incident room, and he had to give permission for Meredith to be allowed in, as the new desk sergeant didn't recognise him. He looked up from the pile of paper in front of him as Meredith pushed open the door and glanced towards his former office.

"I heard you were coming back. What's the story? There's coffee in the pot." Rawlings closed the file and waited for Meredith to pour a coffee. "I thought you might have given me a call."

"I don't know what the story is, Dave. I didn't call as it was all last minute, and the only reason Trump knew was because he called me. What's the latest?" Giving the incident board a cursory glance, Meredith sat at the desk opposite Rawlings.

"Not much, as I'm sure you already know, with Brooker dead there's little or no chance of finding the missing recording, so your mate, who was only up to his neck, is now as good as drowning in it."

"I'm working on that, but I'll fill you in later. Has anyone spoken to the grieving widow? Perhaps she'll be more outspoken now her old man is dead."

"Not yet, Gov. He only died yesterday afternoon, and given Wessex's involvement, better let the dust settle before we piss off the family even more." Rawlings stretched his arms above his head and yawned, "I've made sure everything is up to date for you, got an email with the relevant info ready to send, once it's confirmed you're back and reinstated. I assume you are reinstated?"

"No idea, I think so, I have a meeting in half an hour with the ACC. It was as much a sur . . ." Meredith stopped speaking as Jo Adler entered the room. "Morning, Adler."

"Gov. I heard you were back. Coffee?"

"Have I no secrets anymore?" Meredith got to his feet, "Coffee would be nice, and make a fresh pot, that doesn't taste like old socks."

"Morning, Gov," Tom Seaton called out as he pushed open the door. "I'd say welcome back, but you've not been gone long enough. Can we get a refund on your pressie? You won't have time for coffee, the ACC has arrived with some suits and is asking for you." Seaton shrugged out of his jacket, "Meeting room two, top floor."

"I'd better not keep them waiting." Meredith rolled his shoulders and walked to the door. "When Trump eventually gets in, tell him to call Loopy and get her to send over the contaminator so we can check it against what you've got." Ignoring the confused looks, he left the room and walked slowly up the flight of stairs to the meeting room, composing himself, and ready to make a few demands.

~~~

Patsy dropped her phone in her bag and cursed Meredith. She'd spoken to Sharon Grainger, who assured her she understood Meredith's decision, and that she believed it would all work itself out in the end. The words were accepting, but she'd sounded disappointed, and Patsy wanted to punch Meredith all over again. Tania's laptop was still in the boot of her car, so she grabbed her coat and set off. When she arrived at the house, it was Ben who opened the door.

"Tania's gone shopping, there was nothing in because of the holiday that didn't happen. Come in quickly, I need to tell you some stuff before she gets back." He led Patsy through to the kitchen, opened the door and walked into the garden. "Don't look at me like that. They can't see me from here, and more importantly Tania, if she gets back, won't hear anything. She's been gone a while."

"Sounds intriguing. Get on with it." Patsy stepped out onto the backdoor step.

"You're beginning to sound like Meredith." Ben grinned at the look of horror that flashed across her face. "Don't say anything, just listen."

"Ben, get on with it."

"I don't think it's relevant, but just in case, I'm going to tell you, not Meredith though, because he can be a little insensitive at times, and as I said it's not relevant, but it is connected . . . I think."

"Ben!" Patsy took a step towards him. "Just say it, I'll decide whether it's relevant."

"Tania has been having an affair with Keith Chapman, on and off for seven years. They have a son together, Alex, he's six and is currently on holiday at his grandmother's. Tania should be in Cyprus on a beach with

Chapman, but he cancelled at the last minute, although he did book them into some up-market hotel in Bath as a consolation. He didn't turn up there either, hence the state Tania was in when she got home."

"And you didn't think that was relevant? Because, it is, Ben, very. We're about to put our trust in someone who is heavily involved with Brooker and his family, and you think she'll spill the beans to us, without giving a thought to the consequence?"

"We don't know that Chapman is involved. Anyway, she finished with him. She's had enough. She didn't mind being a secret, and all that goes with being a mistress, but she did get fed up with being let down all the time, not so much for her, but for Alex. He was supposed to go to Cyprus with them, but instead Tania had arranged for her mother to take him to Dorset for a week as her sister is there. He's six, the seaside is the seaside, I suppose."

"I think Chapman is involved, well, Meredith does anyway. Why don't you want him to know about Tania's relationship with Chapman?" Patsy glanced over her shoulder. "We'll finish this conversation later, she's back." Patsy walked back into the kitchen, and helped Tania unload the shopping, before helping make breakfast. "Thank you for this, I didn't realise I was so hungry."

"I can't work on an empty stomach, and although I'm proficient on techy stuff, I'm not an expert so it could take some time."

Patsy smiled, "You may not be an expert, but I know a girl who is. Do you fancy coming into work with me? If you can show my colleague, Linda, what you know, she might be able to do the rest."

"I'm not sure. I'll do what I can, but I don't want to be seen to be involved, Keith has a temper, and this might bring the family into disrepute. He's big on appearances, the two-faced, hypocritical bastard. Can't this Linda come here?"

"Not today, no, she's in the office on her own finishing off some things, and it is Sunday." Pretending that she didn't know about Tania's relationship with Chapman, she added, "I take it you don't like Chapman? Sounds like you've got his measure."

"I don't, no. More accurate to say at this moment in time I hate him."

"Well let's see if we can put a crack in that outward appearance. There's no need for him to know you helped. The police are obviously working on this too, if you find anything, so could they, I just think you and Linda will get there quicker together."

"And what do I do in the meantime? I thought I might help, and . . ." Ben fell silent as the two women looked at him. He sighed, "Okay, television it is, have you got the sports channels?"

Within the hour, Tania and Linda, were sitting side by side, staring at screens and downloading information from BB's security system.

~~~

"Meredith, prompt as always, come in, come in." Charles Frankum, the Assistant Chief Constable, pumped Meredith's hand up and down.

Meredith hid his surprise, he was clearly in favour, he'd never received a greeting like that before.

"I'm not sure if any introductions are necessary?" Frankum looked at the two other men already in position at the table.

"None. Please take a seat, gentlemen."

Burt was clearly in a hurry, and Meredith simply nodded a greeting. He had no idea who the second man was, but knew he probably wouldn't be told even if he asked. He pulled out the chair next to the ACC.

"Tell me what's going on, and why I've been dragged back in here." Meredith glanced around the table unsure of who would be in charge of the meeting.

"Due to cutbacks and other ongoing cases, we were short of an appropriate officer to head up the case now that Wessex is gone." The ACC poured himself a glass of water. "As you are technically employed until the end of the quarter, we -"

"Okay, let's cut the bullshit." Meredith decided he didn't have time to play games. "You'd already put Seaton in charge, why has mentioning Chapman brought me back in? Who is he to you lot, what's he done, and what did he have to do with Aiden O'Brien's murder?" He held back his smirk as the ACC's mouth snapped shut and Burt took over.

"Chapman is old school tie. Went to Eton with a lot of influential people, and was godfather to the former Home Secretary, and his stepfather was close to Maggie Thatcher. He's meddled in politics for a long while, but although he served as an MP for six months back in the eighties, he retired early on health grounds. He -"

"I know all that already, what was wrong with him?" Meredith had taken out his notebook and tapped it with the pencil.

"Nothing that we know of, but it would have been life-threatening if he remained." Burt smiled at Meredith, his eyes letting Meredith know that that was as much as he would be told, for the moment at least.

"What did he do?"

"Nothing at the time, but he was playing both ends against the middle, and causing a lot of waves. Waves that the country didn't need, what with the Berlin wall about to fall, amongst other things." Burt folded his arms on the table and leaned towards Meredith. "All you need to know, is that he has always wanted to be more important than he is, and while we're confident he is not an agent for anyone we know of, he still likes to mingle in political circles, and was around when Harry Knox died."

The name sounded an alarm in Meredith's brain, and he frowned as he brought back what he knew about Harry Knox MP.

"Married, two young kids, went to a party in the Bristol Grand, and was found dead in his room. Had been rumoured to get a top job in the next cabinet reshuffle. There had been calls of foul play, but death was caused by heart failure, and there was a suggestion that sex games had been involved." Meredith looked up, "How am I doing? Because that was about twenty years ago, and I can't see the connection."

"Very well done, Meredith. Chapman was the last person to see Knox alive, other than the young lady who had left evidence that he had had sex shortly before death. We never found out who she was." Burt grimaced, "We have her DNA, but not her."

"And you think she's connected to this current case? Why might this be linked to the murder of O'Brien?" Meredith lay the pencil next to the pad, and crossing his arms, he leaned back against the chair. "Can we cut to the chase, because I'm going to need to know what you're after if I'm going to help you."

"She may have nothing to do with it. Knox had a dickey heart, so all could be as it seems," Burt held a finger up, "*but*, Knox had something on the then PM, and he was being rewarded with the cabinet post for keeping his mouth shut, we believe Chapman knew about that, and was attempting to create a sort of double bluff and blackmail Knox. We can't prove it, we can't cause a fuss, but all efforts to recover what Chapman may or may not have, have proved fruitless."

"*What?* Again, in English please. What has that got to do with why I'm sitting here? What is the information Chapman may or may not have?"

"Can't tell you that, need to know, et cetera. The thing is, Meredith, that Chapman may not know what he has, but whatever it is, it is still too hot for it to come out. If we, and I mean you, can shake Chapman's tree and find out if he has it, it will be job done, case shut, and no one will be any the wiser." Burt shrugged as if it were a foregone conclusion.

"Let me get this straight, not only am I not allowed to know what I'm looking for, you don't know either?" Meredith shot a sideways glance at the ACC, who was rubbing his forehead as he too processed what Burt was not saying. He threw his arms into the air, "Okay, okay, let me summarise this from my perspective, hear me out, and you can chip in again when I'm done, if of course you can find anything to say."

"Meredith! I think a little -" Frankum tapped the table with his finger, if Meredith was coming back, it would do no good if he felt he could call the shots, and he needed to be reminded of that. However, Frankum never finished his sentence as Burt's colleague spoke for the first time.

"Let Meredith speak," he glanced at his watch. "We are wasting time." His authoritative tone brought forth no argument, and he nodded for Meredith to continue.

"Chapman is a naughty boy, but we don't know how naughty, and you'd like to find that out. Aiden O'Brien's murder has nothing to do with what you want, but facilitates a thorough police search of all Brooker's known associates, namely Chapman himself, who by the way was involved in setting up O'Brien."

Meredith ignored the surprised look exchanged between Burt and his colleague, "And despite DI Wessex being called off, following Chapman's interference, you think I may find out what went on . . . how long ago? Twenty odd years by my reckoning, and be able to close the book on Chapman for you. *And,* if I'm lucky, I get my mate out of the shit he's currently stuck in, or not, because that bit is of no importance to you. How am I doing?"

"As always, spot on, Meredith." Burt tilted his head. "Of course, if you can prove your friend's innocence at the same time, all well and good, I wish you luck." Burt pulled a file from the bag at his feet and placed it on the table, "Which brings us neatly to this." He pulled a sheet from the file and slid it across the table to Meredith. "Tonight's headlines in the local paper. You might draw some press interest."

Meredith lifted the copy of the *Bristol Post's* front page. It was dated the following day, and he read aloud the headline above the photograph of him and Ben Jacobs, arms around each other's shoulders, apparently posing for the camera.

Local Police Officer delays early retirement to catch former friend accused of murder.

DCI John Meredith (Left) was due to take early retirement this week, but has delayed his departure from the force, after a former friend, Ben Jacobs, a local singer, was arrested for the murder of Aiden O'Brien, last week at BB's Night Club. Jacobs escaped custody and is now the subject of a manhunt headed by his former school-mate, DCI Meredith.

"Jacobs was wrong to run," Meredith told our reporter. "Justice has to be done, and if he's innocent then I will prove that, if not, he must be punished for the crime. I will find him, and I will bring him in."

Meredith was at a loss for words, and slid the sheet to the ACC who had been attempting to read it over his shoulder.

"Right, we're finished here. We'll leave you to it. Meredith, a daily briefing will be required, more if necessary." Burt got to his feet. "Thank you for your help, Assistant Chief Constable, it won't be forgotten. I'm sure it goes without saying that this conversation remains in this room." He smiled as Frankum nodded, and held out his hand, "Meredith, would you escort us out please."

"One more thing before we go." Meredith's tone was clipped. "Jacobs is innocent, and I will prove that, but I want the help of George Davies. I want his suspension overturned, and his return to duty with no comment on his file."

"But the man let Jacobs escape. Innocent or not, there is a process." Frankum was shaking his head which stopped when Burt announced.

"Don't know who he is, but that seems fair enough. Would you sort that please, Charles?" He nodded his thanks as Frankum agreed without further protest, and recovered the copy of the front page as he walked to the door, slipping it into his briefcase as he left the room.

He turned to Meredith as they approached the stairs. "You don't seem very happy, Meredith. I thought this was what you wanted?"

"Are you surprised? You do know I won't bring Jacobs in until I know we can drop the charges."

"I don't care. You do what you feel is appropriate, get on Chapman's case promptly though. Irrespective of the murder, which, of course, will be investigated, Chapman is your priority. You will have search warrants for all his known premises by lunch-time."

Meredith didn't respond, but walked quickly down the stairs until they reached the door to the carpark, which he held open.

Burt paused as he caught up with him. "I was impressed with your knowledge of Knox, were you involved in some way?"

"Nope, but I'd told my daughter I'd have time off even if the Prime Minister was killed in Bristol, and the next thing I hear is that Knox has dropped dead on my doorstep, luckily, I didn't get the call, but read up on it."

"You have a good memory, I'm much the same. I'll be sending you a file on Knox and Chapman, have a read through and see if you spot something which may help."

"I'm touched. Thanks. I know something about Chapman that hasn't come to the surface yet, but it will do." He stepped to one side to allow the two men to pass him.

"How do you know Chapman had something to do with the murder at the club?" Burt and his colleague had stopped to await Meredith's response.

"Because I'm good at my job." Meredith heard the un-named man snort as he turned away. "I'll be in touch." he called out.

Hurrying back to the incident room, he allowed five minutes of leg-pulling before he called his team to order and issued his instructions.

"Our task today is to find anything and everything we have on Keith Chapman. I'll go with Rawlings to see Brooker's widow, who is also Chapman's daughter, and we'll have another briefing at two-thirty to see what progress has been made. Those of you doing the other properties, remember we are also looking for any indication that Chapman or Brooker have other properties that are not officially connected to them." Meredith glanced at Trump, "Did Loopy send you that spreadsheet?"

"Yes, sir, but I haven't got a clue . . ." Trump held out his hands.

"You don't need one, get her to educate you, then pump in the information that this lot dig up." Standing, he walked to his office, "Give me twenty minutes, Dave, and we'll be off." He pointed at the office, "I'll be back in here." He caught the movement from the corner of his eye and turned to Tom Seaton. "Yes, Tom?"

"What about Jacobs, he's still at large, are we not bothering about him?"

"Not at the moment, no, we'll get to him once we've found out what Chapman has been up to." He held up his hand to halt any protest, "You've had your orders get on with it."

Closing the door, he called Patsy, and found she was in her office, and she told him that Tania was explaining the system to Linda.

"Good. Make sure Ben stays put, wherever that is, and tell him that we've made the front page of *The Bristol Post*. You can also tell him to work on Tania to find out everything he can about Chapman. If she has any joy with the laptop give me a ring. I'm off to see Brooker's widow, so might not pick up. When you've done that, find Sian O'Brien, and establish her side of the story. She might open up now her father is gone."

"Is that it, or do you have more orders for me?" Patsy didn't attempt to hide her irritation, and chose not to tell him of Tania's involvement with Chapman.

"I'm sorry, I didn't say please, but I'm pushed for time."

"And what about telling me what happened at the meeting, why you're back in charge of the case? And, what do you mean you've made the front page? It's all very well that these cases have overlapped, but you will remember you should be out here on this side of the fence, and now you're not. You gave me a promise to explain," she snapped.

Meredith nodded slowly. "And explain I shall. But it's too complicated to do now, you'll ask too many . . . ah there you go, Rawlings is here. I have to go, I'll tell all later." He hung up and slid the phone into his pocket. Standing, he bellowed into the incident room, "Rawlings, get your coat, we're off." He walked to the door and beckoned Tom Seaton, "Get the teams ready to go, once I've spoken to the widow I'll give you a call."

11

Patsy noticed the curtain twitch as she walked up the path, the door was opened before she'd knocked. She smiled at Kathleen O'Brien.

"I'm Patsy Hodge, I believe . . ."

"Yes, I've been expecting you, Rosie called. Come through, Sian is in the garden."

Patsy followed her through the hall and into the dining room, where French windows opened onto the garden, and she called to her granddaughter.

"Sian, Miss Hodge is here, you help her now, none of your nonsense, we need to find out who killed your father, God rest his soul." She sniffed back a sob as she turned back to Patsy, "I'll put the kettle on. If she messes you about let me know. I doubt she knows anything, but manners cost nothing, and she's been leading her parents a merry dance."

Patsy thanked her and made her way up the garden, where a sullen Sian sat fiddling with her phone on a bench.

"Hello, Sian, thank you for seeing me. I'm investigating your father's death, and your mother thought I should speak to everyone in the family." She perched at the opposite end of the bench.

"Are you going to interrogate Gran as well?" Sian didn't look up from her phone.

"I'm not going to interrogate anyone. I'm simply gathering facts. Will you help me?"

"How? I wasn't there. You're wasting your time." Huffing, Sian slid the phone into her back pocket. "Ask away, it's obvious you won't go until you realise that."

"Thank you. When was the last time you saw your father?" Patsy caught the flush as it hit the girl's cheeks. She wasn't much older when her own mother died, and she knew the pain and confusion she must be feeling. She kept her voice light, "What did you talk about?"

"The day he died. We rowed about Gary. He thought he knew it all, he thought Gary was the reason I hated him. He was so shocked when I . . ." Realising she had said too much, Sian clamped her mouth shut.

"When you did what?" Patsy coaxed.

"Nothing. I did nothing. I told him he was wrong, that I hated him because he was a moron. He didn't like it. He stormed off."

"Hate is a strong emotion. Why did you hate him, and in what way was he a moron?" Patsy pulled her shoulders back as Sian turned to face her.

"Fuck off! What are you, some sort of therapist? I hated my father. It happens. I'm not sitting here discussing it with you!" She turned back to her former position, and lifted her feet onto the bench, resting her chin on her knees.

"No, not even close to being a therapist, but other than your mother, you were the last person he spoke to. Your mother tells me he was furious when he got home, and had an angry exchange with Gary's grandfather. Do you know what that was about perhaps?"

"No. I wasn't there."

"But did he perhaps hint he would speak to Mr Chapman. You see the question that's bothering me, is why Gary's grandfather, and not his parents. If your father thought his problem stemmed from Gary, he would have spoken to his parents surely. I think you can help explain that." Patsy watched the shrugged response and tried again, "If I were to speak to Mr Chapman, and tell him we know that something connected to you and Gary had caused the argument between them what would he say?"

"He'd lie, because he's a bastard too. Gary is a wimp and won't stand up to him." Sian turned her head to face Patsy. "This is such a waste of time. Anyway, I thought they had the man that stabbed Dad. Perhaps you should be speaking to him."

"Oh, we will. It's just that he claims he's innocent and he's escaped custody, apparently, he thinks he can clear his name." To her total surprise, Sian laughed.

"That's amazing." She pulled her phone from her back pocket, and tapped away for a minute, before returning it. "Totally amazing."

"Do you not care that he might be guilty. That the man who stabbed your father, and left him to bleed to death on the floor of a nightclub, might be walking around free? Whatever your father did to upset you, I find that difficult to believe."

Sian jumped to her feet. "Well tough shit. There's a lot that happens in this world that's difficult to believe. You learn to live with it." Her cheeks were red, and her eyes blinked away tears. "I used to think he was the best . . . Forget it, have you got anything useful to say?"

"Did he do something to you, Sian? I don't want detail; I'm simply trying to understand why you are being so uncooperative." Patsy was shocked at the vehement response, and leaned back against the bench.

"You stupid fucking bitch. No, he didn't *DO* something to me. He wasn't like that, and don't you dare put it about that he was." A sob took hold of her voice, and she turned and ran off down the garden, narrowly avoiding her grandmother who was stepping out through the French doors.

Patsy remained seated and watched as Kathleen O'Brien carefully negotiated the steps carrying a tray of tea. Placing it on the centre of a bench, she took a seat next to it. Ignoring the tea, she looked up at Sian's bedroom window.

"Was she any help?"

"I'm afraid not. Were you here when Aiden came to see her?" Patsy helped herself to one of the mugs, and sipped her tea.

"I was. He sat on this bench as she marched up and down the garden. I had a word with her after, shouting at the top of her voice like that. No need of it."

"Could you hear what they were arguing about?" Patsy's heart sank as Kathleen O'Brien shook her head.

"Not really. At one point she called him an effing hypocrite, I also heard her ask what her mother would say, but I don't know what she was referring to. I do know that Keith Chapman came into the conversation. The last thing Aiden said, was that she had no idea what she was talking about, and he'd speak to Chapman."

She gave Patsy's hand a squeeze, "We've not been much help, have we. I want to go and stay with poor Rosie, all alone in that huge house, but Sian won't at the moment. She said she needed more . . . Oh, I've just remembered, Sian also seemed to be taunting him with her phone, held it a little out of his reach, waving it at him. He didn't bite though, perhaps he'd threatened to take it away." She rubbed her hands as though soaping them, "I don't know, I simply don't know."

Patsy cupped the woman's hands in her own. "It's an awful time for all of you. Despite Sian's behaviour, it's clear she loved her father. I expect she's feeling guilty that they argued, whatever it was about will seem trivial now." Patsy stood up. "Would you mind if I tried to have another quick word before I go?"

"Carry on. If she'll open her door. It's the one at the top of the stairs." Kathleen made to push herself up, and Patsy held her hand up.

"Don't move on my account. Stay and enjoy the sunshine while it lasts." She handed Kathleen a card, "If you need anything, or are worried about Sian, please call."

~~~

Meredith smiled at the woman who opened the door. He showed his newly reclaimed ID.

"DCI Meredith, I'm here to see Penny Brooker."

"This way. Penny, there's a man here to see you. He . . ." she stopped speaking as her daughter appeared. "Have you been crying?"

Meredith and Rawlings exchanged a puzzled look as Penny Brooker stepped forward and took hold of her mother's hand.

"Go and put the kettle on, Mum, I'll take these gentlemen into the dining room." She watched her mother walk away before turning to Meredith. "She has dementia, she's forgotten about Barry, when she remembers she'll cry again. This way."

Meredith waited until they were all seated before he spoke. "Mrs Brooker, I am sorry for your loss, it must have been a terrible shock. If there's anything we can do . . ." He let the sentence drift.

"Like what exactly? I've just lost my husband unexpectedly, I'm barely coping, and I'd be grateful if you would get to the point."

"Of course, apologies. This is a difficult time for you and, of course, Mrs O'Brien. The purpose of my visit is to advise you that we have search warrants for all properties connected to your husband, including this one, to search, primarily, but not exclusively for his missing laptop. I'm sure he mentioned it to you." Meredith paused, awaiting verification, but Penny Brooker simply looked at him expectantly. "Did he mention it?" Meredith pressed.

"He did. He said it was stolen, so why you think you will find it here or anywhere else come to that is beyond me. I was waiting for you to complete your announcement." She sighed as her mother came into the room. "Mum, will you wait in the kitchen please."

"And leave you on your own, when your husband has just died. No, I most certainly will not." Alice Chapman pulled out a chair and sat facing Meredith. "What do these men want? Are they undertakers?"

"No, they are policemen. Before Barry died," Penny tried to keep her voice level, "a man was killed in the club. They are here about that."

"And it couldn't wait." Alice shook her head at Meredith. "Shame on you."

Meredith smiled at her, "It is atrocious timing, I know, but whereas Mr Brooker died of natural causes, Mr O'Brien was murdered, and we have a duty to his wife, not to mention the public to -"

"O'Brien is dead? When, how?"

Penny Brooker could bear it no longer and she banged the table with the flat of her hand. "Mother, please. Let them tell me what they want, and then I'll explain it to you." Her mother was staring out of the window, having lost interest in the conversation. Penny turned back to Meredith. "I am barely managing to keep my temper. Please tell me what it is you haven't said yet.

You came to tell me you have search warrants, and . . . what?"

"Ah, I see, and . . . rather than come in and disrupt everything without warning, I'm here to ask whether you wish to be present. I thought perhaps you may not want to be here."

"This is my home, are you going to ransack it?"

"Not if I can help it. It may take a while though."

"Get on with it. Just fucking do it!" Exasperated and wanting everyone out of her house, including her mother, Penny found she was going to get the opposite.

"Now?" Meredith glanced at Rawlings, he'd been expecting more opposition.

"Yes. Are you dim? Get it done, and get out of my home." Penny Brooker got up, her chair scraping against the marble floor. "Where's the list or warrant, whatever you call it?"

Meredith pulled a folded document from his inside pocket, and handed it to her.

She skimmed the detail. "Where are you going to start? Some of these premises belong to my father, he won't like it if you simply barge in."

"We're going to start here. Excuse me for a moment, I have to make a call."

Meredith walked back into the hall and called Tom Seaton. "Get those wagons rolling. Rawlings and I will do the home address. Call me if you find anything interesting. But anything you're not sure about bag it and bring it in."

"Will do. I was about to call you, I've taken a call from Frankie, and it looks like the evidence is in Jacobs' favour." As he was speaking, Seaton held up his arm and was moving his finger in a circular motion to get the team mobilised.

"In what way?"

"No blood on the cuff of either the shirt or the jacket he was wearing. Might have been a fluke, but Frankie reckons the way the knife was thrust up, and then dragged down, it would be almost impossible for whoever was wielding it to have avoided soaking up some of the blood, unless the sleeves were rolled up. The footage shows that they weren't. Trump is now arranging search warrants for the faces we do know, and putting pressure on identifying the others. He's gone back to the cars in the carpark, and is running the plates now."

"That is good news, very good. Tell Trump to stay there and keep the momentum going. He can call me with any news."

He hung up and called Patsy so she could pass the news on to Ben. He left a message when her answer service cut in.

~~~

Patsy pushed open the door to her office with her foot, and placed the tray she was carrying on the coffee table. Tania glanced up at her but Linda remained glued to the task in hand. Her fingers tapping away on the keyboard.

"Any joy? I've brought tea and biscuits, actually before you tell me let me check my messages, someone was trying to call me." She pulled out her phone, and listened to the message from Meredith. "Wonderful! The forensic examination of Ben Jacobs' clothes suggests that it wasn't him who stabbed Aiden O'Brien. That's the first bit of good news for the day, are you two going to give me more?"

"Give me a sec . . ." Linda tapped the screen. "Yes, I thought so. Come and look at this."

Patsy walked to stand behind her, on the screen was a list of dates and numbers. "What am I looking at?"

"The lovely Tania gave me the password to . . ." raising her hand, Linda flipped away the comment, "I know, too much info. Anyway, I've run a little program with the data available and I can tell you who has accessed this system and when. Well not actually who, just the IP address of the computer. Now Aiden O'Brien was killed at one thirty-eight according to the recordings, and at one thirty-one, Brooker, or someone using his password, logged onto the system and was watching the live action as it recorded."

She tapped one of the lines of digits on the screen, "That happens here. At one-forty he logs out. At eight thirty the next morning, someone, with a login unknown to Tania, logs in and copies three of the recordings." She glanced up to make sure Patsy had registered the significance, as she was nodding Linda assumed she had, and continued, "Then having made the copies they deleted one of them, which of course would be the missing footage, before logging out."

"And we don't know who that is?" Patsy addressed the question to Tania.

"No, I've always set up the new users to the account, but I didn't set that one up." Tania now leaned forward and tapped the screen, "They were added here at about nine o'clock that evening. I was still at the hotel then."

"So, it was Brooker?" Patsy looked from one to the other.

"Don't know. Because at that time, all of the users, including Tania, had logged on. All for less than ten minutes, and the program isn't sophisticated enough to show who actually added the new user."

"Bugger. We've not got much further, have we?"

"Well, we have, we know someone was watching the bar at the time of the murder, Brooker or whoever, and we've now accessed all the remaining footage which I've emailed across to Louie, as the Skipper wants it checked out. *And*, we know that copies were made of all three recordings so the crucial one may still exist."

"But we don't know who sent the email?" Patsy walked away and collected her coffee, "and by the way he really won't like you calling him that, so probably best not to his face."

"No, to the email. Although it was Brooker's IP address, so shows it was from the club. But the person who did it was logged in as admin. Tania tells me that most of them do that because they forget their own passwords." Linda pointed to the remaining coffee, and Patsy passed it across. "Finally, with regards to the Skipper, he does like nicknames, he's toying with me."

Patsy almost spat her coffee out. "Toying with you? How?"

"The chaps at the station call him Gov, Peggy calls him Merewinkle, and, I therefore, will now be calling him Skipper. He'll soon grow to love it. Was there anything else we needed to do on this? Because if not, I'm going back to the phone records. Now the Skipper is a copper again, he can let us know who some of the numbers I can't trace belong to."

As Patsy told her to wait until she had spoken to Meredith, Linda's hands flew into the air and she gaped at the screen.

"Bloody hell. Come and look at this, someone is deleting every recording on the system."

Tania put her hands over her mouth and leaned forward. "Can you see who it is?"

Linda nodded and turned back to Patsy. "Tania has just deleted all footage from the club's CCTVs apparently."

"What? Do you know where they are?" Patsy hit her palm against her forehead, "Of course you don't." She watched as Linda hit a few keys and leaned towards the screen.

"The club. Whoever is logged in as Tania, is at the club, as it's Brooker's IP address again." Linda flopped back in her chair. "You'd better make that call to Meredith."

~~~

Meredith slid the ringing phone back into his pocket, Patsy would have to wait. He slid the drawer to the bedside cabinet in the spare room shut and looked across the room at Rawlings.

"Nothing here, not even a telephone bill. That's not normal. I'll give Trump a ring and see how it's going elsewhere."

"Maybe he kept all paperwork at the club, some people are like that," Rawlings suggested.

"Tidy, secretive people are. Come on, let's go. A quick word with Mrs Brooker, and we'll see if we can be any use anywhere else."

As they got to the bottom of the stairs, the front door opened and Keith Chapman walked in. Meredith noted he had his own key, he wasn't sure he'd want his in-laws to have such access to his home. He opened his mouth to issue a greeting when Chapman walked forward jabbing his finger at him.

"Name and station," he demanded. "You are going to be very sorry that you've intruded on my daughter's grief like this." He glanced at his daughter,

"I got here as quickly as I could, I had to drop Gary off, you should have made them wait."

Meredith showed his ID. "DCI Meredith, and I did speak to your daughter first. She actually asked us to do this immediately. Why don't we -"

"Dad, it's okay. I told them to get on with it. I thought you'd be at your office now." Penny Brooker looked confused.

"My office? Why? I told you I would help sort things out. You should have called me sooner." He glanced back at Meredith and Rawlings, "Did you find anything?"

"Not here, no." Meredith looked at Penny Chapman and smiled. "We'll leave -"

"What do you mean, *here*? I thought you'd already searched the club." Chapman stepped forward, effectively blocking Meredith's exit.

"They have a list on the warrant. I told them to check here first. I'm going to make some coffee, let them do their job, Dad, the sooner they've finished the better." Penny Chapman turned and left the three men standing in her hall.

"What list? No one has spoken to me about a list." His eyes darted from Meredith to Rawlings.

"We have a search warrant for all premises connected to Barry Brooker. Evidence and information that has come to light would suggest that while Mr Brooker may not have stabbed Aiden O'Brien, he may have been complicit in his death. I'm sorry for your loss by the way."

"My what? Oh, he was my son-in-law, no loss! What premises? Let me see that document," Chapman held out his hand.

"I believe it's through here," Meredith pointed and walked towards the dining room. Alice Chapman was sitting at the table staring out into the garden. "Excuse me, Mrs Chapman." He walked around her and collected the warrant from the sideboard.

Chapman had followed him and snatched it from his hand. His fingers crumpled the paper where he held it, his grip was so tight.

"Some of these are my premises. You will not go in there." He pointed the warrant at Meredith, "Do you hear me?"

"I have to advise that not only can we, we already are." Meredith met his gaze. "I'm led to believe that each property on that warrant is connected to Mr Brooker. Mr and Mrs Brooker, Mr Brooker and Mrs Alice Chapman, Mr Brooker and -"

"That's me. I'm Alice Chapman, but I haven't done anything wrong, have I? It wasn't me, was it?"

Meredith was about to reassure her when Chapman spun away from him, and the warrant was now pointing at his wife.

"Shut up, Alice. Not now, we can't do this now. These policemen are here about Barry. Go to the kitchen and make sure Penny is okay."

"Why wouldn't she be okay?" Alice looked puzzled for a moment, and her hand flew to her mouth. "Are the police here about the navy thing? Have they found out what you did?"

Meredith looked at Chapman, wondering what might happen next. He watched Chapman control his response.

"What thing? Alice, your daughter's husband has died, remember? It was only yesterday. She needs our comfort and support, please try, darling."

There was no compassion in his tone, despite his words, and Meredith watched Chapman rather than look back to Alice who had fallen silent. The silence dragged on until Alice jumped to her feet.

"I'm sorry. I know I get things mixed up. It wasn't you, was it? The thing with the sailors was your father. Poor Penny, has anyone told her?" Alice tutted and left the room.

"As you can see my wife is not well. She has dementia and it worsens by the day. If you've finished here I'll see you out, but mark my words, if any damage has been done to my property you'll pay dearly. I had little to do with my son-in-law's affairs, I don't know what you are hoping to find." Chapman dropped the warrant onto the table.

"I hope there will be no damage, can't be guaranteed though. And what we're hoping to find is why Aiden O'Brien had to be silenced, and I promise you we will find it. I've not failed to solve a case yet." This wasn't quite true, but Meredith wanted the man to worry. He looked at Rawlings, "Let's leave the family to it."

As he crossed the hall towards the front door, Penny Chapman reappeared.

"Is that it? Are you finished here?"

"We are. I'll call if there's anything else, thank you for your time, I'm sorry we had to intrude, if . . ." Meredith paused as Chapman walked into the hall, "Should you wish to contact me, please call."

Meredith placed his business card next to a large vase of lilies on the hall table, and opened the door.

As he pulled it shut behind Rawlings, Penny turned to her father. "Is everything all right at the club? I don't think I want to keep it now."

"Everything is fine, don't worry, darling. I'll deal with the club until the dust settles."

Meredith turned away and followed Rawlings back to the car.

~ ~ ~

Patsy hung up for the second time. "He's not picking up." She paced up and down her office. Coming to an abrupt halt, she turned to Tania, "If whoever is doing this is at the club, we should go and see who's there. I wouldn't get in, but you would. Will you come with me? We can make up a story as to why we're there on the way."

"I'm not sure. If Keith . . . Mr Chapman finds out he might be angry."

Tania looked down at her hands. "I . . ."

"Do you care if he's angry?"

Patsy watched her head snap up, and needed no words to let Tania know she knew about her relationship with Chapman.

Tania's features hardened. "I don't want to be caught in the line of fire. I have my reasons." She gave a laugh, "You know about Alex too, don't you?"

"I do. Nobody's business but yours. This has nothing to do with Alex, this has to do with a murder. If Chapman is involved he needs to be caught, if not, I don't see why he should be angry with you, not that he needs to know anything. We can say I'm looking at the club as a venue for a party." Patsy smiled. "That's it. I'm a client wanting to hire the club. That would work if he found out, wouldn't it?"

Tania closed her eyes, she thought about Ben and how desperate he was, and she thought about how Chapman had treated her. She'd already made up her mind that enough was enough with regards to that relationship, and she doubted he'd care, not really. Nodding, she got to her feet.

"Come on. We might miss them."

Patsy and Tania arrived at the club, five minutes before Meredith. He parked next to her car and walked briskly around to the club entrance.

"I know she'll think she's got good reason, Dave, but I'm buggered if I can guess what it is." When he entered the foyer, Patsy was standing with a woman he'd not seen before, and they were speaking to Big Pete. As one they turned to look at Meredith.

"Thank goodness, it's only you." Patsy beckoned him forward. "There's been a development."

"On Sian O'Brien?" Meredith feigned surprise. "And that brought you here?"

"No, on the recordings. Whoever has been messing about with them deleted the whole lot about thirty minutes ago, so we rushed over to see who was here."

Meredith opened his mouth to deliver a sharp retort, but thought better of it. He jerked his head towards the door, "A word."

Patsy frowned, "Do you not want to know -"

"Now, if you wouldn't mind." Meredith had already opened the door, and Dave Rawlings grimaced as Patsy followed Meredith back onto the street. He paced towards the carpark before turning to face her. "Explain why you are following up such a lead without so much as a by-your-leave."

"I beg your pardon? Explain what exactly?"

"Don't mess about, Patsy, this is serious stuff, and you shouldn't be getting so involved on the Jacobs case. I think you -"

Patsy stepped forward and poked him in the chest. "Stop right there. Do not say another word, or I might find it necessary to punch you." She poked him again as she counted off her explanation. "One, I am still awaiting an explanation as to why you are suddenly back on the force. Two, you have my staff, would have been *our* staff, but as you're carrying a warrant card again, I think mine, looking into your police case. Three, she found something that your lot would have taken hours if not days to find out. Four, I am harbouring a wanted man for you . . . well almost. Five, if you ever picked up your bloody phone, I wouldn't have had to do your job for you. So, after you've apologised for being an unreasonable bastard, you can tell me if you want to know who was here at the club when the data was wiped." She gave one final prod for good measure.

Meredith's lips twitched. "Well that's me told. Who wiped . . . SHIT, if they've wiped the system, we're even more adrift on the Jacobs case. Who was it?"

"I think there was something else you wanted to say, wasn't there?"

"Yes, yes, of course. I'm sorry." His apology was genuine, and Patsy relaxed as he continued. "As always, I jumped in, I should have known, et cetera, et cetera, but can we do this later? I need to know who it was." Meredith frowned, "I also need to know why my men didn't know this was going on, are they in there?"

"There's a list of stuff building up for doing later, whenever that might be, you still have a lot of explaining to do. But, in answer to your questions, yes, Dave Seaton is in there with a couple of uniforms, he was upstairs in Brooker's office when you arrived, and Big Pete believes it was Chapman, as he was supposed to meet him here, but he'd been and gone by the time Big Pete arrived."

She allowed herself a smile, "As to the recordings, due to my interfering, Linda and Tania had already emailed a copy before they were wiped." She turned back towards the club, and continued without looking at him, "Oh and someone was watching the stabbing of Aiden O'Brien, as it happened, probably Brooker."

"He watched it?" Meredith stopped walking, and Patsy paused, her hand on the door. "That explains how he called the police so quickly. Both Ben and Big Pete said the police were there in no time. When I checked, it was Brooker that called it in. I haven't had time to check the time of the call against the time of the stabbing. Was it him who sent the recordings in?"

Patsy turned back to face him, "Okay, so now you're speaking to me like a grown-up, it's unlikely to have been Brooker. Come inside and I'll update you."

"Thank you. I'd appreciate that. Did I tell you that you are looking particularly beautiful today?"

"Overkill, Johnny, don't push it." She smiled as she walked into the club.

Tania made coffee, and they drank it in the locker room, while Seaton and his team completed their search. Patsy updated Meredith on the new user being added, and Tania confirmed that it was unlikely to have been Brooker as his knowledge of the system was too limited. Seaton had confirmed that a silver coloured Lexus was pulling away as he and the team arrived, it had two occupants, possibly three, the passenger was wearing a red top, but he'd not seen their faces. Chapman drove a Lexus.

"The question now is whether I pull Chapman in, or just go for the grandson. He's over eighteen, so although he'll have a brief, he won't have Chapman breathing down his neck." Meredith finished his coffee. "Before I go, how did Ben take the news about the forensics on his clothes. I bet he was relieved."

"I've not spoken to him. I was rather tied up trying to catch Chapman." Patsy gave him a forced smile. "I have to take Tania home, I'll go and see him after that."

Patsy shook her head as Tania opened her mouth, the gesture wasn't missed by Meredith, but he pretended he didn't now know Jacobs was staying with Tania.

Patsy tapped his hand, "May I have a word before I go please."

"Indeed, you may." Meredith smiled at Tania, "Thanks for your help, much appreciated." He turned his attention to Patsy and gestured towards the door, "Shall we?" He led the way back down to the foyer, and held open a door allowing a young uniformed officer to carry out a box of electronic equipment. "There goes the recording system, totally useless to us now I'm told." He smiled, "What did you want to speak about?"

"Gary Mason. When I interviewed Sian, which was a waste of time by the way, she stated that she hated her father, and that Gary was a wimp who wouldn't stand up to his grandfather who, like her father, was also a lying bastard. There was also something else, something to do with her phone, so can you get one of your chaps to find out what's on there. Her grandmother said she showed something to Aiden O'Brien before he stormed off. It might be a waste of time, but worth a check."

"Thanks for the heads up. Doesn't sound like a waste of time to me." He tilted her chin towards him and kissed her. "Duty calls. What are you going to do now?"

"Get Linda to update me on what's happening. See what else needs to be taken care of at the office, *we* do have other clients you know, and as I'm working solo -"

"Enough said, give me a call if anything crops up, if not, I'll see you at home later." He looked away as Big Pete came out of the bar, he was looking worried. "Problem?" Meredith asked as the large man approached.

"Not for me, but I doubt you'll be happy." His eyes darted between them. "Ben's in Cornwall."

"What?" Meredith looked at Patsy as though that was her fault.

"With whom?" Patsy ignored Meredith.

"That bird Hannah. He said he couldn't stay cooped up, Patsy had originally suggested he shouldn't be in Bristol, so he's gone to Cornwall to keep out of the way."

"I'm going to kill that man." Meredith pinched the bridge of his nose and studied the carpet for a moment. Looking up he addressed Patsy, "Call him and tell him to get his arse back to wherever you left him. He needs to turn himself in. With the forensic evidence, he should get bail now."

"What even with that?" Pete held up his phone. It was the front page of the next day's post. "I think Hannah told him about it."

"But how did she get his . . . Oh, it doesn't matter." Irritated, Meredith looked at the phone and the photograph taken some years before. "Patsy, I have to go. Let me know what he has to say for himself. I'm going to get young Mason brought in for questioning."

Already walking to the door, he pulled out his phone, and as he left the club he was instructing Trump to find Gary Mason.

Patsy pulled out a card and handed it to Big Pete. "Here's my card, if Ben calls and hasn't spoken to me, get him to call please, but let me know he's been in touch. I'll get Tania and be off. Oh, and by the way, keeping us updated on comings and goings here would be useful."

~~~

Patsy accepted the offer of coffee and followed Tania through to the kitchen, as she watched Tania busying herself, Patsy decided to address the issue of Tania's relationship with Chapman.

"Ben told me about your relationship with Keith Chapman, if you feel he's not going to be pleased that you've been helping us, you have my card, if you ever need my help you must ask for it." She spoke softly to Tania's back.

Tania spun around. "Former relationship. It's over I have no idea whether or not he's mixed up with Aiden O'Brien's death, but it was over before I came home. I thought I loved him, but I've realised I was forcing it for Alex. I wanted him to know his father." She tilted her head, "I'm assuming Ben told you about Alex too."

"He did, but he didn't say much, just that you were in a relationship with Chapman and that you had a son together. Ben only told me because he didn't want you to find yourself in a difficult position if it turns out Chapman is involved. He told me to help protect you."

"Well, when you speak to him, tell him to keep his mouth shut. Keith has been good to us, considering I'm the other woman, and Alex is his bastard. He's let us down too, but that's mainly because he is paranoid about anyone finding out about us." She held her hand up to stop Patsy saying something, "I mean proper paranoid. He's been here a few times, but mainly we see each other out of the city."

She gave a bitter laugh at the expression on Patsy's face. "Yes, really. We had a day trip planned to Longleat Safari park once, a few years back, and an hour before he was due to pick us up . . . from the bus station, he called to say change of plan, we'd go to the seaside instead and to pack towels. He told me later that his daughter had been talking to her neighbour and it had been mentioned that the neighbour's son might be going there with a friend. A child! He was frightened of bumping into the child of his daughter's neighbour for Christ's sake. When I told him I thought that was ridiculous he became very angry, I mean proper mad. He told me to accept the fact we had to be absolutely discreet or we were through."

She held her hands up, "But no more. If I'm honest I never wanted him full time, I'm happy with it being only me and Alex. It's over, and if he does have anything to do with Aiden O'Brien's murder, then I hope he gets caught."

"And he accepts that it's over?" Patsy asked, hoping that the woman meant what she said. Hanging around for a man to turn up and spare you some time must be an awful way to live. Patsy could think of nothing worse.

"Yes. He wouldn't want me to make a fuss you see." She looked down at her hands, "Unfortunately for Alex, Keith will walk away from him too."

"Does Alex know Chapman is his father?"

"Yes, but he thinks he works abroad, hence the absence of him in our life. I'm not sure how he'll react when he doesn't see him again, but that's a problem for another day. At the moment, I've told him he was called away to Canada."

"Where is Alex now?"

"With my sister. She's on holiday in Dorset, and when Keith cancelled on us, I called her as she has two boys, and she said she'd be happy for him to spend the remainder of the holiday with her. I'm picking him up on Saturday. The new term starts on Monday."

"Do you think Chapman will want to see him in the future?"

"I'd like to think so, but I doubt it, he's too wrapped up in what he once called his own family." Tania looked away, "For me, I'd rather he didn't bother, it will save a lot of aggravation, but for Alex . . . well, I'll do my best to let him down gently."

"For what it's worth, from what I hear you're well rid of him. But he must have been fond of you both for it to last so long, so perhaps I shouldn't judge." Patsy stood and squeezed Tania's shoulder, "I have to get going now, but call me if you need anything."

Once back in her car, Patsy decided Ben could wait until she got to the office, she had little hope of persuading him to come back, even with the forensic evidence. As she drove away her phone rang, it was an unknown number, and although her usual habit was to wait and see if the caller left a message, she hit the answer button.

The caller spoke before she had time to greet them.

"Patsy, is that you? It's Kathleen O'Brien. Gary's here and they are out in the back garden having an almighty row. Sian whacked him a few minutes ago, and he's trying to leave but she won't let him. She's hysterical. I'd call her mother, but she has enough on her plate." Kathleen spoke quickly and was clearly frightened, "I know it's not -"

"Mrs O'Brien, it's fine. I'm in the car already, I can be with you in ten minutes. I'll see you in a little while."

Unsure as to what she would do when she got there, Patsy headed towards Kathleen's home. When she arrived, she hurried up the path to Kathleen who was waiting on the doorstep.

"It's gone quiet, but he's still here," Kathleen whispered, afraid her granddaughter would overhear.

"Okay, let's go and see what's going on. Does she know you called me?"

"No, dear, she'd sulk for a month, please don't let on."

Patsy strode through the house to the French doors leading into the garden. Sian stood with her back to the door, and Gary Mason was lying flat on the bench, his arms raised and his forearms covering his eyes. She tapped on the door, and Sian glanced over her shoulder. She'd been expecting her grandmother, and her shock was apparent. She recovered quickly.

"Sod off, I'm not speaking to you again." She turned away to see Gary sit up.

"Who is it?" He stood and took a step forward.

"Nobody for you. Sit down," Sian snapped, and sneaked a look to see if Patsy was still there.

"Sian is that Gary? If so I'd like a word with him, please." Patsy pushed the door lever down and put her weight against the door. It gave a little but Sian leaned her weight against it too. "Oh, I can't be bothered with this." Patsy walked away, and putting her finger to her lips, hurried past Kathleen to the kitchen, where she unlocked the back door, went into the alley at the side of the house, and walked around to the garden.

"Hello, Gary, my name's Patsy, would you mind if -"

Sian flew at Patsy. "Leave him alone. Just fuck off and leave us all alone, this isn't fair." Tears were now streaming down her face. Her hands made contact with Patsy's shoulders and she shoved Patsy backward. "Go, go now," Sian screamed, but Patsy caught hold of her wrists and pulled them to her side, holding the girl in place. They stood nose to nose.

From the corner of her eye, Patsy was aware that Gary was approaching, and said calmly, "You need to share whatever this burden is you're carrying with someone. You can't keep him trapped in the garden forever. I'm going to let you go now."

Patsy released Sian's wrists, and took a step back. Sian remained motionless, her rounded shoulders bouncing in time with her sobs. Gary pulled Sian to him, she didn't respond, nor did she pull away, and he stroked her back, as her tears soaked into his shoulder.

Patsy smiled at him. "Thank you. Gary, I'm Patsy Hodge, I was asked by Aiden O'Brien to find out why his little girl had changed so much in the last month, he told me she'd finished with you, but it's clear you are together. Now he's been murdered, but before he was he'd argued with your grandfather. Do you know what -"

"You told me you were trying to find out who killed my father, not that you were checking up on me." Sian yanked herself free from Gary's embrace. "You're a liar, why would we want to talk to you?"

"That's why I was employed initially, but your mother has since asked me to look into your father's death. From what we know, the two maybe linked." Patsy looked back at Gary, "Can you help me?" She knew instinctively that Gary did have some sort of information from his expression, so she remained where she was, and let him think it through. Eventually he spoke.

"Are you for hire?"

"I am. Do you want to hire me?" Surprised, Patsy relaxed, and smiled at the troubled young man, "Because, depending on what it is, I don't come cheap."

"Money is not a problem." Gary walked back to the bench, pulling Sian along by the hand. Patsy followed as he continued. "And you are confidential? Whatever we discuss stays between us?"

"Absolutely. Unless you're asking me to break the law. Which I won't do . . . not anything serious anyway. What did you have in mind?"

Gary pushed Sian to sit on the bench. "Can you give us five minutes in private please. I need to speak to Sian first."

"Of course. I'll go and see if I can rustle up some drinks." She made to turn away but stopped. "And for what it's worth, young lady, you owe both your mother and grandmother an apology." She went into the house where an anxious Kathleen waited. "They need to speak privately, shall we make some tea?"

Rather than go back into the garden, she set the tray on the dining room table, and accepted Kathleen's offer of sandwiches. It was hours since she had eaten and it gave Gary and Sian more time. While Kathleen made the sandwiches, she watched them argue. Gary was walking up and down the length of the bench, stopping every now and then to listen. Sian was gesticulating wildly as she put her opinion forward. After another ten minutes had passed, Patsy opened the door.

"Tea and sandwiches are ready in here. Come and sit around the table." To her surprise, they both agreed. Once they were seated, she asked whether they had reached a decision.

"Can you shut the door please, I don't want Gran to hear," Sian whispered.

Patsy nodded and went to close the door. When she returned, she pulled her notebook from her bag. "What sort of job is it?"

"Do you have people working for you? It's not just you, is it?" Gary asked. "And I want you to confirm again that this conversation will remain absolutely, and totally confidential."

"I do, and if necessary I can bring in help depending on the job. And, yes, once again I promise that anything you say will remain confidential. What is it you want me to do?"

Gary looked at Sian, who nodded. Turning back to Patsy, he said quietly, "Dig up some dead bodies."

12

A shocked Patsy studied the two faces awaiting her response. Sipping her tea, she lifted a sandwich from her plate, although her appetite had disappeared. She repeated his words slowly, "Dig up some dead bodies. That's what you want me to do?"

"Keep your voice down," Sian pointed at the door.

"You're serious, aren't you?" Patsy was almost at a loss for words.

"Well, possibly. I can't believe it, and neither can Sian really, but we need to check it out and then we'll know what to do."

"Can I ask how many, and who I'll be digging up?" Patsy wondered if the two were stringing her along for the sport.

"Two. We think, and we don't know who they are," Gary answered.

Patsy scratched her temple, and rummaged in her handbag until she found her tape recorder. She switched it on and lay it on the table.

"Start at the beginning, I'll interrupt if I need to know more."

"It started because I thought my dad was having an affair," Sian began. "I'd come home from school earlier than usual and he was on the phone in the garden, he was waving a piece of paper about and pacing as he spoke. I couldn't hear what he was saying. I opened the door to ask if he wanted tea, and he froze."

"Like he was guilty," Gary added.

"Were you there?" Patsy asked him.

"No, Sian told me." Gary looked sheepish, "Sorry, carry on Sian."

"He did look guilty. He told whoever he was speaking to that he had to go, and that he'd call them later, he screwed up the piece of paper and shoved it into his jacket pocket. He asked if I'd been listening to the call. I told him I'd only just got home, and was going to make some tea." Sian closed her eyes against the memory, but carried on speaking, "He said he'd help, and put on an act of being normal. It was awful, and starting to become embarrassing. When Mum got home with the shopping, he said he had to go out. Which he did." Sian covered her face with her hands, and spoke through them. "I still can't believe it." She fell silent.

Patsy allowed her a few moments to compose herself, eventually it was Gary who coaxed her to continue.

"Come on, Sian, nearly there. No point in not saying it, she knows there are bodies somewhere now."

Wiping her nose with the back of her hand, and keeping her eyes shut, Sian nodded. "I messaged Gary and asked if I should say something to Mum. I thought his lover had written to him or something, and he was angry she'd sent it to our home. I loved them both, but it wasn't fair if he was having an affair. He -"

"I told her she had to be sure, didn't I? There was no point in, sorry . . ." Gary stopped speaking when Patsy shook her head. "I won't interrupt again. Carry on, Sian."

"I knew he was right, so I waited up until Dad came home. Once he went to bed I went downstairs. His jacket was in the hall. I searched the pockets. I found the piece of paper he had been waving about. It was folded neatly, but you could see the creases from where he'd shoved it in earlier. He must have been to the nightclub, I also found a beer mat from BB's with a telephone number on."

She sniffed, and without speaking, Patsy took a tissue from her bag and placed it in Sian's hand. Sian blew her nose. "I opened the paper, and was about to read it, when I heard their bedroom door open. The bathroom light went on, and I knew it was Dad as he always makes . . . made, such a noise when he was peeing. I photographed it, folded it up and put it back. Then, I went to the kitchen and got a glass of water," she opened her eyes, "you know, in case he came down."

Patsy nodded encouragement. "Did he?"

"No, but he was awake, I could hear them talking, so I went back to my room and read the note." Her chin rested on her chest, and she shredded the tissue. "It was so much worse than an affair. I couldn't believe it, I got scared, then . . . well, I freaked out." She looked at Gary, and a tear slid down her face. "I had to tell you."

"I know. Of course you did."

The youngsters' eyes met and they stared at each other, sharing a common hurt.

Patsy's mind was whirring with possibilities. "Can I see the note," she held out her hand.

Sian shook her head. "No. I did have it on my phone. But we've saved it somewhere safe and deleted them from our phones. Once I'd told Dad I had it, I was worried that he'd get hold of my phone and get rid of it, so he could deny it later. Gary said it would be safer if neither of us had it there. I looked for the real one the next day, but it had gone. Perhaps he gave it to Mr Chapman."

"What did it say?"

Sian looked at Gary, "You tell her." Lifting her feet from the floor, she pulled her knees to her chest, and buried her face in her legs.

"It was a letter from her dad to my grandfather. It told him he'd agreed to bury the first body, but now he knew there was a second one, at somewhere called Wendy's Cottage, and they should to go to the police. He asked him to meet him at the pub and if he didn't turn up, he'd go to the police anyway."

Gary looked at Patsy, "I had to ask Grandad, he says it's all crap of course, that we'd got it wrong, or someone was attempting to play an elaborate joke, and after a long speech on loyalty and what have you, he told me I had to trust him."

Patsy's stomach somersaulted, as she realised the danger the two youngsters may be in. "Did you believe him?"

"Yes, at first. I mean it was like something out of a film. Dead bodies, a grave, it was unreal. I don't know if you know my grandfather, but he is a wealthy man, too wealthy, it makes him selfish, no, not selfish, that's not the right word. He's under the mistaken belief that the world should revolve around him. It's his way or the highway, and if he can't have it, he buys it. It took me a while to realise that, because I loved him, he was my grandad and he made dreams come true. But you get there in the end, everyone gets there."

His nose wrinkled as he spoke, "The next day after I'd told him I believed him he bought me a car. A brand-new BMW. My mini is only two years old. It was then that I realised that something was wrong. I'd done nothing to deserve it. He was buying me off. I spoke to Sian, and we decided there were probably bodies. We agreed we'd only meet secretly to keep him off the scent, and I watched him. I went to work with him, went to the house and ate with him and Gran. Poor old Gran. If we're right, I'm glad she's got dementia. She won't have to know."

"I know Sian hasn't said anything to her parents, but have you mentioned any of this to yours?"

"Ha! No. My father hates him, curses, and insults him when he's not around, but creeps and crawls round him to his face to keep him sweet. You can tell by the way Grandad looks at him, the feeling is mutual. I can see now that it's his fault my parents' marriage is so crap. My mother is probably an alcoholic, and my father bounces from one affair to the other, doesn't try very hard to hide it either, and I think that's because my mother always runs to Grandad when she wants something, or has done something, like crashing her car, it makes my father angry. Grandad is big on appearances. Nothing must bring the family name into disrepute, no one must upset Gran. She's the only one he really cares about, so Dad has affairs, and Mum drinks. It's a vicious circle, and once this is sorted out, I'm out of there. I don't want to work for any of the family businesses, I don't even want to stay in Bristol." He took hold of Sian's hand, "As soon as Sian has finished her A levels we'll be off."

Gary had wandered away from the crux of the matter, he was clearly far more affected than he thought by his dysfunctional family, and had a lot to get off his chest. Patsy felt sorry for him, he'd had a pampered life, but all he really wanted was a happy family.

"Did you find anything out, when you were watching him?"

"Not really, not any detail anyway. But he kept leaving the room and ending telephone conversations when I went to find him, something was definitely going on. He was shouting on one occasion but Gran was talking to me, and I couldn't catch it. Oh, and I know he has more than one phone. He had his on charge in the kitchen, and another one rang in his pocket. I pretended I hadn't noticed because I wanted to get hold of the other one. I never managed though."

Patsy thought about his cancelled holiday with Tania, and thought that might have accounted for some of the calls.

"You went to BB's with him today. Why was that? What did he do there?"

Gary's head shot up, "How do you know that?"

Patsy smiled, "Your sweatshirt. You were seen driving away in his car."

"I've not spoken to him properly since all this started, and he called me this morning, he told me he needed my help. Uncle Barry was dead, and Dad was useless. There were things that needed sorting to help Aunty Penny. She's the only sane one in the family, and she's the only one that didn't give in to him all the time." His face fell, "Poor Aunty Penny, I wonder if that will last now Uncle Barry's gone?"

"What did he want you to do?"

"Nothing. Mainly I just listened to him shouting at people. He had a conversation with someone about changing the carpets in the bar," Gary kept his eyes trained on Patsy, hoping that Sian wouldn't pick up on the reason. "He left me to supervise the cleaners in Uncle Barry's office, said he didn't trust them, and he went to collect something, then he came to get me. Said he'd had a call from Aunty Penny and he needed to be there. I assumed I was going with him, but he asked where I wanted to be dropped off. I went home got my car and came here."

"Was anyone else in the car with you?"

Patsy had pulled out her notebook and was jotting down some notes as she spoke. She looked up when Sian groaned, and, releasing her legs she banged her hands on the table.

"Can anyone tell me what this has to do with the bodies? We seem to have lost the plot here."

Patsy placed her notebook on the table. She looked from one to the other. "If I tell you why, you must promise me you'll keep it to yourselves, no challenging anyone. I will get back to the bodies, if they exist, and I will help you solve that mystery, but I think you may be in danger so I need your promise."

Sian's eyes sought Gary's and they nodded in unison.

"My partner is a police officer, he's investigating your father's murder. I was employed by your father to find out why you'd changed so much, why you hated him. He believed that Gary may be the source. He came to see me the day before he was murdered. The two cases overlapped for one reason: Keith Chapman. The police believe he was involved in some way; with what you've told me, I believe we now know why. I think your grandfather is a dangerous man, I think Mr O'Brien died because of that piece of paper, and I think you are in danger because you know about it." Patsy paused to let her revelation sink in.

Sian looked scared, but Gary shook his head.

"I don't like my grandad anymore, and it looks like he may be involved, but I don't think he'd ever hurt me, I'm family. Who would do that?"

"Someone who's desperate. How do you think he'd react if it were him or you? If you were the only person that could link him to all that's been going on?" Patsy spoke softly, it was a horrible thing to have to say, but she truly believed it.

Gary gave a nod of acceptance, unable to voice his agreement.

Sian tapped the table. "But the man in the paper, the one that stabbed Dad, you think Gary's grandad paid him to do that?"

"No, I think he happened to be in the wrong place at the wrong time." Patsy turned her attention to Gary, "Why did the police question you about the recording that went missing?"

"Because Uncle Barry told them I knew how to work the system, and I do, Uncle Barry wasn't very good with IT stuff, so back before all this, when I was going to work for Grandad, he made sure I was able to access everything, he said in case he was ever ill and needed me to get information for him, I think it's because he wanted me to spy on them."

"Did they need spying on, and when you say them, who?"

"Everyone, well, all his business interests anyway. Including my dad. It's how I found out about his affairs." Gary shook his head, "Nothing bad ever happened, it was stuff like, what the turnover was the month before, had this been ordered properly, stuff like that, business stuff."

"Where did you do this, your grandfather's house, or does he have a personal office somewhere?"

"Anywhere," he looked at Patsy as though she were a little slow, "everything is networked or stored in the cloud, you can access it remotely."

Patsy nodded, "Of course, sorry, I work with someone that takes care of all that. I assume you do it from your laptop?" She saw the look of amazement at what Gary clearly thought was another stupid question.

"Or, my phone. It depends what I was doing and what he wanted."

"Did he ever want anything found at Flood's?"

Gary leaned back and sighed. "Not anything unusual. Turnover, lists of jobs booked, aged debtors. But he did cause us to split up a while back," he held Sian's hand. "It's too long a story, but the short version is, business and pleasure don't work. Grandad said that Sian's father was no good at managing the business, and if it transpired that he had to go, it would be better if there were no personal ties. I finished with Sian for a while. I was stupid."

"Can we get back to the bodies, please. If my dad helped him get rid of a body, and there was another one that led to my dad being murdered, let's find them and call the police. That will end it. They will all be gone . . . one way or another."

"If there are any bodies. But you're right, we need to establish that first." Patsy flipped the page in her notebook. "Wendy's Cottage. Any ideas where that might be," she paused, "it would be useful if I could see the actual note."

"I told you, it had gone, I can send you a copy of the photograph. It's not that clear, but you can make it out, for some reason he used a blue font and it was quite faint." Sian grimaced, "He wasn't good at IT stuff either. I have never heard of Wendy's Cottage though, neither has Gary."

Patsy nodded and jotted down a thought questioning the note, and turned to Gary.

"Your grandfather must own a few properties, are you sure it's not one of those?"

"Not that I know of. Most of his properties are business premises, he only had six residential houses. None of those are called Wendy's Cottage, in fact none of them are cottages, we've already checked that out on street view."

Patsy made a note. "*Only* six." She placed her pencil down, "Okay, what I suggest is -"

Gary's phone ringing interrupted her.

He pulled it from his back pocket, "It's Grandad."

"Answer it. See what he wants," Patsy instructed, and Gary accepted the call, and put it on loud speaker.

"Where are you? I've spoken to your mother, and she says you went out after I dropped you off."

"I'm with Sian." They all caught the exasperated huff before Chapman spoke again.

"I don't think that's wise. We've had that conversation; your family needs you. The police have it in their heads that your uncle may have had something to do with O'Brien's death, and are trampling around causing havoc. Come to the house, I need you to do something for me."

"Something like what? Sian needs me too; her dad has just been murdered you know," Gary snapped out his response.

"I have some files I need . . . look, I'm not doing this over the phone. Come home now."

"Your home or my home? Anyway, I can't we've arranged to go out for lunch. What is it, I can do it from my phone."

"No, you can't. You've not got the passwords to this account. Jesus, Gary! Just do as you're bloody told. Come to the house now, I . . . wait a minute."

The three listened to a voice calling in the background, and Chapman answered.

"No, my darling, I'm not cross with Gary. I won't shout at him." He returned his attention to Gary, "Now, please. This is not open to negotiation." Chapman hung up.

More than anything, Patsy wanted to find out what files Gary hadn't already had access to. But believing Chapman to be dangerous, she couldn't bring herself to encourage Gary to place himself in a situation where he may reveal his true feelings.

Gary slid the phone into the centre of the table. "I'm not going to help him. I'm staying here."

"I think that's wise for the moment, let the police do what they have to do and the dust settle. Now, back to this letter, can you access it for me? I really do need to see it."

Gary nodded and retrieved his phone, after a few minutes he held it towards her, "Here it is."

Patsy couldn't read it as the print was too small, and she enlarged the image, enabling her to scroll through the document. She read the words aloud for the benefit of the tape.

"Chapman, I don't care what you do, or what happens to me, but when I agreed to help you with that first body, I warned you. But, now this. The driver told me where you wanted that delivery to go. I followed you to Wendy's Cottage. I saw you open the grave, and I saw you put that young girl's body in there. Two women, dead. Meet me at lunch-time tomorrow at The Turnpike, and we'll work out a story to tell the police. If you don't come, I'm going to the police anyway."

Patsy stared at the final words. Something didn't add up. She looked up at the two faces waiting expectantly for her assessment.

"I'll agree this doesn't look good. Particularly for Keith Chapman, it appears Mr O'Brien wanted to do the right thing . . . almost, not sure what story he thought they might be able to concoct that explained away two dead bodies though. I'm inclined to agree with your grandad, Gary. This appears to be some sort of wind-up." She held up a finger to silence any protest, "*However*, it does need to be checked out. I'm assuming The Turnpike is a pub?"

"Yes, it's not far from Grandad's house, on the main road," Gary replied.

"Okay, and what have you done about finding the location of Wendy's Cottage?"

Sian shrugged, "Not much, Gary did some searching on the internet, and checked his grandad's stuff, didn't you?"

"I didn't find anything. I tried all the estate agency websites, and Google, then I did some searches on Grandad's computers. Nothing. That's why we want to hire you." He leaned back in his chair, "Now you know what we want, will you do it? I don't care what it costs, I've got a new car you can have if you want it, I don't."

Leaning forward in a sudden burst of movement, he pointed at her, "You said your partner was a policeman. You mustn't tell him, not until we know there is something to tell." The colour drained from his face, "You promised this was confidential, and if the police question him about this, or worse, arrest him, and it turns out to be nothing . . . well," he looked her in the eye, "at the end of the day he is family, there's no point in giving him something else to be pissed at, if there's no reason. I might be off, but the rest of them will have to deal with it."

"What if we find that this is true?" Patsy pointed at the phone. "Because if we do, I'll call the police immediately. Probably even before we find any bodies." She wanted to smile to reassure him, but only managed a sigh. "Here's the deal; you," she pointed at Sian, "go home and give your mother a hug, tell her you love her and apologise, whatever your father might or might not have done, she doesn't deserve to be treated in this way. Your grandmother wants to go and stay with her, but won't because of you. Tell your grandmother it's all right." Sian didn't respond, and Patsy tutted, "Agreed?"

"Okay, but she has to let me see Gary. I'm not going home if she doesn't."

"You won't be staying there, neither will Gary come to that, not until we've looked into this. As I said before, if true, you might be in danger, there's no point in putting this to the . . . excuse me." The untraceable phone in the side pocket of her bag was ringing, only Ben had that number. She accepted the call.

"What do you think you are playing at?" Patsy made no attempt to hide her anger.

"Don't give me a hard time, Patsy. Life is bad enough. Big Pete called, he said to phone, what do you want?"

Patsy got to her feet and walked to the French window, opening it she stepped into the garden. "How did he get hold of you?"

"What do you mean? He called."

"On this number?"

"Ah, I see what you mean. Look, Patsy, with Meredith going all heroic and going back to the police, what could I do? I wasn't going to risk him pulling me in. I'm not totally stupid."

"Oh, I think you are. Is Hannah with you?"

"Not any more. She's gone to see her daughter and parents, they're on holiday."

"But she, rather than someone you should trust, someone who has given up a lot, and is risking their neck for you, knows where you are?" Patsy was on a roll, "I'll tell you what I think, shall I? You have the hots for this lady, and you couldn't wait until it was safe to drag her into your world. She is now as good as harbouring you, and it's all unnecessary."

"Did you read the paper?"

"A ploy. Did you read the forensic report?"

There was silence as Ben realised it could only be good news.

"Thought not, well you try and get yourself back to Bristol without being arrested, and give me a call, and I'll share that with you. Now, I'm in the middle of something." She hung up, and returned to the dining room.

Kathleen O'Brien was talking to Sian. She smiled as Patsy returned. "Sian tells me she's going to see her mum."

"Good, did she also tell you she wanted you to go and keep her mum company?" When Kathleen nodded, Patsy retuned her smile. "You go and pack a bag, we're almost finished here, we can lock up and I'll take you over there."

Waiting until Kathleen had closed the door behind her, Patsy turned to Sian and Gary, "Sian, you get your stuff together, I need a couple of hours to come up with a plan of attack."

"You didn't finish what you were going to say. You told Sian what you wanted from her, but what about me?" Gary asked.

"I won't involve the police until I've located this cottage, and had a look to see if there is a possible grave. If there is, I know someone that can help, and if he says there are bodies, then the police will be called. And, given the content of the note, your grandfather will no doubt be arrested and charged."

Patsy slapped her hands against her thighs, "I have to be honest with you, I will do my utmost to locate this cottage, but if I don't, I think we need to show the note to the police anyway. But, as I think he's involved in the murder of Mr O'Brien, I'll give it a week before I involve them, unless of course we find   . . . Oh, God. This is getting complicated. Do you understand, I don't want -"

Kathleen popped her head around the door. "Sorry to interrupt, that was Rosie on the phone, Keith is looking for Gary. He called to see if he was there, she was worried about Sian, so she called to make sure she was still here. I told her they both were, and the news. She was so thrilled, Sian, I told her we wouldn't be long."

"Bugger. Do you think she will tell Chapman that?"

"Oh, no. She thinks he has something to do with Aiden's death. I don't think she'll want to speak to him."

"Good. Give me a shout when you're ready to go." She turned to the other two, "Are you ready, do I need to say more?" They shook their heads. "Give me five minutes to make a call, and we'll be off."

Half an hour later Patsy walked the length of Rosie O'Brien's garden. She'd sent Gary off to Linda at the office, had watched the tearful reunion, and was now trying to explain without scaring Rosie too much, why she thought it would be safer if Sian didn't stay at home for a couple of days. Rosie attempted to get more out of Patsy, but in the end, content that her daughter was no longer angry with her, and had promised to keep in touch, she nodded her agreement.

"Will Gary be wherever she is?" she asked as they walked back to the house.

"I'm not sure. It depends on what I can sort out. I know what you're getting at, but you know, if they were going to do anything they'd find a way wherever they were. If it helps and they are together, I'll insist on separate rooms. For the record, I think Gary is a decent lad, they are clearly crazy about each other, and he's seen through his grandfather's manipulating ways. He doesn't want to be like him."

"Well, at least something good may have come from this." Rosie stepped into the sun room and held open her arms. Sian allowed her backpack to slip to the ground and walked into her mother's embrace.

Patsy allowed them a moment. When Sian appeared, they headed for the office. She wondered what Meredith would say if she told him they were staying with them. The small smile of amusement became a grin as a thought occurred to her, and before they went into the office, she called Peggy Green. As always, Peggy couldn't wait to become involved in something exciting and she agreed immediately. Leaving Sian in the car, she popped into the office to collect Gary, who had pulled up a chair behind Linda, and was engrossed in whatever was on the screen.

Patsy called to him, "Gary, I've found you somewhere to stay, grab your stuff." She paused as Linda held her finger up.

"One sec, please, Patsy." Her finger stroked the mouse, "And finally, there. Half past ten, on Friday night." She shrugged as Gary shook his head. "It was worth a try. Okay, young man, thank you for your help, you are free to go." She glanced at Patsy, "Where is he going?"

"You know better, Linda. It's a secret location, because it's a secret." She glanced at her watch, "Give me an hour and I'll be back to update you. Gary, my car's outside, but we need to take yours too, I'll be out in a minute." She waited until the door had closed behind him. "Key 'Wendy's Cottage' into your contaminator, please. If nothing comes up do a search if you have time. Not sure where you are with the phone records, but Sian is now low priority, they don't seem to be holding back. And, finally, Keith Chapman has two phones, so if an odd number comes up that could be it. Right, must dash."

"What's Wendy's Cottage?" Linda asked as Patsy opened the door.

"Not sure, maybe a wild goose chase, but maybe a crime scene, and possibly a mass grave."

Linda watched the door close. She knew which instruction she'd be following first.

13

Patsy stretched the cling film over Meredith's dinner, and poured another glass of wine. He'd called to say they'd traced one of the key men who'd been drinking with Brooker and O'Brien, and he was going to sit in on the interview. She knew he'd be at least another hour or so, she had so much to tell him, and so much information to get out of him, that she was restless. Deciding to make a list of the salient points to ensure that everything was covered she sat at the table. She had no intention of going yet another day waiting for explanations. Tapping the pad, she wondered how much of the truth he'd tell her. Meredith was good at keeping secrets. Taking a swig of her wine, she drew a circle around Wendy's Cottage. Would she share that information with him? She should of course, but she'd promised she wouldn't. Deciding a long soak would help her decide, she topped up her glass and headed for the bathroom.

~~~

Meredith looked at the man sitting in the interview room, and turned to Trump.

"He's a big bugger, isn't he?"

"He is, not as tall as that doorman, but he certainly wins on the size of thighs and biceps. Nice chap though, very co-operative. Which of course means he's probably got something to hide."

"I think we already know that. What's his surname again?"

Meredith opened the door, and Eric Sampson got to his feet, held out his hand, and introduced himself. Meredith shook his hand, that didn't happen often, the man was certainly confident.

"Mr Sampson, thank you for coming in, hopefully this -"

"Eric, call me Eric. No problem, no problem at all. If I can be of any help, that's good. Although I doubt it. That white guy was smashed, and I know he tried to bottle someone, but it's a shame, a shame he died. The doorman was bang out of order."

"It is a shame, yes. Hold on a minute," Meredith pointed at the recorder, "we need to set this up." He hit the button and the red light pulsed. "Now, Mr Sampson . . . Sorry, Eric. As this is a murder investigation, I am going to caution you, would you confirm for the tape, please, that you have refused legal representation."

"I didn't refuse it, I don't need it. I didn't do anything." Eric smiled broadly.

Meredith announced who was in the room, and read Eric Sampson his rights. He studied the man, as he reeled out the familiar words. Sampson's clothes were smart, his watch expensive, and he was relaxed but alert. If he did know anything about the murder of Aiden O'Brien, it certainly wasn't weighing on his conscience.

"Eric, tell me how you came to be in BB's on the night Mr O'Brien was murdered. I see from the CCTV footage that you arrived late."

"It was convenient. Several friends were out and about, and we agreed to meet up. BB's was the most central place."

"Where had you been before that?"

"At home for most of the evening, then a friend asked if I fancied a drink, and I -"

"Which friend?"

"I'm sorry?"

"Which friend invited you out for a drink, you arrived at BB's with three friends; which one called you and convinced you to go out on a miserable, bleak, evening?"

"Oh, that would have been Marcus." Eric smiled at Meredith. "Marcus White."

Meredith pulled a stack of photographs from his filed and sifted through them. "Is this Marcus White?" he slid a photograph across the table.

"It is, yes."

"Good, and what's his address?"

"He was living on Pembroke Road, but he told me he's taken up with some girl, lives with her now, Coldharbour Road, but I don't know the number."

"Is this a recent thing? If he's a good mate, you'd know, wouldn't you?"

"Yes, last couple of weeks. I've haven't even met her yet."

"Okay, his phone number will suffice." Meredith picked up his pen and taking back the photograph, turned it over to jot the number down.

Eric pulled his phone from his pocket and located the number, he read it out slowly, and added, "It wasn't Marcus, I was with him."

"What wasn't?"

Meredith's eyes locked on Eric's. Eric had just made his first error and he knew it.

He laughed and pointed at Meredith. "Oh, yes, I see. What I was trying to say was, Marcus was with me when the doorman came over, we were at the bar watching Mr O'Brien, and keeping clear of the bottle. Whoever, and whatever wound him up, wasn't Marcus. You see?"

"I know what you were saying." Meredith pushed forward another photograph. "Now I need the names of the other men you were drinking with. Who is this?"

There were a total of eight more photographs in all, Meredith already knew who a few of them were, but wanted to see how many Eric would identify. Eric gave the names of five of the men, but claimed to only have the contact details of two of them.

"They are mates of mates, you know how it is. I don't know them well. I hope that helps, if I bump into any of them, I'll get them to call you."

Eric's eyes darted to Trump as Meredith nodded. Trump got to his feet and switched on a television suspended from a bracket in the corner of the room. He pushed the play button on the machine below.

Turning back, he addressed Eric for the first time, "We're going to show you some footage from the bar, Mr Sampson, and I'd be grateful if you would watch it and answer the questions I ask as we watch."

The clip showed the top corner of the bar. Barry Brooker and Aiden O'Brien were sitting on bar stools and apparently speaking to the barmaid. Eric and another man came into view, they walked up to the two men. Barry Brooker got to his feet, he clearly said something to Eric who responded, and then he walked away, leaving O'Brien shaking hands with the men.

Trump pushed the hold button, "What did you and Mr Brooker say to each other there?"

Eric lifted his massive shoulders, "Nothing." His eyes followed Trump's hand as he rewound the footage a little.

"Watch closely, first watch Mr Brooker's lips and now yours. We can get a lip reader in to tell us, but it would be much cheaper if you could remember." He pushed the play button, and Eric tapped the table at the appropriate moment.

"Oh, that. Just a greeting. You know, good evening, then when Mr Brooker left, he said something like, my friend has had too much to drink, be grateful if you'd keep an eye on him. Something like that."

"I didn't realise you knew Aiden O'Brien," Meredith joined the conversation.

"I don't, I don't know either of them. On my kids' lives," Eric pointed at the screen, "I'd never seen either of those men before that night."

"What a nice chap you are," Trump pushed the play button again. "Here come your other two friends, it appears you are introducing them to Mr

O'Brien. Your friend Marcus is shaking his hand." He moved the recording forward, "And here, you're buying Mr O'Brien a shot, and . . . there you go, helping him back on his stool. Do you always buy drinks for drunks you don't know?"

"He seemed a nice guy, drunk as a skunk, but he was friendly enough at first."

Meredith nodded at Trump, and the recording moved to the next marker, he looked at Eric, "What was said?"

Eric studied the still on the screen, two white men stood in front of O'Brien, one had his arm out, his finger pointing at O'Brien. Eric stood a yard or two away.

Eric looked back at Meredith, "I don't know, it was too noisy, I was speaking to someone else, not paying attention to them."

"But you're looking directly at them. They must have grabbed your attention for some reason."

"I really can't remember that. I did hear the bottle break," Eric glanced at the screen again, "I think I was facing that direction, but not looking. I can't see my eyes clearly enough to say I was looking, can you?"

"Nice scene though, if you ignore the finger pointing, and forget what came next, don't you think?"

"What do you mean? It's a bunch of blokes drinking at a bar. If that's nice to you, then, yes, it's nice." A crease had appeared on Eric's brow, a possible indication he had no idea where Meredith was going.

"A cross section of society, that's what I meant, if clothes maketh the man. I can -"

"I think it's manners maketh the man, not clothes." An extra furrow had appeared, and Eric's eyes were wary.

"You're probably right, but I think the way a man dresses speaks volumes . . . in most cases." Meredith pointed at the screen, "Black, white, definitely a mixture of the two with," he consulted his notes, ". . . there we go, Billy. Smart suits, trousers and shirt, polished shoes, jeans, trainers, not to mention more than a few tattoos. And so far, I've found the following occupations, estate agent, personal trainer, van driver, and bank clerk. Still a few to go, Marcus, for example, how does he earn a living?"

"Is that relevant?" Eric was looking a little uncomfortable, and he twisted his wedding band several times.

"Only if you don't tell me," Meredith smiled.

"He works for Tesco. Manages the warehouse. Is it relevant now you know?" Eric's voice had gained an edge.

"Nope, not really, adds to the diversity though. There were lots of hugs and high fives when the second group arrived," he nodded at Trump who took the recording back a little. "You see."

All eyes watched the enthusiastic greeting while O'Brien smiled aimlessly while watching them.

"How do you all know each other? Clearly good friends."

Eric's plump lips pouted, and he stared at Meredith. "We're friendly people. Sometimes you just click with people, socially. Playing football, at the pub, in the gym. You must have friends that aren't policemen, friends who have become friends with your friends. Life is a wonderful tapestry. You get to know people over time, we didn't go to school together, if that's what you mean. Although I did go to school with Marcus."

"I don't have many friends, and those I do have would be able to say how they met other friends of mine. Are you trying to be evasive?"

Eric lifted his arms, elbows bent, and level with his shoulders, he rotated them. His shirt did nothing to hide, and probably enhanced the movement of muscle beneath. "No. I'm being honest. I'm thirty-four, I know a lot of people, a lot of *diverse* people." Dropping his arms, he pointed at the screen, "For the record, just in case you didn't understand, I did not kill that man, I do not know who killed that man, move that on to where he got stabbed, not only will you see I didn't do it, you will see I was leaving the bar at the time. I could see trouble brewing and didn't want to be part of it. New suit," he added by way of explanation.

Eric Sampson placed his large hands on the table, ready to push himself up. "Do you have any more questions for me, Mr Meredith? If not, I'll get back to work."

"I think that should do for now. Thank you for your time, Eric. We'll be in touch, don't leave the country."

Eric frowned as he got to his feet, "In touch about what?"

Meredith stood to join him and grinned, "Who knows? I've got to question the others before I know that. Have a pleasant evening." Meredith held out his hand, and noticed that the massive palm that accepted it was now moist.

~~~

A long bath had helped Patsy reassess the situation. When she returned to the kitchen an hour later, Meredith had neither appeared, nor called, and she decided that Frankie Callaghan would help her decide. If he agreed to her plan, Meredith would only know the outcome if there were indeed bodies to be found. She called Frankie.

"Hi, Patsy, how are you? Did Meredith answer your questions? Because I have no more I can tell you."

"Why do you assume that every time I call you, I want something?"

"Because you live with Meredith, and he's rubbing off on you, you have, however, maintained your manners."

"I'm sorry, does it really feel like that? Please tell me I'm not turning into Meredith."

"I'll answer that when you tell me why you're calling." Frankie laughed, "I'm kidding. What can I do for you?"

Patsy decide to change tack, and come at the question from a different angle. "Are you still doing freelance work?"

"Not very often, too busy, why? Do you have a client that wants a second opinion or something?"

"No, I have a client who thinks he knows where two bodies are buried. Actually, when I say knows, that's a slight exaggeration. He knows what the place is called, but not where it is, I'm working on that."

Picking up a pencil she made a note to call Linda. "If I can find the location, I need someone to let me know if there are any bodies there. And I thought, who do I know who is an expert in finding buried bodies, who do I know who has all the equipment to look without picking up a spade, who do I know that appeared on the national news and was hailed a hero in Prague?"

"Okay, okay, that would be me. I have to ask, Pats, why is it you asking and not the police?"

Patsy hated being called Pats, as well Frankie knew, but she ignored it, she had a trump to play. If Frankie knew she was keeping Meredith in the dark, he would agree like a shot.

"It's complicated, as always. My client thinks a relative may be involved, if it's true and we find human remains, then he's happy for the police to be called and for justice to take its course. But, if he's wrong, he doesn't want some arrogant police officer, hiking said relative off the street, and stepping on toes with his size nines. Thus, causing a family drama. Apart from which I promised no police until we knew."

"Meredith doesn't know what you're up to?"

"Nope."

"Splendid. Let me know if you find the site, and where it is, and I'll see what I can do."

"And your fee?"

"Depends on how big the site is, and where it's located, but the look on Meredith's face when you tell him should halve it." Frankie laughed, "Seriously, I'll email you some details. There will be a fee."

"Thanks, Frankie, speak soon." Patsy hung up and scrolled to Linda's number.

"What did Sherlock want?" Meredith appeared without warning, and Patsy yelped.

"You frightened me, you don't usually creep around. How did the interview go?"

"Interesting, but as always the more we learn the more we realise what we don't know. Have you heard from Ben?" Meredith kissed the top of her head as he loosened his tie.

"Yes, he's coming back from Cornwall, but won't be here until the early hours, as Hannah had arranged to take her parents and daughter to dinner. I'm seeing him first thing." She pointed at the plate next to the hob, "Shall I warm that up?"

"Yes, and I'll have a glass of that wine too, before you polish it off. I'm going to jump in the shower first." Putting his jacket on the back of the chair he walked back into the hall.

"It will be ready and waiting, and Meredith, the first thing we're talking about is your meeting, in detail, who, what, when, and most importantly, why?"

Meredith kept walking. "That's what we planned."

As he showered he wondered how much he should tell her. He'd not mentioned the arrangement with Burt when they were discussing his involvement with the then Grainger & Co, and he shuddered as he remembered the new fascia. Should he continue to let her believe that he'd managed to agree a leave of absence for a year? It was understandable that she'd believed him, police recruitment was at an all-time low, and he was an experienced and successful officer. He still hadn't decided when Patsy placed his dinner on the table.

"What happened that the wonderful DCI Meredith was urged back into the job? Who was at the meeting? And, how come, one, you're allowed to take this case given your personal ties, and, two, why the hell would they publicise that in the *Post*?" She sipped her wine. "In your own time, I'm in no rush, however long a story it is."

"Your friend Burt has an interest in Keith Chapman, he spoke to the ACC, they spoke to me." Meredith smiled, "It suits them that Chapman can be investigated as part of O'Brien's murder, they can have a poke around at arms-length, and if they find what they want, all well and good, if they don't Chapman is none the wiser."

"That doesn't tell me why you, or indeed why you said yes."

"Because it's Ben. Come on, Patsy, you know I couldn't say no."

"No, I don't. But let's stay with, why you? So, SIS have an interest and can use Aiden O'Brien's death as a cover to poke around. Someone else could have done that. It didn't need to be you, but I'll accept that for some reason you really are indispensable, why did you say yes? You were already being fed information from your team, and *we*," she waved her finger back and forth, "we're already investigating it via our instruction from Rosie. You had more freedom to step on toes as a PI, and yet you decide to go back. Why?" She took another sip of her drink. "Don't lie to me, Johnny, because we both know I've already worked out the answer, but I want it from your own hypocritical lips . . . please."

Meredith stretched his hand across the table, but Patsy pulled hers away, allowing it to drop into her lap.

"Tell me why, after getting an agreement to do your own thing for a year, and then be able to go back if it didn't suit, after making commitments to me, and not forgetting Sharon, who gave you her half of the business because she trusted you and thought you were a safe pair of hands. Tell me why you didn't say no."

"For God's sake, Patsy, don't you think -"

Meredith jumped to his feet as Patsy pulled her arm back, before swinging it forward, and batting the bottle of wine off the table. It smashed against the cupboard.

Patsy's face remained emotionless as she pinched her thumb and forefinger together,

"I'm this close, Johnny, tell me why?"

"Or else what?" Meredith sat back at the table.

"Really. This is what you'd rather talk about, when all you have to do is tell the truth."

"I thought you knew the truth."

"There's a difference between knowing and being told. Is it that painful for you to admit? Can the mighty John Meredith, not bring himself to admit he's a hypocrite? Just bloody say it, Meredith, then we can work out how to move forward."

Meredith was embarrassed, and he didn't like it. But not wanting the 'or else' conversation, his angry eyes found hers.

"The only way I could get to try out the private investigator thing, and be guaranteed a job on the force at the same level if it didn't work out, was to agree to work with SIS. I'm not indispensable, no. It was Burt that sorted it, not me. But you know that, so why does it give you such pleasure making me spell it out?"

"Because you made me promise not to continue taking jobs from them, when you yourself were going to do exactly that. Because you didn't tell me, that you were now a fully paid-up member of SIS, and because I wanted you to admit you were now a puppet, dancing to someone else's tune.

"Now that's out in the open, we'll pretend it's all for the reasons you were trying to fob me off with. I'll get on with my job and you can get on with yours." Getting to her feet, and lifting her glass of wine from the table she walked to the door, "I'll be in the spare room until I've calmed down, you should clean that mess up before Amanda gets home. She might cut her foot."

Meredith had many questions he wanted to ask Patsy, all related to the case, but he knew now was not the time. As he collected the dustpan from the utility room he hoped she'd calm down quickly.

Patsy had already left the house by the time he came down the next morning. There was a note on the table.

I'm sorry I walked out last night, we didn't cover how the business was going to be run, as a fifty percent stakeholder you have a right to have a say. I'd like to get that sorted tonight. I'll have dinner ready for eight, please do me the courtesy of being here. P

Meredith grunted, screwed the note into a ball, and dropped it in the bin.

14

Peggy walked into the hall and bellowed up the stairs, "Come on you buggers, I haven't been slaving over a hot stove for it to go cold you know."

"I see they've settled in okay," Patsy laughed. "Are you sure it will stretch to four? I wasn't hungry but now I've smelt it . . . never could resist the smell of bacon. How were they last night?"

"They were fine, quite good company actually, although, I don't think Gary is a massive fan of *Eastenders*, and they were a bit shocked when I said it was bedtime at ten-thirty, but I made Sian call her mum from my phone before we turned in. And, before you ask, they went into separate bedrooms. Sian got Pablo's room." Peggy poured boiling water into the teapot. "They're back at the end of the week so they'll only be able to stay until then."

"Hopefully it won't be that long, and Peggy, no more calls, I'll bring them a secure phone. If someone does look for them, we don't want it traced back here. Talking of phones," Patsy retrieved the ringing phone in the side pocket of her bag; as she expected, it was Ben Jacobs. She hit the ignore button. "He can wait until we've had breakfast." She looked up as Sian entered the room, "Morning, did you sleep okay?"

Sian returned her smile, "Like a log, first time in ages. I was freaked out when Peggy started banging about this morning though, couldn't remember where I was." She pulled out a chair and sat at the table. "Is there anything I can do?"

Peggy patted her shoulder, "Not until you've eaten, then there'll be washing up. Antony is getting a dishwasher when he gets back, but until then it's down to you. I hate doing the washing up."

It was clear from Sian's expression that this was not a task she was accustomed to, and Peggy gave a snort.

"It's easy, squirt of liquid and hot water. Don't worry I'll give you it back if it doesn't come up to standard. One egg or two?" She glanced at the doorway as Gary appeared, "Afternoon, sunshine. What's that look for, did the cat shit in your shoe?"

Patsy laughed out loud at the look exchanged between the two young people. Peggy looked very demure, but she certainly didn't act it.

"Sorry, Peggy, I was listening to my messages." He looked at Patsy, "Five, all from Grandad, and all increasing in irritation. I think I need to speak to him. I'll tell him I'm not interested and to leave me alone."

"May I listen to them?" Patsy held out her hand and took Gary's phone. She listened to the messages while Peggy dished up the breakfast. As Gary had said, the first message was a polite request for a call and the last, a threat that he'd be out of a job if he didn't make contact within the hour. That had been midnight the night before. Patsy placed the phone on the table. "I'll get a phone you can call him from, and Sian, I'll tell your mum that you will be in touch through me, and to call me if she's concerned. I'll keep hold of your phones if I may, they need to be switched off, I don't want you tracked."

"Do you think he'd go to that much trouble?" Sian asked, spooning sugar into her cup.

"Yes. If we take that letter as read, you two are nothing but trouble for him. The closer you are to him, the easier you are to control. Now, let's eat. I have to get to the office, I'll be back later. Is there anything I can bring you that will make you more comfortable here?"

"What do you mean comfortable? There's nothing wrong with my home, you cheeky madam," Peggy looked genuinely offended.

"I meant to stop them getting bored, Peggy, not comfortable in the literal sense. You have a wonderful home, and they are grateful to be here." She looked across the table nodding, "Aren't you?"

Peggy smiled as she was greeted with enthusiastic endorsement. "Glad to hear it. They can give you a list, but don't worry about them being bored. My back garden is in a state, we'll be attacking that once you've gone. And, if it's a phone you want, I've got the one I bought for Merewinkle when we were under cover."

She looked smug as Sian and Gary looked at her in amazement. "I haven't told you about my life as a spy, have I?" She lifted the empty plates from the table. "When you've finished the washing up, I'll find the spare wellies, and you can decide what you'd like to hear about first, the spying or my tales from the street."

Gary smirked, "*The* street, or this street?"

"I was living on the street for years. Only came back here because of Merewinkle, and I do miss it sometimes. Was more exciting than being a spy too. I could write a book." Lifting the tea towel, she threw it at Gary, "You can wipe."

Patsy checked Peggy's phone, and agreed it could be switched on for Gary to call his grandfather. They concocted a story about Gary running off to be with Sian, and promises were made not to leave Peggy's.

"I must go now, but as soon as you've made the call switch off your phone. No social media, and no contact with anyone else." She collected her bag. "Good. Peggy you're in charge."

"I always am. Let me know if you need feeding, am I all right to drag these two around the supermarket, or did you mean they're totally housebound? I need to stock up."

Patsy pulled her purse from her bag and took out several notes which she passed to Peggy. "I'd offer to do it, but I don't think I'll have time. Go to the one on the ring road, I can't see Keith Chapman or his family going there. But keep an eye out, all three of you."

Peggy flapped her hand. "Get going, I'm practised at checking if I'm being followed. When me and Merewinkle took on the Russian mafia, I was his driver."

"How could I forget. I'll call in a couple of hours."

Patsy left Peggy issuing strict instructions on the order in which dishes should be washed, and drove straight to the office. Linda beckoned her forward before she'd had time to greet her.

"I got your text, I take it that now the Skipper is back on the force we're not telling him everything again?" She tapped her screen, "But you can tell me more in a mo. I think I've found Wendy's Cottage. Actually, I've found three of them."

"Three!" Patsy pulled a chair across the office to join Linda. "And for the record, if Meredith wants the detail on what we're working on, he can come here and ask for it. No more emails, no more texts, no more doing the police's work for them. We're short-staffed in case you hadn't noticed. Now, where are these cottages?"

Linda grinned, "What's he done now?"

"Nothing. Where did you find these cottages? Work to do, Linda."

"But the Skipper is still my boss, what if he asks me for something?"

"Refer him to me."

"But it might not be that easy. You know what he's like. If it's on the phone, great, but if he uses that look . . . the best I can do is promise I'll try."

"Try very hard. The cottages, Linda." Patsy lifted Linda's hand and placed it on the mouse, "Now."

"We have three," Linda clicked away and an estate agent's detail appeared on the screen. "This one was sold about five years ago. It's in Birmingham. Two bedrooms, wood burner, and it retains most of its original character. Is this it?"

"I don't know. Print that off, and the next." She watched Linda click another tab.

"This one is in Newton St Lowe, on the way to Bath. It doesn't appear on any estate agency sites, not that I could find anyway, but it could also have a street address, it's on Apple Tree Lane, so it could also be known as number 10, et cetera."

"But you don't know that?" Patsy mocked, "I thought you could find out anything."

"I can. I've only been at it for an hour. I've found you three, I'd have had more if I'd had more time," Linda sniffed, "What time is the Skipper likely to call?"

"It wasn't an insult, I'm used to reams of information, that's all, and the next?"

"This one I only found because it was in a feature online. It was re-thatched in two thousand and seven, and the thatcher used it as an example of a wrap over ridge on his site. I did take a peep at what that meant, and if my house was thatched I'd go for a copper -"

"Get on with it, Linda."

"You sounded just like the Skipper. It's mentioned by name and street only, no number, no postcode. I'll search public records later." She moved to a different screen, "Finally, Wendy's Cottage, Alveston. That's out near Thornbury."

"And you found it how?"

"I remembered it." Linda tapped the side of her head, "I have a memory you know, a good one."

"From . . ." Patsy wound her finger to encourage more information.

"From the contaminator. Two of the directors of one of Keith Chapman's businesses had it listed as their address for Company's House. That probably means it was for postal reasons only, as I've checked the electoral register, and they both live elsewhere on that. I'm assuming this is the one we want?" She grinned.

Patsy pretended to clip Linda, "Which is why you left it until last of course."

"I need you to know how hard I work. If I simply got it first time every time, you wouldn't appreciate me."

"Email me the details. I need to make a call. I want to know who lives at the cottage now et cetera."

"On it." Linda got to her feet. "I have a couple of iced buns, do you want tea with yours?"

"Had breakfast with Peggy, couldn't eat another thing, thanks anyway."

"With Peggy, why not with the Skipper?" Linda's hand flew to her mouth, "You haven't left him again, have you?"

"No, I had some business with her."

"What business?"

"Make the tea, Linda."

Linda returned with a steaming mug of tea, and placed it on Patsy's desk.

"I take it, that if he asks, I'm not to tell the Skipper that's where you've hidden the kids." She clapped her hands as Patsy's head jerked up, "Ha! I knew it. I told you I'm a good detective."

"Top secret, Linda, top secret. And, I have warned you, he won't like being called Skipper."

~~~

Meredith finished the briefing.

"Finally, how are you getting on with Linda's contaminator, Trump?"

"Very well. She's a genius, sir. I knew she was clever, but this surpasses - "

"All right, all right, save it for when you get home. Sling in all the names from the group in the bar."

"Really? All of them?"

"Yep, there will be a connection. We might get lucky. Start with Eric Sampson, he was the first to show at the club. I want to know of any connection, however insignificant." He turned to Dave Rawlings, "Same with the paperwork brought in from the searches. Get Adler to help when she gets in. His solicitor has already been on to the Super demanding them back. There must be something there Chapman wants, which means we probably need it too."

"Will do."

"Oh yes and find out where young Mason is. I'd like to question him again without Chapman around."

Meredith went to his office and closed the door. Sitting at his desk, he pulled a notepad forward and picked up the phone. Burt answered immediately.

"I'm back in the saddle, there are boxes of documents to go through, and the team are on it. I don't suppose you could give me a clue as to what we're looking for?"

"No. That's why you're detectives, but on a serious note, if anyone does know what it is, then I've not fallen in the 'need to know' group." He heard the frustrated sigh. "What?"

"I don't get all this secrecy crap when you attack things from this angle. Let's say Maggie Thatcher was having an affair with Knox and there was a letter. Because I don't know that, one of my team will get to read it, it'll be a huge joke, everyone in the incident room will know, and there's your secret blown from the water. If you're going to use the police for something like this, surely that's obvious."

"Why did you say Maggie Thatcher? Have you found anything relating to her?"

"No, why should I have?"

"Meredith . . ."

"Chapman's stepfather was an advisor to Thatcher. I chose her name because Knox too was a Conservative. There's a connection. You know all this, *Burt*. You're wasting my time."

Meredith hung up. He drummed his fingers on the desk, pondering his next move. He'd not had an update on Ben Jacobs. Patsy had been in such a foul mood, he'd decided to leave it. He picked up the phone as Rawlings put his head round the door.

"Gary Mason's phone is switched off. Spoke to his mother, she sounded drunk," he glanced at the clock to signify the early hour, "but said he'd not been home, and to check with her father. I called Chapman and he told me to bugger off initially, but when I said we were concerned about Gary, he assumed that Mrs O'Brien had made some form of complaint, and volunteered that they were both old enough, and that if his grandson wanted to take a holiday with Sian O'Brien, it was no concern of the police. Then he hung up on me."

"A holiday. Her father is in the morgue." Meredith remembered Patsy had been going to see Sian the day before, perhaps she could shed some light on it. "Okay, Dave, if we hear anything let me know."

"What about Jacobs, Gov? I know he's a mate and all that, but questions are being asked about why we've not stepped up our search for him. He was holding the smoking gun after all, well, the knife."

"Who's asking?"

Rawlings could see from Meredith's expression that he wasn't amused at his orders being questioned. He shrugged, "Just people in the station. Seems odd. Still, you know what you're doing."

"Well, should any of these people question my priorities in future, point them in my direction. Was there anything else? Good. Shut the door."

Meredith saw a few heads look towards Rawlings as he went back to his desk, he also saw the slight shake of the head, indicating he'd not been successful. He picked up his phone and called Patsy. She hit the ignore button and he left a message.

"It's me. Can I take you out to dinner tonight? We need to clear the air. Let me know, I'll book a table." Niceties out of the way, he got down to business. "Is Jacobs back in Bristol? I know I said I didn't need to know where, but I do need to speak to him. If he has trouble finding somewhere safe, Peggy is always an option worth trying. Also, while I'm on, do you happen to know where Sian O'Brien and Gary Mason are? Chapman thinks they've taken a holiday. I'd like to speak to Mason, so if you could let me know, one way or another, that would be good. Speak later."

He hung up and got to his feet, he'd been looking into the incident room when he noticed Tom Seaton and Jo Adler both hurry to look over Trump's shoulder. He walked up behind them, "What's caused the excitement?"

"Jason's Justice," Jo Adler replied.

"Explain." Meredith leaned forward and peered at Trump's screen. He couldn't make out the text that filled the neat columns of Linda's contaminator. "Aloud, in clear English, Trump."

"Jason's Justice was a group of family and friends established to challenge the police, and other authorities, on the light sentences given to paedophiles, and to keep the story in the press. Most of the group had been affected by a Bristol paedophile ring, which had been exposed when seven-year-old Jason Sampson disappeared. He had never been found. The men arrested never admitted to knowing anything about Jason or what happened to him."

Trump got to his feet and walked to the photographs stuck on the incident board. Taking a red pen, he drew numerous lines between faces that had been in the group of men surrounding Aiden O'Brien, and finally one across to Keith Chapman. He drew an arrow and wrote Jason's Justice.

He turned to Meredith. "That's what came up when I keyed in all the names."

"You're kidding me. Okay, sit back down and tell me how they are connected." He flapped his hand to hurry Trump's progress.

Trump took his seat, and scrolled through to the final column. "Once the first two had that as a common connection, but no other, I thought I'd try a short cut and entered Jason's Justice in as its own entity. It connects those seven people." He pointed at the board. "Chapman put up an initial ten thousand pounds to finance publicity, a meeting place, and then a further seventy-five thousand pounds, for the police to offer as a reward for any information that led to a conviction. Did you know that?"

Meredith shook his head, "Don't think so, but his name did ring a bell, so perhaps that's why. I know from Gerry Matthews, who headed up the enquiry, that having the reward money brought witnesses in. It's probably how I knew the name, and why he managed to have a word with the top brass when we first brought Brooker in." He pointed at the screen, "Carry on, that makes Chapman a goodie, and he's not. Who's next."

"Eric Sampson, uncle of Jason Sampson, set up Jason's Justice with Jason's father, Marcus White. White never married Jason's mother and they split when he was three, he was given his mother's name."

"I think his body is still missing, isn't it?" Jo Adler asked.

"Yep. Must be a living nightmare, how long ago was that? Three years?" Dave Rawlings shook his head, "My Gemma was only gone a couple of days, and she wasn't touched, but to know that . . . well, perhaps we've got this Chapman bloke wrong, Gov. If he helped, he's sound in my book."

Dave Rawlings' daughter had been abducted by a father looking for his missing daughter. She'd simply been in the wrong place at the wrong time, no harm was ever intended, and she was returned as soon as the kidnapper was able to do so. Rawlings knew only too well Jason's family's pain and torment. And that of the other children who had been harmed.

"We'll see, Dave," Meredith patted his shoulder. "Next."

"Darren Fisher. He's the tattooed chap we've yet to question. His son was five. Then there's Errol Hopkins, he was the treasurer. It became a registered charity, they also received donations from the public."

"I need to make a call to Gerry Matthews to see what he can tell us, you keep digging. We need to know everything we can about this group. Do they still meet, are they still active in any way? You know the drill."

"Do you know what this looks like to me, sir?" Trump asked as Meredith walked back to his office.

"I do, Trump. Dig a little deeper on Aiden O'Brien. See if it's likely he was a paedophile." Meredith paused in his stride, "Did Brooker come up as a connection?"

"No, sir. Not a whisper."

"Odd. Get me his phone records again. It's looking as though we've had some sort of vigilante killing, arranged by someone who had no connection. That's not right. In fact, get all their records, those we have names for, and get me a timeline on who called who on the night O'Brien was murdered. If we have any numbers not listed, how often do they appear? Home numbers included." He'd reached his office and turned back, "Anyone here still think we need to have Jacobs as a priority?" A few shook their heads, others busied themselves with what they'd been tasked, and he nodded, "Thought not."

His first call was to Patsy, and again he got her answer machine.

"Patsy, I haven't got time for sulking. I'm an evil bastard and you can punish me in another way, but now I need your help. It looks like O'Brien was murdered because he was a paedophile. You've spoken to his daughter, does it seem probable that she knew, found out, or worse was a victim? Give me a ring." Hanging up he called his colleague Gerry Matthews.

Half an hour later, Meredith brought the room to order. "I've spoken to Gerry Matthews, OIC on the case. O'Brien isn't a name that ever cropped up, but that doesn't rule him out. They believe this particular paedophile ring had at least twenty members. Ten are behind bars, three topped themselves, two were acquitted due to lack of evidence, so that means there are still a possible five out there. Jason's Justice is still active, although it's died off a little. And, in the absence of Jason's body, the case is still open. Over fifty children were involved that they know of. Two of those that were killed in their sick games, and almost certainly Jason. That's a lot of lives ruined. If O'Brien was involved, then some, including a few in this room," he glanced at Dave Rawlings, "will believe he got what was coming, but can I remind you that an innocent man has been framed, and we have to prove that. So, we'll bring those connected with Jason's Justice in again. Tom, you sort that out. I'm going to see Chapman, that way I might get something out of him before he gets his brief involved. Jo, you can be my chaperone. That's it, get on with it."

~~~

Having listened to her messages, Patsy dropped her phone on the desk, "Sod you."

"The Skipper, I take it?" Linda asked.

"The who?" Sharon walked into the office carrying the obligatory shopping bags. She placed them on her desk and waited for an explanation.

"She's talking about Meredith. In the five minutes he was actually her boss, she decided he needed a different name. She came up with Skipper."

Sharon laughed, "Oh, I bet he'd love that, not. Shame he's abandoned us. You'll be pleased to hear that I've come bearing gifts that should cheer you up." She lifted a bag and walked to Linda, "Saw this in John Lewis, and for some reason thought of you."

Linda grabbed the bag and slid the contents onto her desk. It was several meters of folded fabric in a brightly coloured jungle design. She smiled at Sharon, "Thanks, that'll make a fabulous blouse."

"That's what I thought, and with you being a little monkey, well, I couldn't resist."

"There are . . . oh, yes. Patsy, look at the little monkeys peeping out of the branches."

Patsy glanced from one to the other. She was surrounded by mad people. "Fabulous. I'll leave you two oddities together, I need to make a call."

"Not so fast. I have one for you too. I'd have bought it for myself, but there's little point now . . . anyway, Meredith will love it."

Sharon handed Patsy an expensive looking bag. Patsy lifted out the contents. It was a satin negligee in a shimmering gold. She folded it carefully.

"He would if he ever gets to see it, but it is lovely, Sharon, although you really must stop spending money. Especially on us. Thank you. Now I've got to make that call."

Retrieving her phone, she walked to her office. The negligee remained in the reception area. As she pushed her door shut, she heard Linda confide in Sharon.

"The Skipper has upset her. I don't know what he's done yet, but I'm working on it."

"Better have a cup of tea then. I'll be mother." Sharon called to Patsy, "Tea, Patsy?"

Knowing it would give Sharon an excuse to interrogate her, Patsy declined. "No thanks, I'm okay, I'd better get on."

Silently cursing Meredith, she dialled Frankie Callaghan.

"Patsy. That was quick, I'm assuming that we have the location of the bodies, and that you're not calling me to invite me to dinner."

"Oh, Frankie, I wouldn't subject anyone to Meredith's company at the moment. How is Sarah by the way?"

"Well I'm game if you are. We were only speaking of you two last night. Sarah is great, thanks. The wedding plans however . . . still, it's got to be done."

"Let him get this Jacobs thing sorted out first, if not, he's likely to cancel anyway. Are you in front of a computer? If so call up maps."

"Done. What am I looking for?" Patsy gave him the address and he enlarged the image on his screen. "I have it. That's a fair patch of land."

"I know, that's why I wanted you to look. Is it still doable?"

"Of course. We'll do the most probable areas first, then work from the property out in grid formation. Have you actually seen it?"

"No, planning on going there later. We need to get permission from the current owner to go on his land, which brings me to my second question. How soon can you do it? It will be much easier to arrange if I can give him a date."

"I suppose tomorrow is too soon? I've got the day off, but Sarah is now going out shopping for table decorations with her mother. I could escape that delight if I had something else on. Other than that, it's going to have to be next Monday, only available in the morning, or Thursday after eleven."

"The sooner the better. Keep your fingers crossed the owner will agree, I'll give you a ring to confirm later. I'd better dash now. Bye, Frankie, speak later."

Patsy packed her things into her bag and left her office. Keeping up a brisk pace she ignored the glances from Linda and Sharon, telling them she'd be gone for a couple of hours, and that they could get her on the phone. She drove directly to Wendy's Cottage. It took about forty minutes, and during that time she pondered on what, if anything, to tell Meredith.

When she got to the cottage, she parked a little way up the lane and walked back down along the perimeter. It was a large plot, and from what she could see over the hedge, it had been sectioned off with paved walkways joining one area to the next, and was well looked after. A name plaque, suspended by chains from the porch swung in the breeze, it confirmed she had the right place. She was surprised to find a board fixed to the wall by the gateway.

Holiday Lets Available – Call Harriet if interested

Patsy jotted down the number and walked on. The lane looped around to the left, and when she turned the corner, she found the cottage had a detached garage and there was a further outbuilding to the rear of that. She walked until she came to the boundary of the garden of the neighbouring cottage. Retracing her steps to the car she called Harriet.

"Hi, I understand you let Wendy's Cottage; my colleague is looking for something in the area quite soon. Can you let me know the cost and availability please?" Balancing her pad against the steering wheel, she found she didn't have to make notes. The cottage was currently available and subject to any booking coming in, would be for the next three weeks. "Thank you, I'll speak to him and give you a call." Having a sudden thought, she added, "And what's the shortest let you do? He'll only need a few days."

Hanging up, she called Meredith. It went through to his answer service. She left a brief message that she was returning his call, and dialled Frankie.

"Hi, Frankie, I think we're in business. Assuming you have to work through to the last part of the grid, how long do you think you'll need? It's a holiday cottage, and it's available."

"At a guess, anything up to twenty-four hours, depending on the land of course. But if it was longer, I couldn't do the next day. I suggest we make a very early start, and you save your money. Apart from anything else, if we do find bodies, the police will be involved and I'd probably be called out anyway. Shall we say a seven-thirty start?"

"Perfect. You're a star, Frankie. Shall I pick you up?"

"No, the other way around. I'll get my car loaded with all the equipment later, it'll be quicker. See you at seven-thirty, you can buy breakfast on the way. I know the route, there's a burger van that does wonderful bacon baps about halfway there."

"Deal. See you there."

Patsy made her final call before heading back. Peggy confirmed the cupboards were now stocked, the back garden was weed free, Sian had blisters, and was supervising Gary digging over the vegetable patch.

"Okay, glad it's going well. I won't interrupt but can you give them a message? Tell them I've found the cottage, we'll look tomorrow, and to sit tight. I'll call immediately if anything turns up." Her phone vibrated. "No time for questions, Peggy, I've got Meredith calling me. Bye."

"Patsy, I missed you earlier. I take it you got my messages what do you think?" Meredith got straight to the point.

"That I can think of nothing worse than going out and watching you try to force a smile over dinner. You can get a takeaway."

"Okay, but about O'Brien. I haven't got long, I'm sitting outside Chapman's I need to question him again."

"That'll be fun. When I spoke to Sian, I asked if her father did something to her to make her hate him so much. She went ballistic, even at the suggestion, so if he is a paedophile, which I don't think he is, but that's just a gut feeling, he never abused Sian."

"But it's possible she could have found out that he was?"

"I'd say possible, but not probable."

"Thanks. Finally, I don't suppose she said where Gary Mason was hiding did she?"

"No, she didn't."

"Bugger, he's disappeared. You never know, I might find him here. Right, I'll call later and pick up a Chinese on the way home. Bye."

Patsy dropped her phone onto the passenger seat and started the engine. She hadn't lied. Sian hadn't said where Gary was. Why would she, they both knew.

15

Sliding his phone into his pocket, Meredith turned to Jo Adler, who had been speaking to Trump when Meredith called Patsy. "Anything worth knowing?"

"Two things. Trump entered Ben Jacobs' name into the spreadsheet thingy, and the only connection that came up was BB's. But the main reason for the call was because Jason's Justice had also received funding from Flood's Transport. We weren't looking for that connection, and he came across it by chance while checking something else." Jo released her seatbelt. "Seven grand. I don't know about you, Gov, but that's an expensive bluff if Aiden O'Brien was part of the ring, and . . . someone's coming out," she nodded towards the house.

Meredith turned and opened the car door. "That's his wife, Alice. Not all there, might be worth a quick word." He strode up the path, calling to Alice Chapman. "Hello, Mrs Chapman, I wonder if I could have a word with your husband please."

Alice Chapman peered at him, "Do I know you?"

"Meredith, we met at your daughter's house the other day."

"We did, didn't we? What a wonderful party that was. We don't have parties anymore, do we?" She stepped forward and paused, she looked around, "Where was I going?"

"I think to make us a cup of tea," Meredith took her elbow and held his hand towards the open door. "This is Jo. She's with me."

"She wasn't at the party." Alice allowed herself to be led into the house. She sniffed, "Something's burning."

Leaving Alice with Jo, Meredith opened the nearest door and looked in. Not finding the source he opened two others, before finding the kitchen, and the source of the problem. Grabbing some oven gloves, he opened the oven and removed a blackened chicken. Coughing and spluttering as his eyes watered he dropped it into the sink. Alice and Jo stood in the doorway as he opened the window, and the backdoor to the garden.

"A couple more minutes and that would have been flaming." He glanced at the ceiling, "Do the smoke alarms not work?"

Alice Chapman walked into the kitchen, and switched on the kettle. "No, I took the batteries out, they kept going off."

"Your husband -"

"No," Alice spun around to face Meredith. "Don't tell him, he doesn't know." Dropping some teabags into the pot she pointed at the chicken. "It happens now and then, never had a fire, but those blasted things go on and on and on."

"I think that might be dangerous. You should discuss it with your husband, is Mr Chapman not here?"

Alice's eyes narrowed, "Is he with his tart again? I've got to pick the children up from school, and he's doing what he always does." Forgetting the tea, she marched to the telephone on the wall by the door and snatched up the receiver. "That's it!"

Meredith exchanged a glance with Jo, before pointing at the teapot. Jo poured the boiling water into the pot. Meredith continued to watch Alice Chapman. Having put the receiver to her ear she stared at the keypad. She glanced at Meredith.

"What was I doing? Was I calling Keith?" Her forehead furrowed, her chin quivered as she tried to remember.

"You were going to have a cup of tea with us." He pulled out a chair for her, "Take a seat, Jo will be mother."

"Do you take sugar, Mrs Chapman?" Jo lifted the sugar bowl.

"I don't drink tea. I have coffee." Alice tutted, "I seem to repeat myself on an hourly basis. Why does no one listen to me?" She watched Jo look around the kitchen for a clue as to how she took her coffee. "Don't bother. I'll go without."

"You said you had children to pick up, was that today?" Meredith guessed Alice had been somewhere in the past, but felt the need to check. To his surprise, Alice threw her head back and laughed.

"You wonderful man. I know I look good for my age, it's in the genes. But even my grandchildren are too old for school."

"You have more than one? I only know Gary. How many do you have?" He realised he'd lost her when she pointed at Jo.

"Are you Penny's friend? I hope you're not the trollop that encouraged Susie to get drunk at the weekend."

Jo didn't give a direct response, and wondered why Meredith was staying as Chapman wasn't there. "I'm Jo," she held out her hand. "I'm with Meredith."

Alice took her hand and kept hold of it while studying Meredith. "A good-looking chap, you do look familiar."

"We met at Penny's house. You were talking about Keith's father and the sailors." Meredith's smile was short-lived, as Alice jumped to her feet, knocking into the table. Meredith held it steady. "What is it, Mrs Chapman?"

"I never said anything about that. No one knows. No one, you hear me." She pushed her hair from her forehead, and her hand remained on her head, her fingers curled tightly around her hair.

"But you told me last time I was here." Meredith pressed her, "You were also worried that you were in trouble."

"In trouble? Not me. Keith wouldn't allow it. He protects me from such things. The scandal, if you ever told anyone." Her face crumpled. "You won't tell, will you? That was the deal."

"The deal?" Jo stood and put her arm around Alice's shoulder. "Here sit down, you look shocked."

"Why are you here?" Alice ignored Jo, and releasing her hair, pointed at Meredith, "You, why are you here? I don't know you."

"I'm here about Jason's Justice. I understand your husband contributed a considerable sum to bring a paedophile ring to justice. I was hoping he could give me some information about it." He saw her nose wrinkle at the word paedophile.

"Do you know anything about it?" Jo asked quietly.

"What is there to know?" Alice shook her head. "I don't know what you mean."

"Do you know what prompted your husband to make such a generous gesture?"

"Because he's a good man. Someone has to make amends, someone has to make these people pay." Alice looked down at her hands. When she looked up her face was blank.

"I agree. Some say prison is too good for them."

Without warning, Alice's hand flew out and slapped Meredith soundly across the face. "Get out. Get out. Coming here and telling me I'm going to prison. I'm not, get Keith, he'll tell you." Falling heavily into the chair, she covered her face and sobbed.

"Get her some water," Jo instructed Meredith as she rubbed Alice's back.

As Meredith got to his feet, Chapman's voice called from the hall, "Alice, I'm home, can I smell burning?" His feet hurried across the hall and moments later he appeared at the kitchen door. "What the hell are you doing here?" he demanded.

"They are with Penny," Alice explained through her tears.

Chapman ignored her. "I asked what you were doing here?"

"We came to see you, but when Mrs Chapman answered the door, it was clear there was something amiss." Jo pointed at the chicken, "We've sorted it out."

Chapman looked at the chicken, then at his wife, flustered for a moment. Eventually, he held his hand towards the hall.

"Thank you. With crisis averted, I'd like you to leave. My wife is clearly distressed and needs my attention. Whatever it was that you wanted will have to wait."

"It won't take long." Meredith remained where he was. "We need information on Jason's Justice. It would appear that most of the men, if not all, that surrounded Aiden O'Brien in BB's were in some way connected. As you were their main benefactor, I'd be grateful for any information you can share."

"Lack of you mean." Chapman's disgust was evident. "I believed it to be a good cause, I give to many charities, but this one was local and I believed I could help."

"Lack of, meaning . . ." Meredith wanted to string the conversation out, he was hoping that Chapman might volunteer more information.

"He didn't get any, did he? We know from the piece of shit that hanged himself in Blaise Castle, that Jason had been used by them. But have you found out where the poor mite is? No. Have you got any of those my money brought in to tell you? No. So, not an apt name, but a good cause none the less."

"I wasn't involved in the case, but I agree, it appears that your money brought the police information that enabled them to take a few more of that particular ring off the street. I understand Aiden O'Brien's money did too. That's why I'm keen to gather as much information as possible."

"I have no information! Why would I?" Chapman stepped into the hall and pointed towards the door. "Now, if you don't mind."

Meredith decided to take a gamble. "I'm surprised you say that, the information we have would suggest that you've met with Marcus White and Eric Sampson, if not more of those involved." He still didn't move.

"Well of course I did. They didn't have anything formal set up to collect donations," he flipped his hand as though throwing away any relevance. "I attended a couple of meetings, pointed them in the right direction re the finances, and that was it. Have you met these people? Because nice as they might be, we have nothing in common, we don't socialise."

Chapman walked out of view, and Meredith heard the sound of the front door opening. He looked at Jo and jerked his head before addressing Alice Chapman.

"We're off now, Mrs Chapman, we will probably meet again. Thanks for the tea . . . And get that smoke alarm sorted out."

Alice looked up at him, "Who are you?"

"A policeman. You need smoke detectors."

"I thought you were here about Knox. Well that's a relief. Goodbye."

Meredith was about to push her further when Chapman reappeared.

Deciding to do his homework before he touched on the subject, he joined Chapman in the hall.

"Was it you who encouraged Aiden O'Brien to make a contribution? Oh, and I meant to ask, we need to speak to your grandson again, if he appears let him know I'm after him." Meredith allowed Jo to exit the house first.

"It was a company contribution, but of course the other shareholders had to agree. Gary has apparently taken a short holiday, I have no idea where. Good day, Meredith." Chapman pushed the door shut.

"There's something else we need to tie up, I wonder why she thought we were there about Knox. But first, let's go and see Rosie O'Brien, and see what she has to say about Jason's Justice."

"You're not planning on telling her that her husband may have been a paedophile, are you? She's having a tough enough time at the moment." Jo climbed into the car.

"Do I look that stupid?" Meredith started the engine. "I'm offended that you would think that. Get hold of Seaton, and tell him to dig out the files on Knox for me. It may be that that might help, and while he's at it, tell him to find what he can on Chapman's father. That seems like a skeleton that may need to come out of the cupboard, if only to calm that poor woman."

Jo called the incident room, gave Meredith's instructions, and was about to hang up when Meredith clicked his fingers.

"While you're on, get Trump to add all of BB's employees into the contaminator. If there are any other connections, I'd like to know about them. Forewarned and all that."

~~~

Patsy arrived back at the office in a much better mood.

"I'm still not talking about it. It's the same old story, you'd only be bored. I have however bought cakes. I'll even make the tea once you've updated me."

"Sharon made a discovery. I only missed it because I'm too young." Linda looked at Sharon, "Tell her."

"That note the girl found, it wasn't printed in a blue font, it was a carbon copy." She watched Patsy's brow furrow and sighed. "In the olden days, when our lives weren't digital and controlled by computers, we had to use these things called typewriters to make letters appear on paper. Photocopying was very expensive, so if you needed a copy, you put a sheet of carbon paper between the two sheets, or more, but the more you had the fainter it became, and . . ." She opened her top drawer and pulled out the bank paying in book, "Here see."

Patsy walked over and took the book. "Yes, I've used it, but I didn't . . . Linda, call up the image of that note." She walked over to stand behind Linda, and looked from the screen to the book. She smiled at Sharon. "You're right, you know. You see, being old does have its advantages. Which means, of course, why would Aiden O'Brien drag out an old typewriter. He has a computer at home, and I've no doubt several at the office." She walked back towards the door. "I'm going to see Rosie O'Brien, not a subject for discussing over the phone."

"Are you going to tell her about the note?" Sharon asked.

"Not sure, I'll just drop it into conversation. Enjoy the cakes, you'll probably be gone by the time I'm finished, so I'll be in touch tomorrow."

"Are you not in, PHPI?" Linda called.

"Nope, having a day out with Frankie. I'll keep you informed."

As Patsy drove to the O'Brien home, she tried to work out why Aiden O'Brien hadn't simply used the computer and saved or printed a spare copy, and decided he probably knew that even deleted documents could be resurrected by the right person. But why make a copy at all, if he knew the content? That would increase the risk if he was worried it would be discovered, as indeed it had been.

"I'm missing something?" she mumbled to herself as she pulled onto O'Brien's drive. "Something is missing." She pushed the doorbell and fixed a smile. As Kathleen O'Brien opened the door, she realised what it was.

"Hello, dear, come on in, is everything okay with Sian?" Kathleen asked as Rosie appeared in the hall behind her.

"Yes, perfectly fine." Patsy nodded, "You might be amazed to hear that she has blisters from gardening."

"Gardening? Sian doesn't do manual work. What have you done to my daughter?" It was the first time Patsy had seen Rosie smile, and the likeness to her daughter was unmistakable.

"Not me, the lady she's staying with. I only saw her start the washing-up." Patsy laughed as the two women exchanged glances.

"We're in the sunroom, going through some paperwork. Would you like tea?" Rosie asked.

"I'll do that, you to go and settle yourselves." Kathleen walked to the kettle, as Rosie led the way.

"What news? I know you said that you're sure Gary is okay, but there was something else you were working on. I'm assuming that's why you and Mr Meredith were coming. Oh, I've just realised, have you come instead?"

Realising that Rosie didn't know she and Meredith weren't working together anymore, and that Meredith must also be paying a visit, Patsy decided to get on with it quickly.

"I'm not sure what he wanted. I had a few questions that needed clearing up though. Do you have a typewriter by any chance?" She knew she'd guessed correctly when Rosie shook her head.

"Not any more, not for years. What an odd question. Dad loved them, was quite proud of the speed he could work up with his four fingers, I almost didn't get rid of the last one. But they take up space, getting hold of ribbons was a nightmare, and even if you could, there's no spell check on a typewriter. Why do you ask?"

"Something and nothing. As you know we have Sian's phone records and there was a photograph of a document, it appeared to be a carbon copy of something produced on a typewriter, and I wondered if it could be relevant. It didn't mention her or her father, but everything needs to be eliminated." Patsy got to her feet, "I'll not waste any more of your time. I'll apologise to Mrs O'Brien about the tea . . ." Patsy stopped speaking as Jo appeared in the doorway. "Hi, Jo. I was just off."

"Okay," smiled Jo. "It was almost nice to see you."

"Patsy." Meredith appeared behind Jo. "I don't suppose you've managed to find Gary Mason yet?"

"Don't worry, Mr Meredith, Patsy has them both somewhere safe." Rosie had no reason to know that Meredith and Patsy were in a relationship, so she added, "She's obviously not had time to update you yet. She's even had Sian doing washing-up. Miracles will never cease. You're not here about a typewriter, are you? We don't have one anymore as I've explained. You two need to speak more often."

Meredith held Patsy's defiant stare. "No, not a typewriter, I'm glad to hear Patsy has Gary tucked away safely. And you're right, we do need to talk more." He stepped to one side to allow Kathleen to carry in a tea tray. "Are you leaving?"

The way he phrased the question made it sound more like an instruction, and for a second Patsy was inclined to stay, but she nodded, "I am. I've finished, thanks. See you later."

"You will," Meredith snapped.

Rosie O'Brien picked up on the friction between them. "Have you two had a row or something? I'm sorry to pry, but my husband has been murdered, and my daughter was on bad terms with him when he died, so I want answers. If you two aren't sharing information you might miss something." Rosie moved her finger from one to the other, "Whatever is going on, you do your jobs first and foremost. Do you understand?"

Kathleen called to her daughter-in-law, "Rosie, come and sit down. I'm sure everything is in hand." She looked at Patsy, "I'm sorry, it's a difficult time for her."

"No, no. Don't apologise, she's right. She deserves an explanation. It's quite simple and we should have told you to avoid confusion." Patsy pointed at Meredith, "DCI Meredith had decided to leave the police force and take a partnership in the agency Aiden hired to solve the problem with Sian. However, due to Aiden's death, and the involvement of Chapman, and to a degree, Ben Jacobs, he's delayed that, and is still a serving police officer heading the team investigating your husband's death. I am still working on what caused the problem between Sian and Aiden. And there was something, although I've not pulled it altogether yet but I can assure you it was not caused by Gary Mason. Chapman possibly, but not Gary."

Patsy smiled at Rosie, "Please don't worry, both elements are being thoroughly investigated, if from a slightly different standpoint now. Meredith and I simply need to catch up on what's happening."

Rosie nodded, "Thank you. I didn't mean to be rude."

"I know, I'll leave you all to it, and I'll give you a call later about Sian. I'll see myself out."

Patsy walked away ignoring Meredith. Once outside she cursed him. He had blocked her in, and he'd need to come and move his car. He opened the door as she raised her hand to ring the bell.

"Secrets, Hodge. I wasn't expecting that." He stepped onto the doorstep forcing her back onto the drive.

"No, not secrets. You didn't ask me. Those kids need some space, I promise you that Gary knows nothing about his grandfather's possible involvement in Aiden's death. He would have said."

"And you know that how? You've become very trusting all of a sudden."

"I trust no one to tell me the truth, Meredith, as you yourself know, but I know from what he's told me about his grandfather, that if he knew anything he would have said."

"What has he told you about Chapman?"

"Not now, Meredith. We'll trade information later. If you come home at a reasonable hour, and if you go first. Now move the bloody car."

Meredith walked to her. Taking her chin in his hand, he tilted her face towards him, and bending, he planted a kiss on her lips. "There are some games I'd love to play with you, Hodge. But not this one. I won't be late, and I'm still buying a Chinese."

"We'll see." Patsy climbed into her car, and returned his wave as she manoeuvred her car around his. "Bloody man," she cursed as she pulled away.

Meredith returned to the sun room, and sitting next to Rosie, he took her hand in his. "We're not working against each other, Rosie. Just coming at it all from different angles. I now have a full team of detectives trying to prove your husband's murdered was premeditated, and find out by whom. You do understand that, don't you?"

"Yes, of course, I believe what Patsy said. If you're not here about a typewriter, what can I do for you?"

"A typewriter? I'm intrigued. What relevance does that have to Sian?" Meredith really was intrigued, it was a long way for Patsy to come if it wasn't crucial.

"Nothing apparently, process of elimination. She'll no doubt tell you when you get your heads together."

"Indeed." Meredith lifted a biscuit from the plate, "As to why we're here, can you tell me what you know about Jason's Justice?" He popped the whole biscuit in his mouth.

"That was the little boy who went missing. I don't think they've found him yet, have they?"

Meredith's mouth was full and he allowed Jo to respond on his behalf.

"No, not yet. But a couple of the men in the bar at the time your husband died had various connections to the group set up to support the families, and pay a reward for information leading to convictions. We've seen that Flood's Transport made a healthy donation. We wondered perhaps if your husband had fallen out with them in some way?"

Rosie O'Brien was already shaking her head, "No, no. He didn't have any involvement. Keith Chapman was talking, well, boasting I suppose, about meeting with them, and gearing them up properly, is how he put it. Aiden and I simply agreed it was a good thing he was doing, and we agreed that the business could afford to make a contribution to the cause. Chapman organised it. I don't think Aiden or I had anything more to do with it other than countersign the cheque. I can't even remember which one of us did that."

"Thank you, it was worth a shot." Having finished his biscuit, Meredith pulled an envelope from his pocket. "I have some photos I'd like you to look at, if you recognise any of them let me know."

Meredith slid the photographs free and handed them to Rosie. She shuffled through them fairly quickly, setting one to one side. When she had finished, she handed it to Meredith.

"Only this lad. He's a boxer, but I can't remember his name. Chapman knows him somehow, and he arranged a dinner for charity, and the boxing match took place afterwards. We went because Aiden likes boxing, but I stayed at the table when they went down to the ringside. I can't understand how it's entertaining, or even a sport really."

"His name is Sammy Gregory, he worked as a doorman at BB's. Is that how Chapman knows him, do you think?" Meredith replaced the photographs and handed the envelope to Jo Adler.

"No idea. I don't think it was ever explained." Rosie pointed at the envelope in Jo's hand, "Is one of those men my husband's killer?"

"I don't know. Possibly. But I will find out, I promise you that. If you've not remembered anything else that may be relevant, we'll leave you to it." When Rosie shook her head, he got to his feet. "Thanks for your time. Stay and finish your tea. I know the way." He turned back before he left the sun room, "I don't suppose Patsy said why she was looking for a typewriter did she?"

"Not really, something to do with a document on Sian's phone." Rosie's look was penetrating, "You will be speaking to her won't you? I think she thinks the two matters are connected in some way."

"I will certainly be speaking to her, yes. Give me a call if you need or remember anything." Meredith led the way back to the car. "Patsy knows more than she is telling me it seems," he commented to Jo as he started the car.

"Well something is certainly wrong between you two, I could see that a mile away. If it was important, and connected to O'Brien's murder, I'm sure she would have told you."

"You'd think so, wouldn't you, yet she has Gary Mason holed up somewhere, and didn't say. She knew I was looking. She's playing games, and I'm not amused."

"You don't know that, Gov." Jo pulled her phone from her pocket and flipped the screen towards Meredith, "It's Tom."

"Put him on speaker, that way you won't have to repeat it."

"Hi, Tom, you're on speaker phone so the Gov can listen in. Can you hear me okay?"

Tom attempted a response but the line was crackling, he hung up and called back on Meredith's number which was wired into the audio system of the car.

"That's better," he announced when Meredith barked out his name. "You were right, Gov."

"I always am, anything in particular?"

"There are a series of calls which bounced around that group on the night O'Brien was murdered," Tom explained.

"*And . . .*" Meredith hurried him.

"And, it certainly looks like they were planning to meet at the club hours before they actually arrived. Chapman called O'Brien at seven thirty, then Brooker at seven forty-five, Brooker we know arrived at eight fifteen and instructed the staff to keep on their toes, and he already knew that O'Brien would be visiting. An untraceable called Marcus White at five past eight, White calls Sampson at quarter past. Then -"

"In a nutshell, Tom, I can get the detail later." Meredith turned left away from the direction of the station and Jo nudged him. He batted her interruption away.

"It looks like Chapman set up the meeting using his own phone to call Brooker and O'Brien, then he, or someone else instructed by him or Brooker, rounded up the group, some numbers we don't know but I'll guarantee they're the faces we haven't brought in yet. We see O'Brien enter the bar, Brooker is in his office and calls Chapman. Then White gets a call from the untraceable, et cetera, et cetera. Brooker leaves the bar, O'Brien is with the group, and two minutes after he's stabbed Brooker calls Chapman on his mobile, but the police from the club landline. No doubt at all that O'Brien was set up, Jacobs was probably wrong place, wrong time. Shall we bring them in?"

Meredith glanced at the clock on the dashboard, and pondered the options.

"Gov? You still there?"

"Yep, thinking. Get a list of names, Chapman at the top of course, and I want two bodies per person, we'll do an early morning swoop. I want everyone in for six in the morning, we'll hit them between six thirty and seven. I'll be there by five thirty. Send everyone home as soon as they get to a sensible place to stop. Tomorrow is going to be a long day."

"Will do. See you in the morning." Tom terminated the call and immediately began organising the logistics of Meredith's instructions.

Meredith called the station. George Davies answered.

"Hello, George, it's Meredith."

"I've been trying to get hold of you. Thanks for sorting everything out. Not sure what I said at your leaving do, but I didn't mean it. I knew you'd deliver."

"Wasn't aware you'd said anything. Want to share?" Meredith grinned at Jo. "We go back a long way George, it couldn't have been that bad."

"Worse than bad. But it was the drink talking. I even got away with not telling the wife, could have done with another week off mind you, but there, you can't have everything."

"No, so I've found. You on in the morning?"

"I am. Take over from Charlie at eight, why?"

Meredith gave him an overview of what was planned. "We may need some bodies to back us up, we will certainly need the custody sergeant on standby. I can't see that we won't be making arrests. Wouldn't mind a few bodies around in case any of them get excitable."

"Why didn't you just say, you need to come in early, George?"

"That's what I wanted to hear. I'm briefing at six if you want to join us. Thanks, George, bye for now."

Meredith opened the glove compartment and pulled out a packet of cigarettes, he lit it, lowered the window and blew the smoke towards the gap.

"That's not much use you know. I'll still stink of smoke," Jo complained.

"Would you rather walk? I need to think, it helps."

"I might if I knew where we were going."

"Peggy's."

"Your Peggy?" Jo turned to face him, "Why?"

"Not my Peggy, *the* Peggy. And we are going there because that's where Patsy has stored Sian O'Brien and Gary Mason. I still want to speak to Mason, but now the questions might be a little different."

"How do you know?"

"Because I'm a good detective. I hear what's not been said." He blew smoke towards her with a grin.

Jo waved her hand about, and opened the passenger window. "Which was?"

"Rosie O'Brien said Patsy even had Sian washing-up, which surprised her. Patsy didn't make a teenager do that, and we only know one woman who could."

"Peggy Green." Jo nodded approval, "Well done, Gov. Not sure how happy Patsy will be though."

"Patsy will be fine, she knows she should have told me, she's just having a sulk at the moment."

"Patsy doesn't sulk. Don't forget how well I know Patsy. She might be punishing you, but she's not sulking."

"Okay, sister Jo, punishing me. In which case, she knows she's wrong in punishing me this way."

"Can I ask what you did?"

"Came back to work."

"Ah, she's sulking," Jo shrugged acceptance.

"As I said. Here we are." Meredith pulled up outside Peggy's house, as they walked to the door he said, "Don't mention Patsy didn't tell me they were here, for some reason Peggy always takes her side."

"I wonder why?" Jo grinned at Meredith as Peggy opened the door.

"Merewinkle, what an honour. I'm surprised you knew the way." She turned to Jo, "Hello, love, did you have to navigate?"

Meredith stepped inside the house and pulled Peggy into a hug, "Now don't be like that, you know how hard I work."

"Don't kid a kidder, Merewinkle. You just sit at your desk and order your minions about." She glanced at Jo. "No offence intended, but I'm right, am I not?"

"You are, Peggy, yes."

"I know. Always am. Tea, coffee, or something stronger?"

"We haven't clocked off yet, so black with two, please Peggy." Meredith said, "What have you done with your visitors? I hear you've been using them for slave labour."

"They volunteered, but they worked like slaves. Poor old Sian has blisters. Come and see." She walked through to the kitchen and pointed out the window, "I only expected a bit of weeding and the veg patch turned over. They don't shirk, and nice kids too."

Meredith looked out the window. The lawn had been cut, the borders were weed free, and Sian and Gary, were pushing a low picket fence into the ground around a square patch of earth which he assumed was the veggie patch. "Very smart. I might take them around to mine when you've finished with them."

"He's a good lad that Gary. He pushed the trolley around the supermarket, came back and they did all that, Gary remembered that fence had been on offer in the supermarket, and went back and got it. You're not having them." The kettle began to boil and she nudged Meredith, "Get out of the way, Merewinkle, go and see what refreshments they want. They can even have one of those fruity ciders they bought if they want, they're nearly done now."

"Jo, stay here. He might recognise you." Meredith went out into the garden. He waved at the pair as he approached.

"Peggy says you're entitled to refreshment. Soft beverages are on offer, or some cocktail involving cider."

Sian smiled at his joke. "I'll have the cider please." Gary agreed, and Meredith shouted the order back to the house. "Are you her son?" Sian tilted her head, "You don't look like her."

"Don't let her hear you say that, you'll get a clip around the ear. I'm almost family, but not quite."

Gary had pushed the last piece of fence into place and wiping his brow with his forearm, went to sit on the bench.

"She's cool. Never met an adult that says what they mean without some sort of agenda before. When all this is over, I might ask if she wants a lodger. Do you know she makes her own cakes? Better than the crap my mother buys from the supermarket."

"I do. I'm hoping for some with my coffee. Talking of all this, how's it going?" He watched Gary look at him from the corner of his eye as he considered his words.

"How much do you know?"

"About your grandfather, about Brooker, about Patsy placing you here because it was the safest place. Which part?"

"No offence, you could have been sent by my grandfather, I wouldn't put it past him. Have you spoken to Patsy today?"

"Only briefly, I was tied up with something else, but I dropped in on your mum, Sian, she seems a little better now your grandmother is there."

"Yes, I spoke to her earlier. Do we know if Patsy thinks she'll find the bodies tomorrow?" Sian saw the jolt as Meredith pulled his head back to look at her. "Did you not -"

"Merewinkle, get your arse over here. I'm not bloody waiting on you."

"Excuse me." Meredith went to collect the drinks, grateful for the interruption. He wanted to shout, "What fucking bodies", but settled for a moment to collect himself. When he returned, Sian and Gary were grinning at him.

"We know that you've not come from Grandad, not if Peggy likes you, but are you *the* Merewinkle? Policeman, spy, and recruiter of Peggy, call me Lara Croft, Green."

Gary's smile fell away as Meredith's face turned from passive to angry.

Meredith placed the tray on the bench he had recently vacated. He looked from one to the other.

"Yes, I am a policeman, a good one. Yes, I have done some undercover stroke spying stuff in my time. And, yes, I have to admit, Peggy had to become an undercover driver, an eastern European call girl, and all round lifesaver, but, the name is, Meredith, not effing Merewinkle, that's Peggy's attempt at humour. It's not funny. You call me Meredith, get it?"

The two exchanged glances, Peggy had been telling the truth, they were sure Merewinkle would deny her claims.

Sian raised a finger, "Was she also a bag lady? She told us she lived on the streets."

"Yes, she did. For a long time, and that's a long story, which she will tell you if she chooses, word of advice, don't ask, she can turn nasty. When I first met Peggy, the smell was so bad I almost fainted. But, as I say, not my story to tell." He glanced at his watch, "I need to make a move in a minute." He handed Sian a can of cider. "I'm hoping to arrest your father's murderer tomorrow. I'll call if that happens."

Sian ran her finger around the top of the can. "Thanks, Patsy said it wasn't that Jacobs who got arrested."

"Is my grandfather involved?" Gary asked quietly.

Meredith decided to play it safe, after all, family was family, and Gary might have an attack of conscience. "I don't know. As I say, all will be revealed tomorrow. Any messages for Patsy, I don't think she'll make it back tonight."

"Only to let us know if she finds them, Peggy's message was very vague."

"Will do. Behave yourselves, Peggy is unforgiving," Meredith warned as he walked away.

Meredith dropped Jo back to her car and called Patsy. "I've finished for the day. Early start tomorrow, do you still want Chinese?"

"Oh my goodness, what's happened that you feel able to leave your desk? But, in answer to your question, yes, a Chinese would be lovely. Amanda isn't here, so I have no idea whether she'll want to join us. You might want to check with her."

"Will do. I'll be thirty minutes or so. Open a bottle, we have lots to discuss."

Hanging up, he made a second call. Burt answered after the first ring.

"Meredith, I thought you'd forgotten about me."

"If only I could. Not a huge amount to report except that Chapman is almost certainly responsible for orchestrating O'Brien's death. When I prove it, I'm having him for it, I don't care what your agenda is. As you probably know his wife had dementia, and slips in and out of time zones, however, she asked me if I was there about Knox, so there is definitely something there, and, she also mentioned something about Chapman's stepfather and sailors. Don't know anything about any sailors. She said it was a secret that Chapman protected the family from, and it would cause a scandal. I've got my team working on it, but you might want to have a poke around yourself."

"Will do, are you going to question her again?"

"Only indirectly, there ain't a court in the land that would allow me to bring her in without due cause, and even then I'd probably have my hands tied by a doctor. I doubt anything she said would stand up in court, it's like having cryptic clues to work out. Have you got anything else for me?"

"Nothing for the moment. Is that it?"

"Yep. I'll call if and when I get anything else. Let me know if you get anything on Chapman's old man." Meredith knew he should have mentioned the bodies. But as he didn't know what the hell that meant he held his tongue. Tomorrow would be soon enough, if ever. He hung up and headed for the Golden Palace, where he bought a meal for four. He was starving, and if Amanda wasn't there he'd probably eat hers too.

16

Ben Jacobs was standing by the hall table as Meredith opened his door. "What the fuck are you doing here?" Meredith slung his keys on the table as Patsy appeared. "Is this your idea?"

"No. Ben decided if the mountain wouldn't go to Mohammad . . . I did tell him you wouldn't be pleased."

"I am here, you know." Ben rapped the table several times with his knuckles. "I can be addressed directly."

"Not if I'm not talking to you." Meredith placed the takeaway on the floor and hung his jacket on the newel post. "You can go now and we'll say no more about it."

"You've got to be kidding me. I drive all the way back from Cornwall to get the news, and no one appears. I've ruined Hannah's break, and Tania is as stroppy as a cat with a firework up its arse. So, I'd like an update, and if that's a Chinese, I'll join you."

"Oh yes, the heroine of the story. How is Mrs Godfrey, has her husband turned up yet?"

"Fuck off, Meredith, that's over, and it's not our business." With a sudden burst of movement, Ben lunged forward and grabbed the bag containing the takeaway. Turning away from Meredith he pushed past Patsy into the kitchen. "Smells good. I've not eaten since lunchtime."

"Like the rest of the world then? If you stay, Ben, I'm going to have to take you in. You could of course just leave and give me a couple more days."

"I'll go when you've told me what's happening, and as you need to talk, I can eat. It's not difficult, Meredith."

"You, pal, are pushing your luck." Meredith opened the cupboard and placed another plate on the table. "Cutlery is in that drawer." Sitting at the table, he began unloading the steaming cartons from the bag. "I've got stuff to discuss with Patsy, as soon as this is gone you're out of here, or I promise you, you'll be held on remand until your brief can get you bail or the case is dropped."

"And you'll bring me up to date in the meantime?" Ben nodded as Patsy offered a glass of wine.

"Yep, now shut up and I'll bring you both up to date. No questions, just listen."

"Sherlock has confirmed that rather than help prove your guilt, your clothing indicates that it is highly unlikely that you were the assailant. Blood patterns and what have you. Phone records show that Brooker, the blokes that were with O'Brien at the bar, and an A N Other, who is almost definitely Chapman, made a series of calls from early evening up to the point, and shortly after, O'Brien was knifed. Brooker was watching the live action from his laptop, and when O'Brien hit the ground, he called Chapman and then the police. Chapman is connected . . . hang on."

Meredith took the plate that Patsy had heaped with food, and shovelled several forkfuls into his mouth, he carried on eating and speaking with his mouth full.

"Chapman is connected loosely with the men, as they all had ties to Jason's Justice, a group set up by families and friends affected by a paedophile ring operating in Bristol. Most of them are behind bars, some of them are dead, but it appears there are still five that weren't traced. Two children died as a result of their injuries, up to fifty were assaulted and raped, and one boy, Jason, has never been found."

"Shit, and Chapman was involved, he's a paedophile?" Ben put his fork down, his appetite waning.

"Nope, don't think so. He was putting up money as a reward for information that resulted in a conviction. O'Brien, possibly, but Patsy doesn't think so." Meredith looked at Patsy, "Do you?"

"No, I don't. I hinted at it to his daughter, and she was shocked, hated me for even suggesting it, and I know you never know, that they are good at hiding their perversions, but the man I met was desperate to get his daughter back. Until you suggested it, the thought wouldn't have crossed my mind. It's a gut instinct, as I said, not knowledge."

"I'm happy to go with that," Meredith conceded.

"Blimey, I have gone up in your estimation." Patsy couldn't resist the dig, "You trust me?"

"Ah shit. Don't start a domestic until you've got to the punchline." Ben tapped his plate with the rib in his hand, "Save it for later."

"I will." Meredith was still looking at Patsy, "Patsy has a lot of bodies she keeps hidden from me, I'm hurt that the trust is only one way."

Patsy blinked once but held his gaze. Her heart beat a little faster. He knew! How? She cleared her throat. "Perhaps you'd like to explain that later. But for now, let's deal with Ben."

"Good idea." Meredith released her and looked at Ben, "As things stand, it looks like Chapman rounded up this group of men, and wound them up. So much so, that they were prepared to kill. Now, whether O'Brien was or was not part of the paedophile ring remains to be seen, but they certainly thought he was. It was murder, all we have to do is find out which one, but the rest are definitely accessories."

"Tough shout." Ben had forgotten his own problems. He felt sympathy for the families of the boys, and wondered what he would have done had he been in their situation.

"Nope. We don't run this country on an eye for an eye," Meredith held up his finger to stop Ben's response. "Nor do we turn the other cheek. Whatever side of the fence you're on. We catch 'em, and we lock 'em up. Not for long enough, I'll grant you. I don't believe they can be rehabilitated, and these bleeding-heart liberals who say they can are wrong. That's like saying a gay man can be cured. It's bollocks. You are what you are, and once you've acted on it, if it's illegal, then you've got to be locked up. That's the law. That's what I do."

Meredith pushed his empty plate into the centre of the table, and got to his feet. "I'm going for a ciggy, you can join me while you decide what you want." He glanced at his watch, "You have ten minutes to make a run for it, or you can go down to the station, call your brief and reapply for bail. I doubt the charges will be dropped immediately, as we've yet to prove you weren't one of them. I have business to discuss with Patsy."

"You can't be -" Ben began.

"Not me, the law. We've had this conversation. Pass me that lighter."

Ben picked up the lighter, and followed Meredith into the garden. Patsy loaded the used cartons back into the bag ready to bin, and tried to prepare herself for the conversation to come. She gave a nod as she decided on an acceptable explanation. She was loading the dishwasher when Meredith returned. He resisted the urge to grab her, he was still supposed to be angry. Instead he poured them more wine.

"Shall I take these through to the sitting room?"

"Yes." Patsy glanced at the door, "Where's Ben?"

"Who?"

"Okay. Give me five minutes, I'll grab my notebook."

Meredith was lounging on the sofa, his feet resting on the coffee table when Patsy entered the room. She wondered if to sit next to him, but opted for the armchair.

Meredith's eyes followed her. "I won't bite."

"You might. Shall I go first, or is there more you didn't say in front of Ben?"

"I'm done talking, but I think you have . . . Oh shit! Every fucking time!" Meredith got to his feet and went to collect his phone, which was ringing in his jacket pocket. "It's Loopy, I'd ignore it, but she might be coming clean about these bodies." He hit the speaker button and placed the phone on the coffee table, "Loopy, I'm busy, this had better be important."

"It might be, Skipper. Only you will know that," Linda sounded excited.

Meredith ignored the Skipper bit. "Go on then . . . and Loopy, short and sharp. I don't need chapter and verse."

"Of course, Skipper. Louis had a problem with the contaminator and emailed it back to me, so I could sort it. He's gone for a bath and -"

"He sent you a confidential police document? Is that what you're telling me?"

"Calm down, Skipper. I thought we were doing short and sharp. That document is my intellectual property, you only have it because of me, and if any of you can reprogram the formulas, then be my -"

"Okay, okay, point made. Get on with it."

"Thank you, Skipper. Anyway, he'd dragged the wrong box across, so I sorted that, and keyed the possible links in for him. I did all this while he went to take a bath, and when I saw the result, I thought, the Skipper will want to know that. So, here I am."

"Which is where? And stop calling me Skipper. The name's Meredith."

"You love it, Skipper, you can't fool me. But back to the story, I put the names of the staff at BB's into the contaminator, and got some pretty surprising results. This paedophile ring thing, is horrible, I -"

"Loopy, spit it out."

"Skipper! First connection that came up was for Tania Davidson, she has a son, Alex. He goes to QEH and Keith Chapman pays the fees. Keith Chapman is also on the board of governors. Read into that what you will."

Meredith glanced at Patsy her face showed no surprise. She knew.

Linda gabbled on, "But the one I think is most sad, is Sammy Gregory." Linda paused as though she was waiting for Meredith to agree.

"Because . . . Come on, Loopy, I usually have trouble shutting you up. In what way is he connected?" Meredith thought he could make an educated guess, and noticed Patsy drop her head, she clearly thought the same thing.

"Because his name is linked three times. First, working at the club, second, working for a building firm in which Chapman has a stake, and finally, and this is the sad bit, both his father and his uncle were, stroke, are, part of the Jason's Justice group. I've checked and his uncle was there, he's the one with the tattoos. And, finally, Sammy Gregory was a member of the scout troop headed up by one of those convicted as being part of the gang. Victor King. That's not good in any sense, is it? Oh, hello, do you feel better for that?"

"Trump has finished his bath," Meredith murmured to Patsy.

"I was just speaking to the Skipper," Linda carried on the conversation with Trump, despite the fact Meredith was still on the line. "What do you mean, who? The Skipper, DCI John Meredith, Meredith, of Meredith and Hodge Private Investigators. What . . . oh."

"Sir, it's me, Trump. Can I help you with something?"

"She called me, Trump. The conversation is over, except to say give Tom a ring and tell him to add Sammy Gregory to the list for tomorrow. I have something that needs sorting here. Oh and tell Loopy to stop calling me Skipper." For the first time that evening, Meredith's lips almost formed a smile. He avoided looking at Patsy. "Loopy will fill you in on the whys. See you tomorrow." Meredith leaned forward and terminated the call.

He turned his attention to Patsy. "I think I've done enough talking today. Over to you. From the beginning, don't leave anything out. None of it is confidential, I'm a partner, I could just go into the office and ask. I'd rather hear it from you." He emptied his glass, "Let's include the bit about bodies too."

"You would have heard about it tonight. I wasn't going to interrupt your investigation until I had something concrete for you. All I had was a carbon copy of a typewritten note, and the name of a house."

"I thought we'd agreed from the beginning," Meredith pinched the bridge of his nose. "Loopy is rubbing off on you. You used to be good at concise chronological briefings."

"And was always told to cut to the chase. But, because you need it spelt out, I shall oblige, would you like a top up first?" she pointed to his glass.

"Get on with it, *please*."

"Sian found a note in her father's pocket, which basically said, he had helped Chapman with the first body, but had followed him and saw him bury a second one in the same place. I'll show you in a minute. Although addressed to Chapman, it wasn't signed. Sian took a photograph of it and returned the note. Sharon has pointed out that it isn't a letter printed in blue, it is actually a carbon copy of a typewritten letter. I've checked with Rosie O'Brien and they haven't had a typewriter for years. Her father was particularly fond of it." She paused and Meredith nodded.

"So the letter was more likely to be from Sian's grandfather, than her father. Sian jumped to conclusions, scratched her father off the Christmas card list, and Gary did the same with his grandfather. O'Brien, having found the letter somehow, has confronted Chapman . . ."

"Yes, but he only got nasty when Sian showed him the copy on her phone. That was just before O'Brien died. He didn't put her right for some reason, he should have, who knows why?"

"So, Chapman arranges to meet him, also brings in Jason's Justice mob on the pretext he was one of the paedophiles who didn't get caught. One of whom knifes him. All of them knew it was going to happen. Ben got in the way." Meredith sighed, "Well at least now we have a provable motive, and it appears you were right that O'Brien wasn't part of the ring, not so much a gut feeling as knowledge I'd say. What bit haven't you told me?"

"The note said that Flood, and I think we are safe assuming that it was Flood who wrote the note, had followed Chapman to a place called Wendy's Cottage, where he saw Chapman open the grave and add another body. The youngsters tried to find it and couldn't, Linda did." She smiled, "It came up on her contaminator as being owned by someone connected to Chapman."

Meredith clapped his hands, "Good old Loopy. We've got him bang to rights now. Where is it?"

"Out near Thornbury."

"What? You've got that look on your face which says, shall I tell him or not, he's going to be pissed off either way. Spit it out."

"Frankie is going to check it out tomorrow. He's using the equipment he took to find the bodies in Horovice. If he finds remains we'll call the police. You." Unable to outstare Meredith, Patsy got to her feet, "Well I'm going to have another drink even if you're not."

Meredith didn't speak but watched her leave the room. When she had, he leaned forward and released the breath he'd been holding. It was only a ten. He panted gently until he heard her returning. He had to get the ECG done. If these were panic attacks, which he still doubted as he didn't do panic, what had caused that? Patsy held the bottle towards him and he shook his head.

"Bloody hell, Meredith, that's a mega sulk, even on your scale. I was going to tell you tonight. There may not even be any bodies. We weren't going to dig them up."

"Do you promise?" His pain had gone, but he was in no mood for an argument, that would wait until another day.

"Promise what? That we weren't going to dig them up? Of course not. Are you feeling okay?"

"And I have your word on that?"

"Yes!"

"Good. Take me to bed. I've got a very early start in the morning, and I don't want to talk all night."

Patsy couldn't believe her ears. If roles were reversed she'd have gone ballistic. Something was wrong. "Is there anything you'd like to tell me?"

"Nope, I have no hidden bodies." Meredith pushed himself to his feet and collected his empty glass. "Will you not be joining me?"

"Are you feeling okay?"

"Fine, was that a no?"

"Will you be sleeping?"

"Eventually."

"Then I'll be joining you."

"Finally! You lock up, I'll jump in the shower."

Patsy was already in bed when Meredith came into the bedroom, still damp with a towel around his waist. She watched him dry himself.

"How did you know Sian and Gary were with Peggy? You must have been there, that must be how you knew about the bodies."

"Because I'm clever, and I always get there in the end. You'd do well to remember that. Now shut up and move over."

17

When Patsy woke at six o'clock, she vaguely remembered Meredith kissing her before he left. She thought about the previous evening and smiled, perhaps she should keep secrets more often. Showered and dressed in twenty minutes, she went to make some coffee. She could almost taste the breakfast that Frankie had promised awaited them. She saw the note immediately she walked into the kitchen. Meredith had scribbled it on the back of some junk mail and propped it against the kettle.

Thank you – Thought I should mention I've not finished with you. Ring when you find the bodies.

"Bastard. Getting your leg over was clearly more important than a row." She shrugged, "Good choice though." Dropping the note in the bin, she dropped a tea bag in a mug. She'd been sitting for less than a minute when her phone rang. It was Frankie.

"Does Meredith never sleep?"

"I'm not with you? He's called you, why?"

"Several things, not sure I'm allowed to share them with you. The examination of Wendy's Cottage is now a police matter apparently, so there will be no charge."

"He called to say that?"

"Amongst other things. He wants the post-mortem reports on two deaths, and a possible exhumation."

"Who?"

"Can't say, I've already had an ear bashing this morning, quite unjust too. I hung up in the end. That'll have pleased him, he'll notch it up as a win."

"You're not making much sense, Frankie. It's probably too early."

"Hence my call. Meredith woke me at five-fifteen, I've not managed to get back to sleep, so thought you might like to start a little earlier. I'm assuming you're still coming."

"Oh, yes. I'm ready when you are. You can tell me all about the call then."

Patsy dropped the things she needed into her bag, and wondered what had happened between going to bed and five fifteen for him to call Frankie. She couldn't work it out. There had been no calls during the night, and at five fifteen he wouldn't have been at the station. It must be something to do with the case, but what? She began to replay the conversation while she waited for Frankie. She jumped when Amanda appeared behind her.

"God, you lot are noisy. This is supposed to be my day off, a lie in was arranged with my brain, but I get Dad singing and banging about down here, then you chatting. What's happened that no one can sleep?" She dropped a teabag into a mug.

"Sorry, Amanda, your dad has a series of dawn arrests, and I'm off looking for murder victims with Frankie."

"Looking for them with Frankie? Explain."

"I have a case where someone believes their relative may have killed two women. They have a possible location. I had hired Frankie to use his high-tech gadgetry and wizardry, to see if there's any truth in it, but your father has commandeered the case. I'm going anyway, I have a duty to my clients."

"How cool. Can I come?"

"Are you serious?" Patsy looked at her as though she were mad.

"Of course. You know I'm considering doing a Masters in forensic medicine. I get on really well with Frankie, and I've never done a cadaver search before."

"I'd like to say yes, Amanda, but your father will -"

"It's got nothing to do with him. I'm a medical professional . . . almost. He can't choose who Frankie has assisting him."

"But he'll think he can. If Frankie says it's okay, I suppose -"

"You are a star, Patsy Hodge, my father does not deserve you! What time is Frankie coming?"

"I know I am. Frankie's on his way."

"Shit. You phone and tell him I'm coming, I'll go and get dressed." Amanda hurried back upstairs.

"What happened to asking?" Patsy shouted with a smile. She got no response.

Frankie assured Patsy that Amanda was a capable girl, and he'd be delighted to have her to help. Patsy finished making Amanda's tea and poured it into a travel mug.

~~~

Meredith was pleased to note that the whole team had arrived early. He finished giving his instructions to George Davis, and went to join them. He took his usual place in front of the incident board.

"As we're all here, we may as well get on with it. Trump made a few more discoveries last night," he winked at Trump. "It is highly likely that Sammy Gregory, doorman at BB's and the one that let the latecomers in to the club, was abused by his scoutmaster as a child. The scoutmaster was sent down when the Jason's Justice rewards brought forward new evidence. His uncle was part of the group he allowed in. So, kid gloves, but remember this was a murder of an innocent man. Trump and Seaton have a list of who is bringing in who. You'll interview the men you bring in as soon as you get back. George has a list of the solicitors used by those that indicated they had one, and we've put the usual firms on notice that we may need more than the usual number of duty solicitors, so hopefully we won't be kept hanging around. We've also printed a list of questions. I know you might drift off, depending on what the individuals say, but keep going back to the list until you have their answers to those specific questions. We've tweaked them depending on who it is. I'm taking Chapman, Trump has Marcus White, Rawlings is bringing in Eric Sampson, Seaton will get Sammy Gregory, et cetera. Tom, hand out the sheets."

Meredith waited until the team all had a list of questions for their individual.

"Read through them carefully, if you think we've missed anything we should all cover, shout now, because it's going to be mayhem in a couple of hours. You've got ten minutes, before we're off. I'll be in my office."

There were no suggestions for further questions, and they were all on their way to pick up their suspects a little after six o'clock.

Meredith rapped on Keith Chapman's door at six twenty-five. Chapman appeared in his dressing gown, and he looked at Meredith in total disbelief.

"You have got to be joking. That's it, you total bloody nuisance. I'm calling your superior."

"He knows. Keith Chapman, I am arresting you on suspicion of conspiracy to murder. You do not have to say anything, but -"

"Don't be bloody ridiculous. I'm calling my solicitor."

Meredith completed the caution. "No need, he's been notified. Now, would you like to get dressed, or are you coming like that?"

"I'll have your job for this."

Chapman stormed into the house, and Meredith indicated that Rob Hutchins should go with him.

"I don't think you'd be any good at it. Too many people to answer to."

Alice Chapman appeared at the top of the stairs, "Keith, it's too early to get the children up. Keep the noise down." She looked at Meredith, "You were at Penny's."

"I was, Mrs Chapman, yes. Would you like me to call her for you?"

"She's in bed, she never gets up until it's time to leave for school." Alice tutted, and came down into the hall. "I'll put the kettle on. I don't know what you were thinking, Keith, it's far too early to have people around. What will the neighbours think?"

Keith Chapman looked out through the open front door at the police squad car blocking his drive. "I don't know, Alice, but we don't care do we?" He looked at Meredith with total contempt, "That woman needs me."

"She needs someone to be with her, I agree. Shall I call one of your daughters? We need to get moving, I can always bring her in too, and get a police woman to sit with her. This is going to take some time, and to be honest, I doubt you'll be coming home, so something needs to be done." He saw the flinch as Chapman realised he might be held overnight.

Chapman's mouth opened, but no words formed. Turning away from Meredith, he hurried up the stairs. Hutchins followed him. Meredith pulled the phone from his pocket and called Susie Mason. There was no reply so he called Penny Brooker, instead. A male answered the phone.

"May I speak to Mrs Brooker please?"

"She's in bed. Who's calling?"

"Who is this?"

"I think I asked first." There was a hint of amusement in the man's voice.

"DCI Meredith, now please bring Mrs Brooker to the phone."

"She's not having a very good time at the moment, I'm reluctant to wake her. May I help? I'm her brother, Henry Chapman."

"You'll do. Mr Chapman, I have just arrested your father and he will be taken in for questioning, I'm reluctant to leave your mother alone, is it possible for you to stay with her please. I'm not sure how long your father will be away."

"Barry?" Henry Chapman murmured.

"I'm sorry?" Meredith smiled. He was right.

"I'll be there in ten minutes. Will you wait?"

"If it is ten minutes."

True to his word Henry Chapman arrived as promised. Meredith stood on the doorstep with Alice.

Henry looked at his father who was being led to the patrol car by a uniformed officer.

"Dad," Henry nodded acknowledgment.

Meredith thought he was smirking. "Does Henry not get on with his father?" Meredith asked Alice.

"Henry has always been headstrong. Too much like his father, neither will allow the other enough space." She held her arms open. "Henry, come in. I have breakfast on."

Meredith glanced over his shoulder and sniffed. He pulled a card from his pocket, before shaking Henry's hand.

"Should you need to speak to me, leave a message, I have a busy day.

Your mother says she's cooking, last time I was here she'd almost set the kitchen alight. You might want to replace the batteries in the fire alarm. Bye, Mrs Chapman, take care."

"You are coming back, aren't you?"

Meredith had no idea where she was heading, so he smiled, "I expect so. Don't forget your breakfast." He hurried away to the patrol car.

~~~

Patsy screwed up the wrapper which had held her bacon and mushroom bap, and allowed Amanda to wipe the drip of brown sauce from her chin.

She turned to Frankie, "When you said it was good, I didn't think you meant that good. If we're still there at lunch-time I'll come back here for one of their burgers."

"Junk food, Patsy. My body is a temple. I was thinking of something healthier."

"I'll buy an apple to go with it. Now, about these post-mortem reports Meredith wanted."

"What post-mortem reports? Is there something else I can help with?" Amanda asked, and tutted when Frankie shook his head as he responded to Patsy.

"What about them?" Frankie emptied his coffee cup, and collecting all their rubbish, walked to the bin and dropped it in. "Grab the water, we'll make a move."

"Did he say why he wanted more work on his desk? With O'Brien, and another possible two here, I'm trying to understand why he'd look for more trouble," Patsy asked as they walked to the car.

"Perhaps he thinks they're related. It was dawn, Patsy. I wasn't interested in engaging Meredith in conversation." He started the engine and pulled out of the layby. "I was barely civil."

"Whereas Meredith was charm personified? I can't see . . . Related? He wants the report on Brooker, doesn't he? I thought that was a heart attack."

Frankie sighed, he'd not told her, she'd guessed, and it wasn't a secret as there'd been a small mention in the local newspaper. "It was. Barry Brooker died of heart failure. The only other issues he had were a bruised face and a missing tooth. Courtesy of DI Wessex, I believe."

"Ex-DI, yes, but why would Meredith . . ." Patsy fell silent as she tried to work out what Meredith was after.

Frankie knew she'd probably work it out, so he kept silent. If he knew what Meredith thought he knew, it might save some time.

Patsy hadn't worked it out by the time they arrived at the cottage, and she let it go as she directed Frankie to the side of the cottage and the driveway. While he and Amanda began unloading his equipment, she went to the mailbox and entered the code given by the agent. The door to the box sprang open, and she retrieved the key. She waved it at them.

"You get set up, I'll put the kettle on."

Twenty minutes later, with three mugs of tea sitting on the patio table, they were ready to start work. They walked around the garden with Frankie.

"And you don't know how long ago this was?" Frankie asked.

"At least ten years if we're right. What are we looking for?"

"Anything that looks as though it has been changed in the first instance. New patio, an area where shrubs and bushes are not as well developed as their neighbours. Means nothing really, they could have just buried them under the vegetable patch which changes every year. But one has to start somewhere. If you were going to bury someone here, as it is now, where would you chose and why?"

"Oh, it's like being on a quiz show, albeit a macabre one," Amanda laughed.

They were a little off centre to the overall plot and Patsy turned full circle slowly, "Away from the main house. Wouldn't want the body discovered because of a blocked drain, or someone deciding to build an extension or similar . . . and, an area that isn't overlooked by other houses. Nowhere there." Patsy discounted the strip of garden immediately behind the cottage which was overlooked by neighbouring bedrooms. "Probably up by that tree somewhere."

"Following your logic so far, which is good, what if the tree needed to be removed?"

"No one would do that, would they?" Amanda queried.

"They might, it blocks the winter sun from reaching the lawn," Frankie pointed to the top of the side lawn, the growth was sparse and the edges brown, "that area won't get any sun at all in the winter."

"In which case, they'd cut it down leaving the stump for the children to climb on. Sticking with my plot, where would you choose Amanda?"

"I'd probably choose an area where you could lay a patio that wouldn't look out of place, so they were buried and slabbed over. What about you, Frankie?"

"I wouldn't have to, I could never take a life. How dare you?" Frankie laughed. "Grab that blue rucksack and we'll start with Patsy's choice."

Frankie lifted a large square bag and walked over to the area pointed out by Patsy. Opening the bag, he removed a bag of metal pegs and a large roll of tape. He handed some pegs to Amanda.

"Let's get the grid started. We'll start here, marking three-metre square areas. If we have no joy, we'll work that way." He pointed back towards the house. "You see that area where the grass is greener, I'm wondering why?"

"Because nutrients from the body could be feeding that grass, right?" Amanda nodded, "I remember this from a course I did."

"Well done, that and it's a little lower than the surrounding lawn. Which could mean the soil has collapsed a little as a body has decomposed."

"If that's what you think why not start there?" Patsy queried.

"Because you suggested here, and we'll have to do the whole site anyway. You may think there is a body or two, but why not three or four?" He produced a rubber mallet from the bag and banged in the first peg. "No shortcuts, girls, I'm afraid only methodical, continual graft. While Amanda and I get the first grids pegged out, you get on the internet and see if there are any aerial photographs of the area other than Google, which might show changes."

Patsy pulled her phone from her pocket. "I'm going back into the house, there's a code for the Wi-Fi in the kitchen. Shall I put the kettle on?"

"I thought you already had." Frankie tutted, "Can't get the staff."

Frankie and Amanda continued to mark out a grid with the pegs. Once they had set out the first ten squares he collected the roll of tape, tied it to the first peg and wound it out to the second, looped it around and repeated the process, as Amanda finished hammering in the last peg. As Frankie tied the tape off on the last peg, he noticed something sticking out of the ground. He sent Amanda to collect a small scraper and brush. Amanda watched as he brushed away the surface dirt and scraped away at the surrounding soil.

"What do you think it is?"

"Definitely bone, but now I've revealed a little more, I think it's going to be animal not human."

He lay flat to look at the item before he dislodged it. He was right, it was the leg bone from a lamb, probably buried by a dog. Propped up on his elbows, he looked at Amanda, "I should have known it was never going to be that easy. Hang on."

Still lying on the ground, what he did discover excited him. From his low viewpoint, Frankie could see that the apparently flat area of gravel situated between the garage and the shed had a small rise in the centre. Getting to his feet he walked closer. As he approached, the area appeared flat to the naked eye, so minor was the bump. "That'll be next," he told Amanda. "You might want to start pegging here. But do the centre first, but make it larger, say four metres square, dead centre."

Patsy reappeared with fresh coffee, and Frankie sipped it as he explained his plan of attack to Patsy.

"We'll start where you suggested, work down to the greener area, and rather than stick to the garden itself, I want to take a look over there. We'll have to clear back some of the gravel, so your next job is to go back to the car and get a shovel. Check the shed too, see if there's a yard brush. Amanda can start taking soil samples here, and I'll get on the GPR and run the metal detector over the first section."

"What's GPR, and why is that area of gravel of interest?" Patsy asked.

"Ground penetrating radar, that gravel is raised in the middle. You can't see it unless you're flat. Lie down and look."

Patsy smiled as she got back to her feet. "I want to start there now. Mind you, I suppose they might have been lazy when preparing the area before they put the gravel down."

"All in good time." Frankie glanced at his watch, "A little after seven. Let's get going."

~ ~ ~

As the seven arrested men were bought to the station, they were taken to preassigned rooms, before being taken to the custody sergeant and booked in one by one. Meredith didn't want them to have the opportunity of communicating with each other before the interviews got underway. Although Chapman's solicitor had been put on notice, he didn't arrive at the station until Chapman had been sitting in a cell for over an hour. While he waited, Meredith observed parts of the other interviews.

"But, Mr Sampson, in your original statement you said you'd been home for most of the evening, and only went out late because you'd received *a* phone call. As this shows," Rawlings tapped the piece of paper listing the times and order of calls made between the group, "the first call was a little after eight. You then proceeded to make and or receive a further eight calls, all from the group who conspired to murder Aiden O'Brien. Can you explain that please?"

"Call me Eric. So I spoke to my friends arranging to meet for a drink? That's no big deal, and certainly not a conspiracy." Eric's laugh was throaty, "You can't just make these things up."

"I think you'll find that it was Keith Chapman making things up. Aiden O'Brien had found out something that would put him away for life. He used Jason's Justice to do his dirty work."

For a brief moment, Eric's brow furrowed before he shrugged again. "Listen to me carefully, I was nowhere near the man when he was stabbed. Check the footage, I can't keep repeating this. I can't."

"Did you -" Dave Rawlings began, but Eric banged his large hand on the table.

"No, no, no. No more questions, no more answers. I want a solicitor, I want you to show him the footage from that bar. Then I want you to explain why I'm being accused of murder."

"You were arrested for conspiracy to murder. We know Chapman set this up, and if you cooperate, given the circumstances and your personal connection to Jason, I'm sure it will be taken into account, when sentence is passed down. Now, did you or did you not receive a call from Keith Chapman using this number?"

Rawlings tapped the relevant entry on the document.

"I said no more. I want a solicitor." Eric leaned back on the chair, and folded his arms across his chest.

"I'll go and see who's available. Interview suspended at seven twenty." Dave hit the button on the recorder and looked at the uniformed officer sitting in the corner of the room, "Coffee?" The officer nodded. "What about you, Eric? Do you want something to drink?"

"I want a solicitor. Thank you."

Dave left the interview room and was surprised to find Meredith waiting. "No joy with Chapman?"

"His brief is late, I'll have a coffee, I'm going to see how Trump is getting on." Meredith walked back into the room from which all the interview rooms could be monitored. He hit the speaker button for room three, and pulled the screen to face him.

"Were you surprised when Mr Chapman called and said he'd discovered another member of the paedophile gang?"

"I would have been if he'd called." Marcus White did not look as relaxed as Eric, but his voice was calm and level.

"And when you took that call, why did you then immediately call Eric Sampson?"

"Me and Eric, we speak all the time. You have my records, you check."

Trump tapped the document listing the order of calls, "We know this number is Keith Chapman, so I ask again, were you surprised, did you not grasp at the hope you may find out what happened to Jason?" Trump looked down at his pad. He couldn't imagine the pain this man had already gone through, and he didn't want to talk about Jason Sampson if he could help it.

"I know my son is dead. I know it would have been a horrible death, that and the fact that I didn't protect him will haunt me for the rest of my days. I've had a vasectomy you know, to make sure I don't have more children I don't protect, so even if someone had called, the last thing I would want to know is what happened to him. My nightmares are bad enough." Soulful eyes stared into Trump's, "Do you understand?"

Trump cleared his throat. "I do. Was the plan to simply punish him, to take his life as he had possibly taken the life of your son?"

"That's not what I said," Marcus shook his head slowly.

"No, you didn't. You haven't said a lot about anything, and that's what worries me. Others are being far more vocal." Trump tapped the document again, "You get a call from Mr Chapman, and then call Eric, why?"

"I probably wanted the recipe for shepherd's pie. He cooked dinner for me on Monday. It was lovely." He smiled, "Appearances can be deceptive, Eric is an excellent chef. He can make an old recipe new by adding odd ingredients, for instance, a little bit of chilli oil in a chocolate bombe. Wow. Mind you, I wouldn't attempt it, I can only just fry an egg."

"Me too. It's an odd phenomenon, one person can do exactly the same thing, or so they think, to the same set of ingredients, one is a triumph, the other a disaster. One of life's mysteries. After calling Eric, you hung up and almost immediately called Mr Gregory, Sammy's uncle, he then called his brother. Why was that? What did you say he felt he needed to share? I see he called you back after speaking to his brother."

"I can't remember the detail, but it was a hello how are you, type of call, told him I was meeting Eric for a drink later if he fancied joining me."

"Was it a form of reunion, or a meeting?"

"In what way?" Marcus picked up the clear plastic cup of water and sipped it

"All of the people in the group you were drinking with were in some way connected to Jason's Justice, the only one who was involved in the calls who didn't turn up was Keith Chapman, all of them. Everyone. If you didn't go there with the express intention of murdering Aiden O'Brien, one has to assume it was a meeting or a reunion. A jolly one, certainly. I've seen the evidence."

"Have you?" Marcus leaned forward and linked his fingers, forearms resting on the table.

"I have yes. The footage from the camera above the bar shows one and all really having a good old laugh. Whatever the reason you were there, you were certainly enjoying yourselves."

"And this footage shows me near the bloke that got stabbed? I don't think so, as I recall I was leaning on the bar at the time. Have you checked?"

In the next room, Meredith cursed, "Bastards have got this off word perfect." His attention was drawn away from Trump's next question when George Davies put his head around the door.

"Chapman's brief is here. He wanted a word before the interview commenced, so make sure you knock."

"I always do, George. Where is Rawlings with that coffee?"

"He's back in the interview. Duty solicitor went straight in. I'll go and grab one for you."

Meredith thanked George and went to interview room four. A uniformed officer who had been asked to leave stood guard outside. He didn't knock.

He nodded acknowledgement to the solicitor and took a seat.

"Excuse me, I'm taking my client's instruction," the solicitor looked at Meredith as though he were an errant school boy.

"About what? He's been arrested on suspicion of conspiracy to murder, and we've not exchanged a word as yet, therefore it can't be about that." He smiled as he opened his file, "I haven't got time for Mr Chapman to carry out his personal business, that will have to wait."

The solicitor looked at Keith Chapman, "Are you happy to proceed?"

Chapman nodded, and Meredith hit the button on the recorder. He made the usual announcements, and repeated the caution for good measure.

"Now, let's get straight to the point." Meredith slid the telephone listing across the desk. "We know that at the beginning of this trail, the telephone shown here, and highlighted throughout in yellow, belongs to you." He pushed a second sheet forward, "And this, is your listed mobile, highlighted in blue, when we combine both," the final sheet was placed on top of the other two, "we have a clear time line, of who spoke to who and when, and it all began with you. Is there anything you would like to say at this stage?"

"Only that I have absolutely no idea what you are getting at. I -"

"Mr Chapman . . ." The solicitor placed his hand on Chapman's arm.

Meredith sighed. The bastard was going to go no comment. He carried on anyway.

"You will note that the calls you made to Marcus White, and later Eric Sampson, were quite lengthy compared to those that then pinged back and forth between the others in the gang. Can you -"

"Gang? What gang?" Chapman shook his solicitor's hand away. "You've lost your mind. Do you know what those people have been through, what their families have been through?"

"I do, yes, which is why I am shocked, no, disgusted, that you could encourage them to such folly, and just to protect your own back. To clean up your mess."

"What mess?" Chapman spat the words, but Meredith noted the twitch in his cheek.

"Do I need to spell it out, Keith? May I call you Keith?"

"No, you may bloody not. Yes, spell it out." Chapman turned sharply to face his solicitor, "Will you please stop nudging me!"

Meredith held back his amusement. "Let's go back to why Aiden O'Brien had several conversations with you in the week leading up to his death, the final one being early evening on Thursday the third? That was when you called him – here." Meredith indicated the call with his pen.

"It was business. I told you that. We are directors of the same company, we have to communicate."

"And what was that about, I can verify with Rosie O'Brien that you were discussing an ongoing issue."

"A new truck, we were talking about adding to the fleet."

"With what?"

"With a truck! I said."

"You didn't say what make, what size, or why?"

"Ask Rosie, she will know that."

"Funny that, because Rosie O'Brien was present when her husband took that call, she only heard his side of it, but I can assure you, she never heard anything about a truck. Shall I go and get my notes?"

"Do what you want, Meredith."

"We'll be here a while, I'll get them when we have a break. Let's move on to this call. This is Barry Brooker asking Aiden O'Brien to come to the club to speak to you."

"Why? I had no intention in going to the club."

"I can believe that. But that call wound Aiden O'Brien up enough to threaten Mr Brooker. Why was that?"

"How would I know?"

"Because, and this is not complicated," Meredith twitched a smile, "you speak to O'Brien here," he tapped the page, "then you speak to Brooker here," another tap, "Brooker immediately speaks to O'Brien before calling you back here." Meredith drew a line under the call. Are you suggesting that none of these calls were connected, and even if not, that Barry Brooker wouldn't have mentioned to you that O'Brien, your business partner, threatened him?"

"I am. Brooker had a huge ego. He never liked failure."

"In what way would he have failed?" Meredith jotted the word failed on his pad and underlined it.

"In the way that he hadn't intimidated O'Brien enough to be too frightened to make a threat." Once again, Chapman spun around to face his solicitor who had placed his hand on Chapman's arm, "What do you want?"

The solicitor looked at Meredith. "DCI Meredith, I am asking you to suspend this interview to enable me to speak to my client."

"Is that what you want, Mr Chapman?"

Chapman closed his eyes and sighed, "I suppose so."

"Okay. I am suspending this interview at eight forty-five. Shall we say twenty minutes?" The solicitor nodded. "A uniformed officer will be outside should you need me before then." Meredith got to his feet, and hand on door knob, turned back. "Oh yes, just so you have something other than phone calls to discuss, I should let you know I've requested a further post-mortem on Barry Brooker, amongst others."

The furrow in Chapman's brow were so deep his eyes almost disappeared into his forehead. Meredith didn't wait for a response. Instead, he went to the incident room. Rob Hutchins looked up as he entered the room.

"Anything yet?" Meredith asked.

"Not yet, they're all still at it. Chapman?"

"Talking crap, but we'll get there. Solicitor is jumpy though."

"That's a good sign, isn't it? Couple of messages on your desk. One from a bloke called Burt. He said tell Meredith to listen to his effing messages."

Meredith smiled. "Then I better had. Any biscuits to go with that coffee you're going to make." He glanced at his watch, "Another hour before we suspend the interviews and have the bacon butties I've ordered."

He went to his office as Hutchins went in search of biscuits. He'd had two missed calls from Burt. Meredith had called him the night before to let him know Chapman was being arrested the next morning. He listened to Burt's message and jotted down the salient points. He dialled Patsy, she picked up as he was about to hang up.

"What news?"

"None as yet. I did say I'd call as soon as." Patsy glanced around. "At a guess, I'd say we've not even done twenty percent of the garden yet, might be a while before you get a call. How's your day going?"

"Pretty much as expected, Chapman's solicitor asked for a break to consult, euphemism for telling his client to button it. Not that he's said much, but he is getting wound up, so there is hope. To make it more interesting, I gave him something to think about while we were apart."

"Like you're going to be looking a little closer at Brooker's post-mortem? And, before you complain, Frankie said you wanted two reports, and it took me a while but I guessed it had to be related to the case. That's Brooker, but I can't for the life of me guess the second."

"That's because I'm brilliant and you're not." Meredith didn't enlighten her. "Our friend Burt has sent some interesting info through, is that a female voice calling to you? I thought it was just you and Sherlock there?"

Patsy waved her hand at Amanda and pointed at the phone. She ignored Meredith's question and asked, "What was it, the information from Burt?"

"Too long and involved, I'll leave you to it, I'm going back in with Chapman. I'll have my phone on the desk so I'll see if a call comes in. Happy digging."

"Why thank . . ." Patsy realised Meredith had gone, and slid her phone back into her pocket. She called to Amanda, "Sorry Amanda, that was your father, it was easier than explaining. What did you want?"

"Frankie wants to see if there's another shovel and broom in the car so we can start preparing the ground for him, do you have the key for the shed?"

"On the hook in the kitchen I think, I'll go and get it."

Ten minutes later, while Frankie worked his way across the grid, the two women were scraping away the top layer of gravel and placing it outside the grid area. It was hard work the gravel was deep, although they were only allowed to move the top four inches, and they had started running out of space where to put the gravel, when Frankie gave a shout.

"We've got something here," he called. "Spade please."

Amanda hurried forward with the shovel.

Frankie shook his head, "Not a shovel, a spade. I need to take the turf off the top."

"I didn't realise there was a difference. What am I looking for?"

Frankie pointed across the garden to where his own spade was propped against the fence, "That."

Amanda inspected it as she carried it back. "I never knew that before. I can see the blades are different now. You live and learn."

"This is the greener grass, Frankie, it seems you were right."

"Don't get too excited, it's only an indication, but I'm guessing possibly a rib cage. But there is certainly something down there."

The two women stood and watched as Frankie removed the section of turf. He was very careful and rolled the turf and stacked it neatly before doing the next one.

Patsy walked closer. "You're being very meticulous, Frankie. I'm sure if there is a body, and it had nothing to do with the owner, they will understand if their lawn has been damaged, and if they are involved, well who cares?"

"Because, Patsy, if there is something worth finding down here, every inch of soil above will need to be processed, you never know what clues could be hiding there. Neatness avoids mistakes."

"That told me."

"What time is it?" Frankie looked over his shoulder before he attacked the last strip of turf.

Amanda checked her phone. "Almost nine, why?"

"Because I'm hungry again, but we'll give it another hour." He placed the last roll of turf on the pile. "Now we need some buckets for the soil I'm going to move, I've got ten, fourteen litre buckets in the back of the car, I don't suppose there are any more in the shed are there? Otherwise, we'll have to bag some of it, and that's tedious."

Patsy went to look, and Amanda and Frankie began carefully removing the first layer of soil, and spade by spade they dropped it into large sieves and filled the buckets one by one. Patsy paced around, unable to help, frustrated by the delay in discovering what lay beneath.

~~~

Meredith carried his coffee back into the interview room, and smiled at the two irritated men sitting at the table.

"I'm assuming we're ready to recommence, did you want a drink?" he held up his mug.

"No, thank you." The solicitor rearranged his papers.

"Having spoken to my client, I should tell you, that he has no information that would be of use to you. He wasn't at the club, he has no knowledge of this phone number which you suggest brings your case together, and therefore I would respectfully suggest that we call it a day, and that you release my client."

Meredith ignored him, and sitting down hit the recording button. He took a further sip of his coffee before placing it on the table.

"Interview with Keith Chapman recommenced at," Meredith made a show of looking at his watch, despite the presence of a large clock on the wall above the recorder, "nine thirty-three." He smiled at Chapman, "It's all arranged, I'm hoping for the results by mid-afternoon," he lied. "But we'll discuss that then."

"I have no idea what you are talking about – again. But, whatever it is, I have no intention of being here this afternoon. You heard what my solicitor said."

"I did, but releasing you before you tell me the truth would be stupid. Particularly as once you tell me the truth you will be charged. I'm many things, Mr Chapman, but stupid isn't one of them. What do you think the second post-mortem might reveal?"

Chapman sighed and the whites of his knuckles showed as he clenched his fists.

"We both know my son-in-law had some form of panic attack which led to heart failure at the dentist, that's what it will reveal. I have no idea what game you are playing, but it's tedious and unnecessary. I need to get home to my wife."

"Mr Chapman, I am going to say this very, very, slowly. You will not be going anywhere; your children will look after your wife. If you see her again it will be across a table in a visitor's room, or maybe in court. What you need to worry about is cooperating with this investigation, who knows, if you explain your actions then the others who have been dragged into your world may get lesser sentences, but you will all be charged, and you will all serve time for killing an innocent man."

Chapman banged his fists against the table causing Meredith's coffee to slop onto his pad. "I was at home. AT HOME! I refuse to answer any more questions."

Meredith shook his head as he got to his feet. He held up his finger, "One moment." Opening the door, he called to the uniformed officer. "Get me a cloth please, Mr Chapman has spilled my coffee." He closed the door and sat back at the table and looked at the recorder. "For clarity, Mr Chapman's show of temper has spilt coffee over the table, I have requested an officer to bring something to clear it up. We are awaiting his arrival." He looked at Chapman, "Won't be a moment and then we can get on with it."

"No comment."

"On what? The officer's time of arrival, or getting on with it?"

"No comment."

Chapman's stare was cold, Meredith could see that he had brought his temper under control and was ready to follow his solicitor's instructions.

"Taking the no comment route will simply delay the inevitable. Would you like to hear my theory on Mr Brooker's death?"

"No comment."

"I think he knew too much. I think he became a threat. I think you needed him out the way."

"DCI Meredith, you have clearly been doing a lot of thinking, or possibly better described as dreaming. You bring my client in here in connection with a murder he couldn't possibly have committed, and with no evidence of his involvement, you are concocting a reason he may have been involved in his relative's untimely death. This is a waste of our time. Please stop telling us about your fantasies, and release my client." The solicitor gave his pad a sharp tap.

Meredith leaned back in his chair. It was interesting to see the solicitor was getting as wound up as Chapman.

"I can't do that, as well you know." He returned his attention to Chapman, "Was it because you gave him something to hold over you? Was that it?"

Chapman's gaze intensified for a moment, and in that instant Meredith knew he was on the right track.

"No comment." Chapman's shoulders relaxed, and the look or irritation was replaced with boredom.

"I clearly need to spell this out because once your solicitor understands the depth of the shit you're paddling in, he might advise you start cooperating."

"No comment."

"What did Barry Brooker threaten? Or perhaps he asked for something? Did he push his luck a little too far, or did you perhaps ask him to do something that even he wasn't comfortable with?"

"No comment."

"You see, I know you killed him somehow, and I will find out how, I promise you that."

"Are you seriously suggesting that -"

"Keith, please." The solicitor lifted his hand to place it on Chapman's arm, it dropped back in his lap with one glance from Chapman.

"Shut up, I've had enough." Chapman jabbed his finger at Meredith, "This idiot is suggesting that I somehow orchestrated his colleague to seriously assault my son-in-law, to the point that he had to see a dentist, because I knew that being frightened of the dentist may – MAY – mind you, bring on a heart attack. The world has gone mad. Get me out of this fucking place before I go mad too."

Impassive, Meredith continued, "You didn't . . ." he wound his finger in circles, "you didn't do any of that?"

Chapman's head slumped. He sighed and raised his eyes to Meredith, "No comment."

"I'm not sure about DI Wessex's involvement, it might have been a lucky fluke, but I think Brooker's days were numbered with or without that. You simply got lucky."

"No comment."

"So convinced, am I, that you managed this somehow, I have our top forensic man looking into the death of Michael Flood too. I'm hoping he was buried, not had time to find out yet, because then we can take another look at him."

Chapman's teeth were clamped shut and his head twitched with an effort to hold his temper. Eventually, he uttered 'no comment' through gritted teeth. He wrapped one hand around the fist he had made with the other, his index finger tapping it repeatedly.

Meredith glanced at the clock, only a few more minutes and he would leave them to stew. He placed his hands flat on the desk. "I can see you're not happy talking about this, let's choose another subject. What about the Devonshire Boys' Sailing Club? Were you a member?"

Chapman's arms flew wide, one of them hitting his solicitor who was knocked sideways.

"Why is that relevant?" he shouted. "Why are you interested in discussing my childhood? No comment, no fucking comment, you moron!"

"Naturally, I've done some checking into your background, I was trying to understand why you would donate so much of your hard-earned cash to Jason's Justice group. It didn't add up. Mainly, I confess, because that would make you one of the good guys, and we both know how far from the truth that is, and guess . . ." There was a knock at the door and Meredith stopped speaking as George Davies appeared. "What is it?" Meredith snapped.

"Sorry to interrupt, sir. It's just we have a development you need to know about."

"Can't it wait?" Meredith shook his head in irritation.

"Not really, we have a confession for the murder of Mr O'Brien."

Meredith leaned back in his chair. "Well, that does warrant my attention." Smiling at Chapman he leaned towards the recorder, his finger poised on the button. "Sergeant George Davies has entered the room to advise a confession has been given in relation to the death of Aiden O'Brien. Interview suspended at ten-o-five." He stopped the recording. "I'm not sure how long this will take, I'll have some water sent in." He didn't wait for their response, but hurried from the room.

Once outside, he smiled at George, "Is it ready, because I could eat a scabby horse?" he asked quietly.

"Yep, as ordered. I've still got two to do, I'll see you up there," he jerked his head down the corridor.

Meredith nodded, shoved his hands in his pockets, and walked quickly towards the stairs that would lead to his much-needed breakfast.

18

Tania Davidson paced up and down her sitting room, her phone clamped to her ear. Ben Jacobs watched silently. He felt sorry for her, but he knew she wasn't looking for sympathy. She needed to vent her anger, and he had enough on his plate without putting himself in the firing line. Tania hung up and threw the phone onto the couch in frustration.

"Argh! I swear to God. As if I didn't have enough problems!" She rounded on Ben, "You're going to have to go. With Alex on his way home early, you won't be able to stay here, not even on the couch. Phone your girlfriend and see if she will put you up."

"Okay, okay. I will do. I know you can't see it at the moment, but you will come out of this better off you know." His smile lasted seconds.

"Really? I mean, really? They're talking about closing the club. Penny Brooker said it would stay open, but Dan tells me Keith says no. I'm probably out of a job. Keith has not paid this month's school fees and they've written to me, how embarrassing is that? I have to see the bursar on Monday morning. And that bastard thinks he can ignore my calls. On top of which I'm harbouring a wanted man. And I don't give a shit that your friend is a copper. He could be bent for all I know. My life is falling apart, so do I feel I'm better off, strangely enough, no!" She glanced at her phone. "Alex will be home in a couple of hours. I want this sorted before he arrives, it's bad enough his holiday was cut short because his cousin is poorly."

Tania retrieved her phone and called Keith Chapman for the fifth time. His answer machine cut in again. She shouted her short message.

"Enough is enough. I've played the game, and you can't decide when to take the ball home. You have two hours to call me, or then you'll have to do something." This time she placed the phone on the coffee table and looked at Ben. "I'm not having it anymore. I'm not playing." She checked the time, it was nine o'clock, "Pack your gear up, and make your call. I need to change his bed, it'll stink of your cheap aftershave."

Ben nodded and got to his feet, wishing he'd not handed her the post that morning. "It's not mine, it's Meredith's," he nudged her as he walked past. "And for the record, it's not cheap." He smiled his perfect smile and Tania's lips twitched.

"Well he was robbed," she pushed him into the hall, "now get sorted. Apart from anything else, I need to get more shopping in."

"I'd offer to do it for you, but . . . I will strip the bed off though."

"Call Hannah first, she'll need to pick you up, I haven't got time to become a taxi service."

"Will do, I need to let Meredith know too." He pulled the phone supplied by Patsy from his pocket and called her. He was still under strict instructions not to speak directly to Meredith. Her phone gave a brief engaged tone and he was disconnected. He dialled Hannah, it went to answer service. "I think everyone else is on holiday except for us. That or they've been abducted by aliens. I'll leave . . . Oh hi, Hannah, it's Ben. Sorry to ask, but I need a bed for a couple of nights, say no if you don't want to, I wouldn't want to impose. Speak later. Bye."

"You bloody well do want to impose. Go and strip that bed and bring it down for the wash, I need a ciggy." Snatching up her phone she went to the kitchen.

From the bedroom window, Ben watched her pace up and down the path that led to the top of the garden. She ground out the cigarette, and pulled out her phone. Whatever message had arrived, it was clearly not what she wanted and sliding her phone into her back pocket, she lit another cigarette. Ben got on with the task in hand, and ten minutes later was carrying the dirty washing, and his bag of meagre belongings down, when the doorbell rang. He paused on the final stair, glancing over the banister in search of Tania. She was obviously still in the garden. Ignoring the door, he carried the washing into the kitchen and put it in the machine. Tania was halfway down the path when her phone rang. Ben stopped and watched her. He could tell it wasn't Chapman, she glanced up frowning and beckoned him out, before terminating the call.

"My sister is here with Alex. She won't stop as she needs to get her kids home, but I don't want Alex seeing you here. You stay out here, I'll get him sorted and take him out for half an hour. You may disappear in that time. I don't know how, or where, but if you're here when I get back, I won't be held responsible. Do you understand?" Tania was walking back towards the house as she spoke. She stopped at the back door and put her hand on his chest. "Stay here," she insisted and shut the door on him.

Ben took a seat on the back doorstep.

Tania hurried into the hall and opened the door. She knelt to hug her son. "Not having much luck, are we? Are you feeling okay?"

"I'm fine, Mum. Why does everyone keep asking me?"

"Because I'd thought you'd like a trip to the park. What do you think?" When Alex agreed, Tania sent him up to put his rucksack in his bedroom, and stood to hug her sister. "I'm so sorry your holiday was ruined. How's James?"

"Green. He's still got a temperature, but I was lucky with a cancellation so I can take him straight to the doctor. Then it's home and bed. I'd say it was something that he ate, but we've all had the same." A car horn hooted behind her and she tutted, "Tim is worried we'll miss the appointment. I'd better go."

Tania stepped out on to the doorstep and waved them off. Alex appeared behind her.

"Why's my bed got no sheets and stuff on? Have we got any biscuits? I'm starving." He went to the kitchen and lifted the jar out of the cupboard. "Boring," he called with his mouthful as Tania put her coat on. "I'll just get my ball from the garden." His hand was on the door handle as Tania hurried into the kitchen, and Ben, who had been listening, got to his feet.

"Not today. I know the biscuits are boring, we'll do a quick shop. You can choose some different biscuits, and I think we'll have a fried chicken takeaway for lunch. Will that do you?"

"Yes, I'm starving."

"Come on," Tania pulled him towards the hall. "We'll be off. Lock the door." She called out, hoping Ben would hear her.

"What do you mean lock the door?"

"Did I say that? I must be going mad." Tania pulled the door shut and blew out a breath that lifted her fringe.

Once in the car, she decided to get the shopping out of the way and drove first to the supermarket. Shopping done and loaded into the boot, she headed for the park.

"Did you have a nice time?" she asked, as they waited in a queue of traffic.

"Yes, some of it was cool. They had a pool with a slide that was really high, and we went crabbing on the beach. I caught one crab, one fish, and a worm thing which was disgusting. And I don't like Uncle Tim anymore."

"Don't say that, of course you do." Tania turned to smile at him, "Did he tell you off?"

"No, I was good. He was horrible about you, and he used a swear word."

Tania's brow furrowed, and she wondered if her brother-in-law had been put out when Alex became an addition to their holiday. She had promised to cover any expense. "I'm sure he wasn't, what did he say?"

"He thought I was asleep in the car, and he said that you were stupid, I can't remember why, but Dad was . . . and I'm not swearing, I'm only telling you, that Dad was a bastard." His cheeks flushed and he looked at his mother. "That's not nice is it? I bet you don't like him now either."

Tania mumbled an answer and at the next traffic lights, she changed direction. She'd had enough. "I have to go and see someone before we go to the park, it won't take long."

"No chatting, you always say that, and then you start chatting."

Tania forced a laugh. "There won't be any chatting."

Fifteen minutes later she pulled onto the large drive leading to Keith Chapman's house. She parked the car a little way from the entrance in the hope that Alex wouldn't see his father. If he did she'd have to find an explanation, but things needed to be said, and they were going to be said today.

"Stay here, I won't be long."

Tania's feet crunched on the gravel as she marched up to the house. She rang the doorbell and clenched her fist, she had things to say, but not before she'd punched him. He was a bastard, and she was stupid. The door opened and Tania stared at the man standing on the threshold. It took a while before she could string a sentence together.

"I'd like to see Keith please." It came out more like a demand than a request.

"He's not here, I'm afraid, I'm not sure when he'll be back." Henry Chapman looked her up and down. "Is there something I can help you with? I'm his son."

"Have you two kissed and made up? Did he send you out here to get rid of me?" Pushing past him, Tania strode into the hall, she hoped she didn't look shocked. It was huge, and was as far removed from her own home as was possible. She pushed open the door to her left as Henry Chapman, who recovered from the shock, strode to catch up with her. "Is he in here?" She stepped into the dining room and looked around. "No." Turning to leave, she bumped into Henry. She looked up at him, "Your father is a bastard."

"Tell me something I don't know. He really isn't here. I'm going to have to ask you to leave. I don't want my mother upset."

"No, me neither, so he should have had the balls to come to the door himself. What I have to say won't take long."

With an unexpected speed, she stepped past Henry, and headed for the next door. Henry attempted to grab her arm but missed. Tania saw that the study was also empty, so she ran to the next door and found Alice Chapman sitting on the sofa, alone.

Alice looked up at her and smiled, "Hello, are you Henry's friend?"

"Yes, sorry to bother you." Tania backed out of the room and into Henry, who grabbed her arm and pulled her back towards the door.

"I can guess who you are, but I promise you, you won't find him. He's been arrested."

"I don't believe you. What for?" Tania stopped struggling.

"Conspiracy to murder apparently. I have no idea who though. Now, before you upset my mother, who has quite enough on her plate. Please leave, now."

"Why would she upset me?" Alice asked. "Have you two had a row or something? Would you like a cup of tea dear, men can be so insensitive, you're clearly upset."

Henry tightened his grip on Tania's arm as a warning.

Tania smiled at Alice, "Men are all bastards, Mrs Chapman. Your husband being top of the list. When he gets home tell him Tania is expecting a call."

"How dare you, he is not. Strict, yes, but he's a good man. He looks after us and . . ." She looked around her, "Where is he? I can't find him." She started to cry, "He promised me he'd never leave me, has he left me?" Alice walked to Tania and took her free hand, "Do you know where my husband is?"

Tania bottom lip quivered, "No, I'm sorry, I don't. I'll leave you now. I'm sorry if I was rude."

"Don't cry. He hates it when women cry." Her hand flew to her mouth, "Have the police got him? The car was here. I remember a police car." She looked at her son, "Was that today?"

"Yes, Mum. Everything is going to be all right. Tania is leaving now. I'll see her out, and we'll have a cup of tea."

Alice looked at Tania. "Oh, so you're leaving too. Are you Henry's friend?"

"No, I work for Mr Brooker, I needed to . . . it doesn't matter. I'll be off." Tania lifted her chin and pulled her arm from Henry's grasp. She looked at him, "I'm sorry." Thinking of Alex waiting in the car she blinked back her tears.

"Me too, I'll see you out." He turned to his mother, "Put the kettle on." He waited until Alice had turned away, and walked across the hall with Tania, following her out onto the drive. "I take it you're the mistress? We all knew he had one, probably always has, I'm sorry you couldn't get whatever it was off your chest, but he's not worth it." He shrugged, "Of that I'm sure. Be safe."

He hadn't realised his mother had changed her mind and followed him. Alice's brow furrowed as she tried to remember what she had been going to ask. She didn't like it that Henry had a mistress, and she stepped out to tell him so, but her attention was taken by the car driving away.

"Stop. Where are you going with Henry?" She grabbed Henry's arm, "That woman, Tania, she's taking Henry away. Why?" She looked up at her son, "Henry? What's going on? I'm frightened. Where's your father?"

Henry had also noticed the likeness, and he put his arm around his mother's shoulders. If he ever spoke to his father again, he'd tell him exactly what he thought. He turned his mother to face the house.

"I don't know Mum. Let's go and make that cup of tea."

Once in the house, rather than go to the kitchen, Alice headed for the study.

"Where are you going? Don't you want a cup of tea?"

"Coffee, but I have work to do, you can bring it in here."

Henry nodded, if it kept her happy, he wasn't going to interfere. When he returned, Alice was surrounded by files, and he watched her run her finger down a column in a ledger.

She tapped a coaster, "Put it there please. Have you got a pen?"

"Try the top drawer." Henry put the cup down and opened the drawer.

Alice selected a pen. "Thank you, Henry. Off you go, play with your sisters. I need to finish this."

"They're out, Mum. I'll be in the sitting room watching TV if you want me."

"Good boy, Henry."

~~~

Patsy didn't know whether to be pleased or not when Frankie began brushing away the soil around the bone that had been exposed. She pulled out her phone and texted Meredith.

Nothing concrete as yet but we may have found some bones. I'll message as soon as Frankie has excavated them. It's a long process.

"And here's another one," Frankie announced.

Amanda and Patsy leaned forward to see another streak of yellow had appeared in the soil.

"And another. Definitely think this is a rib cage. Amanda pass me that trowel please, the one with the purple handle."

Amanda selected the tool from Frankie's tool box and handed it to him. "Can I do anything? I know there's not room there, but can Patsy and I start the next grid?"

"Are you bored?" Frankie glanced up from his task and smiled, "It's slow work. There that's three exposed, pass the camera again." He took the camera and took several shots of the row of exposed bone and passed it back. "Get the metal detector and go and run it over the grid you marked out on the gravel. Give me a shout if you need help."

Amanda grinned at Patsy, "I've been promoted. Should we clear more of the gravel first?"

"Not until you know it's not got any secrets itself. I'll tell you when." Frankie revealed a further rib, and frowned, but kept his opinion to himself until he was sure.

Patsy followed Amanda down to the gravel, and watched as she slung the strap of the metal detector over her shoulder, and adjusted the settings.

"Centre out, or perimeter in?" she asked.

"Start in the middle. That's where the bump is. You may strike gold early."

Patsy smiled as Amanda walked forward her boots crunching in the gravel. Amanda had only swung the detector in a small arc when she got a positive reading.

"I've got something already, Frankie. Do I look for it before I go on?"

"What do you think?" Frankie called back.

"I think I search as I go."

"And you'd be right. Patsy, you'll need a bucket and the camera. Better get a small shovel too."

Patsy collected the items and returned to Amanda. "Where was it?"

"Here," Amanda swung the detector again, it whined over the original find, and again about a foot away. She glanced at Patsy, "More than one. Hang on, step back a little."

Swinging the detector in a slightly larger arc and walking backwards. The machine whined every ten inches or so over the very centre of the grid. Amanda slipped the harness off her shoulder and placed the detector outside the grid.

"Come on, Patsy. Let's discover what treasure lies beneath. This is a job for two."

Patsy went back to the tool box and collected another small shovel.

"Scoop up just enough to cover the blade, and start a fingertip search," Frankie told her. "Whatever it is there, may be covered in grit or soil. I hope you've both got gloves on, might be some cat poo too."

"Thanks, Frankie. I'll look forward to that. How are you doing?" Patsy leaned over to look. She counted the row of bones so far unearthed. "Oh, my God. I can see it's a ribcage now."

"Getting there, but this is a dog, not human."

"Why are you being so careful? Surely you can just dig it up?" Patsy looked puzzled.

"Because, dear Patsy, we may need to know how it died, it may be related if we find anything else, or, it may have been put there intentionally to hide human remains. Unlikely, but a possibility." He looked away, "Haven't you got something you should be doing?"

"Cheeky. Unpaid labour is what I am. I wonder if Meredith will sign off on my invoice?" she joked as she walked away.

"I said I had a dead dog, not a flying pig," Frankie laughed as he continued his painstaking work.

Patsy knelt beside Amanda. "Ow, this is not good for my knees," she complained.

"Knee pads in box," Frankie called, but Patsy ignored him, keen to get on she scooped up her first section of gravel.

After twenty minutes the two women had found nothing, they had filled the first bucket, and collected a second.

"Are you sure you're interested in this line of work?" Patsy asked Amanda as she stretched out her back. "It's quite tedious."

"I am. Perhaps the detector was wrong. Shall I do it again, do you think?"

"It's not wrong. Keep going," Frankie had walked over to collect the camera. "One side fully exposed, I'm guessing a Labrador, or perhaps German Shepherd, I'm not an expert. Skull is intact." He picked up the camera. Don't let me stop you."

~~~

Meredith glanced at the clock. It was a little past eleven, the men being questioned had been left sitting in the interview rooms for almost an hour. He rapped the table.

"Okay, time to stir it up a little. Stick to the script, only vague clues as to who it might have been. Let's see if any of them will talk." His phone sounded and he read the text from Patsy. That was interesting, but he'd hold off using it for now. He wanted Chapman's confession one case at a time.

Trump was the first back in the interview room, he smiled at Marcus White and the duty solicitor, who seemed quite content working his way through a packet of biscuits. He put them away as Trump apologised.

"Apologies for my absence. There's been a development." Trump hit the record button, "Interview recommenced at eleven-ten. Now, Mr White, you'll be pleased to hear, that someone has confessed to the murder of Aiden O'Brien, but we'd still like to know what you saw." He smiled as Marcus White sat to attention.

"Who confessed?"

"I think you know that already, Mr White. What I need to know is -"

"Whoever it is, they are lying," Marcus White said quietly, and leaning forward Trump held his hands out.

"I'm sorry, did you say they were lying?"

"They are lying," White repeated.

"As you don't know who confessed, how could you possibly know that?"

"Because I did it." Marcus White looked sad, he looked tired, but most of all, he looked what Trump would describe as content.

The duty solicitor swivelled on his seat and looked at White in amazement. He turned back to Trump. "I'd like to consult with my client in private please. He'll be answering no further questions until I've taken instruction. Marcus, hold your tongue a moment."

Trump nodded, "Of course. I'll be outside."

Leaving the interview room, Trump hurried down the corridor to where Meredith was interviewing Chapman. He'd raised his hand to knock when Jo Adler appeared further down the corridor. She was grinning.

"Max Gregory has confessed," she said as she hurried towards him. "Took minutes once I'd said someone else had put their hand up."

"What?" Trump took her arm and lead her away from the door. "I got a confession too."

Dave Rawlings appeared from the room next to Meredith, and they looked at him expectantly.

"You'll never guess what," he looked a little smug.

"Oh, I think we will, Jo, would you like to?"

"Did he confess?" Despite her disappointment, Jo smiled at the look on Rawlings face. "Ours have too."

Trump waved them down the corridor, and waited until they were the other side of the double doors.

"I think we are having a Spartacus moment. Probably best we don't chance any of them overhearing. I wonder who'll appear next?" he glanced through the small porthole window, expecting to see someone else emerge, but all was quiet.

"Bugger," Rawlings shook his head. "Text the Gov, I'll wager Chapman won't put his hands up. He probably planned this."

"Good idea, if he picks it up of course." Trump was already tapping out the message on his phone. "Back to the incident room for now. They can wait until DCI Meredith tells us how he wants to play it."

Meredith's phone vibrated on the table. It was face down. Chapman had just congratulated him on obtaining a confession.

"Now that's settled, and you realise I am not implicated, I take it I'll be free to go?"

Despite wanting to knock the self-satisfied smirk from Chapman's face. Meredith feigned shock.

"Did I say they hadn't implicated you? Mr Chapman, calm, please. Everything will be revealed in the fullness of time." Meredith snatched up his phone as it vibrated again. "Excuse me."

The first message was from Patsy explaining it was a false alarm and the remains were that of a dog. She did say there was another site Frankie was interested in, and she'd let him know promptly. Meredith felt a pang of disappointment. The second message was from Trump. Meredith merely blinked, unwilling to let Chapman see any emotion.

"Apologies, nothing important." He replaced his phone face down on the table. "As I was saying, no one, other than you, has denied your involvement. So, no, you're not free to go. Let's go back to the calls to Barry Brooker. Tell me again, what they were about, and how he knew something was going to happen in the club that night."

"The calls were about nothing, family business and of no consequence. As to how he knew, perhaps he was involved," Chapman held his hands up, "who knows? He can't tell us now."

"You don't seem very upset about the loss of your son-in-law, and yet you had ties to several of his businesses."

"That was business. Have you heard the saying, you choose your friends not your family? I didn't choose him."

"You didn't like him?"

"I tolerated him for the sake of my daughter. The older I get, the more I find I have to tolerate people."

"What was wrong with him?"

"What?"

"Brooker, why didn't you like him?"

"How is that relevant to the murder of Aiden O'Brien?" Chapman demanded.

"Because I believe Barry Brooker died because of Mr O'Brien's -"

"DCI Meredith, whether my client liked his son-in-law or not, and the reasons for that, are irrelevant. Can we please move on to a more productive line of questioning?"

The solicitor looked pointedly at Chapman, and gave a shake of the head. Chapman shrugged. Meredith wanted to go and see if any of the others had confessed. He wasn't going to play their game. He wanted them charged and held until they appeared before the magistrates, at which point he would oppose bail. But what he wanted most was Chapman.

"Let's go back to the beginning. I believe your support of this group is personal. I think it goes way back to the Devonshire Boys' Sailing club. I think that it's highly likely you were abused there, but even if not, that your stepfather was abusing other boys. A shame you've carried, and hidden all of your life. Did he pay them off?"

Chapman's classically handsome face flushed red as he fought to maintain control, his nostrils flared, he bared his teeth and clamped them together, he stared at Meredith for several long moments.

"Are you okay, Mr Chapman? Did I touch a nerve? I asked you a question."

"No – Fucking – Comment," Chapman enunciated slowly.

Meredith asked several more questions and each received the same response. He kept going. His voice neutral, his pitch low. It was the solicitor who asked for a break, and Meredith was glad to agree. He called the uniformed officer in from the corridor before announcing that the interview was suspended and hitting the stop button. Once out of the room, he hurried to find Trump.

"Charge them all," Meredith announced, once he'd had a full account of who'd said what, and finding out that each and every man they had brought in had confessed. "One of them did it, and if they think they can use smoke and mirrors they can think again."

Seaton opened his mouth, but Meredith waved his comment away. "An innocent man was killed to protect Chapman, actually two men. I'm convinced . . . anyway, we'll get back to that. Let's concentrate on this lot first. Their briefs and the CPS can sort out who gets charged with what, but in the first instance charge them all with murder. Not conspiracy, that comes when they start telling the truth."

"And Chapman?" Trump asked.

"Chapman may not go down screaming. But he is going down. I have something I need to look up, you lot get on with it. Any change to their stories come and find me. Oh yes, and someone had better warn George. They'll all be needing a bed for the night."

Meredith walked back into his office and switched on his computer.

M K TURNER

19

Henry Chapman opened his eyes and glanced at the television. An advert with an irritating jingle was urging him to buy better car insurance. Raising his hands above his head, he yawned and swung his feet off the sofa. His stomach was telling him it was time to eat. He glanced at his watch and grunted in surprise, he'd been asleep for over an hour. Still yawning, he went to the kitchen and opened the fridge, he smiled, eggs, cheese, and a nice-looking ham. An omelette was in order. He went in search of his mother.

Pushing open the study door he found it empty. The desk was still in a state of disarray, and the coffee, he'd given his mother, untouched. Walking back into the hall he yelled for her, his voice bounced off the hard surfaces. When she didn't answer, he went up to her room. Empty. He knocked on the door of the en-suite bathroom and pushed it open. Empty.

His hunger was replaced with a gurgle of panic which started in the pit of his stomach. He raced from room to room, she wasn't upstairs, and she wasn't downstairs. He ran out of the back door and into the garden. She wasn't there so he went to the front of the house, and then panic really did set in. The garage door was open, and his father's Lexus had gone.

"Shit, shit, shit," he cursed as he ran back into the house in search of his phone. Finding it on the floor by the sofa, he called Penny and explained what had happened.

"For God's sake, Henry, how hard can it be to look after her? What was she doing before you fell asleep?"

"As I remember it, it was you who insisted on another bottle of wine, and me that left you in bed this morning," he snapped. "I don't know exactly what she was doing, but she said she had work to do. I thought it would keep her occupied, there are files and ledgers everywhere."

"Okay, don't panic. We've told her she has to start writing things down, so that if her mind wanders she can look at her notes and know what or who, et cetera. Check the breakfast bar in the kitchen and see if anything is there." Henry confirmed he was on his way.

"Have we heard anything about Dad?"

"No note, and no we haven't. Bastard, whatever it is, I hope they get him."

"Check the study if that's where she was. Don't be like that, Henry, when all's said and done, he is our father." Penny could hear Henry riffling through the paperwork on the desk. "She had a little red notebook, one with a band around."

"He might be our father, but he's a bully and a bastard, and . . . oh my God. Penny get your arse around here quick."

"What?"

"Do it. Call me when you're in the car, and I'll explain."

Five minutes later Penny called back. "What's happened? Please don't tell me you've found her . . ." Penny's voice broke, fearing the worst.

"No, no. Penny, I'm so sorry, I didn't mean to make you panic." He heard her sigh of relief. "Slow, down, concentrate on driving, we'll talk when you get here."

"No, get on with it. What have you found?"

"Do you know a woman called Tania? She said she worked for Barry."

"She does . . . did. Nice girl. Practically runs the club for him. You'd like her. Why?"

"Not as much as Dad."

"What? Are you saying what I think you are?"

"I am. She came here this morning, I think to give Dad what for, she has a son, he looks like me"

"No!"

"Yes, and it gets worse. Mum saw her and asked why she was taking Henry away, she looked at me, and then . . . well got confused. I calmed her down, made her a drink, and she told me to play with you as she had work to do. I put the TV on and fell asleep. I woke an hour later and she'd gone, along with Dad's car." He thumped the file in front of him, "And I can't find the bloody notebook!"

"I'll be there in five minutes. I'm on the dual carriageway."

Henry was pacing up and down the drive when she arrived. Slamming the car door, Penny grabbed his hand, "Don't panic we'll find her. Let's see what she was looking at." She hurried into the house and headed for the study.

"Bloody everything by the look of it." Henry watched as his sister began moving the files about. She dropped two large red ring binders to the floor. "What are they?"

"Company procedural stuff. Minutes, registration documents, insurance.

Not sure why she got those out. This is the accounts ledger for BB's, that won't help us." Closing the file, she lifted it off the desk. Beneath it was a large ring binder, and it was clear a page had been ripped from the prongs. "Okay, let's see what she tore out."

Henry could see that the next page was a staff registration form. It had the name, address, next of kin, listed at the top, and below various other details relating to that person's employment.

"She's taken her personal details. Could she be going to confront her? Can she hold a train of thought that long? I thought she was getting worse, she puts a teabag in a cup and forgets what she's doing."

"Good days and bad days. But if she's written it down she might remember, it depends how much she wrote down." Penny buried her face in her hands and groaned, "Argh. Where to start." She looked up at her brother, "Do you think we should call the police?"

"I don't know. Probably. She certainly shouldn't be driving. What if she forgets where she's going what will she do?"

"She will call." Penny got to her feet, "She would call. We need to call her." She pulled her phone from her pocket and dialled her mother. It was answered on the third ring.

"Hello, Penny, I can't talk now I'm busy."

"Where are you?" Penny could hear traffic in the background. "Are you driving? Mum, you shouldn't be using your phone while you're driving."

"Then don't call. I have no idea where I am, but the car does, so that's good. I've never used it before, I've watched your father of course, but it's very easy."

"Are you handsfree?"

"What does that mean? Penny, I really should concentrate, I'd better go."

"Where are you going?" Penny heard a horn. "Mum, was that you?"

"Of course not, I wavered a little, the car says I have to turn left, I was in the wrong lane. I wish it would speak to me, it speaks to your father. I have to look at the little screen and I haven't got my glasses on. It would help if I wasn't holding the phone."

"You should have pulled over, you can't be on the phone and drive."

"You're right. Quite sensible. Goodbye." Alice hung up, and peering at the screen looked for the next right-hand turn.

Penny stared at the phone in disbelief. "She's following the satnav somewhere. She hung up on me. I can't call back."

"Call the police, give them the details of the car. I don't think it will help but you never know. We need to find out where this woman lives and go there." Henry lifted his phone to dial out.

"What if she's not going there? You know what she's like. She could be going to pick us up from school for all we know."

"We have to start somewhere, anyway . . ." Henry had dialled the emergency services, the operator answered. After a frustrating few minutes, arguing whether or not it was an emergency, he jotted down the number of the local police station. "Bastards, you'd think they would put you through."

"It would probably tie up their lines. You call the station, I'll call round and see if I can find her address from any of the other staff."

~ ~ ~

Meredith smiled at the screen. "Got you, you bastard," he muttered as he lifted the receiver and dialled Frankie.

Frankie had bagged the dog's remains, and was scanning the area below. There appeared to have been no further disturbances, so he walked across to help the women.

"This is frustratingly tedious work, especially when the detector has told you that you will find something." Patsy brushed her hair away from her face. "This gravel is still at least eight inches deep, this section alone will take the best part of the day if we carry on at this rate."

"Patience is a virtue, Patsy." Frankie lifted the detector and stepped into the grid. "On this one occasion, and to give you something to boost morale . . . I hope, you can shovel one whole section on to tarpaulin, and see if there's anything there. Get out the way."

Patsy got to her feet and Frankie located one of the strongest signals. "Stand there," he commanded, and placing the detector outside the grid, he went and collected the tarpaulin. He lay it on the gravel to Patsy's left. "You will still have to go back and do this properly, but shovel about a couple of feet square around the area you're standing on, until you reach the soil below. Once . . . bugger." Removing one glove, he pulled his phone from his pocket. "That's delightful, it's Meredith, you carry on." Frankie walked out of the grid as Patsy and Amanda started shovelling gravel onto the sheet.

"Meredith, rather busy at the moment, can we keep this brief? And, before you ask, no, we haven't found anything as yet."

"I wasn't going to ask. I've instructed Patsy to call me. I've been doing some research on the internet, and before I go in all guns blazing, I wanted to run my theory by you. I'll tell you what I reckon, and you tell me if we can prove it."

Frankie paced the garden as Meredith explained his theory and asked if Frankie could help him prove it.

"In a nutshell. Highly unlikely, sorry, Meredith, I know that's not the answer you were after. You'll need a witness or a confession."

"I thought you lot could do wonderful, magical, things these days. You can tell what someone ate for lunch a million years ago, but you can't tell me that? Is that what you are saying?"

"Stop exaggerating and I'll tell you why." Frankie looked at Patsy who had called to him, and gritted his teeth. Holding up a finger as he quickly and concisely explained his answer to Meredith.

"Bollocks. Thanks anyway. I'll just have to use my natural charm to persuade him." Meredith hung up and went into the now deserted incident room and looked at the board. He knew he was right, but without proof there was no point in making himself look stupid. All his hopes were now pinned on Wendy's Cottage delivering the goods. He looked up as Tom Seaton came into the room.

"That was quick," he observed. "Lucky though, I've got a job for you." He called to Rob Hutchins, "Pa, come over here. You're going out with Seaton."

"It was quick, because once I'd charged him, the duty solicitor couldn't wait to escape. Apparently, he had other things to do, and we're stuck on no comment. George is processing him as we speak. Where are we going?"

"Give me two minutes and I'll find out." Meredith came back a couple of minutes later, "Pick him up."

Seaton read the note. "On what charge?"

"Murder," Meredith smiled. "Think about it, you'll work it out." He glanced at his watch. "I'm going back in with Chapman."

Leaving Seaton staring at the note, Meredith went back to the interview room holding Chapman. He pulled his shoulders back as he walked breezily back into the room. Chapman glared at him.

"Where's your solicitor?" Meredith asked. "Has he scarpered?"

"In a sense, sir, yes." The uniformed officer stepped forward, "He had prior appointments in his diary, and has gone back to his office for one he couldn't cancel. He assured Mr Chapman, he wouldn't be long." The officer glanced sideways at Chapman. "I don't think Mr Chapman was very happy about it."

"Oh dear, that's a shame. Would you like to continue without your solicitor, or shall we wait?" Meredith smiled.

"No comment."

"That's what I thought. Stick him in a cell and give me a call when the brief gets back."

"You are not locking me up like a common criminal." Chapman jumped to his feet.

Meredith ignored him, and looked at the officer. "You heard the man, remember your manners and shut the door quietly. He's an upmarket criminal."

~~~

"What's got you two so excited?" Frankie stepped over the tape and onto the gravel at the edge of the grid.

"There's some sort of cover. The detector was picking up a stud." Patsy beckoned him forward, "And don't be angry with us, we're novices, but when we cleared the gravel, I pushed my shovel into the earth below and we heard what I suppose you would call an echo. It sounded hollow, so we cleared the earth too." She pointed to a yellow bucket, "We did keep it separate. Anyway, what I want you to say, is that we can get on and expose all of it."

"Let me see." Frankie knelt and inspected the ten-inch piece of wood with a wrought iron stud at one end. He knocked on the wood, and as Patsy had said there was a void beneath it. Standing, he went to collect the metal detector. The two women watched in silence as he swung it over the site. "I think this may be the cover to a well. He replaced the detector and stood looking at the area. Encouraged by a cough from Amanda, he announced, "We'll do it. We'll uncover the whole thing without processing the top matter. But," he held up a finger, "we will keep the materials separate. Get some more buckets over here, and the large shovel."

Twenty minutes later Frankie had cleared the gravel from the thin layer of soil below. As each bucket was filled, Amanda and Patsy took a handle each and lugged it out of the grid. Several empty buckets now sat waiting for the soil. These were filled quickly as more and more of the round wooden cover was revealed. Eventually, they looked down at the circular cover, which was about four feet in diameter, and stood three inches tall. It had a small hole on the end of one of the planks where it had begun to rot.

"That's going to be heavy," Frankie observed. "We won't be carrying that far, let's clear these remaining buckets, and try and lever it up."

The cover was heavy, but not as heavy as Frankie had expected, as it had an inner lip which sat over an inner stone wall. The hole in the centre of the well was a little short of three feet wide. Frankie stepped forward and lying flat put his head into the hole and sniffed.

"Well, not what one would call a pleasant bouquet, but it's not screaming rotten cadaver either. First things first, we need to find out how deep it is. I have an extending pole on the van, I'll go and grab it."

"How are we going to get a body out of there?" Patsy pondered as Amanda also lay flat and stuck her head into the hole.

"It does stink. I think there's water down here," Amanda's voice echoed in the void.

"Well, it is a well." Patsy laughed, "Comes with the territory. I reckon we're going to grind to a halt now. Bugger." Frankie was walking back to them, extending and tightening the sections of the pole. "Amanda thinks there is water down there."

"It's a well." Frankie looked from one to the other. "I'm working with children. Talking of which," he lifted the handle of the bright yellow bucket he carried on his arm. It bore a striking resemblance to one a child would play with on the beach. He secured the bucket to the end of the pole.

"Camera at the ready," he commanded as hand over hand he lowered the bucket. "Each section is two feet long, and . . . two, four, six . . . I have resistance."

The women watched as Frankie pushed on the pole. Frowning, he wiggled it about backwards and forwards with the occasional thrust downwards. After a few minutes, he pulled the pole up. The bucket had an inch or so of sludge-coloured water and some moss from where it had scraped the side of the well. Frankie peered at it, smelt it and detached the bucket from the pole. He handed it to Amanda.

"The well is not full of water. There's some, but that could be rain water that has seeped down. Photograph it, and bag it please. Patsy pass the torch from my bag, the silver one." He lay down again, and having switched the torch on, he lowered his arm into the well, and leaning forwards his head and shoulders followed, obscuring the view from above. "And bingo."

"What does that mean?" Patsy looked at Amanda and grimaced. "We've worked hard all morning to find out if there were bodies buried here, and finding a body would be success. Wouldn't it?"

Amanda didn't answer as Frankie pulled his shoulders out, and placing the torch by his side, held up his hand for the camera.

"Camera. I should've done this first. I blame working with amateurs." Squatting over the well, he lowered the camera lens first into the void. "And take one." The camera flashed and he lifted it up to examine the image, before making some adjustments and repeating the process. "Take two." The camera flashed again.

He repeated the exercise several times, and on take seven, Patsy could contain herself no longer.

"Frankie! What is it?" She stepped back as Frankie grunted and pushed himself upright.

He handed her the camera. "A hand. Which one has to assume is attached to a body. Sorry, Patsy, it appears your clients were right."

"Shit." Patsy looked at the skeletal fingers lying on top of what looked like a sack, small pools of water reflected the flash of the camera.

"How exciting. What happens now?" Amanda took the camera and peered at the image.

"I get a proper team here," Frankie threw her a grin. "And someone has the pleasure of telling Meredith. What time is it?"

"Half past one," Amanda tilted the face of her phone towards him.

"We might get it . . . them, up today if we're lucky. Let's make our calls. I'm assuming Patsy is doing the honours, which means you can start unloading the tent. The two blue bags on the right-hand side." He pointed at his Land Rover with his phone before selecting the number he wanted and wandering off to the corner of the garden.

Patsy peered over the edge of the well. She could see nothing with her naked eye, so she backed away and called Meredith. She left a message.

"We have a hand in a well, which is probably attached to a body. It looks like Chapman did kill one, if not two women. Frankie has called a halt to recovery as he needs more help, I'm going to leave him to it, I need to tell those kids. Call Frankie or Amanda if you need more information, although I think it will be a while before they have anything else."

Frankie finished his first call and Patsy called to him before he made another.

"Hang on, Frankie. I'm going to get a taxi home, if that's okay. I need to go and tell my clients, because this will hit the news once you call the cavalry in. You don't need me, do you?"

"Half a job Hodge. That's what you are. But, no, you are free to go. Are you taking Amanda?"

"No, she's not! I'm staying here. I'll be photographing every stage of this. I take it that's okay?"

"Absolutely, we'll get this crime scene set up, you'd better get down to that shop in the village and get more supplies in. I can't believe we're lucky enough to have facilities on site." He looked at the cottage, as he unzipped his overall and fumbled for his wallet.

"Talking of which, I've left all the keys on the table. I'll try and get back across here, but it will need locking up."

"That won't be tonight, the whole site will be done now, including the house. Call me later, and I'll update you."

~~~

Ross Mason parked next to his wife's car. He'd been hoping she wouldn't be in as he'd not made it home the night before. One drink had led to another, and one lonely divorcee had made him an offer he couldn't refuse. Knowing he had a couple of important clients coming in, he'd gone straight to the surgery. But now he needed something to eat, a shower, and a change of clothes. He opened the door, and stepping inside he listened for movement. Avoidance was going to be his first choice of defence. Hearing nothing, he headed for the stairs.

"Where the bloody hell have you been?" Susie walked out of the kitchen. She looked distraught. "I suppose the question should be, what have you been up to? The police came to see you. I thought they were here because Mum has gone missing with Dad's car -"

"Ha ha. Best thing I've heard all week, bet he's flipping his lid. Good old Alice. I hope she's okay though." He managed another two stairs.

"You don't know do you? How could you, you've clearly been with the latest shag. Dad's been arrested."

"What? Why? There's a long list I know, but was it that Chinese deal?"

"Murder according to Henry."

"Murder! How did they find out?" Ross turned and went to join his wife in the hall. "What's been said?"

"Oh, so now you're interested, and find out what?" Susie lifted her coat from the newel post. "I'll tell you in the car."

"What car? I'm not going anywhere. Tell me now."

"I can't drive, you have to come and help me look for Mum."

"Why can't you drive?" He leaned forward and sniffed her, "Already? Early to be pissed, even by your standards. What did the police say when they arrested the bastard?"

"I had a couple with lunch. I can't afford to be stopped again. If you want to know what the police said you'll have to come with me. *Capisce?*"

"I'm not going anywhere until I've had a shower and something to eat. It would be a needle in a haystack, the traffic is manic out there."

"In which case, you can fuck off and find out what the police wanted yourself. I'm going to call Henry and see if there's any news."

"Henry's back? Bet the bastard was delighted to see him. Was there a punch-up?" Ross was already half way up the stairs. His phone rang in his pocket. "What the hell do they want? I've only just left," he snapped as Susie returned to the kitchen and her glass of wine.

Ten minutes later he crept across the hall, overnight bag in one hand. He could hear that Susie was on the phone. Her pitch was high which meant she was still drinking. He shrugged. Not his problem anymore. Slinging his bag into the back of his BMW he drove off without a backward glance.

~~~

Meredith listened to the message and smiled. He had him. He called to Trump. "Get Chapman's solicitor back here. We've had a development. Tell him we've found another body." He grinned as the incident room fell silent and everyone turned to peer at him. "Briefing in fifteen minutes. Carry on." Turning his back, he dialled Amanda.

"Hi, Dad. How are you. I'm assuming you're calling about our find. Can't tell you much now, actually can I call you back. I'm in the middle of something."

"No, you bloody can't. What are you doing there? I hope it's not to make eyes at Sherlock, he's taken. Don't answer that. Tell me about this hand."

Amanda ignored her father's jibe, and quickly explained the discovery, and its location.

"Good girl. I'll expect a call as soon as you have anything else. Message me some pictures of the scene now, and when they get the body out, I want a photo of it." He looked up as Trump appeared in the doorway. "Got to go. As soon as, Amanda."

"He's already on his way, sir. I've just spoken to him, he'll be ten minutes. May I -" He stopped speaking as Meredith held his hand up, and looked at the messages pinging through on his phone.

"Splendid. Gather the troops, I've got an update. We've got the bastard, Trump. Can't wait to see his face. Close the door, I've got a call to make first."

Burt answered on the first ring. "Meredith, I thought you'd forgotten about me again."

"You're at the forefront of my mind. It's a long story, no detail yet as I have to get back to Chapman, but Frankie Callaghan, Chief Forensic Pathol -"

"I know who he is, we've met. What about him?"

"He's just found a body, possibly two, and there's evidence that Chapman put them there."

"Really? That's better than we hoped for. Put them where?"

"Somewhere called Wendy's Cottage, but specifically, judging by the photographs, down a well. I'm going, but I'll forward what I have so far."

"Hang on a min -" Burt cursed as a recorded message told him the caller had hung up. His phone pinged and he looked at the images sent by Meredith. "Better call the boss. Hope this isn't going to be swept away."

~~~

Peggy Green waved from the doorstep as Patsy walked down the path. Patsy had called ahead to say she was coming, and she could see the faces of the Gary and Sian watching her from the living room.

"Hi, Peggy, hope you're okay."

"I'm fine, but those two are like cats on a hot tin roof. Talk about fidget, they've not kept still since you called. I hope it's good news." The look on Patsy's face told her it wasn't. "Bugger. I'll put the kettle on. They're in the living room."

Patsy dispensed with the usual greeting, and asked the pair to sit down. She started at what she thought was the beginning.

"We believe that some time ago, ten years or so, Sian's grandfather, Michael Flood, helped Keith Chapman bury a body. I'm guessing some form of blackmail was involved to get Mr Flood to agree, but we may never know that. Nor at the moment do we know who the person was they buried."

"My grandad?"

"Yes. That document you photographed wasn't printed in blue font, it was typed on an old-fashioned typewriter, and a carbon copy taken. The blue was from the carbon. Your father didn't write it, your grandfather did, I believe your father found it somewhere. His calls to Gary's grandfather were an attempt to find out if it were true or not."

Sian's hands had flown to her mouth, her eyes glistened, "But, I . . ."

"I know, and I can understand why."

Sian let out a sob, and Gary put his arm around her shoulder. "He thought I hated him." She let the tears flow.

"No, he didn't, but he wanted to know why you were angry. He was frightened for you when you showed him the document. If Mr Chapman had killed . . . twice apparently, he knew you were probably in danger."

"He killed her dad, didn't he? Or arranged it anyway," Gary's face revealed the disgust he felt.

"I think so, yes."

Patsy's voice was low, and she waited until Peggy had placed the tea tray on the table. It sat ignored, Peggy took a seat in the free armchair.

"As you know we found Wendy's Cottage, and we've been searching the site since dawn. About an hour ago, we uncovered a hidden well, and found the skeletal remains of a human hand. We are assuming that the rest of the body is down there, and possibly another below it. The forensic teams are arranging recovery now." She looked at Gary, "I'm sorry."

Gary blinked back his own tears, "Don't be. I hope they can prove it."

"I'm sure they will. As I explained, this is now a police matter, although I will get you what information I can as the investigation moves on. Your grandfather is already in custody, there's no reason for you to stay here now, I have a call to make, but once that's done, I can take you both home."

"Have you told my mum?" Sian sniffed and accepted a tissue from Peggy.

"Not yet. You were my first call. I'll tell her when we get there." Patsy slid her hand into her bag to get her phone, "I'll leave you for a minute, I need to make a call." Her hand swept back and forth in the bag. "If I could find my phone anyway." Tipping the contents on the floor, it was clear her phone wasn't in there. "I'll check the car. Drink your tea."

The phone wasn't in there either, and frustrated she went back into the house.

"May I use your phone please, Peggy? I must have left mine at home. I'll call Linda and get some numbers from her."

"Must have been the discovery." Peggy beckoned Patsy into the kitchen. Once there, she whispered, "Sian's worried about going home. Saying it's her fault her father was killed. I've told her that's rubbish and the only person at fault is whoever started murdering people, but I don't think she wants to go home."

~~~

Alice Chapman pulled over to the side of the road, her heart hammering and her hand shaking. The car had told her to go over a narrow bridge, she hadn't noticed the red light. How the driver of the lorry had stopped in time she didn't know. She leaned back against the headrest and closed her eyes. There was no way she could tell Keith she'd damaged his car. She'd better get home and put it away, she'd not thought about what to have for dinner yet. Deciding she'd go to the supermarket first, she looked to the passenger seat for her bag. It wasn't there, frowning she picked up a piece of paper. Her eyes skimmed it quickly, and her face hardened as she remembered. Keith's mistress had taken Henry.

"Well, Tania Davidson, I'm coming to get him." Alice started the engine.

"At the next roundabout take the first exit, the first exit," the satnav sang out.

"Oh, so now you're talking to me. You didn't tell me about the lorry, did you? That would have been useful. Only five minutes away." Alice tapped the screen. "I'll forgive you. What now?" She snatched up her phone, "Penny, I'm driving. Well not at the moment, but I will be now the lorry has gone."

"What lorry? Mum don't go anywhere. Tell me where you are, and I'll come and drive."

"I don't know where I am, but I'm going to get Henry back, and this is wasting time. He'll be worried, poor mite." Dropping the phone onto the passenger seat Alice drove away.

Penny turned to Henry. "You were right, she says she's going to get you. Someone must know where the bloody woman lives. Give me that file again, we must be able to find someone who'll pick up the phone."

Flipping quickly through the pages, Penny stopped at Ben Jacobs.

"He doesn't work there full-time, just cover at weekends according to this. But it's worth a shot."

Still in an evidence bag at the station, Ben's phone had been turned off, and when the answer service picked up with that message, Penny hit the file to the floor in frustration.

"Get your car keys, we're going to the station."

~ ~ ~

Meredith and Chapman's solicitor were already seated in the interview room when Chapman was brought back from the cell.

Chapman looked at his solicitor, "Very cosy. Am I still saying no comment?" Pulling out a chair he sat with a heavy sigh, "I'll take that as a yes." He looked at Meredith, "No comment."

Meredith ignored him, and hit the record button. He announced who was in the room, and reminded Chapman he was still under caution.

"You 'no comment' away, this is more of an update than an interview. But I felt it best your solicitor was here as he may advise you to speak."

"I'll decide that." Chapman crossed his legs and leaned back on the chair. "Update away."

Meredith nodded. "I have a warrant out for the arrest of Ross Mason, the husband of your daughter, Susie. As far as I know he's on his way to the station."

"I know who he is. Are you suggesting he killed O'Brien too now? I thought you had someone for that?" Despite his smirk, Chapmans eyes narrowed.

"Ross Mason is a practising dentist, and as such has access to adrenaline, which if administered in the right dose, to the right person, will cause death. This is primarily by way of a heart attack, but may also cause a stroke leading to death, et cetera, et cetera."

Chapman opened his mouth to speak, but Meredith held up his hand.

"Hear me out, then you may talk all you like. I haven't actually asked a question yet." It was Meredith's turn to smirk. "Knowing this, many people think it is a foolproof way to murder someone, and so it is, if it's not suspected, and the levels of adrenaline are not checked properly. But I am checking properly. Barry Brooker is undergoing a second autopsy, and as to Mr Flood . . . we'll have to see."

He paused and turned a page in his notebook. He wanted Chapman to believe it was possible after this length of time to trace the origin of adrenaline. Frankie had confirmed it was highly unlikely with either, and particularly with Flood, but how would Chapman know that, he'd only just found that out himself.

"Why, I asked myself, would a respectable dentist want to kill his brother-in-law? What could be the link, I asked myself. The answer is you. So, I've gone back to those phone records, and who should have called Ross Mason, shortly before Barry Brooker arrived for his dental appointment, who was smart enough to grab that opportunity, when former DI Wessex and Brooker had their altercation? Again, the answer is you. I know why you wanted Brooker dead, but I don't yet know what you have on Mason to be able to call on him to despatch people who are a danger to you. Would you like to tell me?"

"Assuming, and it is total rubbish of course, that Brooker did threaten to fabricate some reason I was involved in O'Brien's death, what possible danger do you think Flood posed me? He couldn't fight his way out of a wet paper bag. You watch too many films, DCI Meredith. Your imagination is running away with you."

"No, no. I have the proof on what danger he posed but we'll come back to that. What I'm after first, is what you have on Mason."

"Nothing. You're totally wrong."

"Okay, we'll have to wait and see if Mr Mason is as steadfast as you are. I wonder how long he'll hold out once we've presented the forensic evidence and run through his supply and use of adrenaline?" Meredith cleared his throat and turned another page.

"So, to the reason for the murders of Mr O'Brien and Mr Flood, they knew about the bodies of the two women. The first of which you coerced Mr Flood into burying with you, and the second he found out about and watched you bury in the same location. He was going to tell the police, but you silenced him via your son-in-law and his handy supply of adrenaline. But, he'd taken a carbon copy of the note he sent you." Meredith smiled, "You didn't know that, did you? Not until O'Brien told you. Which brings us neatly to why Mr O'Brien also had to go."

Meredith leaned back in his chair, and stretching out his legs, crossed them at the ankle. Linking his fingers, he stretched and put his hands behind his head, "And that, Mr Chapman, is why you are going to prison, and are unlikely to see the outside world again. How did I do?"

Chapman didn't respond, he didn't even move, except to blink before returning Meredith's gaze.

Meredith looked at the solicitor. "Your client won't be going home tonight, or indeed ever. You might want to let the family know. His wife is not well. Poor old Alice."

"Don't even mention her fucking name." Chapman leaned forward, "This is all conjecture. You have no proof. No adrenaline, no letter, no bodies, NO proof."

"I have Mason," Meredith lied. "I have a copy of the letter," he saw the brief frown and added, "Sian O'Brien thought her father was the one in cahoots with you, and photographed it." He lifted his phone from the desk, "Would you like to see it?"

"If such a document exists, which I doubt, whatever it says could be fabricated. No proof." He ignored the sigh from his solicitor, who had decided it was futile to warn him not to speak.

Meredith smiled, "What about the two bodies?"

"What bodies?" Chapman spun to face his solicitor, "Will you do what you're paid for, and get me out of here? You're a fucking waste of space."

"Mr Chapman, I have advised -"

"I have the bodies." Meredith released his fingers and sat up straight as the two men looked at him in surprise. He was enjoying himself. "When I say have, that's not quite true, but I will do. At the moment, I only have a photograph of a hand. Perhaps you'd like to see that?" He opened the photograph on his phone. "Not long arrived, I'll arrange hard copies for you." He held up the picture for them to see.

"Jesus Christ. You have a photograph of a skeleton's hand. Is that meant to make me fall to my knees and confess?"

"I was hoping so, yes. But, they are getting the bodies out, then there will be DNA tests, et cetera. Eventually, and not necessarily on your knees, I don't see you'll have a choice."

The beads of sweat appearing on Chapman's brow showed he was concerned. But his voice was steady when he responded.

"I'll await your findings. It'll be interesting to hear how you intend to implicate me in that." He pointed at the now blank screen, "Because even if you have genuinely found some bodies, why you would think I had a hand in their death . . . do you not like me, Meredith? I don't think we've met before, I have no idea why you feel the need to fabricate these stories."

"I haven't had time yet, as I've been a bit busy today, but tell me, what am I going to find when I look into whether you have any connections with Wendy's Cottage?"

Chapman paled and became very still. "No comment." He got to his feet, and Meredith hurried to join him. "I refuse to say another word, not even no comment." He looked at his solicitor with contempt. "That useless piece of shit can go, you can lock me up if that makes you happy, but until you put me before a judge and jury with evidence, I shall not utter another word."

"You're still claiming you're innocent?" Meredith inclined his head as though puzzled.

"I am. Enough of this nonsense."

Meredith looked at the recorder, "Interview suspended at three forty-five. Mr Chapman will be taken back to the cell." He leaned over and hit the stop button. "I've got you, Chapman. But as you say, I now need the evidence to back that up. I'd better get to work."

20

A lice Chapman parked at the end of the road. It was narrow, and there were cars parked on both sides of the street, and she didn't want to risk a bump. She glanced at the sheet again. Number twelve. Climbing from the car she looked at the door in front of her. Number forty. Twelve would be some way down. She walked briskly down the road. It was nice to be doing something on her own. Pushing the doorbell, she smiled at the stainless steel numbers on the centre of the door. Her smile fell away as Tania opened it.

Tania froze for a moment. "Mrs C . . . Chapman," she stuttered.

"So you know who I am," Alice's voice was cold.

"Of course, I was at your home earlier."

"My home?" Alice spat, she couldn't believe it. Keith had taken the trollop to their home. "How dare you go to my home."

"I know, it was wrong of me. I'm sorry. I did apologise to Henry." Tania pulled the door behind her, not quite shutting it, hoping Alex wasn't listening. "It won't happen again."

"No, it will not." Alice paused, if she were to get Henry, she'd better not annoy the woman. She smiled, "We need to talk."

"No, I don't think so." Tania leaned out a little and looked up and down the street. "Who brought you here?"

"No one. I drove. I'm not incapable you know."

"I wasn't suggesting . . . how did you know where I lived?"

Alice was flummoxed. How did she know? Her brow furrowed as she tried to remember, when she did, her smile was triumphant. "The car told me. Now may I come in? I'm not accustomed to doing business on the doorstep."

Tania relented, "Go straight through, the kitchen at the end." She held open the door, and when Alice had entered the kitchen she called to her son.

"Alex, I have some business to take care of, play upstairs for a while." Hurrying to join Alice, she decided she'd allow the woman to insult her, and then apologise, and explain it was all over. Pulling her shoulders back she walked into the kitchen. "Mrs Chapman, there's little I can say, except to apologise, and promise you it's over. Finished."

"What is?" Alice screwed her face up. "I don't understand."

Tania was well aware of Alice's illness, and she pulled out a chair and sat next to her. "Can I take you home, Mrs Chapman. Your son will be worried."

Alice banged the table, "That's why I'm here. I'm here about Henry."

"Henry? Let me phone him."

"You can't have him. I won't let you." Alice pictured the face looking out of the car at her. "It's not fair."

Tania naturally assumed she was speaking about her husband. "I know. I don't want him."

"Then why take him?" Alice screwed her hands into fists.

"I'm not going to. Really, Mrs Chapman, I promise you that. He's yours, forever."

"I know he's mine forever. He's my son. But you took him. It's wrong, so wrong."

Tania picked up her phone. "I'll call the house, Henry will be worried." She gasped as Alice's hand flew out and hit the phone across the room.

"Of course he's worried. What did you expect you stupid woman?"

Alice's voice had an edge that made Tania feel uncomfortable. Illness or not, she didn't want her in the house, not with Alex upstairs.

"Mrs Chapman, I'm going to have to ask you to leave. I'm expecting guests, we'll have to speak another time." Getting to her feet she opened the door to the hall.

Alex looked over the banister. "May I have a drink please? I don't want to wait until you've finished. That new programme is on soon."

"Give me two minutes. Back upstairs."

"Are you having a party, I love . . ." Alice saw the boy's feet disappear through the spindles. Without warning she grabbed Tania by the hair and dragged her into the kitchen. "You will not take my son. You will not." She pushed the door shut with her foot. "Don't you make a noise."

Tania struggled to free herself, but Alice was surprisingly strong and she pushed her forward so that she was bent over the table.

"Mrs Chapman, I don't want your son. I came to your house to see your husband Keith." As the words left her lips, Tania wondered if she hadn't stepped out of the frying pan. But it seemed to have worked, she felt Alice's body relax, and the grip on her hair lessened. "Call Henry, he'll tell you."

"HENRY!" Alice bellowed at the top of her voice. "HENRY!" she called again when she received no response.

"He can't hear you. Henry's not here. He's at your house, he'll be worried about you. Why don't you get my phone and call him? It's over there by the sink."

"Do you think I'm mad? The rest of them do. They treat me like some kind of imbecile, and I'm not. I saw him, I saw Henry. I saw him in your car, and I saw him on the stairs." She retightened the grip on Tania's hair. "I'm not leaving here without him."

"That wasn't Henry." Tania's heart thundered in her chest. She had to keep Alice Chapman away from Alex. "That was another boy. Please let me sit down and I'll explain."

Alice yanked her upright, and Tania stifled the groan as she felt her hair being pulled out by the roots. Shoving Tania down onto the chair, Alice darted across the kitchen and pulled a large knife from the block next to the kettle.

"Explain away. Whore."

Anger had contorted her face, and Tania knew she had to keep her talking.

"When I came to your house this morning, who was the man you were with? I thought that was Henry. It's probably why I'm confused."

Alice tilted her head, "That was Henry, my son."

"That's what I thought. Who was the boy in the car? I'm sorry I'm being so stupid." Tania clamped her hands to her cheeks and screwed her eyes shut as though trying to work it out.

Alice didn't speak for a while. She didn't know how that was possible, all she knew was she was right. Her bottom lip quivered and she pointed the knife at Tania.

"You're trying to confuse me on purpose. Well it won't work." Pulling out a chair she sat so her knees almost touched Tania's. She stretched out her hand, and the cold steel of the knife touched Tania's throat. "Tell me why you took my son. Did Keith tell you to do that? Were you going to take them both?" She sneered as a tear travelled down Tania's cheek. "Stop being such a baby. I'm not going anywhere until this is over. I want what is mine. You are not having him."

"Please put the knife down. Ow!" Tania gasped as the knife nicked her skin.

"Don't tell me what to do, don't. I'm in charge."

~~~

Meredith whistled all the way back to the incident room. He'd have a coffee, see what news there was on Ross Mason, and then drive over to Wendy's Cottage. He'd let Trump have the pleasure of interviewing Mason. Rawlings was on his way to find Meredith and met him in the corridor.

"Gov, I've got Chapman's son and daughter downstairs. She's near hysterical. Mrs C has done a runner in the Lexus, and given she's not always compos mentis they want our help in finding her. They've reported it to the local station, but they want the address of a Tania Davidson, and say we should have it."

Meredith frowned, "Tania, you say? Where are they, in the visitor's room?" When Rawlings nodded, Meredith told him he'd deal with it, and hurried down the stairs. He held his hand out as he entered, "Mrs Brooker, what can I do for you?" He shook Henry's hand, "DCI Meredith."

"Is our father here?" Henry asked.

"He is, but he won't be going anywhere. He's facing serious charges. What did you want? I understand it's something to do with your mother."

"Throw away the key," Henry responded, "but first ask him where a woman called Tania lives."

"Do you know who she is?" Meredith asked quietly.

"Apparently his mistress," Penny answered. "That makes little difference, that's where my mother is going, or is there, we have no idea. She's not answering her phone, and she's taken what records we had on the woman. Actually, you'll have it, you questioned all of BB's staff."

"Not her unfortunately. She was away at the time, she didn't witness anything. Why has your mother gone there?"

"Shit," Penny cursed. "Then go and ask Dad. Mum saw her . . . their son, in the back of the car. Apparently, he is the spit of Henry when he was that age, she thinks the woman has kidnapped him." Her eyes searched Meredith's for some compassion. "Please, she's not well as you know. We need to find her."

"Unfortunately, your father has decided he's not going to talk to me. But I may know someone who can help." His phone rang, and he pulled it from his pocket. "Excuse me." Stepping outside he took the call. It was from Peggy, and he knew Patsy was going there, "Peggy, I haven't got time at the moment is -"

"It's me. I'm calling from Peggy's. I've left my phone at home."

"What's Chapman's mistresses address? It appears Alice Chapman thinks she's kidnapped her son. Long story just need the address."

"I don't know it. Ben directed me. It's in Kingswood, off the Downend Road, number twelve I think, but call Ben. Do you have Hannah Godfrey's number?"

"I do. What's he doing there? I thought -"

"Does it matter? Tania kicked him out, couldn't get me, couldn't get you, blah blah. He's not far from Tania's she might need some moral support. I'm taking Sian and Gary home in a moment, I'll call you once I've done that and have my phone."

"Better leave young Mason where he is. We're about to charge his father with murder."

"What?"

"Haven't got time, got to go." Meredith hung up and called the Godfrey house, Hannah answered. "Hello, Hannah, it's Meredith. I understand you have a lodger again. Can I speak to him please?"

"He's in the shower, shall I -"

"Get him out," Meredith smiled.

"I beg your pardon?" Hannah also smiled.

"I don't know why he needs a shower at this time of day, but I, and Tania need his help. It's urgent."

"But -"

"Hannah, do as I say. Walk into the bathroom and give him the bloody phone."

Hannah did as he asked without further comment. Meredith heard her knock on a door, and announce she was coming in as Ben had an urgent call. He didn't see Ben hide his modesty behind a hand towel, or him allow that towel to drop to the floor when he realised Tania may be in trouble.

"Fuck, I don't know it, Meredith. I know where it is, and that it's number twelve, but not the street name. I've never looked."

"Is everyone bloody blind to sign posts. Get your arse over there, and call me as soon as you have a proper address."

"I haven't got a car . . . Oh, okay, I do have a car. Get off the line, Meredith, I have to get a move on."

Meredith hung up and went back into the visitor's room. He smiled at Chapman's children, "I can't give you the address, but I do have someone on the way. They know where it is, but not the street name. They're not far from the area, and they'll call as soon as they get there."

"That's no good. She might be confused. Will you please at least try my father?" Henry paced up and down. "I'm very concerned, very."

Meredith shrugged, "Wait here, but I don't think he will help. He's not feeling co-operative."

"He'll do it for Mum. She's the only one he really cares about. Please hurry."

Meredith cursed as he walked briskly to the custody office. George Davis was sipping a mug of tea.

"I hope you're not bringing in any more. We've only just processed the last lot. I'm knackered and as soon as I finish this, I'll get the missus to pick me up. No bloody bike yet. Your mate Jacobs had better put his hand in his pocket."

"I'll speak to him. Grab the keys for Chapman's cell. I need a quick word."

"You want him in the interview room you mean?"

"No, I mean I want a quick word. You can be my witness," Meredith jerked his head towards the cells.

George led the way to Chapman's cell and looked in before opening the door. Chapman was lying on his back and ignored the clanging of the hatch.

"What do you want him for?"

"His wife has found out about the mistress and she's not all there," Meredith tapped his temple. "She needs to be found, there could be trouble."

"You've had a day and a half, haven't you? I'm hearing tales of bodies in wells." George slid the key into the lock, it made a satisfying clunk as the bolt slid free.

"Tell me about it." Meredith stepped into the cell, "Sorry to bother you, I can see you're busy." Unable to resist sarcasm he smiled at Chapman who ignored him. "I need the address of your mistress, Tania."

"Go away, Meredith. Or have you come here to give me a hiding? I see you've brought a friend."

"Your son and daughter want to know where your mistress lives. It's of no consequence to me."

Chapman sat up and swung his legs over the side of the bunk. He looked at Meredith with pure hatred. "Why? How do they know about her? You small-minded little bastard, did you have to tell them? Did it make you laugh? Tania has nothing to do with my family, and nothing to do with this business. Now fuck off."

Meredith held his gaze, "I didn't tell them, they worked it out all on their own. She paid you a visit, at home." He smirked when he saw Chapman stiffen. "She met Alice, and Alice met your other son. Only she thinks it's a young Henry. She took the records you have at home, and is the only one with Tania's address. She is there now, or very soon anyway. I'm not sure how long she's been gone. She took your Lexus." Meredith stepped back and bumped into George as Chapman jumped to his feet.

"Go and find her. Now. Twelve, Hawthorn Road, Kingswood." Chapman quoted the post code and now stood immediately in front of Meredith. "Quickly man. Quickly. None of this should involve Tania or Alex. What are you waiting for?"

"None of what?" Meredith didn't move.

"O'Brien, Flood, those women. None of it. She knows nothing." Chapman's eyes were wide, and raising his hands, he grabbed hold of his hair, his arms framing his face. "Go."

Meredith knew he couldn't miss the opportunity. "And you do know about it."

"Meredith, please." The plea came via a sob. "I'll tell you whatever you want to know."

"Okay, you tell me, I'll go and find your wife." Meredith turned away.

"George, have Rawlings meet us in interview five, and get Mr Chapman's solicitor back here."

"We don't have time for that. I don't want a solicitor. Quickly now." He almost pushed past Meredith in haste to get to the interview room. "I don't need anyone else there, I'll tell you here."

"You will not," Meredith held the door open, "You'll do it on record. Properly." He pushed open the door to the interview room and Chapman paced to the table. "Two minutes. I need someone else in with us." Closing the door on Chapman, he walked back to George who had already called Rawlings, "You know what to do."

"Twelve Hawthorne. Got it." George nodded.

Meredith went back to Chapman, and encouraging him to sit they waited for Rawlings who arrived a few minutes later.

"Sorry, Gov, I -"

"No need. Sit down." Meredith pushed the button on the recorder. He announced the time, who was present, and that Chapman had refused a solicitor. "For the tape, Mr Chapman, please confirm you have refused legal representation."

"I have. Get on with it," Chapman snapped, his foot beat out a tattoo on the cracked tiled floor in frustration.

"And you are aware that you are still under caution?"

"Yes. I killed Michael Flood. I got a supply of adrenaline from my son-in-law, and pinned Flood down and injected him underneath his tongue. It was not my best day."

"Clearly, and O'Brien?"

"Is that not enough for now, go and get Alice," Chapman thumped the desk.

"I will, I want everything. Who killed O'Brien?"

"I don't know. I knew if I told those men that he was part of the ring that abused and killed their children, his days would be numbered. I didn't know they would do it in the club, I thought they would take him somewhere, I told Brooker to ply him with drink so that he'd go quietly. They decided not to wait."

"But you organised it, knowing full well an innocent man would be killed because of your lies?"

"Yes. Now, can -"

"And Barry Brooker? What and why?"

"He knew what I had arranged and why. O'Brien told him everything, the idiot. He was supposed to simply get drunk while he waited for me. Not that I would arrive of course. Brooker tried to be clever, told me he wanted me out of his life. I had to sign over my interests in all his businesses, and he'd keep his mouth shut. Common council estate fodder, he wouldn't have kept his word. He had to go. Do you see?"

"No, not really. But I suppose having killed once, the next time it gets easier. Is that how it is?"

Chapman considered his words, his eyes filled with moisture, "I'm going to say yes, because that's what you need. Go and find my wife."

"How did you get Mason?" Meredith was amazed, the man who had killed all these people was going to cry. How great must his love of his wife be, to confess to all this when he didn't even know if she was in danger. He pushed home his advantage, "Exactly how did you get Mason to agree?"

"I'd already worked out that was how it was going to happen. Brooker was scared of the dentist, Mason took great delight in teasing him whenever there was an opportunity. Your colleague simply brought it forward, I couldn't believe my luck." Chapman put his hands flat on the table, "There, is that enough?"

"No. Why would Mason agree? I accept, although I don't understand why he would give you the adrenaline, but to kill a man?"

"Oh, I see. Because I owned him. Lock, stock and barrel. He is a gambling, drinking, womanising moron. He put his head in the noose. He got to keep the house, the family, the practice, and I got him." Chapman shrugged, "Simple as that. Fear of what he might lose. He'd never much liked Brooker, it didn't take much persuasion."

"And Ben Jacobs had no part in this, he was simply in the wrong place at the wrong time?"

"No, he didn't. I'd never even heard of the man until Brooker called."

"And finally, Wendy's Cottage. Who did you put down the well, and how was Michael Flood involved?"

"No, no more. Not until you go and find Alice. Not another word." Chapman got to his feet, "Take me back to my cell."

"Sit down, Mr Chapman. I've sent someone. But I'm not going to tell you how she is, or what happened until this is done. You've come too far now. Let's get it done." He saw the hesitation, and watched Chapman pace backward and forwards. "You told me all this to keep her safe. Surely you want to know if she is? Sergeant Davies despatched a car before Rawlings had put his backside on that seat. Now sit down, and tell me about Flood and Wendy's Cottage."

Chapman looked at Rawlings,

"For the purposes of the tape, and I will have you if you lie, is someone on the way to find my wife?"

"Yes, Mr Chapman, they are." Rawlings nodded at the vacant chair, "Please, sit down. The sooner you tell us, the sooner we can find out if they've found her, and how she is."

Chapman sighed, and resigned to his fate dropped down onto the chair. "Where do you want me to start?"

"At the beginning. You talk, we'll ask questions if you miss anything we

252

need to know," Meredith answered. "Was Flood involved in the first murder?"

"No, only in as much as he became involved after the event." Chapman raised a shoulder, "I suppose he was what you'd call a good man, but he got caught between a rock and a hard place."

"Which were you?" Meredith asked.

"Both." Chapman looked at Meredith, "He'd taken delivery of the first five trucks, and I was surety for the finance. I could have pulled the plug. He had nowhere to go, not really."

"Actually, change of plan. Tell me about the sailing club. I know it's involved, but can't for the life of me work out how. Probably doesn't matter much in the scheme of things, but it might help me understand."

"You're right, it's where it started really." Chapman looked at his hands. "My mother was widowed when I was very young. It left us destitute. I didn't understand what that meant when she'd say it, not until she married again. Then it all became clear. We had warm rooms, food on the table, clean clothes that didn't need to be darned. A house with more rooms than we could ever use, and fun. People coming and going, parties, theatre, outings. I was living the dream." He lifted his hand and held his finger against his eye before flicking away a tear.

"What happened?" Rawlings coaxed.

"The bastard that she married took me to the sailing club. He had his own yacht, not huge, but enough to impress a small boy, and he taught me to sail. Being a pillar of the community, they, my stepfather and his friends, took out boys from the local orphanage and those in less fortunate circumstances, to teach them a skill, and give them a treat. I loved it. They were a good bunch. They'd take five or six of us out at a time. Sometimes I went, sometimes I didn't. It was a constantly changing crew. I got the first whiff of trouble when I overheard some of the boys talking. Young and innocent as I was, it didn't take a genius to work out that my stepfather was touching them, and more. I was disgusted. So, I told my mother. She asked if he'd ever touched me, and I assured her he hadn't. Do you know what she said?"

Meredith shook his head.

"Then it must be lies. Dirty lies, I think she said. I was to find out who was lying and tell my stepfather, and he'd put a stop to it."

"Did she confront him?"

"I don't know, something changed in their relationship though. There wasn't so much laughter and fewer parties."

"And you didn't go to the club anymore?"

"I did. It all died down, no one said anything else, and I assumed it had been a lie. But a few months later one of his friends asked me to touch him. I refused and he tried to rape me. We were in the galley, and I grabbed a knife. He laughed at me, and told me not to be so touchy, and backed away. I went up on deck and stayed there. I was bloody freezing, but couldn't risk going down below again. But one of my closest friends from the club was already down there, and I guess he raped him."

"What do you mean, guess? Did he indicate something had happened?" Meredith's tone was soft.

"He did. He came up on deck and he was crying, I could guess what had happened, so I asked him. He told me the man had hurt him. That he was dying. I said we'd tell my stepfather, and he'd sort it out. He laughed through his tears and snot, and told me he'd been there. That he'd watched."

Chapman closed his eyes and rubbed his forehead. "We didn't realise my stepfather had come up on deck. He called to him, told him to stop his stupid stories, or else. The boy, Fredrick Proud, his name was, he was ten, froze, when my stepfather came towards him, he grabbed my hand and I held it. I stepped in front of him and told my stepfather to 'bloody well leave him alone', I think it was. It was brave of me, I was not only standing up to him, but swearing too." Chapman smiled, "It was a small thing, but I felt brave, until he gave me a back hander. Cut my lip, knocked a tooth out, and I was spread-eagled on the deck. They say it's character building. As you know, it didn't do much for my character. Are you enjoying this, Meredith?"

"Not really, no. What happened to Fredrick?"

"He jumped overboard. Once I had been knocked out of the way, he grabbed hold of Freddie. I don't remember the exact words, but to the effect that he'd show him what happened to boys that talked. Freddie managed to wriggle free somehow, my stepfather chased him, and Freddie jumped overboard to escape. My stepfather panicked at first, but then realised it was probably for the best. He told me to look where tell-tales ended up, and to think about that. He went down below to announce to the other boys and his friend that Freddie had fallen overboard. I got up and I couldn't see him, I threw the lifebuoy over where he'd gone in. A futile gesture I thought, but at least I tried."

"Did no one ask about him? There must have been questions asked." Rawlings didn't believe that even fifty plus years ago, no one would have noticed a missing boy, orphan or not.

"The authorities were told. They changed course and called it in ten minutes later. The coastguard came out, and they were questioned once back in port. I heard him tell my mother several weeks later, 'that poor boy has never been found, God rest his soul.' I think if I hadn't heard that, things may have turned out very differently." Chapman fell silent.

"What happened?" Meredith still couldn't see the connection.

"I ran into the room, and screamed liar at the top of my voice. As he chased me around the furniture, I told my mother what his friend had tried to do to me, and subsequently did to poor Freddie, and I told her that he'd watched. I was sobbing as I told her how I really received the injury to my face, and I told her I didn't know whether Freddie jumped or was thrown off by him."

Chapman laughed, "I remember calling him 'your husband' rather than he, or him, I rarely called him father before, although they wanted me to, now I spat the word husband like an insult. At some level I suppose I wanted her to feel guilty too." He cleared his throat. "Then, as they say, the shit hit the fan. She picked up the phone, and told him she would call the police if he didn't tell the truth. And he did. Do you know why he allowed that animal near us? Because he had promised him a decent job within the party. Maybe ending up in Number Ten. At that time, I had no idea what number ten was, but when he told my mother who his friend was she put the phone down."

"Who was the friend?" Meredith asked, knowing he'd probably have been long dead.

"Wilbur Axminster. He was a senior civil servant, a Sir. Knighted for his services to children's welfare. Unbelievable. He was lost at sea himself, several months later. But I'm not convinced he wasn't pushed. I was eighteen or so, before I found out who he was. Immediately after that showdown I was sent away to boarding school, my stepfather was never around during the holidays though, I rarely saw him. They'd bought a flat in the city so he could further his career, and that's where he lived most of the time. For the most part my mother lived in Devon." He glanced at Meredith, "I'm sure you're wondering if I'll ever get to the point."

"Nope. Take your time. What happened when you left school?"

"I went to Exeter University, and there I met Alice. Beautiful, brilliant, wonderful Alice. Alice was everything that had been missing in my life. She was funny and kind, she was loving and sincere. She was with me when I bumped into Freddie Proud. I didn't recognise him at first, but when I saw he was watching us, I stared back. He had a mole, here," Chapman touched a spot below his eye, "and very long eyelashes. He was a good looking young man. I went over and asked if it were him, he confirmed it was."

Chapman smiled at the memory. "I hugged him, I cried, and with a little coaxing from Alice we told her what had happened. It turned out my lifebuoy had saved him. He'd been carried out to sea a way, and was picked up by a French boat. He didn't understand the language, and luckily for him they were going to France. Even when they spoke to him in English he didn't respond. He was mute for four months. He was taken into care in France, eventually adopted by a couple in Bordeaux, she was English, he was French. He laughed when he told me how bright they thought he was learning English so quickly."

"And . . ." Despite his previous assurances, Meredith was becoming impatient.

"And . . . we blackmailed my stepfather. Freddie was a bright boy, he'd written everything down in a secret diary as soon as he had a home. He said it was because he intended coming back and killing them both, but he found out that Axminster had died, and that my stepfather was working with the government. His adopted family were of limited means, and he didn't intend to be. Anyway, long story short, my stepfather gave him a one-off lump sum to enable him to buy a cottage overlooking the sea; despite his experience he was a keen seaman, and, he gave us both a generous monthly allowance. Alice negotiated that. Strange, my stepfather was a bully with boys and men alike. Loved asserting his authority, but terrified of educated women, he didn't argue, she should have asked for more."

"I'm sorry, but again I have to ask, *and?*"

"It worked. Alice fell pregnant, we got married, happily so, and he was working for Thatcher, which helped me get a leg up here and there. I tried politics but didn't take to it. Too much like hard work for too little money. If I was going to work that hard, I wanted a real income. I wanted more than he had. Alice and I bought little businesses here and there, and eventually moved to Bristol. Which was where it all started to go horribly wrong."

If he saw the glance exchanged between Meredith and Rawlings, he passed no comment on the exchange. Now the barriers were down, he seemed glad to get it off his chest. Meredith resisted the urge to glance at the clock again.

"Alice was the perfect wife, perfect mother, perfect everything, but I ruined everything. I began an affair with a woman who was an acquaintance. She was sweet, but edgy, didn't want me for anything other than a light-hearted companion, and, of course, sex. Good sex. She was happy with her life, in fact she was happy with pretty much everything. Alice, while almost perfect, became wrapped up with making everything just so. Perfect home, perfect children, perfect everything, but it wasn't very exciting. Elizabeth was simply a diversion from everything mundane." He stopped speaking when Meredith banged the table and pointed at him.

"Elizabeth Ingle, am I right?"

"You are, how on earth do you know that?" Shocked, Chapman fell against the back of his chair.

"I was involved in the investigation into her disappearance. I knew your name was familiar for some reason. You called it in, didn't you? We were instructed to be discreet about questioning you as you were married. Is she in that well?"

"Yes," Chapman looked at his hands. "She threatened to tell Alice, it turned out she wanted more than I would give. We argued. I killed her."

"Now, we're getting somewhere, who was the other woman?"

"A prostitute. She was someone Knox had picked up to have sex with. Knox had been close to my stepfather in Downing Street, and he asked me to meet him at The Grand, where, believe it or not, he was trying to turn things full circle and blackmail me. In his dotage, my stepfather had shared his secret. I went back later that night to kill him. I knocked on his room door expecting him to answer and this scrap of a girl does, they were both drunk, so I killed him." He looked directly at Meredith, "Adrenaline. I'm predictable. I told her she'd done it by having kinky sex with him. She got frightened, and I told her I'd help her get away so no one knew. I killed her too. I can't give you her name, I never asked. There you have it. Everything." He folded his arms across his chest, "Now, as promised, go and find out what's happened to my wife."

21

Ben Jacobs opened the letter box and peered into the hall. He was sure he'd heard a shout, but all was quiet. Both the kitchen and living room doors were shut so there was little to see. Stepping off the path, he peered into the living room window. Empty. Deciding to go around to the back, he hurried to the end of the street and up the back lane. Keeping his body close to the fence he approached the back of the house, stooping to go under the kitchen window, and to the back door.

Ben listened to the end of the conversation between the two women. Alice Chapman had a knife, and by the sound of it intended to use it. Deciding confusion was the best course of action, he drew back his shoulders and put his hand on the back-door handle, praying it wasn't locked.

"Hi, honey, I'm home." He pulled down the lever and the door opened. He quickly took in the scene, and ignored the knife. "Sorry I'm late." Walking past Alice Chapman, he pulled Tania to her feet, Alice placed the knife in her lap. "Give me a kiss. I've had a bit of day I can tell you," he leaned towards Tania and kissed her full on the mouth, then turning her, he pushed her away towards the hall, "Go and get my boy ready, we'll need to leave soon."

Tania gulped back a sob and ran from the room. Ben turned to Alice Chapman and held out his hand, "Hello, I'm Ben." He placed himself between Alice and the open door to the hall. "How can we help you?"

"Who are you?"

"Ben."

"I don't think I know a Ben." She squinted at him, "Are you Henry's friend?"

"Yes. I work with him." Ben rubbed his hands together, "I don't want to be rude, but we're off out in a moment, family outing. Can I give you a lift home?"

"Not yet. I have things to do. They have to be sorted."

"You've done everything you need to do here, Mrs Chapman. It's time to go now."

"Have I?" Alice looked around the kitchen, not knowing where she was. "I don't know where I am. I need to phone home."

"I can take you home, don't worry." Ben held out his hand, "Can I take that for you?"

Alice frowned as she looked at the knife in her lap. Lifting it, she held it out towards Ben, but something caught her attention in the hall, and she lurched forward. "She's taking him, she's taking him."

Alice ran forward and tried to sidestep Ben, but he was too quick for her, and blocked her path. The knife sliced through his sleeve and went into his upper arm. He gave a shout and with his other arm, tried to grab hold of her, but Alice was focused. Pulling the knife free, and with Ben clinging to her cardigan with his good hand she forced her way past and into the hall. Tania opened the door and the sound of sirens filled the air as a squad car skidded to a halt blocking the street outside.

"Run, Alex. Run to the policeman." Tania shoved Alex forward, and the boy did as he was told.

Alice called out, "Henry, Henry, Mummy's here, don't worry." She relaxed as she saw one of the policemen take Henry and put him in the back of the car. Another man walked up to the open door, he wasn't wearing a uniform. He smiled broadly.

"Who are you?" Alice demanded, one hand on her chest, the other holding the knife.

Trump quickly took in the scene, judging by the blood running down his arm, Ben Jacobs had a significant injury, but was still holding onto Alice Chapman's cardigan. Tania, knowing her son was safe, had stopped short of the door, and allowed her tears to flow.

"I'm DS Louie Trump. Henry and Penny are very worried about you, and have asked that we come and bring you home."

"They mustn't know about this. Keith wouldn't like it, we never tell the children." Alice waved the knife in her hand.

"It will be our secret." Trump held out his hand. "I'm going to take that knife before you leave, it wouldn't do waving that around in public. Then we'll get you home. May I come in?"

Trump lifted his foot to cross the threshold as Alice nodded, and he was unprepared for what happened next. Alice released the button holding her cardigan in place and surged forward towards Tania.

"I won't let you take him," she screamed, trying to raise the knife.

Fortunately for Tania, the knife became tangled in the cardigan, and Trump threw himself at Alice Chapman. They landed awkwardly at Ben's feet, and Alice screamed in agony, as the arm holding the knife twisted beneath her, and the bone snapped. Ben moved forward and stepped on the knife. Trump got to his knees, and took both the cardigan and knife away from Alice, who screamed again. The uniformed officer stepped into the hall, and told Tania to go to Alex, before calling for an ambulance. Ben clamped his hand around his injury, and walking around Trump, went to sit on the stairs.

Trump smiled at him, "Jacobs, I am arresting you for absconding, stay where you are, the ambulance won't be long." He looked down at Alice who was weeping. "Alice Chapman, I am arresting you for grievous bodily harm, you do not have to say anything . . ." He finished the caution, and added quietly. "I'll leave you there until the ambulance comes. I'm not sure what damage has been done."

Two hours later, Trump arrived back at the station with Ben Jacobs. Meredith was waiting for them. He held out his hand.

"I won't if you don't mind, this arm is throbbing already, you can man hug me though, to show you care." Ben smiled as the officers watching sniggered.

"No, you're all right. I'll wait until the arm is better. Thanks for today, who knows whether Trump would have been in time." He glanced at Trump, "Alice Chapman?"

"Held in hospital, sir. I'm afraid her arm snapped in two places, they have to wait for the swelling to go down before they can plaster it. I landed on top of her, we might get a complaint. Jo is waiting with a WPC, they'll bring her in when it's done. We will need to get the doctor to give us the okay to interview her. Her daughter, Penny Brooker, turned up. I've allowed her to stay with Mrs Chapman, who is understandably distressed, and keeps asking for her husband. She's convinced the whore has taken him."

"Good. We've had a full confession from Chapman. Still need some bits filled in, but now he knows his wife is safe, he's going to wait for a solicitor. That will be tomorrow, so he's on his way to Horfield nick."

"Good news. Mrs O'Brien will be able to arrange the funeral now. What news at the cottage?"

Meredith's nose wrinkled, "They've pulled one and a half bodies out so far. Sherlock reckons they'll be done in an hour or so."

"Excuse me, much as all this is interesting, and I'd love to know why my life has been turned upside down. I'm in bloody agony here. Can we do what needs doing so I can be on my way."

"Sorry, mate, of course." Meredith lifted the clear plastic bag containing Ben's personal effects down from the counter. "Here you go. Ben Jacobs, the charges previously brought against you have been dropped, although we're waiting for confirmation about you doing a runner, but that's just paperwork. George Davies won't press charges regarding the bike, as long as it's replaced. You are free to go. Give me ten minutes and I'll give you a lift."

"No need, I'm being picked up," Ben grinned and took the bag with his good hand.

"By whom?"

"Now that would be telling."

"She's only just out of a marriage, it could all end in tears."

"Possibly, but nothing's started yet, you keep interfering. I'll take that risk though, now you lot have stopped chasing me."

Meredith stepped forward and hugged Ben, being careful to avoid his injured arm.

"Be lucky my friend."

Ben smiled at him, "Well it's got to start sometime. I can't survive on looks alone." He held up his bag. "Which way is out? Tell George, I'll be in touch."

When Ben had gone, Meredith walked up to the incident room with Trump.

"Gather the troops, briefing in ten minutes or so. I've got a phone call to make, then we'll call it a day. It's been too long already."

"Will do, sir. At least we got a result, and given the number of bodies that were stacking up, all cleared up quickly. Not to mention your friend getting his liberty back."

"Hmm."

"Problem I don't know about."

"I reckon. But I don't know about it either. Everything stacks up. Chapman went from no comment to spewing information. Life is never that simple. Would be nice though, still, we have what we have, CPS is in first thing to work out who to charge with what."

"I heard. Would be nice if that recording turned up. Otherwise they'll have a hell of a job."

Meredith didn't answer. "I'm going for a smoke," he announced and wandered up the corridor while Trump prepared for the briefing. Once on the fire escape, he called Burt.

"It's over. Chapman has confessed, get a pen, there's a list." He gave a shudder, all those lives and he was making light of it, "Chapman killed Knox. That's the main thing you want to know, because his stepfather, and some knight of the realm, Axminster, were paedophiles. Chapman had been blackmailing them. Knox found out and tried to turn the tables. Unfortunately, he also killed a girl Knox had picked up. Flood helped him bury her for some reason. Oh yes, and he also killed his mistress who had threatened to go to his wife. He dropped them both in a well, they're being recovered."

"Busy boy. What about O'Brien?"

"O'Brien found out as Flood left the note, so Chapman set a vigilante group on him, telling them O'Brien was a paedophile. Brooker tried to blackmail him, and he got son-in-law, Ross Mason, to do the honours. Adrenaline is his weapon of choice. Trying to find Mason as we speak. All done and dusted bar the shouting. I'll send you a copy of the report with dates and details when it's ready. Can I assume that now I've given you your man, I'm free to go?"

"Don't be silly, Meredith. Two things, one, your time's not up, and two, you haven't finished yet. There's more to it than Knox trying to blackmail him. Find out what, and where the evidence is or he'll walk."

"What? Fuck off! I had another officer listen to his confession, I've briefed my team," he lied. "Chapman is going nowhere."

"He'll say he did it under duress because you were holding back information on his wife, so he made up a story to placate you."

"How the hell do you know that?"

"I know everything, Meredith. You'll get used to that."

The pain that shot through Meredith's chest came without warning, and quite literally knocked him sideways into the railing of the fire escape. He doubled up and counted to twenty. He could hear Burt calling him in the background, but was unable to respond. When the pain subsided, he stood up and drew in several deep breaths before looking at his phone. The call was still connected.

"Are you still there?" Meredith asked.

"I am, what just happened?" Burt sounded puzzled.

"I had something I needed to do, unavoidable," Meredith ignored the question. "I have to go, and let me tell you this, Chapman is going nowhere. If you're so bloody clever, you can find out what you think is missing." Meredith went to hang up, but had a thought, "You already do know, don't you? You want him to confess and hand over the evidence."

"Something like that. He will walk if you cock up, Meredith. But you never do that, do you? That's why I allowed you to go back. Keep in touch." Burt terminated the call, and rubbing his chest Meredith pulled another cigarette out of the pack.

It was another twenty minutes before he went into to give the briefing.

Seaton took hold of his arm. "Are you okay, Gov? You look funny." There was genuine concern in his voice, and he placed his hand on Meredith's arm.

"Then, why aren't you laughing? I'm fine thanks, Tom, let's get this done and we can all get home."

Shaking off Tom's hand, he took his usual position on in front of the board. "Good result today. Well done, this really will be brief as it's been a long day."

He gave a brief resume of the charges brought so far, explained what CPS would want the next day, and what the team should work on as soon as they got in.

He concluded, "Alice Chapman will remain in hospital overnight, and with her doctor's permission Jo Adler and A N Other, will interview her in the morning. She likes Jo apparently. Sherlock will get cause of death, if possible, and send off for DNA results. Elizabeth Ingle will be on record as samples were taken when she disappeared, identifying the other woman might be a long shot if she's a prostitute, but you never know, at least we can match the DNA. Once we've got the CPS off and running, our priority will be to bring in Mason. He's done a runner, but we've an APW out, and his bank accounts are being monitored. Hopefully he'll need petrol, or a bed at some stage. I need to tie up some loose ends with Chapman, and apart from several ton of paperwork, it will be case closed. Now go home, I'll see you bright-eyed, and bushy-tailed in the morning."

When everyone had dispersed, he went to his office and called the doctor's surgery. The receptionist took great delight in telling him that he'd only just caught them, and gave him the number of the hospital to change his appointment. He called the hospital, only to get a recorded message telling him the department would reopen at eight the next morning. He grabbed a pad, wrote himself a note and left it on the centre of his desk.

When he arrived home, he found Patsy slicing vegetables in the kitchen. She called to him as he emptied his pockets.

"I couldn't decide what to eat, I don't want another takeaway, so I'm doing a stir fry. You can open the wine."

Meredith walked to the doorway, "That's fine. Don't rush, I'm going to shower first. I'm so bloody tired I might fall asleep at the table."

"I'll come and watch. This won't take long once it's prepared. I want a full update. Amanda tells me they've recovered both bodies. Frankie is going to let her watch the post-mortems tomorrow."

"Lucky old Amanda, Sherlock had better not try and get her to go across to the dark side. She'll make a fine doctor, a proper one. And, before I tell you anything, I'll expect an apology, a proper one." He smiled, but knew he hardly had the strength to climb the stairs let alone anything else.

"And you'll get one." Patsy turned to face him, "I know what you think about Amanda's future, but like her father, Amanda knows what she wants to do. I'm sure she'll make the decision that's right for her."

"She will if I have anything to do with it." Meredith walked away unbuttoning his shirt.

"I'll be up in a minute."

Meredith threw his shirt in the direction of the washing basket and unbuckled his trousers allowing them to fall to the floor and stepped out of them. He'd hooked his thumbs in the side of his boxers to pull them down, when a wave of nausea came over him. He sat on the bed, gripping his knees waiting for it to pass. He closed his eyes as the room spun around him, and collapsed backwards onto the bed.

It was fifteen minutes before Patsy found him, apparently sleeping. She gave him a shake, "You must have been knackered, you've passed out."

Meredith forced open heavy eyelids, "What?"

"You fell asleep getting undressed." Patsy lifted his trousers and folded them. "Lift your feet, I'll pull your socks off."

Meredith groaned and tried to sit up, "I don't have the energy."

"Don't be such a baby. I've had a long day too." Patsy tapped his knee, "Up."

Meredith forced, first one, and then the other leg up, and she removed his socks. He kept his eyes shut as he tried to remember what had happened. His heart raced as he remembered. That wasn't a panic attack, that wasn't his normal pain either. Rolling onto his side he crawled up the bed.

"I'm so knackered, Patsy. I'll have an hour before we eat. You go on if you can't wait."

"Are you okay?" Patsy walked to the side of the bed and felt his forehead. It was clammy. "I think you might be getting man flu. I'll bring you up a drink and some paracetamol."

By the time she returned, Meredith was asleep again. He didn't wake up for food, and his stir fry was gratefully received by Amanda.

22

Gary Mason paced up and down the hall as he waited for Patsy to answer the phone. His mother got up and immediately turned her ankle.

"Stay there, sit back down," he hissed. He stopped pacing when Patsy answered. "Patsy, what's going on? You didn't tell me that Gran had been arrested."

"I didn't know she had. I knew she was in hospital."

"And they won't let me see her. Some bitch with a ladder in her tights wouldn't let me go in. What's she done?"

Hoping the call had his full attention, his mother attempted to leave the room again.

"Fucking sit down, before you do yourself damage," he shouted at her without moving the phone.

"Gary, what's going on? Where are you?"

"At home. After you left us at Sian's, I decided that I really should be at home, what with Dad and   . . . Anyway, mother was drunk when I got here, so little change there, but she told me this long-winded story, and the only bit that made any sense was that Gran was in hospital with a broken arm. I called Aunty Penny, but she wasn't picking up, so I went to the hospital. At first, they wouldn't even tell me she was there, so I got angry, and they called this woman police officer to see me. She told me Gran was under arrest, and that I might be able to see her tomorrow. We had a bit of a row and I came home. What's going on? Your husband is a policeman, can he find out?"

Patsy sighed. "He's not here," she looked up at the ceiling, Meredith was wiped out, and it was only a white lie "He's not my husband either, Gary. I'll tell you what I know, but don't panic, given your grandmother's illness, I'm sure she'll be home tomorrow. With your grandfather unlikely to come home, she's going to need a lot of help."

"So, you do know something. Why didn't you tell me earlier?" Gary was becoming angry again.

"Because I didn't know then. I only found out myself a little while ago, and that was second-hand. Perhaps you should speak to the police in the morning," Patsy snapped.

"I'm sorry, please tell me."

"Your grandfather has been having an affair, and it appears he has a son with the woman. Your grandmother went to her house and assaulted her, although that was minor, but she did stab a man that was trying to help. He's okay, he's been stitched up, but the police were called and she's been arrested. She'll be charged, or probably not, tomorrow. She fell during the struggle and broke her arm, hence the hospitalisation."

"A son? He has a son?" He looked at his mother, "Did you know Grandad had another son?" His mother looked genuinely shocked, and mouth open, shook her head, so he returned his attention to Patsy, "How old is he?"

"Six, I think."

"I can't believe this. Do you think he even knows how much trouble and hurt he's caused?" Gary asked quietly. "Bastard."

"I expect so. Gary, look after your mum, call the station in the morning, and they'll keep you updated. Get a good night's sleep, because when your gran comes home tomorrow she'll need you."

"Will you ask your boyfriend if I can see her tomorrow please? Whether anything happens to her or not. She'll be scared if none of us are there."

"I'll ask him first thing and give you a call. 'Night, Gary."

When Meredith woke the next morning, he felt much better. Starving, but better. "I hope that's a major fry-up you're preparing," he announced as he entered the kitchen. "I can't believe you didn't feed me last night. I feel like I have a major hangover with none of the fun that went into making it. Is a fry-up a possibility?"

"Sit down, I'll grab the bacon."

As Patsy cooked the breakfast, Amanda appeared and stole a piece of toast and Meredith's coffee.

"Oi! What's your hurry?" Meredith asked.

"Working with Frankie. We're examining the bodies." Amanda put the coffee back on the table. "See you later. Have to go, already late."

Meredith followed her into the hall. "In which case you might actually be of use to me. As soon as you know anything let me know. Text me, because I may not be able to answer, you can drip feed me anything that comes up. I'm interviewing the murderer again today."

"Well kick that bastard in the nuts for me. Dumping bodies in wells is not a proper send off."

"I think his biggest sin was killing them in the first place." Meredith laughed, "I doubt they worried much after that."

"You know what I meant, don't be cheeky or I won't drip feed you titbits, I'll make you wait for the report." Stepping forward she kissed his cheek. "You look pale, don't work too hard."

"Is there any other way?" Meredith closed the door behind her and went back to the kitchen. Patsy placed a full English on the table in front of him. "That looks bloody marvellous."

"I have a favour to ask, this is your reward for saying yes."

"What favour?" Meredith's eyes narrowed.

"Gary Mason wants to see his grandmother, I said I'd ask nicely on his behalf."

"I doubt it will be a problem. I'm not convinced the doctors will let us interview her anyway, and even if they do her brief won't. She's not going to make a very reliable witness, can't see much will be achieved in charging her. Except of course she's clearly in need of twenty-four-hour care. I'll see how the land lies when I get in and give you a call."

When he arrived at the station, Trump was busy organising the CPS people with coffee and files.

Meredith called over to them, "Morning, everything all right? I'll be in my office if you need me."

Trump walked across to speak to him, "I wasn't expecting them at the crack of dawn, they're keen."

"Good. The sooner they're out of here the better. Any news on Mason? I'm guessing not as I didn't get a call." Meredith slumped into his chair. "I am knackered already. Knowing my luck another body will turn up."

"You do look odd, sir. Do you feel all right, there is a bit of flu going around?"

Meredith looked at the note on his desk. "I'm fine. What news? I've got some calls to make." He pulled the note forward.

"Not much. No word on Mason. I've messaged Jo to come here rather than go to the hospital. Alice Chapman won't be plastered until at least lunchtime due to the swelling. Jo will be more useful here. I've left a uniform with Mrs Chapman. She caused a bit of a fuss in the night, but all's quiet now. Chapman will arrive back here about nine thirty, and the rest of them are before the magistrates this afternoon. They'll do them all immediately after lunch."

"We can get on without too much hassle then. Depending on what they say." He looked out at the CPS people, "Rawlings and Seaton can go to court." He looked at the empty coaster on the corner of his desk, "I'm sure you made enough coffee for one more cup. Anything else?"

"Not at the moment."

"Good, I'll make those calls while you make my coffee." He was already dialling the hospital as Trump left. He was in luck; his call was answered quickly. "The name's Meredith, my doctor wants me to have an emergency ECG." He was asked for full name, address and date of birth, which he provided. He was given a date for his appointment. "What? I could be dead by then. That's a week away."

"Are you having chest pains?" the receptionist asked. "It says routine on the doctor's note, but if you're still having chest pains, I can give you an emergency slot."

"When would that be?"

"Are you having chest pains?"

"No. Yes. Sort of, but I'm not sure if it's related. Are you medical, or just a busybody?"

"I'm a nurse, sir. I work in the cardiac department, specialising in heart failure. Are you having pain, or just a time waster, because I have three more calls in the queue already?"

"Are you allowed to speak to me like that?"

"Only if you're rude. You were rude. So, pain or no pain, if you do have pain we can get you in at eleven this morning."

Meredith thought about Chapman, the hearing at magistrates, and the meeting with the CPS. "It's not that bad, I'll come next Wednesday." Meredith hung up and called Patsy. "Alice Chapman won't be seen until at least this afternoon, she's not been charged yet, so I'll make a call and you can take Gary Mason into see her. If he asks, there's still no news on his father."

"Thanks, I'll give him a call now. How are you feeling, any better?"

"Fine, thanks. Got to go." Meredith hung up, and accepted the coffee offered by Trump.

"I think you need to see a doctor, sir. I take it Patsy was asking after your health too."

"I need a lot of things, Trump. Starting with this coffee." He took a sip. "Better already." He looked out at the now bustling incident room, "You ready for me? I've one more call to make, Alice's grandson wants to see her. I've said yes. Patsy is taking him in."

"Might keep her calm. Ready when you are."

~~~

Gary Mason waved as Patsy pulled up outside the house. He was wheeling a dustbin down the path, and when he'd positioned it to the side of the gate he got into her car.

"I've binned all the booze. Aunty Penny is on her way over, so we might keep her sober until lunchtime." He patted his pocket, "I've taken her purse too, so she can't sneak out and buy some."

"It sounds like she needs professional help if she's not trying to help herself." Patsy grimaced, "It's a huge undertaking for you to try and cover."

"Well, perhaps once the police have dealt with Dad, she won't feel the need to drink so much. Any news on him?"

"Nothing as yet." Patsy started the engine. "Your grandmother was a bit distraught last night, so they sedated her. Not sure how much sense you'll get out of her."

"Never got much anyway." Gary lifted his hand and waved at a passing car. "That's Aunty Penny, she wants to see her too. I said I'd ask."

"I'm sure it can be arranged. Let's get you there first."

Patsy called the number Meredith had given her, and a policewoman came down to collect them. She looked exhausted. She recognised Patsy, and once she'd shown them to Alice's side ward, she asked if Patsy would stay until she'd got back. She needed a coffee and a comfort break. Patsy assured her that would be fine, and followed Gary into the room.

"Gary. Thank goodness. They won't let me go home. Your grandfather will be worried. Have you seen him?" Alice held out her hand, Gary took it before sitting next to her. Alice looked at Patsy. "Is this your young lady?"

If it had been anyone other than Alice suggesting that, Patsy would have been flattered. She walked forward holding out her hand "I'm Patsy."

"Nice to meet you. Do you know where Keith is?"

Patsy looked at Gary. His face was solemn. "I'm going to tell her. She won't remember in half an hour anyway."

"Tell me what? Has he gone away on business again, with me stuck in here?"

"No, Gran, he's in prison. He's been arrested."

"Don't make bad jokes Gary, where is he?"

"I wasn't. He's been arrested for murder." His grandmother's free hand shot to her mouth, and he took hold of it. "Don't worry, I'll look after you."

"It's Knox, isn't it? I always thought they would find out. It's all my fault."

Patsy had taken a seat on the other side of the bed, and rummaging in her bag she found her recorder. She switched it on, and placing the bag next to the bed, she placed the recorder on top. Gary was as oblivious as his grandmother.

"No, I don't think so. Who's Knox?" he asked.

"Henry, don't ask impertinent questions. How long am I going to be in here?"

Gary ignored the fact she thought he was his uncle, it was a common occurrence. He pointed to the arm strapped to her body, "They have to plaster that when the swelling has gone down."

Alice stared at her arm as though she were seeing it for the first time. She looked up, puzzled, "I'd forgotten about that, I was getting Henry back and a man jumped on me. Your grandfather will not be happy. Did he get Henry, has he had his dinner?"

"Henry is with Aunty Penny, the boy you thought was him wasn't. It was a boy called . . ." he looked at Patsy.

"Alex. His name is Alex."

"It is not," Alice said firmly. "That was my Henry, and that trollop had taken him. Is she dead?"

"No. You stabbed her friend, not her." Gary squeezed her hand, "But we'll sort that out, you didn't mean too." He wiped a tear from her face. "Don't cry, it was probably an accident, I know you didn't mean to."

"I probably did," Alice sniffed. "I get these rages, Henry. It's not fair, I've always been good, always. But these women come along, and they want him. They want to take your father, it's not fair."

"Grandad is in prison, no one will be taking him anywhere. He's safe." He moved his face closer to her and smiled, "I'm Gary. The cheeky one."

"I'm sorry, I do get confused. I think it's getting worse. Although I did make the car talk to me." She laughed, "What would he say about that?" Her eyes widened. "Did someone put it back. I can't remember putting it away. He'll want it when he comes out of prison."

Patsy was impressed with how well Gary handled his grandmother, no frustration, no patronising, he was simply himself. She did, however, think he'd be wise not to give his grandmother too much more to think or worry about. She decided to step in.

"It's back in the garage, he'll never know it's been moved." She smiled, "Nothing to worry about."

"Who are you? How do you know my husband?" Alice looked at Patsy, disgusted she was even in the same room.

"I don't know your husband. I've never met him, I'm here with Gary." Patsy pointed at him, and Alice turned to look, the scowl replaced with a smile.

"My Gary, he's a good boy, if a little cheeky." She patted Gary's hand, "Go and get Grandad, he can drive me home now he has the car back."

"Gran, listen to me, listen and then be quiet and think," Gary tapped his temple. "Grandad has killed people. He's in prison, but you still have Mum, Penny, Henry and me."

"I killed them, and don't be ridiculous, my mother has been dead for years."

"I meant my mum, Susie. Not your mum. You didn't kill anyone, Gran."

"Susie is too young to have children, Henry. She's your sister stop being silly. I killed that girl. Tart! I thought she was with your father. But Keith was only there to see Knox, that's why he had to go too. Horrible man." She gave a nonchalant shrug, "They won't be missed."

Gary's eyes darted to Patsy, "Is that one of the women?"

"I think so, yes. This is important, Gary. Your grandfather might get the blame for something he didn't do." Patsy smiled at Alice who was frowning at her. "Alice, how did you kill her?"

"I hit her with the table lamp in the hotel. There was no blood. She just crumpled. My rage passed, and I had to tell Keith. He came with . . . a man." She looked at Gary, "Your father. He was there too. They got a packing box, and a van. Michael was driving it." She closed her eyes. "I only remember the row."

"What row?" Patsy asked quietly.

"His father is a coward, Keith told him so. He wouldn't stay, that's why Keith called Michael. Michael caused a fuss too, I cried. I remember crying."

"What happened?" Patsy could see the look of fear on Gary's face, but knew she should keep her talking before he spoke. She was surprised when Alice beamed.

"We had a party, it was glorious. All the children were so well behaved, and Mr Thatcher came. Like Keith said I suppose, if we carry on as normal, everything will be normal. Michael was quiet, and Keith wouldn't let his stepfather come. He died a few weeks later." She turned to Gary, "He didn't touch you, did he?"

"Touch me? What do you mean, I didn't know him?"

"Good. Keep it that way, he's a horrible dangerous man. Horrible." She glanced sideways at Patsy. "You're safe, he doesn't like girls. Especially me." She put her head back on the pillow and closed her eyes. "I can't remember why though."

"What did they do with the body?" Patsy asked.

"What body?"

"The girl in the hotel. What did they do with her?"

"Shh. We don't talk about that. Keith said, 'Least said, soonest mended'."

The door opened and a nurse came in, "I'm going to have to ask you to leave for a while. Doctor will be in to check the swelling. Alice may have to be sedated, she doesn't like him." The nurse smiled at Alice, "You caused a fuss, didn't you?"

"Why are you speaking to me like I'm an idiot? Bring me your manager now. Scrap of a thing like you being so familiar. Were you not taught any manners?" She turned to Gary, "Henry, go and get your father now. He'll sort this out."

"Alice, we have to go and wait outside. We'll see if we can find Mr Chapman. But before I go, how did you kill Elizabeth?"

"Don't you dare mention that woman's name. EVER!" Alice sat up straight and it caused her broken arm to move as she yelled. "Get out, get out now, or I'll take a knife to you too. I hid that one, I know where it is."

Patsy apologised, grabbed her bag, and taking a shocked Gary by the arm led him out into the corridor.

"Do you think she killed them both? Shit what sort of family do I come from?" He made a fist and thumped the wall. "I can't believe any of this, is she making it up?"

"I don't think she's capable of that." Patsy sighed, "Do you want me to take you home?"

Gary shook his head. "Not really, I'll probably find Mum burying the window cleaner. You can drop me at Sian's if you like."

"No problem. I have to wait for the WPC to come back, why don't you go and get us a coffee from the café to drink on the way?" Patsy watched him go, she walked to the end of the corridor and called Meredith. She was surprised when he answered on the first ring.

"Keep it short, I'm about to go and talk to Chapman."

"Good, I've caught you in time. Alice Chapman has just told us she killed the girl who was with Knox by hitting her with a table lamp, and Elizabeth by stabbing her, she said she hid the knife. I don't think he killed them, although he certainly killed Knox to cover it up. I've got it all recorded. If you . . ."

"Good girl! Got to go, bring the recording in, I need to speak to Amanda." Hanging up, he paced up and down his small office waiting for Amanda to answer.

"Dad. What it is? We're just at an interesting bit."

"How interesting? You haven't texted me."

"I was waiting for this next result, but so far one of the women has a fractured skull, blunt trauma possibly a bat or similar."

"What about a table lamp? Ask Sherlock." He listened as she asked the question and he heard Frankie's answer. "Good. What about the other one, Elizabeth Ingle, how did she die?"

"Hard to say for certain, as there wasn't much left of her, but Frankie thinks probably stabbed, there's a small nick in her rib that isn't typical of animal teeth marks. Dad, you won't believe how interesting this -"

"They're dead people. I'm going now, thank Sherlock for me." Meredith sat heavily in his chair. He was exhausted. He called Burt. "Quick update for you. It appears that Chapman didn't kill the women in the well, although he doesn't know I know that. His wife, the one with dementia, says she did it. Hodge has a recording. I think he's taking the blame for her."

"Suggest it, and call me back with his response."

"I can't stop a bloody interview to give you a ring."

"Yes, you can. You'll think of a reason, it's why you're there, Meredith. I'll await your call."

Meredith slid his phone into his pocket. He didn't like having his strings pulled, he had to find a way to sever them without losing his job. He walked down to the interview room slowly, pondering when he had become so stupid.

Chapman and his solicitor were waiting for him. Meredith announced who was present, reminded Chapman he was under caution and fell silent. As much because a hot flush which had started at his feet and was now making its way up his body, as to unsettle Chapman. It was the solicitor who broke the silence.

"I assume you have questions, DCI Meredith?"

"Too many for him to answer. But let's start with these: What did Knox have? Where is it now?"

"I have no idea what you're talking about. I explained yesterday. He was blackmailing me," he sounded each syllable of the word blackmailing slowly.

"You did, but that was a lie. What was it?"

"Why are you persisting with this, I won't change my answer?" He watched Meredith's eyebrow twitch, but Meredith gave no response. "I think we'd better see each other in court, if it gets that far." He smiled and turned to his solicitor, "Am I right in thinking that now I've been charged I don't have to speak to this man?"

"You are. They can bring you here of course, or interview you at the prison. But these days they can't *make* you speak." The solicitor looked at Meredith, "Did you hear that DCI Meredith? My client will save what he has to say for the judge." He closed his notebook and placed his pen back in his top pocket. When Meredith didn't respond, he tapped the table with his fingernail, "DCI Meredith, are you all right, are you playing some sort of game here, because if you are, it is pointless and infantile."

Meredith looked at him, "I'm sorry, my mind was elsewhere. What did you say?"

The solicitor looked disbelieving. "My client is refusing to take part in further interviews, he will speak only in court."

"If it gets that far," Chapman looked smug.

Meredith leaned back in the chair. "How did you kill the prostitute, and why?"

"I've told you, because she knew I'd killed Knox."

"No, no, no. It was the other way around. Knox died later."

"How can you possibly know that? I . . ." Chapman snapped his mouth shut as the possibility of how presented itself.

"How did you kill her?"

"I hit her."

"What with, your fist, or did you use a weapon?"

"What does it matter?"

"Because we know what the weapon was and I need to know if you're telling the truth or protecting someone. What was it?"

"A table lamp. I disposed of it in a dustbin I was passing. I don't believe you have it."

"Then ask yourself how I would know? What did Knox have and did you get it?"

Chapman was now almost as pale as Meredith. "He was blackmailing me."

"How did you kill Elizabeth Ingle?"

"I stabbed her. Here," Chapman put his hand in the centre of his ribcage."

"With what?"

"A samurai sword! A knife, Meredith, a knife."

"Where did you put that?"

"I disposed of it."

"Where?"

"I don't remember."

"Ah, well someone does. Who could that be do you think? And whose fingerprints will be on it when we collect it?"

Chapman clasped his hands together, Meredith glanced down and wondered if they were shaking because he was becoming angry, or simply scared.

"I asked, whose -"

"I know what you asked. Mine. Mine. Mine."

Meredith leaned forward and placed his finger on the switch of the recorder. "Interview suspended at ten twenty-seven." He hit the button and looked at Chapman, "Would you like your solicitor to go and get you some refreshment?"

Chapman chewed his bottom lip, and blinked rapidly. When he looked up he was perfectly calm, "I think that would be a good idea."

"But, I -"

"A cappuccino would be nice. But if they don't run to that, a plain coffee will suffice. Thank you, Charles."

Meredith stood up and opened the door for the solicitor to leave.

Before he'd closed it, Chapman snapped, "Who's pulling your strings, Meredith? What is it they want?"

"Whatever it was Knox had. I know Alice killed those women, I know how, and I know why. If Ben Jacobs hadn't stepped in, she would probably also have killed Tania Davidson, and possibly your son. Why are you protecting her? We'll come back to Knox."

"Because she is my world. Was. I owe her my sanity, my fortune, and I cheated on her. I was discreet, very, but she was an intelligent woman. She could have done anything she chose, but she chose to be my wife. Poor old Elizabeth could never have taken me from her, even if she'd wanted to. But the girl in the hotel . . ." he shook his head, "Alice was under the mistaken belief that I had an interest in her. She'd followed me to the hotel, I'd arranged the woman for Knox, I was attempting to set him up. She was going to do a tell all if he didn't play ball . . . for a large sum of cash of course. She even got a photograph of him naked, bound up, and fully erect. She was good. I had waited in the adjoining room, but Alice saw me let her in to mine to discuss our transaction. She knocked, I let her in, she was shouting accusations, and she picked up the lamp and hit the girl. Just the once, but it killed her. It was not intentional."

"Why did you kill Knox if you were next door?"

"He'd heard the fuss, realised it was Alice, and at the time thought I'd been enjoying myself with someone else. The door hadn't closed, he came in as I told Alice that she'd killed her." Chapman placed his fingers on his temple and moved them in a circular motion. "I quickly explained what the girl had been doing, and that her death had been an accident, he knew differently of course, but I showed him the reel of film. I said I had people that could deal with the body and he was to wait next door. To be on the safe side, I removed the phone from his room."

"And Mason? Why did he agree to do it?"

"He didn't at first. I lied, told him a friend of a friend had asked for some, it was his own fault. He'd been boasting a few weeks earlier how he'd saved the life of someone who'd had a heart attack at the surgery. It helped that I told him they paid well. Suffice to say he did it in the end. I held Knox, he administered the injection. Mason panicked and ran, and I had to get Flood to help me." He dropped his hands onto the table, "Meredith, I want your word that if I give you what Knox had, you won't charge Alice."

Meredith rubbed his chest. "You're a very trusting man. I could lie. I could be just like you."

"You're not. You're a straight down the middle company man, as we used to call them. I don't think you would lie. Believe it or not, I'm an excellent judge of character."

"I need to make a phone call."

"I thought you might."

There was a thud on the door and Meredith opened it. The solicitor stood there with a steaming cup in each hand.

"I thought I'd have one -"

He didn't finish the sentence as Meredith fell forward and knocked the cups from his hand. He hit the floor unconscious.

It took the solicitor one and a half minutes to gather himself and raise the alarm. Four minutes for George Davies to take a look and call an ambulance, seven minutes for him to give continual CPR until the paramedics took over, and cleared the corridor before taking Meredith to hospital. Trump waited anxiously with Seaton at the end of the corridor, and they held the doors open for the trolley to be wheeled out. One paramedic running alongside, puffing air into Meredith's lungs with a manual resuscitator. George followed it slowly, and when they looked to him for news, all he could manage was a shake of the head.

.

23

atsy parked the car and grabbed her handbag. It was clear that Alice was genuinely ill, and therefore questioned if she should be held responsible for her past actions. What good would it do? But if she was of sound mind at the time, and when you took into consideration her actions the day before, she was certainly a danger to others. Her phone rang in her handbag and she ignored it, an ambulance had a siren going and she wouldn't be able to hear anyway. She'd give the recording to Meredith, and then find out who wanted her. Running up the steps to the station, she pushed the buzzer, looking up at the camera as she did so. The door clicked open.

A young female officer was manning the front desk. She didn't know Patsy, and asked if she could help.

"Would you buzz DCI Meredith please. Tell him Patsy's here."

"Is he expecting you?"

"Yes. I'm his partner," Patsy smiled. "He'll probably tell you to send me up. I used to work here. If he's interviewing can you ask Louie Trump or Tom Seaton, please."

Patsy wandered to the other side of the small lobby, and looked at the *Crimebusters'* display. There was a gap on the right-hand side and she idly wondered if that's where Ben's photograph had been. Realising the officer hadn't given a response to her request, she turned to see what had distracted her. Patsy's stomach somersaulted at the look the woman gave her.

"What?" Patsy asked. "Why are you looking at me like that?"

"Sergeant Trump is on his way."

There it was again, that half smile of sympathy. Her pulse increased. "Why, where's Meredith?" She spun around as a flushed Louie Trump opened the door into the reception area. "Louie, what's going on?"

"Patsy, I tried to call. Come with me, DCI Meredith has been taken to hospital." Taking hold of her arm, he led her back the way he had come, and towards his car in the rear carpark.

George Davies was on the staircase. He took hold of Patsy's hand, "I'm sorry, love. I tried, I really tried."

"What? What does that mean?" Trump still had hold of her arm and was pulling her down the steps to the exit. Patsy grabbed the handrail and they ground to a halt. "Not one more step until someone tells me what's going on."

"I think he had a heart attack. George did CPR until the ambulance arrived. He's in the best hands." Trump's chin quivered as Patsy sank to the floor. He sat on the step next to her. "Would you like a coffee before we go? They've only just left so it will be a while before you'll be able to see him."

"It passed me, the ambulance passed me. It's why I didn't answer your call. The noise." Patsy covered her face with her hands, "I can't lose him, Louie."

"I know. Sit quietly, catch your . . ." He leaned to one side as Patsy jumped to her feet, the bag slung over her shoulder hitting the side of his head.

"Louie, we're wasting time. Take me now, please."

When they arrived at the hospital they were taken to a room and asked to wait while doctors treated Meredith, and told that someone would come to see them as soon as possible. Patsy called Amanda who rushed to join her.

After ten minutes of pacing the room, Amanda could bear it no longer. "I can't do this. I have to go and find out what's happening."

As she opened the door a nurse appeared with a clipboard. She looked at Amanda's scrubs and assumed she was part of the staff and not a relative.

"Oh, I didn't know someone was here, have you completed the form?" She held up the clipboard, "Is the next of kin here?"

Amanda was Meredith's next of kin, as he and Patsy had still not married, but Amanda pointed to Patsy. "That's the next of kin. I'll be back later."

As the nurse, who was unable to give details of Meredith's condition or prognosis, asked Patsy for basic details, Amanda slipped into the emergency department. She found Meredith in a side ward, a ventilator pumping oxygen into his lungs and various medical staff responding to the sharp instructions of the consultant. It didn't look good. She swallowed back the lump in her throat, and stepped inside the open door. No one took any notice of her.

"I think this is a PE. Let's get a CT scan done," the surgeon announced, he glanced at Amanda, "Call and let them know we're coming."

Amanda nodded. Picked up the phone and made the call. She kept out of the way while the team prepared and moved Meredith for the scan. Knowing there was nothing she could do, she went back to Patsy and Trump.

"They think it is a PE, not a heart attack." She dropped heavily onto the chair next to Patsy, "If they've caught it in time, I think that's better."

"What's a PE?" Trump racked his brains for medical knowledge.

"Pulmonary Embolism. A blood clot, from what you tell me, it sounds like it's blocked his lungs. That would explain the pain and temperature, et cetera." She gave Patsy's hand a squeeze, "It's treatable, and he can make a full recovery."

"If . . ."

"If they can dissolve it or thin the blood to travel around it while the body does its thing and removes it naturally. But, if what you tell me is true, he may suffer scarring to the tissue. Of course it doesn't help that he's a bloody smoker, and depending on how long the brain was without oxygen there is always a possibility of brain damage." Amanda covered her face, "He wouldn't want to live with that."

"He will be fine. He will make a full recovery and spend months telling us to stop fussing. He will be irritable and unreasonable because he won't be working, and he'll try and sneak out for cigarettes and unhealthy food. In short, he will be even more of a pain in the arse than he is now, but he will not have brain damage." Patsy stood and faced Amanda, pointing at her, "Don't you say that. Don't you dare." She allowed her hand to fall to the side. "I need to get some air, come and get me if there's any news."

Amanda nodded, and forced a smile, "You're right."

Patsy pulled open the door and found Burt. His hand outstretched ready to turn the knob. She looked him up and down.

"The vultures are circling, I see." She tried to step past him. He placed a hand on her shoulder and opened his mouth to speak, he closed it again as her open palm flew at him and his head jerked back. "Fuck off. I am not speaking to you." Patsy hurried away, not knowing that Trump was now manhandling Burt.

Trump dragged Burt into the room by the lapels, and pushed him up against the wall.

"Who are you? What are you doing here? This is a time for family."

"Let go of me, I'm a friend."

"Patsy didn't seem to think so," Trump glanced over his shoulder, "Amanda do you know this man?"

Amanda walked closer. "No. I don't know who you are, but I think as Patsy suggested it would be best if you left."

"No, no. First, he needs to say who he is, and apologise for intruding." The usually mild-mannered Trump was emotional, and unable to help Meredith, he was at least going to protect his family. "What's   . . ." Having calmed a little, Trump looked at the man more closely, and his arms fell to his side. "It's you. I didn't recognise you. Have you coloured your hair?"

Burt straightened his jacket. "How's Meredith?"

"Having a scan for an embolism. Why are you here?"

"To see how Meredith is. I'll come back. Where was Patsy going?"

"To get some air. Leave her alone. She clearly didn't want to see you." Amanda walked closer, "Who are you?"

"A friend, like I said. I'll leave you to it." He stepped towards the door, "Trump, a word if I may." Burt had no idea whether or not Patsy had given the recording to Meredith. If it was at the station, Trump would need to get it. "Patsy has a recording she was going to give to Meredith. If she has already done so, then I need you to find it. Let's go and ask her."

"I'm not sure I understand, you're with SIS, what is this recording?"

"If, and when you need to know, I'll tell you. Just take me to Patsy."

They found her sitting on a wall near the entrance to the emergency department.

"I assume you want the recording." She got to her feet, "It's somewhere safe. Until I speak to Meredith, it'll stay there."

"This is no time to play games, Patsy. Give me the recording."

"No. I think I know why you want it, and it's not right. What is it this time, protection of a government paedophile? Tough shit. No one is that important. He might be hit by a bus tomorrow."

"I'm not quite sure if it is, I might not play ball. I need that recording or Chapman could walk."

Patsy snorted. "You want something but you don't know what it is, and yet you know it could secure Chapman's release? Give me a break, Burt. You know exactly what it is."

"I know it could damage the government, and if Chapman gets to use it, he'll walk. If he gives it up to save his wife, it can't save him too."

Patsy jabbed a finger into his chest. "But who else will it save? Have you considered that? Perhaps everyone that deserves punishment should receive it! Get a new job, Burt, your conscience must be near to breaking point."

Trump looked from one to the other, "I have no idea what you are speaking about, although I could take an educated guess now that Mrs Chapman has been mentioned. If you want my opinion, I think that SIS do protect too many people and for spurious reasons. Perhaps whoever it is needs to be brought to book. But, Patsy you are naive if you don't realise that sometimes doing what appears to be right simply starts a domino effect that could bring the house down. No, I think what we should do -"

"We? I know we're supposed to live in a democracy, Trump. But last time I looked you weren't on the payroll. Your opinion isn't required."

"I have always paid my taxes, which means I pay your salary, so yes, my opinion counts." Trump looked at Patsy, "What I think we should do, is whatever Meredith would have done."

For the second time in less than twenty minutes, Patsy's arm flew out and slapped a man. This time it was Trump. His hand flew to his cheek and he stuttered out his rebuke.

"That was totally unnecessary. What did I say?"

"You used the past tense. Meredith will decide what to do. Now you can both fuck off." Patsy walked to a bench on the other side of the road where several smokers looked across at the hospital. She stopped at a large lady, whose dressing gown only just managed to encase her large breasts. "May I have a cigarette please." She smiled and thanked the woman who seemed only too eager to share, and cupped her hand while Patsy lit the cigarette.

Trump and Burt watched Patsy walk away, small puffs of smoke rising every few steps. She stopped walking when she had finished the cigarette, crossed the road and walked back to them.

"Louie is right, we'll do what Meredith decides when he's well enough. In the meantime, I suggest Chapman is left behind bars, and you two find something useful to do. I'm going in to see how he is. You two don't need to come."

Trump sat on the wall vacated by Patsy. "I didn't mean it like that."

"Yes, you did." Burt sat next to Trump. "We'll wait here for a minute while she calms down."

"Really? You're not going to search her home and car et cetera?"

"Not yet. Let's see what happens in the next couple of hours. I promised Meredith I wouldn't go into his house again without telling him."

"Quite right."

It was three hours and thirty-eight minutes later that Louie Trump ventured into the room where Meredith lay attached to various monitors. Patsy was sitting on one side, and Amanda the other.

Meredith nodded at him, and lifted the oxygen mask off his face. "How's the cheek? I hear Patsy owes you an apology," his voice was low, but there was a twinkle in his eye.

"No, she doesn't, I was being insensitive. How are you feeling, sir?"

"Like I've been hit by a bus. I had a blood clot on my lungs, all under control now. How are things at the station?"

"I have no idea, I've been here. But I've not had any calls, so all must be well."

"That's a long time to hang about, tell me you've not been with Burt."

"I have, quite an interesting chap, says more by what he doesn't say, which makes for an interesting conversation."

"Is he still here?"

"Yes," Trump shuffled awkwardly. "It was him who told me to come in to see if it was safe."

"Send him in," Meredith grunted as he pushed himself up the bed.

"Meredith, you can't be serious." Patsy tried to grab his hand, but he pulled it away.

"Very much so. When he arrives, you lot can go and find me something to eat. I'm starving." Although he was addressing all three he looked at Patsy, "It won't take long."

Burt dropped a bag of half-eaten grapes onto Meredith's midriff. "Heard it was touch and go, glad you're still with us, Meredith."

"I'm not. I'm done, it's over. I should make a full recovery, maybe immediately, which I'm aiming for, or it could take years. Whichever it is, much as I love you, our relationship is over," his lips twitched into a smile.

"We have unfinished business, Meredith. Patsy is playing silly buggers. Do you know where the recording is?"

"I do, and you shall have it, if I think it shouldn't be made public."

"You've been speaking to goody-two-shoes. It's way past its sell by date, something that happened when Thatcher was in power. Most of the players will be dead."

"So, why not publish and be damned?"

"Because, it is believed our poor beleaguered country has enough on its plate, with BREXIT and the rise of right-wing parties across the globe, and let's not forget Donald Trump. There were threats of someone finding the UK's very own grassy knoll when he visited. Obviously he didn't pass it. All in all, it's considered that further distraction from sorting out the mess is not needed."

Burt pulled several grapes from the bunch and popped one into his mouth. "You get what you want. Chapman will be behind bars, and Alice, naughty, naughty Alice, will be held in a secure hospital. You can't go around stabbing handsome singers and get away with it." Burt ate the remaining grapes while Meredith considered his words.

"And I have your word that no one walks who shouldn't?"

"You do."

"In which case go and get Patsy. I'll tell her to give you the recording."

Burt grinned, "Good man."

Twenty minutes later, Burt had Patsy's recorder tucked into his inside pocket. He'd listened to it with Meredith, while the others waited outside. Neither of them spoke, simply exchanged a nod as the recording ended. Burt wished Meredith a speedy recovery as he straightened his blanket, and ate the remaining grape.

Meredith called to him as he opened the door, "We're done here, Burt. I'd like to say it's been a pleasure, but it hasn't. Now you have that tape, I'm released from your grip, irrespective of whether or not I keep my job on the force. I have other options, a near death experience makes you take stock. And as a by the by, keep away from Trump."

"I hear you, Meredith. I'll see what I can do. But, nobody walks, not really, don't be under the mistaken belief that any of us are free. One day your phone might ring when you least expect it."

"Do you know, it's on days like this I'm glad I get a crap reception on my phone. Bye Burt."

ABOUT THE AUTHOR

Having worked in the property industry for most of my adult life, latterly at a senior level, I finally escaped in 2010. I now dedicate the bulk of my time to writing and, of course, reading, although there are still not enough hours in the day.

I began writing quite by chance when a friend commented, "They wouldn't believe it if you wrote it down!" So I did. I enjoyed the plotting and scheming, creating the characters, and watching them develop with the story. I kept on writing, and Meredith and Hodge arrived. In 2017 the Bearing women took hold of my imagination, and the Bearing Witness series was created. I should confess at this point that although I have the basic outline when I start a new story, it never develops the way I expect, and I rarely know 'who did it' myself until I've nearly finished.

I am married with two children, two grandchildren, two German Shepherds and a Bichon Frise. We live in Bristol, UK.
I can be contacted here, and would love to hear from you:
Website: http://mkturnerbooks.co.uk/

Printed in Great Britain
by Amazon

79616800R00169